Typewriter Pub, an imprint of Blvnp Incorporated
A Nevada Corporation
1887 Whitney Mesa DR #2002
Henderson, NV 89014
www.typewriterpub.com/info@typewriterpub.com

ISBN: **978-1-64434-201-5**

DISCLAIMER

This book is a work of fiction. The characters, incidents, and dialogue are drawn from the author's imagination and are not to be construed as real. While references might be made to actual historical events or existing locations, the names, characters, places, and incidents are either products of the author's imagination or are used fictitiously, and any resemblance to actual persons living or dead, business establishments, events or locales is entirely coincidental.

CHANGING FATE

Changing Fate Trilogy

BOOK ONE

C.J. ALEXIS

To my momma,
the first person to read my books and the one who has supported me endlessly since the day I told her I wanted to be a writer.

Trigger Warning

The following story contains strong language, violence, and adult scenes.

Reader discretion is advised.

CHAPTER ONE

"Kendall, can you come down here for a minute?" Dad called from somewhere downstairs; likely his home office.

I sighed and rolled off my queen-sized bed, throwing aside the book I was reading. I strolled out of my bedroom and down the stairs. I enhanced my hearing to listen to my Dad. I could hear his and two other heartbeats in his office. No surprises there. I quickly let my hearing go back to normal and strode the rest of the way to his office.

I opened the door without knocking; not something I would usually do except for when he calls me. I pushed the cherry oak door shut behind me and took in my surroundings. Dad was seated in his desk chair and casually leaned back. I didn't let his nonchalant body language fool me though; his face was pinched with tension.

Brody, my oldest brother, and future Alpha, stood to the right and slightly behind Dad. His six-foot, four-inch body leaned against the wall parallel to the door, his muscular arms crossed over his chest and a blank look on his face, although I could see a look of hesitance in his eyes that usually wasn't there.

My other brother, Matt, was sitting on the couch on the right side of the office. He looked prepared for a fight, which startled me.

All three men looked eerily similar. They all had the same shade of espresso-brown hair and russet eyes. The only real difference between them was that Matt had shoulder-length curly hair and a crooked nose while Brody had thinner lips and a wider face. Dad had a few gray hairs peppered in his locks, with lines deepening in the crease of his eyes. All this, and he still didn't look his real age.

With the slow aging of werewolves, once they reached adulthood, he looked to be more in his late thirties instead of nearly 200. Brody certainly didn't look twenty years my senior.

"What's going on?" I asked apprehensively.

"Sit down, Kenny," Dad said, gesturing to one of the two chairs in front of his desk.

I glared at him for the use of my childhood nickname but didn't comment on it. Now wasn't the time, I could tell.

As I took a seat, I oddly felt like a child again. Anytime we needed reprimanding as kids, we would have to sit here across from our stern Alpha father. I had spent countless amounts of time here during my teenage years along with my sister, Selena. It felt like I was seventeen again instead of twenty-three.

I raised an eyebrow at each of the men, waiting for one of them to start.

My father began, "As you probably know, I've been working on earning a seat on the council for some time now." He paused.

I was quite aware of this fact. The council was made up of the strongest Alphas of the kingdom. They helped the king to make decisions about werewolf matters. I didn't completely know what those matters entailed but I did know that they were important, and being asked to join the council was a huge honor.

Dad had been trying for years to receive an invitation but to no avail. He was a strong Alpha, there was no doubt about that. However, we didn't have the largest pack compared to others. Dad had always sort of straddled the line of power. While he was never the most powerful Alpha, he wasn't the least powerful either.

The king was very specific about who he added to his council. He had completely disbanded the original council his father and deceased former king had created when he took the throne almost twenty-five years ago. He started from scratch, forming his own council that he vetted and trusted. Dad had been trying to make the cut ever since.

I nodded, and he continued.

"Well, I have received a letter that I am finally being considered. They've asked that I send representatives to stay for a few months. I can't possibly leave the pack that long, so they want me to send someone I trust in my place to try and earn a spot for the pack."

"Congratulations, Dad! I'm so happy for you. I know how much this means to you." I smiled brightly at him, a weight lifting off my shoulders. This wasn't bad news at all. "Is it going to be Matt? Or is it Brody?" I asked as an afterthought.

"That's what I wanted to talk to you about. Brody can't go; he's needed here. Instead, I'll be sending Matt. Of course, Kat will be joining him," he said, referring to Matt's mate and my best friend since kindergarten. She was also the daughter of the pack's witch. She was a strong witch in training.

"I'll miss you guys." I looked over at Matt with a frown. He averted his eyes, refusing to make eye contact as he rubbed the back of his neck.

"That's the thing, Kendall. You'll be joining them," Dad added in a *this-isn't-up-for-discussion* tone.

Just like that, the weight settled back on my shoulders and in my stomach. I felt defiance bubble up inside of me—the Keating family temper coming into play.

"Are you kidding me?" I gripped the wooden chair handles, my claws extending and puncturing the dense oak. Wouldn't be the first time.

"I assure you, I am not kidding," Dad replied, still calm and collected.

"You can't do that. Why the hell do I need to go?" My voice had taken on the shrill tone for when I got angry.

"I can, in fact, do that. I need you there. I can't have Selena go, for obvious reasons. That leaves you."

I knew Selena couldn't go. She would just embarrass him. I loved her to death, but she wasn't exactly reliable. She cared more about partying and finding her next boyfriend than she did helping Dad with the pack business. It was no secret in our family that he was perpetually disappointed in her.

"Why aren't Matt and Kat enough?" I demanded.

"I need to show the King that I'm serious about this. Sending two of my pups, along with my daughter-in-law and pack witch, will show that. I need as much representation as I can get, and I don't trust anyone with else with this. Well, aside from Dalton. He'll be accompanying you as well."

I threw my head back and groaned dramatically. I couldn't stand Dalton. He was the pack's future Beta, being the current Beta Wes's son. He was also the pack's current douche bag. We grew up together and never got along, although he and Selena were somehow best friends.

"You can't do this to me, Dad. Please. You know I hate that asshat," I spat.

"Language, Kendall," he warned.

I rolled my eyes.

"Daddy, please." I went for a different tactic. I widened my green eyes and blinked a couple of times, feeling them mist over slightly. I pouted my lower lip and put on the saddest look I could muster.

"That might have worked when you were ten but you're an adult now. You said you wanted to be more involved with the pack. This is your chance."

I dropped the act. "That isn't what I meant and you know it. I just spent four years in college getting my accounting degree. I didn't do all that work to go kiss the King's ass. I did it to help with pack finances and to run your businesses," I said.

In the werewolf world, Dad was Alpha Jefferson Keating. To the human world, he was businessman and entrepreneur Jefferson Keating. He owned several businesses around the state. It's

"Maybe not. Keep an open mind, Kendall. You might actually like it there."

Always the voice of reason. She had kept me out of a lot of bad situations. As a witch, her intuition was never wrong. I had still managed to find trouble, but I'm sure I avoided the worst of it because of her. When I wasn't being stubborn at least.

"I don't need to keep an open mind. I know this will suck."

Before she could say anything else, the door to my bedroom burst open and Selena stormed in, glaring daggers at me. I rolled my eyes at her.

"You bitch," she spat.

"What now?" I glared back at her, not in the mood.

I couldn't exactly kick her out. This was her room too. We had lived in the same bedroom since I was born. One of us could have moved into Brody's bedroom once he moved out, but we just never did. We had lived together for so long, it just didn't feel right.

As much as I hated her sometimes, the thought of not bickering with her every morning made me sad. A pang went through me at the thought of being away from her for two months. I would actually miss her.

"What now? You get to go stay at Castle Cahill for two months, that's freaking what. Why the hell do you get to go and I don't?" she demanded to know. She crossed her arms over her chest, much like I had in Dad's office.

"Maybe if you weren't such an embarrassment, Dad could trust you to go." I raised a mocking eyebrow at her.

"She's got you there," Kat added, chuckling.

"You two are both bitches."

We just laughed at her. Kat and Selena bickered too, but it was all in good taste since they were friends as well. Kat was our sister. Maybe not our blood sister, but she was a part of the family. She would be even if she and Matt weren't mates. Kat, Selena, and I had grown up together. We may have fought a lot, but at the end of the day, we loved each other and had each other's backs.

"Maybe so, but at least no one has to worry about us jumping the King," Kat told her, grinning widely.

"I am so going to enjoy a break from you two," Selena muttered as she walked past me. She threw herself on her queen-sized bed at the other end of the room.

Her side of the room was messy, but I couldn't really criticize her for it; mine was just as cluttered. Maybe that's why we could tolerate sharing a room together. Clothes were strewn across the room, some of it hers and some of it mine. Both of our beds were messy and wrinkled. Dust covered our entertainment center and bookshelf. Our bathroom didn't look much better; it was clean but very disorganized.

"That's mine," she said with a growl. She was looking at the tank top I was folding.

"Um, no it's not. You just take whatever clothes I own whenever you please," I argued back.

"Yes, it is. And you wear my clothes all the time too."

"No, I don't. Your fat ass stretches everything out so I can't wear it."

"It's not fat, sweetheart. It's called having curves and not looking like a twelve-year-old boy."

"Oh really?" I drawled, throwing the tank top in my bag anyways. "Is that why Grandma gave you that dieting cookbook?"

Kat snickered and Selena growled.

"You know she only gave me that because I said I was going to start eating healthy," she defended herself.

I didn't really feel bad about insulting her. This was the type of relationship we had; we were bitches to each other. We could give as much as we could take since neither of us was overly sensitive. The one thing we had done for each other was give each other thick skin. She knew she wasn't really fat, just like I knew I didn't look like a pre-pubescent male.

"You sure you can't leave tonight?" she whined.

Our bickering continued back and forth for a while. It helped take my mind off the next few months. Eventually, she went downstairs to help Mom cook.

She was the one who helped do stuff around the house. She didn't like school, even though she was smart, so she didn't go to college after high school. She didn't get a job either. Selena wasn't really made for a real job; she was too rebellious and had authority issues.

She and Dad butted heads a lot because of it, although he let her get away with a lot. Because of her lack of schooling and employment, our parents agreed to keep supporting her so long as she helped out around the house and Mom with her Luna duties. She did it since it was really her only option until she could find her mate. Lord help the poor guy when she did find him. She was going to be a handful.

After an hour or so and another suitcase, I was all packed and ready to go. I had two big suitcases and a smaller bag with toiletries and beauty products. I didn't know what I would be doing exactly, so I packed for any occasion.

By the time I was finished, Mom was calling us down for dinner. I frowned, knowing that it would be my last family dinner for a while.

Kat walked down beside me and plopped down next to Matt, who immediately kissed her cheek lovingly. I sat next to Kat and across from Selena.

We all fixed our plates, passing around the dishes and making small talk as we went. Once all of our plates were fixed, we all started eating hungrily. As werewolves, all of us, except for Kat, had a big appetite. It made for a hefty grocery bill.

"So, are you three excited about tomorrow?" Mom asked, looking down at my side of the table.

"I am. I heard that the castle is beautiful. And they have a Petrova witch. I'm hoping I might be able to study with her while I'm there," Kat said excitedly.

I could tell why she was excited. Kat was from a powerful witch line, the Abara's, but the Petrova's were the most powerful witch line. They had been working with the Royal Family for centuries—back before they even relocated from Europe to America in the 1700s.

"Actually, they have three Petrova witches. I'm sure it will be no problem studying under one of them. I'll make a call in the morning," Dad told her happily. Having Kat become a strong witch could greatly benefit the pack, especially if she impressed the right people while we were there. Kat's mom was powerful, but she didn't have the patience and compassion that Kat had. Which meant, in my eyes, she was already better than her mother.

"Really? Thanks, Jeff." She bounced in her seat a little. Matt looked at her adoringly.

"What about you, Kenny? You excited?" Mom turned her attention to me.

"Not really," I muttered.

"Why not? I'm sure you'll have fun. And you'll get to meet the King. I'm so excited for you." She sounded so enthusiastic. I wanted to make a sarcastic comment, but my Mom was the sweetest woman ever. I didn't want to hurt her feelings.

"That doesn't really excite me. Plus, I'm sure I'll only meet him for, like, a few seconds."

"Maybe not. Besides, he is very handsome," she hinted. Dad growled at that but she ignored him.

"So? It's not like it matters. We both have our mate out there somewhere. His looks aren't going to help me in this situation."

If I was honest, I had no idea what the King looked like. I had never been to the castle before. All of my family members, besides Selena, had. The King threw a mating ball every year. It was basically a giant party that anyone could attend to help them find their mates. I never cared enough to go.

"Well, that's something to look forward to. Maybe you'll meet your mate while you're there." She always tried to find the bright side of things. I was a little more pessimistic than her.

Truth be told, I didn't want to find my mate there. I wanted a mate, sure. What wolf didn't? They were the other half of your soul. But I knew that if I met him at the castle, then he was bound to be important. I'd have to leave my family and pack; the only life I've ever known. I wasn't ready for that. I just wanted my mate to be someone who could join my pack, not the other way around. As selfish as that sounds, I didn't want to leave my family.

I just hummed in response to her. I didn't dare say I didn't want to meet him. That would lead to a long lecture about the importance of mates. That was not something I wanted to hear tonight. I just wanted to have a sleepover with Selena and Kat like old times. We were going to binge-watch some Netflix shows and eat junk food all night.

She soon moved on, and dinner continued for a while. Soon enough, it was over. We helped Selena clean the kitchen up and loaded up on junk food.

Now we were all seated on my bed, watching some crappy horror movie while we ate ice cream. We also had a pack of Oreos and three different kinds of chips spread out on the comforter in front of us.

"I'm really going to miss you two," Selena said from beside me, having one of her rare moments of sincerity.

"I'm going to miss you too, Sel," I told her honestly.

"Me too. The Three Amigas have never been separated before." Kat pouted.

"I really wish I could go with y'all."

I was stunned into silence when I saw tears fill her eyes and spill over. She wasn't a crier, so this was unusual. She angrily wiped them away.

"I wish you were too. I'm nervous about going," I admitted.

"Me too," Kat told her.

"Maybe Dad will change his mind," I added, and Kat nodded in agreement.

"You know he won't. He thinks all I'm good for is cooking and cleaning. He doesn't trust me with this; he doesn't trust me with anything. He trusts everyone but me." A few more tears fell. Her voice cracked, sounding so sad that it broke my heart. I had no idea she felt this way.

"Sel, that's not true. You don't give yourself enough credit."

"I give myself the credit he gives me."

"I'm going to be completely honest with you right now, okay?" She nodded, so I continued, "You're so smart, Selena. You have so much to offer, you just don't act like you do or believe that you do. If you want Dad to take you seriously and let you get more involved with pack duty, you have to show him that he can trust you. Dad will come around eventually."

"You really think so?" she asked, her tears drying up.

"I do."

"You're right."

"Never thought I'd hear you say that to me," I joked, lightening the mood.

"And you never will again." Kat and I both laughed at that. "Now enough of this sentimental crap. My ice cream's melting."

The rest of the night went by smoothly. We got back to bickering like usual. It was like the emotional outpour never happened, but something seemed different about her. I hoped Dad would go easy on her.

After two more movies and a ton of junk food, we all laid down to go to sleep. They surrounded me, leaving me in the middle of my bed. They were both asleep, but I stayed awake.

Matt came in about thirty minutes after they fell asleep and took Kat back to his room. I shook my head at that. Alphas were ridiculous. He couldn't be away from her for one night.

I couldn't help but think about tomorrow. I had this feeling deep in my gut, my wolf antsy. I couldn't explain it, I just felt anxious about the whole thing. Eventually, I gave up on sleep and decided to go for a run. I needed to let my wolf out and get rid of some of this pent-up energy.

I quickly snuck out of my bed and down the stairs. Luckily, everyone was already asleep, so I was able to leave without interference. I walked from the back patio to the tree line. I stood behind the biggest tree, just in case someone decided to come outside, and stripped off my pajamas.

I called my wolf forth, which she happily complied with, and let the shift take over my body. It didn't hurt; it actually felt freeing. It happened quickly and within seconds. I was small, but I was a lot stronger and faster than I appeared.

I shook my glossy brown coat and started running. As I darted through the forest, swerving around trees and bushes, I started to feel better. The restless energy was wearing off, but for some reason, I still had a nagging feeling in my gut.

I ignored it and decided not to worry. I'd find out soon enough anyway.

CHAPTER TWO

"No. I refuse," I stubbornly told my father, who was currently starting to lose his patience with my defiance.

Waking up this morning had been a struggle. I stayed out late last night running, so I only managed to get a meager three hours of sleep. I had dressed nicely, wanting to make a good impression. My curls were smoothened, not frizzy like they normally were, and my body was adorned in one of my favorite outfits, an emerald green dress that matched my eyes with a thick black cardigan.

"Do you always have to be so difficult?" Dad finally snapped, sending a glare my way.

We had been arguing back and forth for about fifteen minutes now. He had informed me when I came downstairs this morning that we would be going to the airport at noon. That led me to promptly inform him that I would not be taking a plane.

There were two reasons for my refusal. One was that I was terrified of planes. I had only been on one three times and every time it scared the shit out of me. Now, I would only travel by car or I wouldn't travel at all. It wasn't so much about a fear of crashing. It was a fear of being so far from the ground with nowhere to run. You couldn't very well shift in the middle of the clouds, but you could stop the car and get out at any time. If you couldn't fight back and fleeing wasn't an option, that only meant freezing in place.

The second reason I wanted to drive was because if I was going to be stuck at the King's castle for at least two months, I wanted to have an easy escape route. I wanted to have either mine or my brother's vehicle there so that I could leave at any time. I didn't want to depend on anyone there for anything except a place to stay.

"Who do you think I get it from, Dad? Sure as hell ain't Mom."

He growled at that.

"That's true, hun," Mom added, walking into the living room with us.

Dad glared at her, but he didn't dare growl at her like he did me. She may have been the more submissive of the two, but she still expected respect from Dad. He knew better than to piss her off. It was a rare occasion to see her angry, but whenever it happened, you'd better run. She had only ever been truly angry with me once, and it was more than enough for this lifetime.

I wasn't the best kid in high school, so she was disappointed in me plenty of times, but it wasn't until she found out that I had let my high school boyfriend go down on me that she became furious at me. In her mind, it didn't matter that it was only oral. She thought I shouldn't do anything sexual until I found my mate. She was old school like that.

"Must you two gang up on me?" He sounded exasperated, and I had to repress a smile.

"Only when you're being unreasonable, Jeff. Kendall is willing to go and help even though she doesn't want to. All she's asking is that they drive there instead of fly," Mom jumped to my defense. I shot her a small, appreciative smile. She returned it, then turned her attention back to my Dad. I could tell he was wavering slightly.

Both of their eyes glazed over and I knew they were mind-linking each other.

Mind linking was an easy way for werewolves to communicate with each other. It's a mental connection that members of the same pack have with each other to be able to talk with one another. It wasn't something I used a lot; I preferred a phone usually.

But it was helpful to have during emergencies. I typically only used it with my family. It took a lot of mental energy to lower the shield you create in your mind to keep people out and then put it back up afterward. The only wolves who could force someone's mental shield down were an alpha and, of course, the king.

The mind linking between Mom and Dad continued for a minute, Dad's face showing a wide variety of expressions. At first, he looked frustrated, and angry. Then he looked surprised, then disgustingly lustful at Mom, who had a small teasing smile on her lips. I absolutely did not want to hear what they were saying. Finally, he sighed and looked accepting.

"Fine, you'll take Matt's Tahoe. Your car is too small for all the luggage you'll be bringing," he said when he finally looked back at me, the glazed-over look leaving his eyes.

"Thank you, Daddy," I told him happily, running up to him and throwing my arms around him tightly. He lost his annoyance and hugged me back tightly, kissing the top of my head.

"You're welcome, sweetheart."

I pulled away, looking at him with a grin on my face. I turned to Mom and pulled her in for a hug as well.

"Thanks, Mom," I whispered to her, even though I knew Dad could still hear.

"No problem. I'm gonna miss you so much, Kenny. I can't believe my pup is leaving me." Tears gathered in her eyes and my smile wavered. Mom was a bit of a crier and it always made me nervous. I wasn't good in situations like these.

"It won't be for long, Abby." Dad saved me from consoling her. He pulled her away from me and into his arms, letting her sob on his chest.

"Go," he mouthed to me.

I didn't need to be told twice. I quickly left the living room and shot up the stairs. I stopped in front of Matt and Kat's bedroom door and knocked quietly. Not two seconds later, Matt pulled the door open and stepped to the side, allowing me to step in. Kat was finishing lining her cat-like green eyes with some eyeliner. She saw me in the mirror's reflection and smiled at me, which I returned.

"So, you convinced Dad to let us drive, huh?" Matt asked, plopping down on his bed. I did the same.

"Actually, that was Mom. Don't ask me how she convinced him. I don't even want to know." I shuddered dramatically. Matt made a sound of disgust while Kat just laughed at us.

"What time are we leaving?" I asked him.

"As soon as Dalton gets here," he answered me. He pulled out his phone, tapped on it for a minute, and then shoved it back in the pocket of his black dress slacks. "He's on his way."

"Why does he even need to come?" I complained.

"Dad trusts him and he works closely with us. He's familiar with pack policies and procedures. He's going to help me with the political side of this trip," he explained.

"I have an idea. How about he flies there while we drive?"

He chuckled. "I don't think so, Kendall. He'll be riding with us. I hope you realized that when you fought with Dad. Also, this is going to be a five-hour drive."

"That far? This is gonna suck." I flung myself back on their bed, groaning loudly.

"Don't worry. I'll be controlling the radio." Kat grinned at me. This time Matt released the groan.

"Good. I'd have to throw myself out of the car if I had to listen to bad music as well."

"What kind of friend would I be if I didn't help take away the urge to fling yourself out of a moving vehicle?"

"A crappy one," I grumbled.

"Well, I'm a damn good one because I also have snacks." She grabbed a bag from the floor and lifted it. It was a large paper bag so I couldn't see everything, but I could make out a pack of Oreos poking out of the top. My favorite.

"I could seriously kiss you." I grabbed the bag from her and immediately tore into the Oreos. I had eaten breakfast with my family before I had gotten ready, but I was pretty much a bottomless pit. I could always eat more.

"You'd have to fight me for her," Matt joked. He tried to steal an Oreo, but I slapped his hand away and growled at him warningly. He lifted his hands in mock surrender.

As I dug through the bag, I could tell Kat had a variety of snacks. There was everything from Oreos and Cheetos to grapes and oranges. This was why she was my best friend.

"We wouldn't need to fight. She'd choose me," I teased him. "Wouldn't you Kat?"

We both turned to her expectantly. She held back a smile and tried to look serious.

"Sorry, babe. I knew her first." She sounded apologetic.

He stood and walked right up to her, wrapping his arms around her waist and leaning down to whisper in her ear. "Guess I'll have to change your mind tonight then." He even took it a step further and started nibbling on her ear lobe.

"Woah, party foul, guys. Save that for your alone time," I told them, feeling thoroughly disgusted.

He chuckled again and pulled away from her. She looked ready to jump on him. She grasped the pink quartz crystal hanging around her neck and rubbed it gingerly with her thumb. She wore it every day since it was the first gift Matt had ever given her.

"I'm gonna leave before you get it on right in front of me." I took one last Oreo and left the room. Kat called out an apology while I was walking out. I just waved a hand at her over my shoulder.

I made my way to my room. Selena was sitting on her bed, looking gloomy still but not as much as last night. Before we could say anything, we both heard a voice yell from downstairs.

Dalton. Gross. He was announcing his arrival as if anyone would care. Apparently, Selena did, because she jumped off her bed and happily clambered downstairs.

I rolled my eyes and grabbed my bags. I threw my purse on one shoulder and my smaller bag over the other. When those were secure, I grabbed a suitcase handle in each hand and followed Selena down the stairs. It took me a while with all the extra weight, but I eventually entered the living room. Everyone was already in there except for Matt.

I placed my stuff next to the front door and walked towards everyone. Dad was holding a tearful Mom. Brody was standing next to Dad, his hands stuffed in his jean's pockets. Kat was talking to Mom while Selena was speaking to Dalton, who turned his attention to me.

"You ready, Kenny?" he asked mockingly, mirth dancing in his muddy brown eyes.

I snarled at him. Have I mentioned how much I hate that name? He said it just to piss me off.

"Are you, jackass? By the way, you're riding in the back with the luggage like the dog you are."

Instead of getting pissed off, like most werewolves would when they were called a dog, he just threw his head back in laughter.

"You're such a sweetheart, Kendall. Really," he said sarcastically.

"And you're an idiot. If we're done stating the obvious, can we get this show on the road?" I asked.

"We're leaving now," Matt said, walking back into the room. He grabbed my luggage and walked right back out.

I turned to my family and a pang of sadness ran through me. I turned to Brody first, since he was nearest to me. He dropped his usual harsh, serious exterior and pulled me into a hug.

Brody and I weren't particularly close, mainly because of the large age difference. He had always acted like my father and was ridiculously overprotective. It used to irritate me to no end, but I loved him nonetheless. And I knew deep down he was just looking out for me because he cared.

I hugged him back tightly. "I'm gonna miss you, Brody."

"I'm gonna miss you too, kid." I pulled back and playfully glared at him.

He ruffled my hair and pushed me away, right into Dad's big form. He pulled me into a giant bear hug. His hugs always made me feel safe and protected. As much as we butted heads, I was still a daddy's girl through and through. Maybe because I was the baby of the family. That always helped me get away with a lot.

Matt used to complain about how unfair it was that Selena and I got away with stuff that he never would have been able to. I knew he was right. Dad was harsher on the boys than on us.

Selena and I took after our Dad in more ways than not. Not looks wise; we looked more like Mom. But in personality. We had Alpha blood running strong through our veins. We weren't the least bit docile like Mom tended to be. All three of us could argue with a brick wall and win. It made for a lot of frustration for Mom. I think Dad felt a kinship with us, which made the others say we were the favorites. Frankly, I always thought the boys were his favorites, but I guess it was just a difference of opinion.

"I love you, baby girl. Thank you for doing this. I'll make it up to you, I promise." He pressed a kiss on my forehead and pulled away from me.

"I love you too." I smiled up at him.

Before either of us could say anything, Mom pulled me away from him and practically threw herself at me. I managed to find my balance before we both tumbled into the wooden coffee table. She clung to me like she was dying and I was her lifeline. She sobbed into my shoulder as I awkwardly wrapped my arms around her. I grimaced. I wasn't good at this, so I just patted her back and let her cry.

Finally, after a few uncomfortable minutes, she pulled back to look at me, her face red and blotchy.

"Be safe, my baby girl. Call me every day. I love you so much." She started pressing kisses on my face after that, which caused my grimace to grow.

"I will. I love you too, Mom," I told her once she pulled away from me.

Dad stepped in for the second time today to pull a tearful Mom away from me and into him.

They then moved on to Kat and Matt while I moved to Selena. She rolled her eyes but still pulled me into a hug anyway, which I returned.

"Stay away from my side of the closet while I'm gone," I told her playfully when she pulled away.

"They look better on me anyways."

"You're delusional, but I'll miss you anyways."

"Me too, Kendall. Call me every once in a while, okay?"

I nodded and hugged her again one last time. Dalton came and stood next to me while we waited for Kat and Matt to finish their goodbyes. Mom currently had a hold of her "baby boy."

"You nervous?" Dalton asked me, for once sounding serious.

"A little. You?" If he could act civil, I could as well.

"A bit." He looked down at me. "I've only been to the castle once. A couple years ago."

"What'd you think?"

"The place is beautiful. Definitely fit for a king. I didn't meet King Finnian, but I did meet the Head Enforcer of the Royal Army. Seemed like a good guy. Had nothing but good things to say about the Royal Family."

"What were you there for? The mating ball?" I asked curiously.

"Yeah. I haven't had a chance to go again since then." Dalton had also been in school for the last couple of years. Plus, he was training to take over as Beta one day.

I nodded at him and my attention was brought back to my family. They had finished their goodbyes and quickly made their way outside. Mom pulled me into one last hug and Dad spoke with Matt and Dalton, going over a few last-minute things.

After a few minutes, Mom finally released me. I hopped into the back seat and frowned at what I saw.

"Hell no. These seating arrangements suck," I told them.

Matt was in the driver's seat and Kat was next to him. They both looked back at me, amused. Dalton smirked from the seat right beside me, and I glared over at him. "Can't you sit up front?" I asked, or more like demanded.

"He could, but then I can't control the radio. I don't really trust them with the job either," Kat told me.

I rolled my eyes and sighed heavily. She did have a point. So, I settled for the next best thing: threats.

"If you cross the middle seat even a little, I'll take away your ability to reproduce," I threatened.

"You're so feisty," he told me, sounding amused. We all buckled up and waved goodbye as Matt pulled out of the driveway. "I love it."

"Yeah well, we'll see how much you love it when I neuter you like the dog you are."

"I look forward to it." He wiggled his thick black eyebrows at me.

"I feel sorry for your mate," I muttered harshly.

"I could say the same. He's gonna have quite the challenge domesticating you." I reached over and punched him in the arm as hard as I could. He didn't seem fazed by it because he just continued, " 'Course, your fiery attitude could come in handy in the bedroom."

That received two additional punches from me and a loud growl from Matt, ever the overprotective big brother. Kat just chuckled at us and changed the song on her phone, which she had plugged into the car radio.

"At least my mate will want to touch me. Yours probably won't come near you with a ten-foot pole. And even that would be too close."

"Please, she won't be able to resist this." He gestured at himself. He was handsome, something I'll only admit in my head, but he was just so obnoxious.

"Yes, because girls love arrogance. That will change her mind in no time."

"Glad you finally see things my way, Kenny."

"Don't call me that," I spat between gritted teeth.

"Aww, don't like it, Kenny?"

"I'm seriously about to beat the hell out of you," I growled to him, balling my hands into fists.

"Both of you knock it off. I don't want to listen to you two argue for five hours," Matt said, authority filling his voice.

I glared at him for bossing me around, but I stopped nonetheless. I didn't want to speak to Dalton anyway.

We fell into silence after that, munching on snacks and listening to the music. Kat talked to all of us, but I didn't communicate with either of the males in the car. They didn't speak to each other as well. Soon enough, I dozed off, leaning my head against the small pillow I brought.

* * *

By the time we reached the Royal Territory, it was already dark outside. We had gotten a late start, not actually leaving until the afternoon. We had made a few stops along the way as well. We had a late lunch when we reached the halfway point, then we had to stop to get gas and use the restroom.

Dalton and I had bickered a few more times, but not enough for Matt to tell us to stop. It had mostly been just me and Kat speaking because the closer we got to the castle, the more both men started acting like the Alpha and Beta that they were. They knew to take this seriously.

I had slept for about two hours along the way and was feeling better because of it. My lack of sleep from the previous night was making me cranky, so a little nap helped a lot.

Entering the Royal Territory was quite the experience. When we reached the first gate, they checked all of our IDs and searched the car. After about fifteen minutes of searching and confirming our identity, they finally let us through. We drove for another ten minutes or so, dense forests on both sides of the small concrete road before we came to another gate.

They repeated the same process as before. Once they let us on our way, we drove for ways again. I thought we were finally through, but much to my exasperation, we reached yet another gate. This time, it opened up to a huge, medieval castle in front of us.

It was a dark stone castle, which was probably five or six stories tall. Forests surrounded all three sides and a snow-covered mountain sat right behind it. A thin layer of fog covered the land and the walls were bathed in moonlight, making the castle as eerie as it was beautiful. The property that it sat on was bare of any trees and was enclosed by a wrought iron fence.

The large gates creaked open, and Matt slowly drove through the small road. The yard was probably two or three acres, so it took a minute or so to reach the end of the road.

It was a round driveway with a large stone fountain in the center. There was a road off to the side, which I'm assuming leads to a garage. We stopped in front of the fountain as the last guard had directed.

By the time we opened the doors, we were already surrounded by people. Someone grabbed my hand and helped me out, closing the door behind me. I thanked him. He nodded curtly and walked away.

Someone else helped Kat and the two guys out as well, and two more opened the trunk to get our suitcases out. We didn't need to tell them whose were whose; they could detect our scents and separate them.

We all gathered in a group. Kat and me in the middle, Matt next to her, and Dalton next to me. I didn't shy away from his proximity, purely out of nerves. The next man to greet us was very intimidating. I shivered, partially from him and partially from the cold air that now surrounded us. My legs were fully exposed to the biting wind and the cardigan did little to shield me.

He stopped a few feet from us, a relaxed look on his handsome face. He was a Latino with warm, tanned skin, short black hair, and honey-colored eyes. He was tall—taller than all of the men in my family, which was saying something. His muscular body was encased in a pair of black slacks and a dark blue button-down shirt, the sleeves rolled up to his elbows. He was handsome, but for some reason, I didn't find myself attracted to him.

He stepped closer to us. For a split second, he got a weird look on his face and sniffed the air. A second later, it was gone. He shook his head, an easy smile gracing his lips.

"Welcome, Keating Pack. I'm Royal Gamma Tyler Guzman. It's a pleasure."

"The pleasure is all ours. I'm Matthew Keating. I'm here to represent my Father, Alpha Jefferson Keating." He shook hands with the Royal Gamma, then gestured to each of us. "This is my mate and our witch-in-training, Katerina Abara; our Beta-in-training, Dalton Collins; and lastly my sister, Kendall Keating."

Dalton shook his hand first, then Kat. Lastly, I placed my hand in his. He brought it up and pressed a kiss to the back of it. I didn't view it as inappropriate, instead respectful. I'm sure that was how the Royals greeted women. I had a feeling he would have done the same to Kat, had she not been mated.

"If you'll follow me, I'll take you on a short tour, then show you your rooms before dinner. Your bags are being delivered as we speak. You'll be able to freshen up, then you'll dine with King Finnian tonight."

My mouth went dry and a knot formed in my stomach at those words. I wasn't ready to meet the King yet. Dalton noticed my hesitation and gently pushed me forward to follow Royal Gamma Guzman. I was slightly surprised to see that he was the one greeting and giving us a tour. The Royal Gamma was the third in command of the King. Didn't he have better things to do?

We all followed him up the stone steps into the castle. He opened both of the tall wooden doors and gestured for us to enter. As we stepped inside, my breath got caught at the sight of the interior.

It was just as medieval looking as the exterior, but I could tell it was still modern and up to date. The floor was made of shiny dark colored marble and an expensive large chandelier hung from the ceiling of the foyer. The walls were made of stone and had large paintings hanging from them. There was a staircase, also made of smooth dark colored marble, on both sides of the foyer. A balcony in between the tops of the stairs overlooked the room.

The area between the staircase was cloaked in darkness. I didn't get to figure out where it led, because he guided us up the stairs and took a right. We followed him down a dimly lit corridor. He took several turns and we finally ended up in a large kitchen.

"This floor is the guest floor. This kitchen is free for your use. A chef will be available to you whenever you request. You are also free to dine with us whenever you please. The royal kitchen and dining area are three floors up."

I was curious as to who "us" included. I was a little surprised by the open invitation to dine with them. By a little, I mean very.

The kitchen was large. The interior was made of cobblestone, but the appliances were modern stainless steel. There was a kitchen table off to the side, and I could tell the room next to the kitchen was a large dining room. He led us out of the room and continued down the same corridor.

"Royal Gamma?" I asked timidly, which was highly unlike me. He looked over at me and smiled slightly, so I continued. "Out of curiosity, how many floors does this place have?"

"It has six. This is the east wing, which is the residential wing. The first floor has a lot of empty rooms. It's not currently in use. The second and third floors are for guests. The fourth and fifth floors are for the Royals. They are the only people who live here. The Royal Army has separate housing to reside in, as do the rest of the workers. The sixth floor is King Finnian's personal quarters. No one but him is allowed on that floor," he explained.

"And the west wing?" I inquired.

"That area is for a variety of things. It holds the ballroom, which is its own separate floor. Several meeting rooms are located on that side of the castle, along with the king's private and public office. Basically, any event or meeting takes place in the west wing. I'll show you around tomorrow if you'd like."

"Thanks, that'd be great."

He stopped in front of an open room. It was a large living room. Couches and chairs surrounded it, and a large stone fireplace was against a wall. A television was mounted above it. The area seemed cold, unused. It was clean, but it lacked the warmth of the living room at my home.

"This is the living area. There are televisions in your rooms but if you want to use the fireplace, you'll have to come in here."

We followed him back out. He led us down the rest of the hallway, which led to another. We turned left, which ended in a dead end. He stopped at the first door and pushed it open.

"Beta Collins. This will be your room during your stay here. Each bedroom is equipped with a full bathroom and a large walk-in closet. If you need anything else, there are speakers next to the door on every wall. Just press the talk button and someone will assist you."

Dalton nodded and entered his room. We continued walking and I heard the door shut behind us. The next door he opened was for Kat and Matt. I could tell Kat was pleased with her room, but I didn't get to see it before I was whisked away to the end of the hall.

Royal Gamma Tyler pushed it open and gestured me inside. I, once again, lost my breath as I took in the room in front of me. The floor had plush white carpeting and, like the rest of the castle, the walls were made of stone. A king-sized red canopy bed sat on one wall. A TV was on the opposite wall in front of a sitting area, which had a sectional black couch. Double doors were on the wall opposite the exit. I assumed the closet and bathroom were in there.

"Is this satisfactory, Miss Keating?" He looked like he already knew the answer.

"It's amazing. And it's just Kendall."

"Okay, Kendall then. I'll be back to retrieve all of you in an hour for dinner. Just use the speaker if you need anything before then."

"Thank you, Royal Gamma." I bowed my head in respect.

"It's just Tyler," he mimicked my words.

"Okay, Tyler then," I mimicked him as well.

He grinned at me and left the room, pulling the door shut behind him. I noticed my bags were sitting on the bed. I grabbed them and carried them to the bathroom, wanting to unpack before dinner.

I opened one side of the double doors and pulled my bags inside. The bathroom was just as magnificent as the bedroom. It had a large Jacuzzi tub and a walk-in shower, the door made of glass, and the walls inside lined with stone. There was a vanity area with a chair and a lighted mirror next to the sink. The closet was inside, as I predicted. It was huge but empty.

I quickly got to work unpacking my bags. I was just about done with the big pieces of luggage when I heard my door open and shut. I took in a deep breath, sniffing for the scent. Dalton. I rolled my eyes and continued unpacking my toiletries until I saw him in the bathroom doorway.

"Your room is even nicer than mine."

"That's what happens when you're a likeable person. You should try it sometime."

I left the bathroom after I finished unpacking my bag of toiletries. He followed behind me. I sat down on the bed and he leaned against one of the bed posts, crossing his arms and ankles. He smirked down at me.

"You know you secretly like me. You don't have to pretend you don't."

"You make me want to stab myself in the ears with a fork so I don't have to listen to you. That's how likable you are." I smirked back at him. I crossed my own arms.

"I see you want your eyes still intact. Must mean that you want to look at me," he said cockily.

Before I could give him a smartass reply, something shifted. Something that neither of us could prepare for because it all happened so fast.

I opened my mouth to speak just as the door to my bedroom flew open. My eyes widened and I stood up quickly, my arms falling to my sides. Dalton did the same and turned towards the door, looking as startled as I felt. We didn't even hear anyone coming.

In the doorway stood the most perfect specimen of a man I've ever had the pleasure of laying my eyes upon. He was the epitome of tall, dark, and handsome. He had dark brown hair, which was pushed back stylishly. He had a layer of dark stubble covering his strong jaw and surrounding his full, perfect pink lips. He had a long, strong nose and high cheekbones. His body was strong and muscular, adorned in black slacks and a black button-down shirt which, like Tyler's, was rolled up to his elbows and had the top button undone.

He towered over both Dalton and me, standing at least six foot six, maybe taller. Lastly, I took a look at his eyes. They were glowing molten gold now, but somehow I knew they were blue when his wolf wasn't taking over.

As much as I felt like the moment of taking him in happened in slow motion, I know it didn't. He briefly took me in as well, then turned his attention to Dalton and snarled. He looked lethal like he could crush Dalton in a second and not think twice.

It didn't take me long to figure out my reaction to him and why I wasn't scared for myself, only Dalton. He was my mate. My wolf was freaking out inside of me, trying to claw her way out and towards her mate. Her need to mark and mate with him was so strong. I nearly shifted right there but somehow, I pushed that part of myself back.

He stalked over to us, still looking deadly. Dalton looked terrified. Even though I hated him, I still felt bad for him and was ready to jump in to help him.

I gasped as my mate, whose name I still didn't know, grabbed Dalton by his throat and lifted him. Werewolves were strong, but this was crazy. He was lifting a grown man, who was well over 200 pounds of pure muscle, with one hand, without even looking like he was struggling even a little. Dalton just hung there limply. His wolf was probably telling him to submit instead of fight.

"Don't ever flirt with her again," he growled out. His voice was rough and gravelly, which happened when our wolf took over but it still caused goosebumps to erupt across my flesh.

Just like that, he dropped Dalton, who fell to the floor and scrambled to his feet. His eyes stayed low and he bared his neck to him.

"Get out. Now. Speak to no one about this," he commanded. I knew Dalton wouldn't be able to defy him.

The sheer power that came from the command left me baring my neck in submission as well. It was something I had never done or experienced before. I was of Alpha blood and wasn't the least bit submissive but the power he exuded was almost too much to handle.

As Dalton shot out of the room without so much as a glance in my direction, it suddenly hit me what was happening. Just as a large, warm hand grabbed my chin firmly but gently and tilted my head up to look into his eyes, I realized who this was.

As I took in his now cerulean eyes, I said the only thing that was rattling around in my brain.

"King Finnian . . ."

CHAPTER THREE

As soon as his name left my lips, his eyes glowed gold again. A deep growl rumbled in his chest, but I had a feeling it wasn't out of anger this time.

He let go of my chin and instead grabbed my hips to pull my body as close to his as possible. Not an inch of space was left between us as his hard, warm body pressed against mine. Chills ran down my spine, leaving me breathless. My wolf continued to fight to the surface of my consciousness, refusing to be ignored, my own eyes resembling his.

A loud gasp left me when he buried his face in the crook of my neck, inhaling deeply. His lips skimmed the sensitive flesh where his mark was supposed to lay. The sensations I felt increased and a haze of lust clouded my mind, cutting off all reasoning. He gently nipped at the area that his lips were just at, causing molten heat to accumulate in my lower belly. I had never felt like this before.

I had kissed guys before, sure, but their lips could never do to me what this man was doing. I had apparently underestimated the mate bond, because never in my wildest dreams would I have imagined this.

Suddenly, he grabbed the back of my thighs and lowered me to the bed, my back pressing against the plush mattress. He settled himself between my nearly completely bare thighs since my dress had risen dangerously high up my legs. He held himself up with his muscular arms, but his body was still flush against mine. My hands weakly gripped his shirt, and his hands were tangled in my hair, which was fanned out against the pillow under my head. He tugged gently on my curls, but not in a painful way.

His lips inched closer to mine. I pulled him down by the back of his neck and our lips collided in a desperate, lust-filled kiss, moving in a passionate synchronization. I nipped on his bottom lip, tugging it gently. I opened my mouth for him and our tongues collided.

He pulled away when I started getting lightheaded. I breathed in a shuddering deep breath as he moved down my jaw and to my neck. He nipped and sucked at the skin, eliciting a breathy moan from me.

Before I even realized what was happening, I felt his elongated canines against my neck, threatening to break the skin. I didn't have time to react before he pushed himself off of me completely.

I pushed myself up with my elbows, looking around the room in confusion. I breathed heavily and pulled my dress back down over my legs. I noticed he was several feet from the bed, his back turned towards me. I heard deep, rumbling growls emitting from his chest. His hands were fisted by his sides, his knuckles turning white and his body was shaking like he was fighting off a shift.

I wasn't sure what to do, so I sat there nervously, tugging my fingers on my lap, waiting for him to calm down. I didn't want to say or do anything that would set him off again. As my breathing slowed, the lustful haze died down, and the reality of the situation returned to the front of my mind. I hadn't wanted to meet my mate here, which I was ashamed to admit now, but now that I had, it wouldn't change a thing. He was perfect.

Finally, after what felt like hours but was probably only minutes, he turned back around. My smile widened at this but dropped just as quickly when I saw his face. My brows knitted together, confusion and anxiety spiking once again.

His now blue eyes regarded me rather coldly. His lips were thinned in a straight line and his jaw clenched. He looked every bit the king now. As much as I hated to admit it, I was feeling slightly intimidated. That didn't happen often.

"Dinner will be served in twenty minutes, Miss Keating. Clean yourself up and don't be late. This stays between us," he told me, or more like commanded me, with no emotion in his voice whatsoever.

My mouth opened in shock and my heart felt like it was ripped to shreds. Why was he acting like this? Like nothing happened and I wasn't his soulmate?

Before I could respond, he gave me one last look, a glint in his eyes showing up that I couldn't decipher, but soon it was gone. He strode out of my room, not once looking back.

I felt my eyes misting over, but I quickly blinked the tears away. This wasn't me. I didn't cry, especially over a boy. Mate or not, at the end of the day, he was still just a boy.

With that thought, a new determination filled me. I wasn't going to let him get to me. If he didn't want me, that was fine. I'd show him that it didn't bother me and that I didn't want him either. He wasn't worth my tears and heartache. My wolf begged to differ, but I quickly pushed her away; into the deepest recesses in my mind, and she went willingly.

With my new mindset, I walked to my bathroom to get ready for this dinner.

* * *

"You look hot," Kat commented as I stepped out of my room.

Tyler had knocked on my door exactly twenty minutes after King Finnian left. He had Kat, Matt, and Dalton in tow. Dalton wouldn't even look at me. I felt somewhat bad for him. I mean, I didn't like the guy but Finnian took it too far. He accused him of flirting with me, which was a preposterous notion in and of itself. Dalton had been mocking me, not flirting.

"Thanks, you do too!"

Kat was wearing the same tight, long-sleeved red dress that she had been wearing earlier, but she had straightened her wavy hair and had touched up her make-up. Her pink quartz still sat lightly against her chest.

I, on the other hand, had changed completely. Gone was the modest green dress and black cardigan. In its place, I was now sporting a tight, lacy black dress. It was sexy but classy enough that I could get away with wearing it to a fancy dinner with royalty. I had pulled my curls back into a low bun, revealing the smooth curve of my neck, which King Finnian's teeth nearly pierced twenty minutes ago.

I knew I was being immature wearing something so sexy but I couldn't help myself. After how coldly King Finnian had treated me, I wanted to get a reaction from him. At the very least, I wanted to show him what he was missing. I wasn't conceited, but I felt comfortable with my body and in my own skin. I didn't mind showing off my curves every once in a while. Hence why I had this dress to begin with. I knew I was beautiful; I didn't think it was wrong to think like this. I sure as hell wasn't going to let him make me think otherwise.

"You okay? You seem different . . ." Kat asked me as we began walking. We trailed a few feet behind the rest of the group. Matt and Dalton were both speaking with Tyler and paying us no mind.

"I'm fine. Just a little nervous, I guess," I lied.

She gave me a look that told me she knew I was lying but wasn't going to push me right now. I knew she would later.

"I'm a little nervous too," she admitted. She linked her arm with mine and we continued following the boys.

I wondered who would be attending this dinner. Obviously, Tyler and his mate, if he had one. King Finnian as well, but I wasn't sure who else. I didn't really stay updated on the Royal Family. I knew of King Finnian, but that's as far as my knowledge went. I wasn't even sure who the Royal Beta was. It was sad really; I was a werewolf who was unfamiliar with the Werewolf Monarchy. Like I said, I hated politics.

We walked up another set of stairs, down a long hallway, then another long hallway, before we went to another set of stairs. Before I knew it, we were on the fifth floor. Tyler guided us through hallway after hallway, and we finally made it to a huge dining room. It looked more like a ballroom though.

There was a long table sitting right in the middle of the stone room. It was made of dark wood and stretched across the room. It looked like it could seat at least thirty people. The chairs surrounding it had high backs and were made of the same dark oak with red velvet detailing. The chair at the head of the table looked fit for a king. No doubt, that was Finnian's chair, who wasn't actually present.

The table had centerpieces all across it. Tall white unscented candles were scattered everywhere, and the smell of burning wicks overwhelmed my olfactory senses. There wasn't food on the table yet, just empty wine glasses, glasses of ice water, a small empty plate, probably for salad, and a butt load of silverware. I couldn't possibly know what fork went with each meal. Why couldn't I just use one fork for both salad and the main course? The world may never know.

Although King Finnian wasn't here yet, other people were. Tyler led us to the table, and we sat across from the four other people already seated. Tyler sat next to the chair King Finnian would sit. He pulled out the chair next to him for me, and I took a seat. Kat sat next to me, Matt next to her, and Dalton beside him, as far away from me as he could get.

Once seated, I took in the people across from us. Directly across Tyler was another man. He had an air of authority around him, but not like the King. I sensed that he was the Royal Beta.

He had short black hair and piercing blue eyes, which were currently on me. I smiled tightly and he nodded once in acknowledgment.

The woman next to him was beautiful but her face was pinched with a look of disgust; her delicate features morphed in repulsion as she took us all in. By the way, the man sat as close to her as possible, I knew they were mates.

Next to her was a similar-looking girl, although she looked around ten or fifteen years older. She smiled kindly at us, which I returned. She pushed her black hair over her shoulder and I looked at the last girl. She looked young and timid. She smiled shyly at us and I did the same.

As I took in all three women, I knew they were related. They were all tall and willowy, with the same black hair, olive skin, and sharp, high cheekbones. Their eyes were dark, but only one of them lacked any warmth.

"It's truly a pleasure to meet you, Keating Pack," the one in the middle said. She had a happy, knowing smile playing on her lips. My curiosity grew as she looked at me longer than necessary as she spoke, before moving her gaze down the line. "I am Nikolina Petrova. You may call me Niki."

I saw Kat perk up beside me upon hearing that she was a Petrova witch.

"I am King Finnian's Royal Witch. These are my sisters, Emiliya and Liliya. Emiliya is mated to the Royal Beta Kieran Cahill. He is King Finnian's brother," she spoke gracefully, something I lacked, and gestured to each person she introduced.

"I am Alpha Jefferson Keating's son, Matthew Keating. This is my mate and our pack witch in training, Katerina Abara; our Beta in training, Dalton Collins; and my sister, Kendall Keating," Matt introduced before anyone could speak.

"I know exactly who you all are." She smirked. She spoke like she knew something we didn't. "I hear you'd like to study under one of us while you're residing here, Katerina. Is that correct?" She turned her attention from me to Kat.

"Yes, that would be such an honor," Kat spoke politely, but I could hear the hope and enthusiasm in her voice. It seemed Niki could as well.

"The Abara line is a very powerful Coven. They are normally very closed off from the outside world, so you are the first I have had the pleasure of encountering. The honor would be all mine to teach and guide you."

Emiliya made a disgusted sound in the back of her throat, but Niki ignored her so we did as well.

"Really? Thank you so much. That means so much to me." Kat smiled widely at her.

"You are most welcome, Katerina. We'll begin tomorrow," Niki informed her.

I was so happy for Kat. I immediately took a strong liking to Niki. My wolf approved of her as well.

"You can just call me Kat, ma'am. No one really calls me Katerina except for my Mom."

"Alright, Kat. And please, just Niki. I am infinitely too young to be called ma'am," she told her lightheartedly. Then she turned her attention back to me. "So, Kendall. Tell me about yourself," she asked me with a glint in her eyes.

I felt stunned for a second. I wasn't exactly sure what she was looking for. I felt like she was fishing for something.

"Well, I'm twenty-three. I'm the youngest of four children. I just finished college. I help my father and brothers with pack finances and with the family business," I finally told her.

"I already know all that dear. I want to know about *you*," she emphasized. I felt so confused. I wasn't sure what to say and what she wanted to hear, but thankfully I was spared.

King Finnian chose that moment to make his entrance. I felt him enter the room before I even saw him or smelled his musky, masculine scent. I felt him as both my mate and the King.

Before I could turn to look at him, everyone stood up and bared their necks to him, eyes on the ground. This was a sign of respect. I didn't want to do this; I was supposed to be his equal. But I have to keep this a secret for now. I hesitated briefly, which Matt glared at me for, but I stood as well and submitted. I could feel his eyes burning a hole on me, moving up and down my body, taking in my change of clothes, but he never said a word to me.

Once King Finnian sat at the head of the table, we were all seated as well and conversation resumed. Luckily, Niki stopped questioning me. She started a conversation with Kat, Matt, and Liliya. I remained silent. I had to bite my tongue. I wanted to comment how Finnian was late for dinner so badly, despite telling me not to be late.

It pissed me off that I couldn't speak my mind. I was always one to voice my thoughts. I was of Alpha blood. I hated suppressing my true nature, especially since my mate was being a royal douchebag, pun intended.

I felt bitterness settle over me. He made me feel this way. That chased any pain away, although I know it still lingered deep, deep down.

I had been so lost in my thoughts that I didn't pay attention to the conversations around me until I heard my name.

"Wouldn't it be great if Kendall or Dalton here found their mates during their stay?" Niki spoke joyfully, speaking to no one in particular.

I gulped. Someone shoot me.

"That would be great. There are a lot of wolves here. It's very possible. The mating ball will occur during your stay as well," Tyler spoke.

Waiters came out at that time, filling our wine glasses and serving us salad. They didn't deter from the conversation, unfortunately.

I glanced at King Finnian from the corner of my eye, making sure no one realized I was looking his way. He looked like the epitome of calm, but I could see the fire burning in his eyes as he glanced my way as well.

"As likely as that may be, I'm keeping my fingers crossed that it doesn't happen," I said as I turned my attention back to Niki. I couldn't help myself.

"Oh?" Her eyes slid sideways to Finnian, then back to me. No one else noticed because they were looking at me as well. I had everyone's attention, including his. I could feel possessive anger coming off him in waves. "Why is that, dear? Most werewolves can't wait to meet their soulmates."

"I don't think he'll be able to handle me." I stabbed at the salad, probably with the wrong fork, and brought it up to my mouth. I held back a grimace. It was coated in some kind of fancy vinaigrette which smelled horrible and tasted even worse. I was an old-fashioned ranch-dressing kind of girl. I ate it anyway and washed it down with the white wine.

"What do you mean?" She tilted her head slightly in curiosity.

"I'm a hard person to please. I don't think he'll be up to the challenge."

Niki looked slightly surprised at this and glanced nervously at King Finnian. I did the same. He sat stiffly in his chair, the fork in his hand bending from his tight grip. His jaw was clenched and his eyes were filled with fire, but he didn't speak. I looked back at my plate and smirked slightly, hiding it by taking another bite of salad.

"I think what she means is that he won't be able to handle her stubbornness," Matt joked.

"You do strike me as rather willful," Niki added knowingly. I liked her, but the speaking in riddles was getting to me.

"That's putting it lightly," my brother told her.

"Obstinacy is a very unattractive quality to possess," Emiliya spoke for the first time tonight, her pretty face twisted up in an ugly sneer. I glared back at her.

"It takes someone with many unattractive qualities to comment on those of others, Emiliya," King Finnian also spoke for the first time, his voice deep and sexy. He spoke casually, but everyone clearly heard the warning in his tone. It warmed my heart that he was defending me, but it seemed to piss Kieran off because he glared daggers at him, which was ignored.

"That quality is called honesty, Your Highness," she drawled out almost sarcastically.

"No, it's called insolence. And I won't tolerate you speaking to my guests in such a way," he growled out.

"My apologies, King Finnian," she sneered.

"Watch your tone. And I'm not the one you should apologize to," he sneered back at her. I somehow guessed there was no love lost between these two.

"Please accept my most sincere apologies, Miss Keating," she told me through gritted teeth. I think that actually caused her pain.

"Uh, sure," I mumbled.

I realized quickly that I sounded like an idiot compared to these people. They spoke with such grace and eloquence, meanwhile, I spoke like I barely completed fifth grade. Emiliya seemed to notice this too because she gave me another look of disgust before turning back to her salad.

After a couple of minutes, the servers came and took the salads away and brought us the main course, which was medium rare ribeye steak, rosemary potatoes, grilled asparagus, and a roll. It was much better than the salad.

"So, what do you all think about the castle? Is it to your liking?" Niki asked, delicately cutting into her steak, putting a small bite into her mouth, and chewing slowly.

"It's amazing. It's so beautiful," Kat answered first.

"It is quite lovely. Perhaps King Finnian can personally give you a complete tour of the grounds tomorrow?" She raised an inquisitive eyebrow, looking between King Finnian and me.

"You know that would be a waste of my time, Nikolina. I have better things to do than explore my own property," he said calmly, after swallowing the food in his mouth. I swallowed a growl.

"That's quite alright. Tyler here has already offered to give me the grand tour." I rested my hand on his shoulder and smiled up at him, which he returned.

I looked back at Niki, who looked quite amused. Finnian, not so much. I could hear him grinding his teeth when I listened carefully.

"That sounds lovely. Tyler is such a sweetheart, isn't he? Always going above and beyond, especially for a beautiful girl such as yourself."

I started to wonder if she somehow knew. She seemed to not only be baiting me, but Finnian as well. She was the most powerful witch in the castle, so it wouldn't surprise me if she knew. Maybe she had a vision about us.

"Royal Gamma Guzman will be occupied tomorrow. I'll have Melanie show them around instead." Tyler looked confused at this but didn't interrupt.

"Nonsense, King Finnian. You shouldn't have a maid showing your very special guests around. Royal Gamma Guzman would be more appropriate, I'm sure."

"Well, I'm not. I said no," he suddenly snapped, losing his cool demeanor. He growled at her and glared gold-colored daggers in her direction.

"As you wish, Your Highness." She didn't look scared at all. In fact, she looked smug; like she was trying to make him lose his cool. "Perhaps you'll let Liliya here show them around?"

The girl, who I hadn't actually heard speak yet, looked up shyly from her dinner, looking between the King and her sister.

"That would be fine," he finally spoke after mulling it over for a minute.

"Excellent. You wouldn't mind showing our special guests around, would you, Liliya?" She turned to her sister.

"Of course not, Nikolina. It would be my pleasure," she said in a soft voice, which I noticed Emiliya roll her eyes at. Bitch.

"Excellent," she repeated. "You'll receive your tour in the morning, then you can join us for lunch?"

"Sounds great," I told her.

"Afterwards, Kat, we'll begin your training. You're welcome to observe, Kendall. Or if Tyler is no longer . . ." She paused, laughter dancing in her eyes. "Occupied, maybe he can occupy your time."

"No. She'll stay with you and Liliya," Finnian answered before I could.

"As you wish," she repeated.

* * *

"Was it just me or was that really weird?" Kat told me once she closed my door behind her.

The rest of dinner had gone by quickly. Niki had stopped her probing questions and Finnian hadn't spoken again. Once we finished the main course, we had some kind of fruity dessert. Niki bid us farewell for the night, with the promise of Liliya giving us a tour at nine sharp. Tyler had led us back to our rooms. Dalton went straight to his room, still not even looking at me. I was starting to feel really bad for him. I didn't know if he was embarrassed or mad at me, but I didn't like it.

Matt tried to pull Kat to their room, probably having something inappropriate in mind, but she ignored him and followed me instead. I had given him a smug grin just to mess with him. He mumbled something under his breath and went to his own room.

"Wasn't just you. That was the very definition of weird." I flung myself down on the couch and she did the same.

"It's just us now. Spill. You seem weird too. What's going on?" She looked at me seriously.

I bit my lip, trying to decide if I should tell her. He had commanded me not to but, for some reason, his command didn't really work on me. On every other wolf, they would have no choice but to listen. Our wolves instinctually knew who our superiors were and they wouldn't allow us to not listen to their commands. But since I was technically supposed to be his equal, my wolf didn't see it that way.

I wanted to tell her, but in all honesty, I was embarrassed. My own mate didn't seem to want me. That was the lowest form of humiliation.

She was my best friend though. I never hid anything from her. She knew every embarrassing thing about me and had never once judged it. I knew that if I could trust anyone to tell this to, it was her.

"This stays between us, okay? I don't even want Matt to know yet." I knew I was asking a lot, asking her to practically lie to her mate, but if he knew, he would come to my defense and do something stupid. I couldn't let Finnian hurt my family. Dalton was bad enough but not my brother.

"I promise," she said with no hesitation. That's why I loved her. Despite being with my brother, she was still, first and foremost, my best friend.

"He's my mate," I whispered, just in case we had any prying ears. The stone walls made it hard to hear through rooms, even with werewolf hearing, but Finnian had somehow heard Dalton and me talking earlier. And who the hell knows where in the castle he had been.

He was the King though. Everything about him was enhanced. His senses, his strength, his speed—everything basically—far exceeded that of even the strongest Alpha. He could probably hear every pin that dropped in this massive castle if he tried hard enough.

"Who? Tyler? He's cute. You could definitely do a lot worse. Was that what all that mate talk was about? You were messing with him weren't you?" she said all in one breath before I could get a word out.

"It isn't Tyler," I said before she could say anything else.

"Then who . . ." she trailed off, a look of understanding settling on her face. "Kendall . . . You've only met three guys since we've been here. Tyler's not it, and the Royal Beta has a mate . . ."

I nodded in confirmation at her unspoken question.

"Kendall, what the hell were you thinking with your answers tonight? He's the king for crying out loud. Were you trying to piss him off?" she whispered loudly.

"Pretty much," I told her honestly.

"How in the hell did he not react to seeing you? Even a psychopath would react to seeing his mate for the first time."

"He did react. That wasn't the first time I saw him," I confessed.

"We were only separated for an hour before dinner. Did he come to you?"

"He did. It was crazy, Kat. Dalton was in here and he just stormed in and choked him. He freaking choked him! And accused him of flirting with me. It was ridiculous. Then he kicked Dalton out and was all over me just like that. I don't know what I did wrong, but he suddenly just stopped and turned into the world's biggest douchebag. It was like it never happened," I confessed everything to her.

"Well, at least that proves he feels something. He got jealous, so that's a good start I guess." She tried to sound optimistic. "And he defended you during dinner."

"He wasn't jealous. And if he was, then he had no reason to be." She gave me a dry look, raising her eyebrow at me. "What?"

"He had every reason to be jealous," she told me like it was the most obvious thing in the world.

"What the hell are you talking about? I'm so over people talking in riddles tonight."

"Dalton obviously likes you. Has for years."

I couldn't help it. I laughed. Like, to the point of tears.

"Why are you laughing?"

"Because that's the craziest thing I've ever heard, Kat."

"You're so blind. He's had a thing for you since we were kids. You were always so mean to him, so he's never acted on it."

"He's mean to me too," I defended.

"Not really. He just does that to get a reaction out of you because you wouldn't pay any attention to him otherwise." She shrugged her shoulder like it made all the sense in the world.

"If he's into anyone, it's Selena. They've been hanging out since they were like ten."

"He and Selena are like partners in crime; they don't feel anything towards each other—other than friendship. You know her. She would have told him."

"That's true I guess, but it doesn't mean he doesn't feel that way about her."

"He doesn't. You don't see the way he looks at you when you aren't paying attention. It's actually kind of sad."

"Why didn't you tell me this before?" I demanded.

"Wasn't my place to. Besides, I knew it wouldn't mean much coming from me. You wouldn't have believed it unless it came from him." That was true I guess, although I still wouldn't have believed it then.

"Well, fuck my life . . ." I mumbled. I definitely didn't want to deal with Dalton now. I had absolutely no feelings for him whatsoever. "Why didn't he ever tell me?"

"He knew you didn't like him, like at all. And even if you did, it wouldn't have changed anything. You both have mates out there. I guess he figured he'd just hold out until he met his and got over you," she explained.

"Hmm . . ." That was all I could muster in response.

"Doesn't matter now though. You have your own mate. He'd never act on it now. I'm sure after what happened the flirting will stop. At least he'll leave you alone now."

She shrugged and stood up. I stood up with her.

"Well, I have my own mate to get to. Don't worry about this, Kendall. He has the strongest wolf in the world; he can't hold it back for long. It'll all work out. Goodnight."

She hugged me and left the room after I told her goodnight as well. I decided after that to try out the Jacuzzi tub in my bathroom. Mine and Selena's bathroom at home didn't have a bathtub, just a walk-in shower, so I never got to enjoy soaking in a tub. I filled it with hot water and added some of the lavender bath salts that surrounded it. They were a little overpowering to my heightened sense of smell but I quickly adjusted and it died down a little.

Once the tub was full, I stripped out of my dress, shoes, and underwear. I slowly lowered myself into the warm water and felt my muscles immediately relax. I closed my eyes and leaned my head back.

I thought about everything Kat had said. I couldn't believe what she said about Dalton. I had thought for years that he was my nemesis, but apparently, only I felt that way.

I couldn't say that what she had told me changed my thoughts about him though. I still thought he was an arrogant jackass. Now I could add coward to that list too. If he had feelings for me, he should have either told me or got over it. Mocking me wasn't the way to go about gaining my affections.

I couldn't help but let my mind drift to King Finnian. I feel like Kat was wrong. Dinner only proved that he didn't really care. No one but me and Niki even noticed his anger. I was expecting more of a reaction, but he'd given me practically nothing . . . like I was nothing. It pissed me off.

Before my Keating temper could come out, my phone started ringing. I dried off one hand and grabbed my phone. The screen just said "Home." Someone's using the house phone.

"Hello?" I answered, wondering who I was going to get first.

"Why didn't you call me when you got there?" Mom asked, sounding disheartened. Should have guessed. I probably should have remembered to call . . .

"Sorry, Mom. It's just been a busy day. I figured Matt would call you."

"Well, he didn't. I had to call him. I've already scolded him and Kat. Now it's your turn."

I held in a long sigh, but I did roll my eyes under my closed lids.

"I am your mother, Kendall. When you're traveling, you're supposed to call as soon as you get there and let me know you made it safely."

"Relax Mom. It's not like we died. You would have felt something if we did anyway, so you knew we were safe."

"Kendall Taylor Keating! Don't talk so frivolously about death. It's no joking matter. If anything ever happened to you kids . . ." she trailed off and I heard her sniffling.

"Sorry, Mom," I blankly replied to her dramatics.

"You should be. I can't even talk to you anymore right now. I love you. Here's your sister."

"Love you too," I muttered, waiting for the transfer.

"Kendall, you should be ashamed of yourself for making Mom cry like that," she reprimanded. I knew Mom could hear her and was appreciative of her, but I also knew she was mocking me.

"Screw you, Sel. Besides, she's cried more tears over you than the rest of us combined."

She didn't have a response to that, so she changed the subject. "So, what's it like there?" Excitement now filled her voice.

"It's alright."

"That's it? 'It's alright'? Give me details, you bitch."

"I don't know what else you want me to say. The castle is nice . . ."

I knew what she wanted. She wanted to talk to boys. I couldn't tell her about my mate, so I was trying to avoid that topic.

"The men, you idiot," she finally spat, just like I knew she would.

I sighed heavily. So much for my relaxing bath.

"They're fine, Sel."

"You know what, you're no freaking help. I'm done talking to you. By the way, Dad says he loves you and he'll talk to you tomorrow."

Before I could say anything else, the little bitch hung up. I growled at my phone and dropped it down on my pile of dirty clothes.

I finished bathing and got out of the tub, going through my normal nighttime routine. I threw on a t-shirt too large for me and a pair of panties.

Once I was ready for bed, I turned off the light and opened the door to my room. I froze at what I saw. King Finnian was lying on my bed, his hands tucked under his head. His eyes looked me up and down, suddenly glowing tawny, and he sat up.

"You were testing my patience tonight, mate. That wasn't a wise decision."

I gulped, not really out of fear; more like excitement, as crazy as that was.

Looks like I won't be going to sleep quite yet.

CHAPTER FOUR

"I don't see how," I denied, crossing my arms over my chest.

I didn't feel particularly self-conscious. He was looking over my bare legs up and down, heat filling his eyes, but it didn't bother me. I couldn't bring myself to hide my body from the man I was designed to be with. It didn't feel right. So instead, I cocked an inquisitive, yet mocking, eyebrow and let him look all he wanted.

"My patience is nonexistent at this point, Miss Keating. Don't make me prove that," he threatened. He stood up and took two steps closer to me, but I stayed rooted in front of the bathroom door.

"Mine as well, King Finnian. What do you want?" I got straight to the point, tired of the mind games today.

"I can think of a few things I want . . ." He looked down at my body again before settling on my face once more.

"Hmm, I see . . ." I drawled out. "Well, you're in for quite the disappointment because you won't be receiving those things here."

Two steps closer. "Is that so?" It was his turn to lift a taunting eyebrow at me, his lips pulling up into a smirk.

"It is. Although, maybe you could send me a real man instead."

Before I could even comprehend the words that had left my mouth, he was right in front of me, growling lowly from deep within his chest. He pulled me into his hard body, his hands gripping my hips. I could feel his claws elongating through the thin material of my t-shirt but they didn't puncture it.

His canines were poking into his bottom lip and his eyes glowed. His wolf was in control right now. I knew he wouldn't physically hurt me so I wasn't afraid of him.

"I assure you, Miss Keating, the only man who will be pleasuring you is me. If any other male even thinks about putting their hands on you, I'll rip out their throats and show you who you belong to."

He ran his nose up the side of my neck, the heat from his breath burning deliciously against my cold skin. Goosebumps rose across my flesh and a quivering heat ignited inside me. Somehow, I managed to keep a cool exterior, much like he had at dinner.

"Careful, King Finnian. We wouldn't want anyone to know whose mate I am, now would we?" My voice came out surprisingly strong.

He hummed, peppering kisses on my jaw. "I suppose not," he played along. His voice came out as a deep, husky rumble.

"I am rather excited about the mating ball though. I'm sure there will be plenty of eligible bachelors who are actually up for the challenge." I pressed my own lips to his jaw, teasingly, before pulling back and smiling innocently up at him.

"A challenge that is meant for me and me alone. Don't make me follow through on my threats."

"A challenge that I don't believe you're man enough to handle," I taunted.

"If you keep questioning my manhood, I'll be forced to prove you wrong. It's you who I'm not sure is up for the challenge." He nipped at my earlobe. I held in a moan.

"Maybe. I guess we'll never know since you're a coward who's too scared to claim—"

I didn't get to finish my sentence. My feet left the ground, and I was slammed into the wall behind me, his mouth covering mine. I responded immediately despite my better judgment.

As I started kissing him back, I wrapped my legs around his hips with my feet resting above his tight, sexy ass. My arms wound around his neck, and I pulled his head closer by tugging on his hair harshly. He growled in response and bit my lower lip, not enough to hurt, just to sting a bit.

He slipped his tongue into my mouth. This time, I couldn't stop the moan of pleasure. It was muffled by his mouth, but I knew he heard it when he slipped his hands from my hips to my ass and squeezed roughly.

I ground my lower half into him, trying to create friction to sooth the ache between my thighs. He pulled away from my lips and trailed open-mouthed kisses from my jaw to my neck, and then my shoulder. My head fell back against the wall at the foreign feelings he was creating in me.

"I'm the only one who will ever make you feel like this," he mumbled into my neck, biting playfully before sucking at my sensitive skin.

His words were like a bucket of ice water. I stopped grinding my hips against him and my hands released their hold on his brown locks. This wasn't right.

It may feel more than right, but it wasn't. He had hurt me. He acted like he was ashamed of me. He can't just do this in private while acting like there was nothing between us in public. I was stronger than this. I was better than this.

With that in mind, I pushed him off of me as hard as I could. He didn't go far. He stopped his assault on my neck and looked up at me with confused, lustful eyes. My legs unwrapped themselves, as did my arms. All of my limbs just hung limply. The only thing holding me against the wall were his hands, still squeezing my butt, and his lower torso still pushed against mine.

"Let me go," I said with a hiss, my eyes blazing with anger.

He growled at the command, but surprisingly, he did just as I asked. My legs felt a bit like Jell-O but I managed to stay upright.

He now stood about two feet from me while I still had my back against the wall.

"What the hell is wrong with you?" I demanded, my temper flaring.

"Don't speak to me that way," he growled again.

"You get the respect you earn, and you have yet to earn mine," I said through gritted teeth.

"I'm your king," he said menacingly.

"Either you're my king or you're my mate. You don't get to act like both whenever it suits you."

"I am both. I am the king, and you don't get to command me."

I laughed bitterly at how childish he sounded. He was like a glorified toddler telling me to not boss him around.

"I do when it comes to me. Either you want me or you don't. You don't get to play mind games with me," I said after the laughter stopped.

"I'm not playing anything." The hands at his sides balled into a fist.

"Yes, you are. You have to make a decision. You either accept me—in public," I emphasized, "—and we can do this whenever you want. Or you don't and you don't get to touch me."

He stood in silence, his back ramrod straight and his body shaking in anger. He stayed that way for a few minutes, just staring at me; his face unreadable. I held his gaze, not backing down or submitting to him.

Somehow, his silence gave me my answer, so I finally broke mine.

"Fine. I'll keep my distance, and I would appreciate it if you would extend me the same curtesy, King Finnian," I said decisively, my voice coming out even and emotionless.

That's far from what I was feeling on the inside. On the inside, my heart was shattering to pieces. My wolf was howling in despair in my head; a hollow, numb feeling encasing my whole body. But I refused to cry.

He must have felt my inner turmoil because he took a step towards me. I held up my hand to stop him.

"I've had a long day, Your Highness. I'd like to get some rest." A nice way of kicking him out of my room.

He looked at me for a few more seconds before finally nodding. He turned on his heel and walked towards the door. On his way out, he slammed his fist into the wall, causing it to crack. I winced. The wall was made of solid stone. That had to hurt.

He didn't act like he felt it though. He just continued his way out and shut the door behind him, not once looking back.

Deep down, I had hoped that if I gave him an ultimatum he would choose me. I was mistaken.

I bit my lip to keep the tears at bay and walked to my bed. I slid under the covers and pulled them up to my chin. I couldn't even enjoy the softness of the mattress, my thoughts purely focused on him.

I never thought this was how it would go. Mates weren't supposed to be like this. It was supposed to be love at first sight and all that gooey crap. I wasn't much of a romantic but, for some reason, I still wanted that. I wanted someone who would love me unconditionally. Someone who would be my rock when I needed him and vice versa.

Guess that just wasn't in the cards for me. Eventually, I drifted off to a restless sleep, dreaming of my blue-eyed King all night.

* * *

A knock sounded on my door just as I finished getting dressed. I went for a more casual look today. I was wearing light-blue skinny jeans, a loose grey heather V-neck which was slightly tucked into the top of my jeans, and a thin berry-colored blazer over it. My feet were encased in a pair of matching berry-red close-toed pumps.

"Coming," I called to whoever stood on the other side of my bedroom door.

With one last look in the mirror, I deemed myself ready and went to the door. I pulled it open to see a timid-looking Liliya. The hallway was lined with windows, letting the sunlight stream in and allowing me to take in her striking features much better than I was able to in the lowly lit dining room last night.

She had inky-raven hair and dark onyx eyes. Her skin was a deep olive and she had sharp, high cheekbones. She was tall, even taller than me with my four-inch heels. Her body was lanky and willowy, encased in a flowy white long-sleeved dress.

"Good morning, Liliya. I really appreciate you giving me a tour," I said to her, a friendly smile gracing my lips.

"It is my pleasure, Kendall. You can call me Lili," she spoke quietly.

I nodded to her. There was something about Lili that I liked. It wasn't like it was with Niki. I liked Niki because she was kind to me and spoke her mind, something I really appreciated in a person. But with Lili, I almost felt protective over her. She had an air of innocence and naivety around her.

"How old are you, Lili?" I asked curiously.

"I am twenty-six years old."

"Wow, I wouldn't have guessed that you were older than me. No offense."

"I'm often mistaken to be younger than I really am. No offense taken." Her lips pulled into a shy smile.

"So, I guess we should get going then?" I asked her, stepping out into the hall with her and pulling the door shut behind me.

"Yes, we should. Lunch will be served in three hours, and we have much to see before then."

I nodded. We walked halfway down the corridor, stopping in front of Kat and Matt's room. I rapped my knuckles a few times against the hard wood.

"Morning," Kat said cheerfully as she opened her door.

She had also gone for a casual look today; sporting jeans, a long-sleeved red chiffon shirt, and tall brown leather boots. Her hair was straight and half pulled back.

"Morning," I returned her greeting. "Where's Matt?" I asked as she pulled her door shut before I could look inside.

"Tyler came and got him and Dalton about an hour ago. They are doing their initial interview today," she explained their absence.

It made sense, but I didn't realize they would start so early. The process of being vetted for a seat on the Council was a lengthy one. I didn't know all the ins and outs of it, but I knew there were a series of interviews. The first one usually lasted twelve hours. There was also a series of tests that had to be passed but, again, I didn't know what they were. That was Matt and Dalton's job.

I was relieved that I wouldn't see Dalton for most, if not all, of the day. I didn't really know what to say to him. What do you say to someone who you had just found out had a huge crush on you for most of their lives but was then strangled by your mate? Hell if I knew.

"Where to first Lili?" I asked as we began walking, Kat and Lili on either side of me.

"I thought we could start in the ballroom since it is on the second floor was well. There is not much to see on the first floor. Most of it, except for the gym, is not in use. We'll end up in the gardens where we will be dining for lunch. The gym is closest to the gardens as well, so I'll show you that at the end of the tour."

I nodded at her explanation and we continued walking. We had just passed the living room and kitchen that Tyler had shown us last night, so I knew we still had a ways to go. I decided to make conversation as we walked. "So, Lili, have you always lived in the castle?"

"I have. My mother was the Royal Witch for the previous King and Queen. When they passed, Mother retired in our native land of Bulgaria. Her mother still lived there before she passed away. Nikolina became King Finnian's witch when he took the throne."

"What was it like growing up here? Where'd you go to school? Is there even a school around here?" I asked.

"There are no schools here for miles. The children who reside in the Royal territory are either homeschooled or attend a boarding school that King Finnian controls. Only students he allows are let in. It's disguised as a very prestigious school, so it doesn't look suspicious when human students aren't admitted."

"Did you go there?" Kat asked her, joining in the conversation.

"I did not. I chose to be homeschooled instead. My mother left when I was just two years old. I stayed under Niki's care until I reached adulthood. She trained me while one of the teachers in the territory homeschooled me."

"Why didn't you go with your mother? If you don't mind me asking," I quickly added.

"I don't mind at all. Niki volunteered to take care of me, so mother took her up on that offer. From what Niki has told me, mother wasn't very . . . maternal."

"What's the age difference between you two? She doesn't look that much older," Kat asked, probably to not be reminded of how her own mother had a poor sense of parenting.

"She is twenty years my senior. Emiliya is ten. Niki was twenty-two when Mother left, and then she took over as Head Witch."

"Are you telling me that Niki is forty-six?" I stared at her, dumbfounded. She did not look that old.

"A combination of good genetics and powerful ancestry," she said with a snicker. She seemed to be coming out of her shell a bit.

"Woah, hold on. She was able to cast an aging spell? It normally takes three strong witches to complete that. Did someone help her?" Kat asked in shock.

"No, she completed it herself. She only wanted to shave a few years off, so it wasn't too difficult for her."

"That's insane. Could you have done it?"

"Hmm, I doubt that I would have been able to. I'm certainly not as powerful as Nikolina. My body would likely shut down before I could finish."

I was lost during the talk about magic, but I understood that part. When a witch does a powerful spell, especially if they do it alone, it tends to drain their powers. It's like a recuperation of sorts. If they were to do too much at once, it could actually kill them. Their powers drain automatically to protect their life force.

I didn't know certain kinds of spells and how much power they took, but I did know a few things about witchcraft. Kat had taught me the basics but a lot of it was beyond my understanding.

I knew that witches had several different abilities. Casting spells was probably their most known ability. It also took the most power. Some spells were easy, such as starting a fire. Other spells, like the aging spell apparently, were more difficult and something not every witch could complete.

There were some things that even witches couldn't mess with though. They couldn't change death. They could heal, but once someone's life left their body there was absolutely nothing a witch could do to change that.

They also could not mess with the mating bond. The bond between mates was the most powerful thing there was, and a witch couldn't touch that or come between it. It made me want to laugh. It didn't seem that powerful to King Finnian. I was sure he would destroy our bond if possible.

Witches also had visions. They couldn't control them and were often difficult to understand.

It wasn't what most people thought it was. They didn't always see a clear picture. It wasn't like a movie playing in their heads. It was more like a feeling and knowing what was going to happen, even if they didn't see it clearly.

They couldn't control when they had visions or what they saw. Kat had described it as more of a sudden thought or remembering a memory that hadn't happened yet.

Visions almost always come true. It was a very rare event that a vision could be changed, although it was not impossible.

"I'm so excited to train with her. I still have so much to learn." Kat's words brought me from my thoughts.

"She is the best. She will have much to teach."

"Will you be training with us as well?"

"I will. I'm still learning as well. I hope to be able to eventually match her power. I've set the bar very high, so I don't know if I'll ever reach it but one can still try."

"That's a good attitude to have. I'm sure you can do it," Kat encouraged.

"Thank you, Kat," she replied gratefully.

Before the conversation could continue, she stopped in front of a giant double door. They were in front of a giant foyer with a crystal chandelier hanging from the ceiling.

"This is the ballroom," she informed us as she opened one of the doors and ushered us in.

I gasped in awe. This room was huge and much more elegant than the rest of the castle. Instead of a gothic, medieval look, it was much more sophisticated. The floor was made of shiny white marble, and the walls were white with intricate gold designs.

One wall was lined with vast portraits of past Kings and Queens and the wall across from it was lined with giant windows that were rounded at the top and had gold drapes hanging above them and pulled to the side, allowing sunlight to filter in. Directly across from us on the other side of the room was a wide staircase right in the middle of the wall. I wasn't sure where it led, but I guessed that important people made their entrance down those stairs.

The room seemed like it could fit hundreds comfortably. It seemed even bigger because it was so empty. Other than us, there was nothing in here. No tables, no chairs, nothing.

"The band sets up over there." Lili pointed to a corner of the room next to the staircase. There was indeed a short stage for performers. I assumed they usually had classical performers at these things. "That door over there leads to the bar and kitchen." She pointed at the door to the left. "It's for workers only. They bring out drinks for people during mingling and dancing. Then they serve the food during dinner."

"This is amazing. I'm sure it's beautiful during an event," I said to her.

"It is. You'll see next month, during the mating ball."

Kat gave me a look, but I ignored it and smiled a tight-lipped smile at her. I didn't want to discuss mates. She must have noticed my hesitation because she changed the subject.

"I'll be going to the nearest city next week to find a gown. If you two don't already have one, you're welcome to accompany me and my sisters."

"Sounds great." I smiled at her. It did sound great, except for the fact that Emiliya will be there. But I needed a gown, so I'd have to tolerate her.

"Yeah, we'd love to," Kat added.

"Excellent. It'll be a girl's day out." She sounded so excited.

I briefly wondered if Liliya had any friends. She had lived in the castle her whole life. She hadn't even gone to school, which is where most kids made their friends. As far as I knew, there weren't many people who actually lived in the castle. It wouldn't surprise me if her sisters were her only companions.

I made the decision then to befriend the youngest Petrova witch. She was a sweet girl; a little shy, but I think she'd get along great with Kat and me.

"So where to next?" Kat asked her.

* * *

After a long three hours, we had finally seen everything. The inside of the castle was far larger than it looked from the outside. After the ballroom, she showed us the main kitchen, the library, the old dungeons—which were scary—the indoor garden and sunroom, several meeting rooms ranging from small to extremely large, King Finnian's public office, which we didn't enter, and Lili and Niki's workrooms. She even showed us the secret passageway that the castle workers used.

The castle had many workers. Some chefs also served the food. They cooked in the main kitchen, not in the private kitchens in the residential wing. The main kitchen was massive and industrial. It had to be though; they sometimes had to feed hundreds and hundreds of people.

There were also maids. They were all assigned to different sections of the castle. Even the rooms that weren't often used were still kept clean and tidy. It took a lot of people to keep this place running.

I found out that despite their low status in the werewolf hierarchy, they were all treated very well. They were paid generously and given free housing in a separate mansion. They could also buy a house within the territory for a reduced rate if they wanted to live alone. Other than being treated well financially, they were also shown respect as well. They had nothing but great things to say about King Finnian. I could tell they all meant every word.

It warmed my cold heart to him slightly. It showed a different side of Finnian that I hadn't seen yet. A lot of people would let the power go to their head and treat workers like dirt. Not him.

He seemed rather compassionate actually. Too bad he couldn't show that side of himself to me.

Even though Lili showed so much of the castle to us, I knew there was a lot we still hadn't been shown. For example, we hadn't gone anywhere near where the guys were. I hadn't smelled, heard, or seen them.

As much as I hated to admit it, I had also been looking for King Finnian. We hadn't gone anywhere near the sixth floor. That entire floor, in both wings, belonged to Finnian. No one was allowed up there, not even Kieran, his brother and Beta. It made me curious about what was up there.

The last place we looked at was the gym. It was more than just one room though. There was a room that had all kinds of exercise equipment, such as treadmills and stationary bikes. Another room was dedicated to weights while another was strictly meant for combat training. There were mats covering the floor and punching bags on one side.

There was even an indoor pool. It was settled in a glass room, letting the sunlight shine in. It was something I wanted to use while I was here. Lili informed us that the gym was available to us whenever we wanted.

We were able to get to the gardens from the door in the pool room. The gardens were absolutely breathtaking. I couldn't name all of the flowers but there were a lot of them, and they all bloomed in different colors. A fountain sat in the middle, enhancing the beauty of the area. The scents of the flowers were overwhelming at first, but eventually, I got used to it.

Lili led us up the concrete path to a small area. It was a wooden gazebo with trimmed vines and flowers threaded through the rustic, hand-carved oak. A small round table with eight cushioned chairs sat in the middle of it. Two of the seats were already filled. Niki and Emiliya.

I sat next to Niki, who was seated across from Emiliya. Kat sat next to me and Lili across from me, next to Emiliya. It was chilly outside, but the wind was none existent and the sun warmed the air, making it tolerable.

The view from the table was beautiful. On one side, there was the walkway, where we could still see the fountain. On the other two sides of the gazebo, it was flowers and plants as far as the eye could see. And lastly, sitting behind the table, was the view of the large snow-covered mountain. It was a ways away, surrounded by trees, but it was seen.

"Good morning, Kendall, Kat." Niki nodded to me first, then Kat. "I trust your tour went well?" she asked, taking a sip of her lemonade. I noticed there was already lemonade in front of us as well, even though we just joined them.

"Good morning, Niki. Yes, it went well," I told her. Then I turned my attention across the table. "Good morning, Emiliya," I said, looking directly into her eyes as I spoke.

I couldn't help but want to size her up a bit. I didn't trust her. My wolf sneered inside of me, wanting to be let out to attack her and put her in her place. After her attitude and disrespect last night, I couldn't exactly blame my wolf.

"It's Royal Beta Female to you." She glared as she spoke. I didn't think she liked my continuous eye contact.

"Emiliya, can you not act like a proper Royal Beta Female for even a day?" Niki asked lightly, still sipping her lemonade. Her tone and actions made it seem like she was commenting about the weather, not slighting her sister.

"I wasn't aware of that, Nikolina. Perhaps you think you could do a better job? Do I sense a bit of envy about my title, sister?" she sneered. It made her pretty face so damn ugly.

"On the contrary," Niki spoke, keeping her cool demeanor. She even looked a tad amused. "I'm very pleased at being chosen as the Head Royal Witch. It is quite the honor to be considered the most powerful witch by the King."

Damn. Even I was feeling that burn. I could tell it was a sensitive subject and that it was Emiliya who harbored the jealousy, not Niki. Emiliya practically growled and stood up, her chair hitting the floor in her haste to stand. She gave Niki one last glare and stormed off.

I looked over at Niki and was surprised to see a small smirk pulling on her lips.

"I'm sorry about that, ladies. My sister can be rather temperamental," she said as she turned her attention back to us.

At that time, the waiters came out to serve us our meals. My stomach growled in anticipation. I hadn't bothered with breakfast, which I had started to regret about two hours ago.

On the menu today was a small side salad, which thankfully had better dressing than last night, grilled herb chicken covered in a lemon cream sauce served over a bed of wild rice, and roasted potatoes. We quickly dug in after thanking the waiters. It tasted even better than it looked. The chefs here sure could cook.

"Are you ready for your training to begin, Kat?" Niki restarted the conversation.

"Very. I meditated this morning, so I'm ready to go."

Meditating is something all witches would do. It helped them get back in touch with nature, which is where they drew their power from. They didn't meditate daily, but they did do it regularly. Kat usually did it once a week, maybe twice if she was casting a big spell.

I never knew exactly what she did when she meditated. She had to be alone. All I knew was that she didn't need anything around to do it. No candles, no potions, nothing. Just herself. It usually took her about an hour. If she went too long without meditating, her powers weakened. Eventually, a witch would lose their powers if they didn't do it for an extended period of time but that took a while.

"As did I. It seems we're on the same page." She paused, then looked at Lili. "Liliya, darling, have you meditated lately?"

"Yes, Nikolina. I meditated last night in preparation for today."

"Good girl. Liliya here is coming into her powers nicely. Almost surpassing me when I was her age," she bragged about her younger sister.

"I believe that. I can sense her power," I said.

As a wolf, I could sense certain things instinctually. One of those things is sensing how powerful someone is, be it a werewolf or a witch. It was how I knew that Finnian was King without being told.

I could sense that Lili was a very powerful witch. Not quite was much as Niki or even Emiliya, but she was getting there. Kat wasn't as strong as a Petrova, but she was as close as a witch her age could get. They had both only gotten more powerful with time and practice.

"Liliya, there is no reason to act embarrassed. Embrace your power, don't be ashamed of it," Niki lightly scolded when Liliya blushed, seeming uncomfortable with the compliments.

"Yes, Nikolina," she repeated her earlier words, still blushing. Niki let it go.

"So, did you girls enjoy your first night in the castle?"

"Yes, it was great. The bed was so comfortable. Matt and I both slept great."

"And you, Kendall?" There she goes again. Looking at me like she knows something.

"Um, it was good. I slept good too," I answered.

I didn't want to speak about what happened last night. What happened between Finnian and me was our business. The less others knew, the better. I did not know her well enough to trust her with this information.

"That's good to hear. I know dinner was a bit . . . unusual. I had hoped it wouldn't ruin the rest of your night."

"And what are dinners here usually like?" I couldn't help but ask.

"Well, for one, King Finnian usually doesn't dine with us. I suppose he thought last night's dinner was of importance," she hinted.

"Who does he dine with then?" A shot of jealously ran though me, picturing him eating dinner with some other girl, my thoughts taking a ridiculous turn.

"Himself, dear. Not exactly a social butterfly, that one." Those words eased my fears, which I was positive she realized. She knew what I had been thinking.

"Doesn't he get lonely?" Damn. Why couldn't I control my questions? I shouldn't care about him being lonely.

"I'm sure he does. Perhaps he'll find his mate soon to remedy that problem."

Okay, now I was 100 percent sure she knew. The knowing glint in her eyes was too obvious to ignore.

"Maybe he will. I'm sure many are awaiting the arrival of the next Queen. Too bad I probably won't be around anymore by that point."

I was trying to get my point across without being obvious. Finnian didn't want me. I'll be going home after the two months are up. When that happens, one of two things could occur.

The first was that he would continue as he had done now. He will be lonely, having no one to rule by his side. Eventually, after many, many years of loneliness, he will die, leaving no heir behind. In which case, the next in line will be Kieran's first born.

The second possible outcome would be that he will meet someone else. He will make that person his Queen. He would die with some woman who wasn't his mate. Both options broke my heart.

Niki regarded me sadly, but she looked reassuring as well. "You never know, dear Kendall. Maybe he'll find her while you're here. He needs a strong Queen by his side."

"I'm sure he does," I agreed.

She stopped questioning me after that. We had easy conversation for the rest of lunch. Liliya finally warmed up and contributed as well. I learned more about her and Niki, realizing that

Niki was more of a mother figure for Lili instead of a sister. I could easily see the love Niki held for her.

They talked magic with Kat and asked us about my siblings and our home. I told them about Brody and Selena. Niki put the idea in my head about inviting them all to the ball next month.

Kat and I both thought it was a great idea. I knew I'd be rather homesick by that point and a visit would be long overdue. I just had to convince my stubborn Alpha father.

Once lunch was finished, Niki led the three of us back to her workroom, which was located on the fifth floor. My feet were still killing me from going on the tour in heels, but I followed without complaint.

Niki's workroom was rather large. There was a big table in the middle, a couple of books and artifacts sitting on top. She had shelves around the entire room, filled with more books and artifacts, along with potion ingredients and other witch-related items. There was another table in the corner that held a bowl and ingredients around it. I knew that's where she did her potion mixing. One corner was bare, save for a few lone cushions. Her meditation area, I presume.

Her workroom resembled Kat's but bigger.

Niki, Kat, and Lili all took a seat around the main table. I, however, sat on the couch on the other side of the room. I was just here to observe; I didn't want to get in the way.

"Have you learned to harness the wind yet?" Niki began.

"Not yet. I've mastered earth and fire. I'm still a little shaky with water. I've only tried wind once; it was a tracking spell. I blacked out before I could complete it," Kat explained.

Elemental magic. The most common kind. Since witches had to harness nature to fuel their powers, the elements were what they most commonly drew from. Kat usually preferred fire. Some powerful witches could also draw from someone's life force. It wasn't something that was often done, just in serious situations where the elements weren't enough and there weren't other witches around to help.

Someone's life force provided more power than the elements, although it was very dangerous to use, for the witch and the werewolf. It couldn't be done with humans; their life force wasn't strong enough. That left werewolves.

The danger was, that it drained the wolf rather quickly. If it took too long, it would kill them, which in turn would kill the witch as well. They became linked during the spell, so if one half died, so did the other. It wasn't a common practice, and most witches weren't taught how to do it and therefore never even attempted it.

There was also dark magic, but Kat never talked about that. Mainly because she didn't know much about it.

"We'll first master water. Mastering three of the four elements will help you master wind more quickly."

Niki stood and walked to one of the shelves. She grabbed a small bowl and poured water from a canteen into it. She carried it back over and placed it in front of Kat.

"Do you have a spell you're comfortable with doing while harnessing water? I just want to see where you're at.," she asked her.

"Healing small wounds."

It was true. I had sliced my palm many times for her. I had been her guinea pig of sorts. It worked out because, even if the spell didn't work, my werewolf healing would quickly close the wound. I didn't particularly like cutting the palm of my hand, but she had always been there for me so I was glad to help her. Besides, Matt wouldn't let her cut herself, so it was me or him.

"She can use me," I volunteered automatically.

"Am I safe to assume you've helped her many times in perfecting this spell?" she asked, looking over to me.

"Yeah . . ." I replied hesitantly, not knowing where she was going with that.

"Then no, I'm afraid she can't." She turned her attention back to Kat to explain, "You'll use me. You're used to and comfortable with Kendall. You need to push the boundaries of that comfort. It might not always be her who you'll have to heal. You'll need to be able to heal anyone, not just those close to you. Do you understand?"

Niki had lost her playfulness and instead sounded like a full-blown teacher and mentor. This was a serious matter and it needed to be treated that way. During training, she was not Kat's friend. She had to push Kat to her limits. That was the only way she'd get better.

It was something Kat's mom had done for years and drilled into her head. Her mom could only teach her as much as she knew. Since Niki was more powerful, she would be able to push her further.

Kat nodded to her. Niki grabbed a dagger and sliced it across her hand. She didn't even flinch. She wiped the blood away and held it out for Kat. Kat let one hand hover over the bowl of water and the other touch the top of Niki's cut.

She started chanting in the ancient witch language, a language witches were born to speak and didn't have to be taught. It was never anything I understood or would ever be able to. This continued for a few minutes.

Finally, she stopped. She lifted her hand and we all glanced at Niki's palm. She wiped away the remaining blood, but underneath it, the skin was smooth and free of injury.

"Good job, Kat. I expected that to take twice as long. You harness water better than you let on." She praised, which elicited a proud grin from Kat.

"Now let's take it up a notch."

* * *

At some point, I had fallen asleep. I had carefully watched for a while, but eventually it was less spells and more lecturing. I couldn't help but doze off.

I was awoken by Niki, who was now alone in the room. I sat up confused, wondering where Kat and Lili went.

"They retired to their rooms. They're both rather worn out after performing so many spells. I told them I would wake you and get you to your room," she explained without me having to ask.

"Oh, okay. How long have you guys been done?" I yawned. I pulled out my phone to check the time. Six o'clock.

"Only a few minutes. I wanted a moment alone with you."

"Oh?" Now I'm fully awake. I stood up and slipped my heels back on.

"I just wanted to let you know there is more to him than meets the eye."

I froze and looked up at her.

"What do you mean?" I hesitated.

"Finn, dear girl. I mean Finn."

It didn't slip my attention that she called him Finn. Somehow, it gave me a weird reaction. I pictured myself calling him Finn and I shivered. It sounded much more personal and intimate than King Finnian. I suddenly found myself wanting to test it out on him. I was getting carried away though, so I pushed the thought away.

"How do you know?" I asked her, dropping the denial.

"I can't discuss any more than that, unfortunately. Just try to give him the benefit of the doubt. I've known Finn for many years. There is more to him than you think."

"He doesn't want anyone to know. Frankly, I don't either. We shouldn't be discussing this. Someone may hear us," I explained to her.

"I assure you, My Queen," My eyes widened at the title. "No ears are on us. I've cast a spell on my workroom. No one from the outside can hear what is being said. I've done the same on Finn's floor of the castle. I also did it to your room last night immediately after dinner. Both areas are safe for you to speak freely now. No one will be listening."

"You placed a spell on my room?" I was shocked.

"Indeed. I knew Finn would be visiting you last night. You two needed your privacy." I blushed at that.

"Uh, well, thanks for that I guess."

"It was my pleasure. Be careful though. This room, your room, and Finn's floor are the only safe areas. Not everything is as it seems. Be wary of your words when you're not in those places."

That made me nervous. What the hell was going on? I nodded to her absentmindedly.

I told her I could find my own way back to my room. As I followed Kat's scent to our quarter of the residential wing, the only thing on my mind was this.

No matter what the hell was going on, I was going to figure it out.

CHAPTER FIVE

It had been four days since we arrived at the castle.

I hadn't done much since I arrived. I wasn't sure what exactly I should be doing. Everyone had found their groove . . . everyone except for me, that is.

Kat had been training every day. I hadn't been with her since the second day at the castle. She had invited me, but I felt like I didn't belong there. That was her thing, not mine. That kept Kat, Niki, and Lili busy for the majority of the day.

Matt and Dalton had been spending their days with Tyler. He was guiding them through the recruitment process. They didn't tell me exactly what they were doing. Whatever it was, it kept them the whole day.

That took away everyone I knew and liked.

It had also been four days since I saw King Finnian. He hadn't shown up in my room since that day. He also hadn't been to dinner either. I had stupidly showed up to dinner every night in hopes of seeing him, but I never did.

I tried to lie to myself, tried telling myself that I didn't want to see him . . . that I was glad I hadn't. But I knew the truth; I knew that deep inside, I was craving his presence and attention.

I couldn't have that because he was doing just what I told him to do; keeping his distance. It hurt . . . It honestly did.

I felt so alone in the Royal Territory. I didn't do well on my own. I liked to be surrounded by people. Growing up, I had always been around someone. I shared a room with my sister and a house with five people. Besides the people who lived there, there were always people over as well.

My pack was a close-knit one, and the alpha's house was always open to anyone. It used to bother me, never getting any time for myself, but eventually I found comfort in it. I hated being alone; hated not having someone to talk to. I hated it here.

I had been talking to my family daily. I think they were getting sick of hearing from me. I just needed something to occupy my time. I explored the castle and the woods surrounding the Royal Territory. I loved the crisp, fresh mountain air.

Today would be the same—start with a run in the forest behind the castle. After that, I planned on checking out the pool in the gym area.

With that in mind, I got dressed for my day after a quick breakfast with Kat before she left. I put on my most modest swimwear, a forest green bikini with high waist bottoms and a halter top. I pulled a white fringed cover-up over it and tied my curls in a messy bun.

After I slipped on a pair of flip-flops, I made my way out of my room. I had asked Tyler the second night where I could run. He told me I could run anywhere on the property, but that he preferred the area behind the castle. It was my favorite part of being here so far.

Once I was outside, I made sure no one was around and stepped behind a thick tree. I stripped off my swimsuit and cover. I folded them next to the tree and began to pull my wolf forward. Within twenty seconds, I was no longer human. I shook out my brown fur and slowly began to trot forward. Eventually, I gained speed and maneuvered around trees and brush as fast as I could.

I had to focus on my running. My instinct as a wolf was to fight me to get to Finnian. I fought it off as I pushed my body as far as it could go.

I guess at some point, I had become so focused on controlling my wolf that my other senses dulled. I was startled when an ashy-colored wolf suddenly appeared and ran right next to me.

I stopped dead in my tracks, nearly falling over from the abruptness of it, and turned to the unfamiliar wolf, raising my hackles and snarling at him. He seemed unaffected; even looked a bit entertained.

I finally took a deep breath, breathing in his scent. Tyler.

I relaxed once I knew he wasn't a threat. I growled playfully at him for scaring me and continued to run. He followed me and soon enough, we were racing.

We even started playing dirty at one point. We would knock each other over or try to trip each other. We were both very competitive, but eventually, after over an hour of running, we called it a tie and made our way back.

I stopped behind my tree while he stopped behind another. I shifted back and got dressed. I walked out to the front of the tree line and saw him already standing, waiting for me to finish, now dressed in jeans and a t-shirt. It was the most casual I'd seen him dressed.

"You're faster than I thought you'd be," he complimented.

"Thanks, you too." I ran a hand through my unruly curls, pushing them out of my face and tying them back into a bun.

"It's nice to have someone to run with," he added. We slowly started walking the long distance back to the castle.

"You don't usually? I rarely run alone."

"Not really. I used to run with *mi hermana*, but she found her mate a few years ago and moved away."

"You don't run with King Finnian or Beta Kieran?" I nearly shivered when I said his name aloud.

"No, not since we were pups. We ran together all the time when we were young, but ever since Finnian took the throne, he has chosen to run alone. Kieran too. They usually run at weird times, like the middle of the night when no one else is awake. Though they never do it on the same night," he explained.

I didn't know what to make of that. Wolves were social creatures, we did better in groups. I didn't know anyone who preferred to run alone. Finnian was a mystery, that was for sure.

"What about pack runs?" They didn't exactly have a pack per se, but they did have more wolves here than the three largest packs combined.

"We do those once every three months. The three of us lead the run; other than that, we all run alone."

"Well, I'll run with you while I'm here. I hate running by myself."

"I run daily. You sure you can keep up?" he teased, bumping his shoulder against mine lightly.

"The real question is, can you keep up with me?" I joked back.

"I think I can manage. So, what are you going to do now?"

"I thought I'd use the pool for a while. You want to join me?"

"Sure. I have a couple of hours before I'm needed."

By that time, we had made it back to the pool room. Tyler excused himself to change. He didn't take long, since he kept a bathing suit in a locker in the gym. I stripped off my cover-up and slid off my flip-flops.

I didn't want to jump in, so I sat down on the concrete and slipped in slowly. I ducked my head underwater for a few seconds. When I came back up and wiped the water from my eyes, I saw Tyler already in the water as well.

"So, what exactly have you boys been doing every day? Matt won't tell me," I asked him, floating on my back lazily. I turned my head over to look at him. He leaned against the edge of the pool and looked at me bemusedly.

"If he won't tell you, what makes you think I will?"

"We're friends, right?"

"I suppose we are."

"Well, friends share information. That's the most common rule of friendship."

"I see your point." He faked looking serious. "I suppose I could indulge you a bit."

"Really?" I pushed down my legs and lifted my torso, moving my body to be vertical again. I swam up to him until we were just a few feet apart, trying to keep myself afloat in front of him. I couldn't touch the bottom like the lucky bastard in front of me.

"I don't see how it could hurt. They're basically still in the interview process. It won't get too difficult until King Finnian starts testing them."

"How much could they possibly be interviewed about? I'm sure there's only so much you guys could want to know, right?"

"It's a lot more than you think. King Finnian wants to know everything about your pack, all the ins and outs. He gives scenarios and asks how they would handle it. There is a lot he's looking for."

"Does he do it himself? The interviewing, I mean."

"Kieran and I do most of it. Niki does part of it as well. King Finnian is a remarkably busy man. He's not only the king, but a very powerful businessman in the human world as well. He only steps in when he feels it's important. We report back to him at the end of the day for any progress," he explained.

"If he's so busy, why such a long process?" I asked curiously.

"He is not the most trusting man. His father and mother died because a Council member betrayed them. He almost disbanded the whole thing, but it was more beneficial to keep the Council. So, he created an extensive process for packs to prove their trustworthiness.

"If they fail, not only do they not get to join, but their leadership is also questioned. We even had one incident about ten years ago where we had to execute an Alpha who was physically abusing his pack. It was discovered during the interview process."

"He killed him?" I queried in shock.

"He did. He deserved it, though; I can assure you of that."

I knew executions were something that had to happen. If they wanted to act like a rabid dog, then they needed to be put down like a rabid dog. Some of them deserved it. Still, the thought of being the one to follow through with it put my stomach in knots. I didn't know how Finnian did it.

Tyler continued when I didn't say anything, "Finnian is a harsh but fair King. He's been through a lot, but his number one priority is always his people. He goes above and beyond to take care of everyone but he also does the same when he has to punish those who deserve it. He has no qualms about disciplining those who have done something wrong. Maybe he's too harsh, that's debatable, but he's a hell of a King, and my loyalties will always lie with him."

That was a lot to take with him. My feelings for King Finnian were all over the place. My experience with him was that he could be cruel at times, yet he is loved by his subordinates. I had never heard anyone question his leadership. I was glad he had such a loyal friend and Gamma.

"You mentioned that you haven't run together since you were pups, how long have you two known each other?" It sounded like it had been a while.

"Me and Finn? We go way back. We grew up and went through extensive training together."

"He's your Kat," I stated.

He laughed. "I guess you could say that. You and she have been friends for a while?"

"Oh yeah. Since we were young. We called ourselves 'The Three Amigas."'

"Three?" he asked, tilting his head sideways.

"Yeah, me, Kat, and my sister, Selena. We've been raising hell for our parents since we were babies." I grinned at him, which he returned.

"Why am I not surprised? If your sister is anything like you, I'm sure your parents were miserable."

"She was worse. She is the *worst* but I love her to death. I miss her most, although I'd never admit that to her."

"Maybe you'll see her at the ball? I'd like to meet this sister. Somehow, I can't picture anyone having more sass than you."

"I hope so. I mentioned it to my dad, but he just said he'd think about it. That usually means no, but I'll keep trying. Hey, I've been thinking about something," I started, changing the subject.

"About?"

"I need something to do while I'm here. I don't want to wander around all day and bother everyone. I need something to keep me busy. Do you have any suggestions?"

"Like what? You're a guest. It's not like we're going to put you to work."

"It doesn't matter to me. I just need something to do. I'm going crazy, and I don't see Matt letting me get involved in the vetting process," I explained to him.

"How do you feel about answering phones?"

"Expand on that."

"It's hard to get any work done when your phone won't stop ringing. Kieran, Finnian, and I could use someone to sort through our phone calls. Take down messages from the calls that aren't that important and transfer the ones that are. You could set up in my office with me if you want."

"What are the hours?" I asked, mulling it over.

"Whenever you want. It's not a real job, so you can do it whenever you feel like it or whenever you get bored. It won't bother anyone if you aren't there, but it will be helpful if you are."

"Where is your office anyway?"

"Right next to King Finnian's public office."

A devious thought hit me right then. I had told Finnian I would keep my distance if he would. I didn't think he would though. I wanted to see how he would react if I was around him a lot. I wanted him to react. It was immature. I should just let it go and forget about him, but I couldn't. Which lead me to my next words.

"I'll do it."

*   *   *

"We need to talk right now," I ordered him, grabbing his arm before he could shut himself in his room.

We had just finished dinner, which King Finnian was yet again absent from. It was time for this confrontation. I was tired of the awkwardness and the silence.

I pulled him to my room and shut the door behind us. I was suddenly extremely grateful for Niki's spell. No one needed to hear our conversation right now.

I pushed Dalton down on the couch and sat on the chair directly across from him. He, reluctantly, allowed me to pull him here but now he wouldn't look at me.

"No one likes a coward, Dalton Collins. At least look at me," I told him, crossing my arms over my chest.

He growled but still looked up at me, glaring daggers.

"Are you mad at me for what happened?" I got straight to the point. "And feel free to speak freely. Nikolina cast a silencing spell in my room. No one can hear you."

His anger deflated. "No, I'm not mad at you, Kendall. I'm . . . disappointed, I guess."

"Disappointed? About?"

"The King is your mate, isn't he?" he probed.

"Why would that disappoint you?" I wanted him to admit his feelings willingly.

"I just think you deserve better. You deserve to be treated like the queen you are, and I haven't seen him do that."

I swallowed my anger at him questioning my mate. He was right, and it's not fair for me to remain mad at him for something legitimate.

"And you think you could do that?" I raised an eyebrow at him.

Fire filled his eyes once again. "Actually, I could."

"Why didn't you ever tell me?" I didn't need to explain what I meant. He knew.

"Would it have mattered, Kendall? You hated me anyways."

"I hated you because you were an arrogant bastard. You could have gone for flattery instead of mockery. Not the best dating strategy."

"You and I both know that, that would have been worse. You hate guys who act like love-struck idiots. That would have been a good way to get you to ignore me altogether. At least this way, I still got you to talk to me."

"You could have at least told me. Cowardice is also a trait I can't stand."

"It wasn't cowardice. I just knew it was pointless. It wouldn't have mattered to you anyway. You never would have felt that way about me. I was just biding my time until I could get over you."

"Why me anyways?" I still didn't understand why.

"Hell if I know. Maybe stubborn bitches are my type," he grumbled, though it wasn't filled with hate.

"Well maybe if assholes were my type, it would have worked out," I said, laughter in my voice.

He laughed, but it soon died down when he looked at me seriously. "I hope we can still be friends. I know you hate me, but I always considered you a friend. I don't want this to change anything."

"Well I do hate you, but I look forward to continuing to let you know that. Things will only change if we let them, and I won't allow that."

Despite my words, I knew deep, deep down that I cared for him as a friend. He had been in my life for over two decades. He annoyed me like no other but so did Selena, and I still loved her. I guess you could say that I saw him as a brother of sorts. A brother I didn't want nor need, but a brother nonetheless.

"I won't either. Maybe we can hang out this weekend? We're getting Saturday and Sunday off. If King Finnian will let you, that is."

"I don't need that douchebag's permission. We'll go for a run or something?"

He smirked at my words. "Sounds like a date," I growled at him and he raised his hands. "Kidding, kidding. Jeez."

"You better be. Now get out so I can take a shower and get ready for bed."

"You need help?" I threw my flip-flop at him. "Sorry, I'm going. Goodnight." He laughed and started walking out.

"Goodnight," I grumbled back.

Once he left, I went to the shower. I had spent the morning in the pool with Tyler. We continued to talk and laugh until he had to leave.

After that, I lay down beside the pool, letting the sun warm and tan my skin through the glass ceiling. I had fallen asleep for a while and when I woke up, I actually swam a few laps around the pool instead of lazily floating around.

I hadn't gotten a chance to shower before dinner, so my hair and body still smelled like chlorine. I didn't know how anyone managed to sit at the dinner table with me. It was giving me a headache with its potency.

I quickly showered and got ready for bed. When I walked back out, I got a sense of déjà vu. King Finnian was lying on my bed, just like last time, while I was just in my t-shirt and panties again.

I gulped at the sight of him. I felt like a piece of my heart that had been missing was now firmly back in place. I took in his scent and had to stop a moan of pleasure from leaving my lips. He smelled so damn good and he didn't even try.

He looked even better. His hair was in mild disarray like he had been running his fingers through it all day. His eyes were a swirling mixture of gold and blue, which was mesmerizing. They drew me in and held me captive.

For as good as he looked, I couldn't help but notice a few imperfections as well. He had dark circles under his bloodshot eyes, and a shot of worry ran through me at his obvious lack of sleep. His beard, which had been a short and neat stubble, was now unkempt and in need of a trim. His jaw was clenched so hard that it looked painful. He looked like he had a rough few days.

"Is this gonna be our thing from now on? Because I prefer it when people knock before making themselves at home on my bed," I commented.

He was still lying down, his head rolled to the side to look at me. I ignored him and walked to the other side of my bed. I was going to act like his presence in here meant nothing to me, just like how he acted like my presence in his castle meant nothing to him. I slid under the covers and turned on my side, my back facing him.

He still didn't speak for a few minutes, but he also didn't take the hint to leave, so I spoke up again.

"What do you want, King Finnian? I haven't even seen you, so I don't know what I could've possibly done to piss you off," I said lazily, shutting my tired eyes.

I figured that, that was why he was here. I had done something he wasn't happy about. That was the reason for his first two visits. I raked my mind and couldn't think of anything . . . unless maybe agreeing to be Tyler's unpaid receptionist.

"You know . . ." He pushed my wet hair over one shoulder, leaning his chest right against my back. I stiffened and gulped nervously. "I don't appreciate you prancing around half-naked in front of my Gamma." He pulled my t-shirt to the side and pressed a soft kiss to my shoulder.

"Are you talking about us swimming together?" I turned around to look at him, trying to hold in a laugh, but I couldn't hold back the huge smile. Was that what this was about? I wore a bathing suit in front of Tyler? That was nothing short of comical and ridiculous.

He growled, but once he took in my face, he stopped. His eyes glazed over with a look I couldn't decipher, his hardened features softening considerably. He raised his hand and cupped my cheek, his thumb stroking my cheekbone.

Before I could figure out what changed in him, he pulled his hand back, taking his heat with him, and his face hardened once again.

"That's exactly what I'm talking about."

I didn't hold in my laugh this time. This whole thing was absurd.

"Why are you laughing? This isn't funny," he demanded.

"Actually, it's hilarious. Are you seriously jealous about this?"

"I'm not jealous," he insisted.

"I think you are. Maybe it's warranted." With that, I turned back around with a small victorious smile on my face. I ignored his enraged growls.

"Don't make me hurt my best friend, because I will," he threatened right in my ear, kissing the skin right underneath it after.

"Why would you need to do that? You don't want me, remember?" I pushed away the hurt. I was testing him. I wasn't trying to make him feel sorry for me.

I was suddenly flipped over and he was on top of me. His eyes glowed golden.

"I would need to do that . . ." He peppered kisses along my jaw. "So he'll know to stay the hell away from you." He moved to my neck.

"Why would he need to know that?" I asked breathlessly.

He didn't answer right away. He kept kissing my neck and shoulders. I was about to push him away, but he pulled away on his own, amusement dancing in his eyes.

"I don't want that pup in here with you anymore. I'll know if he is. I know everything that happens in my castle," he said, referring to Dalton this time. "I'll see you tomorrow, Miss Keating." He pressed one last sweet kiss on my lips and then pulled away. He was out of my room before I could blink.

CHAPTER SIX

"Are you sure you want to do this, Kendall?" Kat asked as I slipped on my second shoe.

"I'm positive. I need something to do, and Tyler offered," I explained my reasoning.

She didn't think it was a smart idea playing receptionist to the Royals. She figured that whatever was going on between King Finnian and I was better handled privately with just the two of us. She didn't think anyone else needed to know our business.

Apparently, she had a vision about this after I told her my plans last night. She wasn't completely sure what she had seen. Visions were sometimes . . . blurry, for lack of a better word, and hard to decipher. From what she could make out, King Finnian had a reason for his coldness towards me. What that reason was, she couldn't say, but she felt it was safer to keep things a secret until we could find out more.

"Are you sure you're not just looking to get under a certain someone's skin?" She gave me a knowing look.

"No," I lied. Well, partially lied.

I was honest about needing something to do. I didn't want to just sit around all day, and there was only so much exploring I could do around here.

I couldn't tell myself that the thought of being near Finnian all day didn't cross my mind, but I would have accepted Tyler's offer even if his office wasn't near Finnian's. That was just a perk.

"How do I look?" I changed the subject before she could call me out on my lie. She knew me so well; I could never get away with anything less than the truth with her.

I held my arms out and twirled around slowly in front of her. I was dressed in a burgundy sweater, a high-waisted, flared short black skirt, black tights, and heeled black ankle boots. My sweater was tucked neatly into my skirt. I had pulled my hair up into two messy space buns. My eyelids had a simple winged liner and my lips were painted in a lipstick that matched my burgundy sweater.

"Beautiful like always. You'll get the reaction you're looking for," Kat quickly commented, crossing her arms over her chest in annoyance. "Just be careful, okay? I think there is a lot more to this story than either of us realizes. I don't want you to get in over your head."

"I'll be careful. I promise," I assured her when her voice went from stern to worried.

"Okay, good. Do you want to walk over together? I'm meeting Niki in a few minutes."

I nodded in response to her request. We left my room and made our way to the west wing of the castle.

"So, how's training going?" I asked her as we walked.

I hadn't had much of a chance to talk to her about this. The only times I had seen her since we'd arrived were in the morning and during and after dinner. We hadn't really been alone to discuss this.

I also hadn't seen much of Matt or Dalton either. Even after my heart-to-heart—well, something as close to it as we can— with Dalton last night, he had been absent this morning. They left before we could even eat breakfast. Kat said they often left before the sun even came up.

"It's going great. I've almost mastered water. We're going to start with wind after that. Today I'm going to harness water to see a past memory from someone's mind. It's a very complicated spell, so I'm a little nervous. I've never tried it before."

"You can do that? Go through someone's memories?" That seemed a little too invasive for me.

"Yeah, but like I said, it's difficult to do. Most witches can't perform it. I know it seems intrusive but think of its tactical benefits. You can see what the enemy has planned before he can follow through."

"That makes sense. Is there any way to block a witch from digging through your mind?" I asked curiously. Most spells like that had a blocking spell that went with it, to protect someone.

"Of course. No one can do this to any of the Royals. Niki placed a shielding spell around their minds. No one can enter unless she lifts it. She's going to teach me that tomorrow. I'm going to shield your and Matt's mind first. Probably Dalton's too, just in case. When we go home, I'll do everyone else's."

"Good. The thought of someone going through my memories freaks me out. Whose mind are you going to look through today?"

"Matt's. Niki doesn't really want me performing spells on you or him since I'm so familiar with you two, but she's making an exception for this. Mainly because it is very invasive and she wants me to practice on someone who doesn't mind the intrusion."

"Well, I'm sure anything you can find in Matt's head, you already know about." I laughed. They didn't keep secrets from each other. Except for when Kat was keeping a secret from me, but other than that, they were completely open with each other.

"He better hope so," she joked.

"How do you not get overwhelmed with memories?" I inquired.

"You have to search for a particular memory. You will get overwhelmed if you just start going through someone's memories without a clear idea of what you're looking for."

"Ahh, okay. What are you going to look for?" I wondered as we walked up another set of stairs. My heels clicked against the stone floor, echoing around the empty corridor.

"Well, it has to be something that I wasn't aware of at the time. If it's something that I experienced with him, my memories will get mixed in with his. So, I'm going to look for the memory of when he found out I was his mate. I was there physically, but I wasn't aware of what was happening with him. Besides, he never really told me the whole story. That makes me curious."

Come to think of it, I didn't really know the story either. I knew that he knew for a few years before they got together, but he never really spoke about the particular moment that he realized. It would have to have been when she was at least thirteen or so. Mates couldn't be recognized before puberty.

"Let me know when you find out," I was half joking, half serious about it.

"I might. We'll see. I'll have to actually complete the spell first, which is easier said than done."

We slowed down, stopping in front of Niki's workroom.

"You'll do great, don't worry. I'll see you at dinner. Good luck."

"Thanks. You too."

She walked inside where Niki and Lili were already waiting. I waved to them, which they returned. I then walked in the direction of King Finnian's public office.

I didn't really remember where exactly it was, so I sniffed around until I caught a faint trace of his and Tyler's scent. I followed it up a floor and stopped in front of the door where it was the strongest. Sure enough, there was a sign on the door stating that this was the Royal Office. I twisted the brass knob and walked inside.

It opened into a big room that was filled with plush leather chairs and tables. There was a TV mounted on the wall, which was turned on but remained muted. There was even one table that held a fresh pot of coffee, coffee cups, and an assortment of snacks such as muffins and pastries.

It was by far the fanciest reception area I'd ever seen. Also the biggest.

There was a long hallway on both sides of the reception area. To the back of the room, there looked to be a place where conferences would be held.

Before I could decide which hallway to go down, Tyler came from the hall to my right.

"Morning. I'm glad you're here. You look cute today." He motioned to the space buns on top of my head.

"Morning. Thanks," I said, unconsciously bringing my hand up to fiddle with one of the buns but then dropped it soon after.

Before he could say anything else, the overwhelming presence of my mate entered the room. I felt his eyes look me up and down, before leaving me. I could feel the anger rolling off of him, but he remained outwardly calm. At least I think he did. I was refusing to look at him.

"Could you please refrain from flirting with my guests, Royal Gamma? Your dalliances are neither wanted nor appreciated," he said tightly.

I was surprised that he spoke to Tyler with such coldness and unfamiliarity. Weren't they best friends? Why didn't he call him Tyler?

"My apologies, King Finnian." Tyler bowed his head, but I caught a glimpse of confusion on his face. "Flirting wasn't my intention."

"See that it doesn't become your intention." The warning was clear in his voice. I felt his eyes move back to me. "Take Miss Keating to begin the interview."

That got my attention. "What interview?" I finally looked over to King Finnian, taking him in with my eyes. He was wearing charcoal grey slacks and a crisp white button-up shirt rolled up to his elbows, showing off his muscular forearms, with a matching grey tie around his neck. His hair was messy but hot. His eyes smoldered blue as my green orbs met his.

I quickly looked away from him and back to Tyler. As someone below the King, I wasn't supposed to maintain eye contact unless we were familiar with each other. As far as Tyler knew, we weren't, so I needed to keep up appearances.

"I was just about to tell you," Tyler began explaining to me. "We need to interview you today for the Council position."

"Umm, why?" I asked out of confusion.

"Just a formality. It won't take long."

"Okay, but I don't really understand. I thought this was Matt and Dalton's job."

"Do you have something to hide, Miss Keating?" King Finnian sounded mocking but a dark undertone was in his voice that was impossible to miss.

I gritted my teeth to stop myself from glaring at him. "Not at all, King Finnian. I'm an open book. Ask me anything; I have nothing to hide."

"Is that correct?" I nodded. "Then you wouldn't mind if I conducted this interview instead of my Royal Gamma?"

Tyler's mouth pulled down into a puzzled frown, his eyebrows knitting together. "Not at all, Your Highness," I countered, not backing down.

"Tyler, I'll take it from here," he said while still looking at me, dismissing Tyler without even glancing his way. Tyler left, despite his perplexity over the situation. "Follow me, Miss Keating." His tone held slight amusement now, losing the darkness from before.

He led us completely out of the office area and back into the hall. I had to walk fast to keep up with his long strides. He slowed down slightly when he realized this.

As we walked, I couldn't help but admire the form of his back. His back muscles tensed and flexed against the tight fabric of his shirt as he moved. My eyes trailed lower. Whoever said girls couldn't enjoy a nice ass had obviously never seen his. It was definitely a nice view.

He stopped and turned around after a few minutes, an eyebrow raised and his eyes holding a slight twinkle. Now that no one was around, I met his eyes and smirked, unapologetic. I wouldn't feel embarrassed about looking at something that was mine. The twinkle in his eyes grew, and he looked forward once again to continue walking.

After a few more turns, he stopped in front of a door. He held it open and allowed me to walk in before him. I smiled inwardly at this. As the king, he usually didn't hold the door open for anyone. It filled me with warmth that he would do it for me. It was a sign of respect.

We were now in a small conference room. There was a round table surrounded by black leather rolling chairs. I took a seat in one of them and he sat directly across from me.

"Why did we come all this way when you have a conference room by your office?" I queried.

"This is my private meeting room. It's spelled so no one can eavesdrop inside. That one wasn't."

"And why exactly would we need to be in a room where no one can hear?" I probed.

"You sure are inquisitive," he commented. Since he ignored my question, I gave him a look that said I was waiting for an answer. "Any interview I conduct, I do so in this room. You never know when you will need the extra privacy," he finally explained.

"Why, King Finnian . . . Planning on asking me questions that require privacy?" I lowered my voice and looked at him through my lashes. I bit my lip innocently.

His eyes swirled golden now.

"Don't tempt me, mate," he warned.

I gasped, faking horror. "King Finnian, that is highly inappropriate. I'm starting to question your motives for bringing me to this empty, private room." I faked being innocent like I hadn't been goading him before.

"As you should, Miss Keating. My motives are very questionable," he played along but I knew he was somewhat serious.

"Perhaps my motives are questionable as well. Maybe Tyler should have conducted this interview after all," I teased.

A loud snarl left his mouth, all teasing gone from his face. I smirked inwardly. It was so easy to get under his skin; a little too easy.

"I'll kill him." His voice was more animalistic now, less man.

"Don't be so dramatic, your highness." I snickered. Even though he looked on the verge of shifting, he didn't scare me. I knew it was his wolf pushing him towards me; he would never hurt me. Not physically at least.

"Don't be so promiscuous," he countered. My jaw dropped.

A laugh that I couldn't suppress escaped my throat. "I assure you, I'm not the least bit promiscuous. You can calm down." My lips curled up in a large grin.

His growls immediately died down. His eyes still burned gold but his face had taken on a tender expression as he took in my features. His eyes glazed over, but I could tell it wasn't from mind-link. My smile dropped as I wondered why he was looking at me like that.

After a few seconds, he closed his eyes tightly and shook his head. When he looked at me again, his eyes were cerulean and his face was serious, his light and playful mood evaporated, as had his rage. I sighed inwardly.

"What is your role in the Keating Pack?" he asked, his voice all business now.

"I'm the Alpha's daughter and I assist with pack finances." My tone matched his.

"What is your pack's financial status?"

"We're a wealthy pack. My father is a successful businessman, as was my grandfather."

"How are those finances distributed throughout the pack?"

"We make sure every pack member is cared for. We provide housing and job opportunities for wolves in need. My father raised us to know that greed was not an option. Wealth meant nothing if you weren't respected, and the only way to gain respect is to care for every member of the pack."

"So, the alpha's family isn't frivolous with their wealth?" he questioned.

"No, we're not. My siblings and I have always had to earn the money we were given. My parents instilled work ethic into us."

He nodded, seemingly pleased at what he was hearing.

"What jobs do the other Alpha offspring have?"

"Brody is the future Alpha. He has been training since he reached adulthood. He is the most tactically knowledgeable of my siblings. He works closely with the Head Enforcer. He helps train wolves and keep the pack safe. Matt is more business-minded. He helps Dad run his chain of restaurants across the country. He's more hands-on now than our father is. He's the main one who's helped me become familiar with pack finances."

"And your sister?" he inquired when I paused. I wanted to roll my eyes. He already knew all of this. I didn't know why he needed to question me. I refrained from pointing this out and answered nonetheless.

"Selena helps our mother with her Alpha Female duties. She's hoping to get more involved with pack issues though."

We haven't discussed it again since I left, but I still remember our heart-to-heart my last night home. I truly believed that she was trying to turn over a new leaf, and show Dad that she could be trusted.

"How many of you continued your education after high school?"

"Just Matt and me."

"How does your Alpha handle punishments? And what warrants punishment?"

"The type of punishment depends on the infraction committed. Our pack has rules, like any other. If those rules are broken, he handles it accordingly."

"What kind of rules? And what punishments?" He wanted a more in-depth explanation. His cerulean eyes drilled holes into my face, making me slightly uncomfortable with the power emanating from him.

"Well, like, no fighting between members. Violence, other than when it occurs during training, is punishable. For serious violence, he will lock someone up in our pack cells. No one has ever killed another member but that would be punishable by death. For less violent acts, he assigns them to some kind of community work."

"How would he handle a traitor within your pack?"

"I can't answer that."

"And why is that?" He looked suspicious now.

"We've never had a known traitor. I have no idea what he would do. I'm not completely sure how someone would betray us anyway. We're neutral to outer pack disagreements. We have no enemies."

"That's a naïve thought process, Miss Keating."

Being called promiscuous didn't offend me but being called naïve did. I felt my hackles rise.

"I'm not naïve," I spat out. My eyes narrowed on his face, causing him to do the same. He was the king right now, not my mate. He didn't seem to appreciate my disrespect, but I didn't care because I didn't appreciate his either.

"If you think you or your pack have no enemies, then yes, you are."

"We don't. We're on good terms with all surrounding packs."

"That doesn't matter. The worst kind of enemy is the kind you'd never suspect. You'd do well to remember that," he advised me.

My anger deflated. "Did that happen to you?" I asked softly.

"That is none of your business, Miss Keating. My personal life does not concern you. Remember your place."

Hurt bubbled in my chest, but I pushed it down and focused on the anger and resentment.

"I'm sorry, Your Highness," I spat out bitterly. "I'll try and remember my place from now on." I stood up furiously, my chair falling to the stone floor behind me. He did the same, wanting to use his height advantage to intimidate me. "As long as you remember yours as well. You're my King, and that's it. That is all you'll ever be to me. I'm done here."

I turned and stormed off before he could speak. He let me go. Perhaps if I hadn't been so irate, I would have noticed the look of pain in his eyes at my words. But then again, I'm sure my eyes mirrored his.

* * *

"This is the Royal Office, how may I help you?" I asked into the phone.

"I need to speak to the King," a gruff voice answered confidently.

I rolled my eyes. "About?"

"It's between me and the King. It doesn't concern some little receptionist. Transfer me through, little girl," he growled.

My temper flared at the audacity of this stranger. Tyler made a move to get up and take the call, but I handled it before he could.

"The King is a very busy man. He doesn't concern himself with little commoners. Can I take a message?" I feigned being polite. This seemed like a man who thought very highly of himself. I knew calling him a commoner would get to him.

Another growl rumbled through the phone. "I'm no commoner, you little bitch. Do you know who I am?"

"I'm afraid not. I can recognize the voice of most important people in the werewolf community, I don't recognize yours though. Are you sure you didn't mean to call the Help Center?"

The Help Center was a place that low ranked wolves could call with their concerns or questions. Higher wolves, such as Alphas and Betas, had direct access to the Royal Office, but everyone else had to call the Help Center and talk to a regular castle worker. Actually, they didn't even work in the castle. They worked in one of the mansions on the Royal property.

"I'm the Alpha of one of the biggest packs in the country, you pathetic servant. Get me the King. Now," he demanded. The arrogant jackass sounded like he was on the verge of shifting. I held back my snickers.

"And which pack would that be?"

"The Chandler Pack, you ignorant bitch. I'm Alpha Derek Chandler."

"I'm afraid I'm not familiar with a Derek Chandler." I purposely left out his alpha title. It was a sign of either familiarity or disrespect to drop the title. I definitely didn't do it because I was familiar with him.

"That's Alpha to you, servant. Don't think I won't inform the King about this treatment I've received from you," he said haughtily.

Before I could say another word, Tyler grabbed the phone from my hand. I didn't even notice him walking towards me.

I was sitting at a small table with just an office phone, my cell phone, a mug of hot chocolate, and a plate of muffins. His office was rather large. His giant work desk was at the back, giving me plenty of room at the front.

I had been here for about seven hours. After my abrupt departure from my interview, I had been holed up in here. I haven't seen King Finnian since the incident, which I was grateful for. I'd probably try to claw his eyes out if I saw him right now.

Tyler helped take my mind off of it though. He hadn't asked any questions, but I think he knew that Finnian had upset me. We talked and joked around to keep my mind off of Finnian. He still worked but he made time for me, which I appreciated. He also supplied me with food all day, making me like him even more. Food was the way to my heart.

I hadn't seen Matt or Dalton all day. I figured I would since they were usually with Tyler, but they were being tested with Royal Beta Kieran today. Apparently, it was their physical training that was being examined. They wanted physically strong packs on the Council.

"This is Royal Gamma Guzman speaking. I don't appreciate you calling and speaking to my receptionist and friend that way."

"Why in the world would you be friends with some irrelevant servant bitch?" He sounded disgusted. I could still hear him clearly with werewolf hearing.

"She's no servant, Chandler." He also dropped the title. Ouch. "She is the King's guest, an alpha's daughter, and a good friend of mine. Your condescending insults are not welcomed."

"If she's an alpha's daughter, she should know how to properly respect her superiors. Apparently, her father isn't a very good father or Alpha. If I heard my daughter speak to anyone like that, I'd—"

Tyler cut off his caustic, hateful words. My body shook with fury at his words about my father.

"Alpha Keating is a damn good Alpha, Chandler. And he's the next to join the Royal Council. Both he and his children will be superior to you once he has his seat. I suggest you show respect to your superiors, not the other way around."

My rage simmered down upon hearing Tyler put him in his place. Chandler was stunned into silence.

"Since you have refused to leave a message with Miss Keating, do not expect a callback. It was a pleasure, as always." His voice oozed sarcasm, then he hung up without another word.

"That was amazing." Laughter erupted from my mouth now that I didn't have to hold it back.

"Sorry about that. He's a pendejo. He calls here every couple of months trying to bother Finnian, who never even gives him the time of day. He won't give up though."

"Don't worry about it. He didn't get to me until he brought up my dad." I took a bite out of the blueberry muffin in front of me and washed it down with the now lukewarm hot chocolate.

"You don't get offended easily, do you?" It sounded more like a statement rather than a question.

"When you grow up with three older siblings, one of them being Selena Keating, you learn not to wear your feelings on your shoulder."

"I admire that. Most wolves would have let their pride get in the way; just like Derek did." He leaned against the front of his desk and crossed his arms over his chest.

"I'm a lot of things, but sensitive isn't one of them. Choleric on the other hand . . . Definitely." I swallowed the last of my muffin and hot chocolate.

"I can tell."

"I am curious if you've ever investigated Chandler."

"We haven't. I suppose we should."

"I definitely think you should."

"I'll speak to King Finnian about it. We'll have it taken care of," he assured me. "In the meantime, dinner is in an hour and a half. Care for a run before that?"

"For sure. Let's see if you can keep up." I grinned at him as I stood up.

"Let's see." He returned the grin.

* * *

"Okay, I would have won if you hadn't cheated," I whined as I walked out of the locker room, securing the last bobby pin in place.

We had run for the entire hour and a half and were now late for dinner. We hadn't had the time to go back to our rooms to clean up and for me to fix my hair properly, so we stopped by the locker room in the gym. I didn't have time to shower like I wanted, but I was able to secure my hair in two messy buns again and straighten my clothes out.

We had been racing again and unfortunately, Tyler won. It was close but he pulled ahead at the end. I was convinced he cheated somehow.

"How did I cheat exactly?" He snickered and straightened his tie. We quickly made our way to the dining hall.

"I haven't figured it out yet. We're having a rematch tomorrow though."

"Sure. I actually wanted to ask you something about tomorrow."

"And what would that be?"

"Well, tomorrow is a Friday, so the castle usually shuts down early as long as nothing is going on. I was thinking of going into town for the night. Maybe grab a drink and a bite to eat. Would you and your pack be interested in joining me?"

"Sure, sounds fun. I could use a beer. Who else is going?"

"Probably just Lili."

"You and Lili are friends?" This surprised me. I'd never even seen them talk.

"Si. She doesn't talk much, but I still try to include her when I go out. I think she gets lonely here. She always goes with me, mainly just to get out of the castle for a while. She's a sweet girl so I like the company."

"Are you two . . ." I trailed off, hoping he got my implication.

"No, definitely not." He laughed. "I'm waiting for my mate, and Lili isn't her. It's purely platonic between us. Things get lonely around here sometimes. We just provide each other with some company," he explained.

"Are there others here that hang out with you two?"

"Not really. Nikolina claims she's too old for such things, and Kieran and Emiliya are so stuck up each other's asses that no one else concerns them. Finnian always locks himself away on the sixth floor whenever he's not working. Occasionally, some of the top

Royal Enforcers will come, but they're usually so tired by the end of the week that they just go home and rest and spend time with their families. Everyone else is too intimidated by my status to go. That just leaves me and Lili."

"That's actually really sad. I hope you find your mate soon."

He smiled sadly at me, but his eyes looked far away. "Me too."

"The mating ball is coming up, maybe she'll be there," I tried encouraging him.

"Hmm. Maybe."

"Don't worry. I'm always up for a night on the town. I'll go with you whenever you want while I'm here."

"Gracias, Kendall. You're a good friend."

I smiled at him as we walked into the dining room. Our seats were the same as always; Kat and Tyler on both of my sides and Niki directly across from me. King Finnian was absent as usual. I figured that the appearance he made for the first dinner was a rare occurrence and wasn't going to happen again anytime while I was here.

"Sorry we're late," Tyler said as we slid into our seats. As soon as we were seated, the salads were brought out and the wine was poured.

"You are most certainly forgiven, Tyler. Two powerful wolves such as yourselves need to run often," Niki excused us.

"Well, I certainly try, Nikolina." He sent an apologetic smile to her.

"So how was training today?" I asked, looking between Kat, Niki, and Lili as we all started eating.

"It was great. The spell went perfectly," Kat said, sounding proud of herself, which she should be.

"Indeed. Katerina is progressing even faster than I anticipated. She's going to be very powerful once her training is complete," Niki bragged about her newest pupil.

"Would you mind coming tomorrow afternoon so I can place a shield around your mind?" Kat asked me.

"Of course. We'll do it before we go into town with Tyler."

Niki perked up. "You're going out with Tyler tomorrow?"

"Yeah, he asked if we wanted to join him."

"Lili, will you be joining as well?" She looked at the youngest Petrova witch to her left.

"Yes, Nikolina."

"I see. So, it will just be the six of you?" she inquired.

"As long as Kat, Matt, and Dalton decide to come, then yeah," I answered her. I looked at my packmates for confirmation. They all nodded to me; even Dalton, who grinned at me.

"Perhaps King Finnian will join you all? He could certainly use a night in town. He has seemed rather tense lately, no?"

"I'll extend an invitation, but I highly doubt he'll join. He never does," Tyler said to her.

"Maybe this time will be different. Maybe he'll want to accompany his guests." Her gaze lingered on me discretely.

"Like I said, I'll ask him about it. You never know."

"That is certainly correct. He may surprise us all."

Dinner went by quickly after that. All talks about King Finnian ceased. When it was over, I bid everyone goodnight and retired to my own room. I showered and prepared for bed in the bathroom.

Once I was finished, I stopped at the door and took a deep breath. I twisted the door open.

I released my breath as my shoulders slumped in disappointment. I guess I expected King Finnian to be waiting on my bed again. He wasn't. My room was completely empty.

I swallowed the lump in my throat and curled up in my bed. My last thoughts before going to sleep were that maybe he took my angry words to heart. Maybe he was done being my mate and was strictly my King now. The thought hurt more than it should.

CHAPTER SEVEN

"Hey, Mom. What's going on?" I asked into my phone, holding it to my ear with my shoulder as I pulled my black combat boots over the hem of my dark blue skinny jeans.

"Nothing much here. Grandma and Grandpa said hi. They were just over for dinner last night," Mom replied.

"Tell them I also said hi and that I love them," I said as I sat up straight and switched the phone to my other ear.

"I will. So how are you doing?"

"Pretty good, I guess. I miss home, but I've made a couple of friends here. We're actually heading to town with them in a few minutes."

"That's great, honey. I'm glad you like it better than you thought you would. I know your dad really appreciates you going."

"Yeah, well, whatever I can do to help," I muttered, chewing on my bottom lip.

Part of me wanted to spill everything to her right now. I wanted to tell her about meeting my mate and how he didn't want me. She was my mom; I knew she would understand. But I couldn't bring myself to utter the words. Shame and embarrassment sat in the pit of my stomach, tying it in knots.

Obviously, something was wrong with me. I didn't want to hear the disappointment in her voice if I told her. I couldn't handle that. Not from my mom; not from anyone in my family.

"So, have you met anyone? Your mate maybe?" She sounded excited.

Ouch. It's like she read my thoughts.

"No, Mom." I sighed heavily, the lie easily tumbling from my lips.

"Oh . . ." she trailed off. "Well that's okay. You'll meet him eventually. When the time's right."

I couldn't take her cheerful optimism anymore. "Is dad around?"

"Sure, sweetheart. Let me get him." She paused for a few seconds, probably finding dad. "He's right here. I love you. Talk to you soon, okay?"

"Yeah, sure. Love you too."

"Hey, Kenny. How is everything?" Dad's deep voice echoed through the phone after I said goodbye to Mom.

"Everything is good. And don't call me that," I warned, not that it would do any good. They'd never stop.

He ignored my last comment, as expected. "Matt told me you were interviewed yesterday. How did that go?"

Ugh. Maybe I should have asked for Selena instead. I didn't want to think about that interview, although it was burned in my mind. I hadn't seen King Finnian ever since. I had been in Tyler's office all morning and into the early afternoon. He hadn't even made a brief appearance in his public office. I desperately wanted to know where he was, which was pathetic. But I didn't dare ask; I didn't want Tyler asking questions.

I thought about Niki's comments at dinner last night. She made it seem like he would go, but I knew he wouldn't. Tyler didn't mention him going, and I knew well enough to know that he would have told me if Finnian was going. I shook the thought of him away and focused on my dad.

"Kendall? Did everything go okay?" He asked worriedly when I took too long to answer.

"It went fine, Dad. He was just asking questions about the pack. Nothing special really. Mostly about finances and about our family."

"And what did you tell the Royal Gamma?"

"Royal Gamma? Tyler didn't interview me. And I just told him the truth."

"You're calling the Royal Gamma by his first name?" He sounded surprised.

"Yeah, we're friends."

"Interesting . . . I knew there was a reason why I sent you. If it wasn't him, then who was it? The Royal Beta was with Matt and Dalton all day."

I bit my lip again. "It was the King," I reluctantly admitted.

"The King interviewed you personally?" he breathed out.

"Yeah . . . What?" I asked, amusement thick in my tone. I didn't understand why he was acting so weird. I'm sure the King interviewed people all the time.

"Kendall, sweetheart. I'm not sure you understand. King Finnian doesn't usually get involved in the recruitment process until the second month. You've only been there a week. This is either very good or very bad." He sounded apprehensive now.

"Well, we're still here, so I'm sure it can't be that bad. Besides, it seemed to go fine. I'm sure Tyler was just busy with something else," I tried to downplay it.

"You haven't gotten in some kind of trouble, have you?"

"No, not that I know of."

"You haven't insulted or disrespected the King somehow?"

I absolutely had. "No, Dad. I've only seen him a couple of times. I've barely even talked to him." More lies. The thought of my dad sounding disappointed in me was even worse than if my mom was. I couldn't tell them yet. Maybe not ever.

"Okay, well, let's not worry yet. Maybe you're right. It could be nothing," he said like he was trying to calm me down.

"You're the only one worrying," I muttered dryly.

"I suppose you're right. Just keep me updated on any future interactions with King Finnian."

"I will. Is Selena around?" I hadn't talked to her in a couple of days and sorely missed our verbal spats.

"Sure. I love you, kiddo."

"Love you too."

I waited as the phone was passed yet again. I heard muffled arguing, probably coming from Selena. I held in a chuckle. I missed watching their quarrels as well.

"What?" She sounded irritable. Lovely.

"Looks like I got away from you just in time. Eat a Snickers, you PMSing bitch."

"Eat a dick, you whore."

"What's up with you?"

"Your father is a huge douchebag," she said loudly. I could imagine her turning her head towards the door, wanting him to hear her. With my sensitive hearing, I could hear a muffled growl but nothing else.

"My father is your father. What'd he do?"

"I've been trying to get more involved in pack stuff. You know, show him he could trust me like you said? But he won't even give me a chance," she whined.

"What are you trying to get involved with?"

She didn't respond, which gave me my answer.

"Selena, bugging him about coming here wasn't what I meant. Try asking him to let you join Brody for a day. That would go a long way with him. Just show interest in something other than coming here."

"I just miss you guys. I hate it here with just dad's little puppet that we call an older brother and the gruesome twosome that we call parents." I heard three different growls that time.

"You haven't seen a real gruesome twosome until you meet the Royal Betas." I laughed. This was another time I was glad Niki had put a hearing spell on my room.

"I'll bet you otherwise."

"Easiest money I've ever made."

"You really think that will work?" she asked, referring to my advice about shadowing Brody for the day.

"I think it'll be a good start. You have to do something. I really want Dad to let you come to the mating ball, so you need to show him he can trust you."

"That gives me a month. No problem."

"Well, you're nothing if not determined. Just follow my advice and I think he'll give in."

"For the first and last time in our lives, I will follow your advice. Don't expect it ever again though."

"Wasn't planning on it. You'd have to be somewhat intelligent to do that. Everyone knows your brain could triple in size and you'd still be stupid," I teased.

"I guess that's another thing we have in common." She laughed, sounding less irritable than before.

"What? That we're both bitchy and stupid? I'm sure our family is envied by everyone. Mom and Dad must be so proud," I drawled out sarcastically.

"At least we're fun to be around."

"I'm fun to be around; you're a pain in the ass."

As I was talking, I decided to stand up from the couch and stretch my legs. I had been sitting all day.

"You're getting us confused again."

"I don't think so. You're the confused one, which is nothing new. With your lack of—"

A startled cry left my lips as I turned around, cutting off my own sentence. I dropped my phone in surprise but managed to catch it with my fast reflexes before it smashed against the stone floor. I gulped nervously.

"Are you okay?" I heard Selena yelling.

I lifted the phone back to my ear. "I'm fine. I'm gonna have to call you back though." I hung up before she could say anything else.

As I shove my phone roughly into my back pocket, I tried to calm my racing heart as I took in the man in front of me.

King Finnian was leaning against the closed door frame, looking more than relaxed. His arms were crossed over his chest, making his biceps stretch against the fabric of his t-shirt. He looked casual now, unlike yesterday. He's just wearing a T-shirt, jeans, and black combat boots.

It unnerved me a bit that I never heard him come into my room. If I hadn't turned around, I might not have even realized he was there. God only knows how long he had already been standing there.

"How long have you been standing there like a creeper?" I demanded.

"You lied to your mother about meeting your mate," he stated nonchalantly.

My jaw unhinged. I had talked to both my dad and sister after my mom. How in the hell have I not heard him, smelled him, or sensed his presence?

"Has anyone ever taught you how rude eavesdropping is? I would expect the King to treat his guests better than that." I ignored his comment about my mom, which he returned by ignoring mine as well.

"Do you and your sister often speak to each other with such malice?"

"My relationship with my sister is none of your business," I hissed. My hackles were raised. I didn't take well to people criticizing my family. My relationship with Selena was weird, I knew that, but I loved her dearly. I didn't appreciate him questioning that.

"I'm not criticizing you or your sibling. Although you did criticize mine." The playful gleam in his eyes told me he wasn't really upset. "Gruesome twosome? Clever."

"I wouldn't have said that had I not been under the impression that my conversation was private," I defended myself, even though he wasn't angry.

"My mistake, Miss Keating. I had just assumed that, as a werewolf, you would have heard me enter the room." Now he was making fun of me.

"Maybe if you'd try knocking for once, I would have."

I knew that deep down the real reason I hadn't heard him was because my wolf realized he was here and didn't deem him a threat. Had it been anyone else, she would have forced me to notice their presence to assess if they were a danger. I think he realized this too, which would explain the pleased look in his eyes. I was sure he loved that he had my wolf on his side.

"I'll keep that in mind for next time." His lips curved up slightly, which shocked me since I had yet to see him actually smile. I bet it'd look good on him.

"Are you saying there will be a next time, King Finnian?" I raised a taunting eyebrow at him.

"I just can't seem to stay away."

That warmed my heart slightly. "I can tell. Am I that irresistible?" I asked flippantly. His response was completely serious, all teasing leaving his eyes, his eyebrow furrowing and his smile dropping.

"Yes."

I swallowed the lump in my throat. My emotions were going haywire and I couldn't tell what exactly I was feeling from his answer.

"You look beautiful, by the way," he said to me when I didn't say anything back. Mutant butterflies flapped their gigantic wings in my stomach.

"Umm, thanks. I guess that makes one of us," I said to lighten the mood around us, which had started to make me uncomfortable.

He surprised me even more when a deep, husky chuckle escaped his lips in response to my words. My lower belly filled with warmth at the sound. I felt my eyes glaze over as I looked at his smiling face. I was right. It did look good on him; too good.

"You never cease to surprise me, Miss Keating," he said when his laughter died down.

"I could say the same about you, King Finnian." My voice sounded slightly breathless. I cleared my throat.

He walked closer to me and stopped a foot in front of me. He made no move to grab me. He just lifted his hand and stroked my cheek with his thumb.

"I just wanted to tell you to be safe tonight." He dropped his hand. I refrained from grabbing it and holding it in place.

"So, you're not going," I stated rather than ask. I didn't need to.

"Afraid not. I've taken the proper precautions though."

"Those would be?"

"I had Nikolina cast some spells on you."

"What spells?" I asked through gritted teeth. I didn't appreciate spells being cast on me without my knowledge or consent. I had a lot of spells cast on me, all by Kat. But she had always asked my permission first. I had never unknowingly had someone do it. I didn't like the thought of someone controlling me without me even knowing.

"The first will let me know if you are in distress. Since we aren't fully mated, I need a way to know if you're hurt or in trouble," he explained calmly. My fury didn't seem to phase him.

"Have you ever heard of a cell phone, Your Highness?"

"The second is to prevent males with questionable motives from approaching you."

"Are you fucking serious?" I walked forward and poked him in the chest. He glared down at my finger, then my face. "You had your witch cast a spell on me to keep guys from hitting on me? You have some real issues."

"Is that so?" I could tell he was reining in his anger due to my disrespect.

"It is so. You're a jealous psychopath. You need a royal therapist," I sneered.

His lips tilted upwards again and he started walking towards the door slowly. He stopped right in front of it, hand clasped around the knob but not turning it, and looked back at me.

"That's where you're wrong, Miss Keating. I'm not jealous, I'm territorial."

"Is there a difference?" I narrowed my eyes at him.

"Indeed, there is. Jealousy is wanting something you don't have. Being territorial is protecting something that's already yours." My mouth dropped open in shock. "Have a good night, Miss Keating."

With that, he twisted the knob and left my room before I could say anything else.

In that moment, I realized something important. This man was going to be the death of me.

*   *   *

"So where are we going exactly?" I asked Tyler as he started driving away from the castle.

Matt had driven his car, Kat and Dalton with him. I was in the passenger seat of a black SUV with Tyler driving and Lili in the back seat behind him.

"Mountainside Bar and Grill," he answered as he pulled through the heavy wrought iron gates.

"Are they any good? I'm starving."

"Best in town. Not that there's much to choose from."

"It's a small town?"

We hadn't driven through a town on the way here. We must have come in from a different direction. Tyler confirmed my thoughts when he veered off the pathway that we had originally come through. I could see guard posts every once in a while but no one stopped us.

"It is. It's part of the Royal Territory. Most of the residents work in either the town or for King Finnian."

"I thought you had separate houses for workers and enforcers on the Royal Territory?" I asked.

"We do. Not everyone chooses to live there though. Which is a good thing, because they're not big enough to house even half of the workers and Royal Army. It's mostly just unmated wolves who decide to live there. Wolves with mates and families prefer the privacy of their own home," he explained to me.

"Everyone in town is a part of the Royal Pack?"

It wasn't really a pack per se, but that is what everyone called it. It sounded better than saying a large group of wolves who work for the Royals.

"Si."

I nodded and started fiddling with the radio. I settled on a station after a while and stared at the thick greenery blurring by the car. I felt a pang of longing, and wished for Finnian to be next to me instead. I sighed and looked back out ahead of us.

We drove for about fifteen minutes before we were surrounded by civilization. It was a small town, like he said. It was quaint. There weren't any franchise stores. Everything was a mom and pop type place. Thankfully, it had all the necessities.

There weren't many restaurants to choose from. There was a fifty's style diner, a bakery, a coffee and donut shop, a seafood place with a drive-thru, a little Italian place, and finally, a Mountainside Bar and Grill, which we turned into.

It was pretty packed; it was a Friday night after all, but we were able to find a couple of parking spots in the back. Tyler maneuvered into one, while Matt took the other.

I jumped out of the vehicle. The cold wind blew my hair back and bit at my exposed skin. I pulled my leather jacket tighter to my body and shoved my hands in the front pockets. A cold front had blown through the night before and I could definitely feel it. I may have had a higher body temperature than humans but I still got cold.

Matt pulled off his jacket as they walked over to us and wrapped it around Kat's shoulders. Another shot of longing ran through me. It didn't seem like Finnian and I would ever have that. The only thing we seemed to be able to do together was fight, kiss, and mock one another. Never care for the other like them.

I pushed the longing away. I was going to have fun tonight. I was determined. I linked arms with Kat and Lili, pulling the former away from my brother which earned me a glare. Tyler walked with Dalton and Matt as we trailed behind them.

I sighed in relief when we walked inside. It was so much warmer. I thought at first we would have to wait for a table because of how packed it was, but they led us to a big rounded booth right away. I assumed it was because Tyler was with us. I felt bad for all the people standing around and waiting for a table.

I sat in the middle of the rounded seat. Kat was next to me, Matt next to her, then Dalton. On my other side, Lili was next to me, and Tyler was on the outside, across from Dalton.

We didn't have to wait that long for the waiter. I barely opened the menu when he walked over to us. We ordered our drinks first. Tyler, Dalton, and I all got a beer. Matt got a Jack and Coke. Kat and Lili stuck to iced tea. Witches didn't like to drink; something about it throwing off their connection to nature or something, but werewolves sure as hell didn't need to connect to nature.

We also ordered several appetizers for the table. We got everything from chips and queso to wings to stuffed shrimp. I was tired of all the fancy food lately, so once our waiter returned with our drinks I settled on a bacon cheeseburger and fries.

Once the waiter finished taking all of our orders, we started sipping on our beverages. I took a long sip of the ice-cold beer.

The last time I drank something alcoholic was the night of my college graduation. That's not including the wine at dinners, but I wasn't much of a wine person so those didn't count. I've only had one glass every night, and that was just so I didn't seem rude by refusing. It was nice to have a real drink.

"I had a feeling you were a beer kind of girl," Tyler said, sipping on his bottle.

"Really? Why's that?"

"I could tell you've been having trouble drinking even one glass of wine every night."

"You pay that close attention to me?" I snorted.

"Well, you do sit right next to me."

"I suppose I'm nicer to look at than Royal Beta Kieran."

"You can drop the Royal Beta when he's not around. Although I'd suggest using it when he is. He's not exactly the type to drop titles like that. He's very formal."

"And you're not. Why is that?" I sipped at my beer some more.

"I'm no better than anyone else. Why should I have a title when other people don't?" He shrugged.

"Well, I'm glad to see the power hasn't gone to your head. It would have for a lot of people."

"It would have, and it has in the past."

"Oh?" Kat joined in the conversation.

"Finnian's grandfather's Beta. He led the previous rebellion against him. He did it all behind his back. When the former king found out, he had his beta executed. His whole family too.

"Then he went to war with the rebels. They didn't stand a chance against him and his Royal Army without the Royal Beta. He slaughtered hundreds, maybe thousands. The Royal Beta line died with him. Finnian and Kieran's father was the first to appoint someone of Royal Alpha blood as his beta. It was his younger brother. Finnian continued it in the next generation of the Royals."

I was in awe of what I had heard. What kind of Beta could betray their Alpha? The role of the Beta was one of the most sacred roles to an Alpha, besides his Alpha Female of course. It was supposed to be someone the Alpha could trust and count on. If you couldn't trust your own Beta, you really couldn't trust anyone.

As irritating as Dalton was, I knew that when the time came, Brody would always be able to count on him the same way Dad had always counted on Dalton's father.

As I looked around the table, I realized no one other than me looked surprised by this history lesson. Did they already know?

"How come no one else seems surprised to hear this?" I asked.

"How you managed to graduate high school, the world may never know." Matt laughed at me.

My jaw dropped. "What is that supposed to mean?"

"Did you ever pay attention in Werewolf 101?"

Werewolf 101 wasn't really a class, per se. We still had to follow the human government's rules and regulations, so what most packs did was add in disguised electives, but what we were really being taught was everything wolf-related. This included history, government, combat training, senses and strength control, and everything else a young werewolf needed to know to function in a werewolf society. We usually had two of these classes a year along with normal classes such as English and Math.

Kat snorted this time. "Never."

"Hey, I did sometimes. Most of the stuff they taught were things Dad had already taught me," I defended myself.

"Apparently, he didn't teach you werewolf history," Dalton added in.

"I distinctly remember Selena used to help you cheat in Chemistry. So, you can't make fun of me. You have absolutely no ground to stand on."

"I didn't get a chance to study," he defended himself.

"Sure." I dragged out the r. "Let's go with that." I swallowed the last of my beer.

"The only reason I didn't study was because you were a menace back then. Still are."

"How did she prevent you from studying?" Lili asked, joining in for the first time.

"I'm glad you asked." He looked at Lili, then turned back to me. "She hit me with her car," he said with a deadpan voice.

Everyone started laughing at this. Even Lili giggled a little. I just glared.

"If you're going to tell the story, tell it right."

"By all means, Kenny, tell them about your attempted murder."

"Fine, I will." At this time, the waiter brought us our appetizers and another round of drinks. We thanked him as he walked off. "So first, let me start by saying, Dalton and Selena were completely at fault."

"I'll give her this one; it was more Selena's fault than anyone else's," Kat added.

"Thank you. Finally, someone with some sense," I said in relief.

"Well, what happened?" Lili asked, smiling slightly.

"It was a few weeks before Halloween, and I had just gotten my driver's license. Kat and I were on our way to a bonfire some of the teenagers in the pack were having. Selena, who had told us about the bonfire, was supposed to come with us but decided to hang out with Dalton instead. We thought they were just going to wreak havoc on everyone like usual, but they decided to target us that night."

"We did not wreak havoc," Dalton stated.

"You did. You two were the real menaces." He rolled his eyes and I continued the story, "So anyways, we were driving along this dirt road. It was pitch black except for the car lights. No one was around the area. Turns out, Selena gave me the wrong address. She said Carly Teller decided to host it in her backyard instead of Dani Monroe. We stupidly believed her and went to Carly's instead who, by the way, lives in the middle of nowhere. It's like ten miles down a dirt road."

"We should have known better right then. Selena never would have gone to Carly Teller's party. They didn't like each other at all." Kat chuckled.

"I know. Remember their 'fight' in fifth grade?" I did air quotations.

"How could anyone forget? Selena was on top of Carly, pinching the shit out of her cheeks, so Carly bit her on the wrist like a freaking vampire."

We both were laughing so hard now, tears were gathering in our eyes. That was single-handedly one of the greatest memories I have. I still tease Selena about it to this day. Both girls had ended up crying and covered in dirt. It was hysterical.

"You two can't finish a story for anything." Matt shook his head, but he looked between us fondly.

"Right, my bad." I sobered up from my fits of laughter. "So anyways, we were just driving along and suddenly we saw this ghost-like thing falling down from this tree and this screeching noise. We legitimately thought it was a real ghost. The damn thing looked so realistic."

I paused, thinking back on it. They had told us after that they bought it online a few weeks before. They had the whole thing planned for like a month.

"After it fell, we slammed on the breaks. It was just like an automatic response. We were so focused on it that we didn't see anyone walking towards the car. All of a sudden, something was right in front of the car. It was Dalton, of course, but he was dressed in this scary-ass ghost costume. Selena was too and she popped up next to my window and started beating on it and screaming at me. They thought we'd be scared, realize it was them, and all would be good and we'd go to the real party. Well, it did not go as planned."

"No, it went horribly, horribly awry," Kat said, dripping a chip in the warm cheesy queso. I grabbed one as well, chewing and swallowing quickly before speaking again.

"Very dangerously awry. My fight-or-flight reflexes kicked in. Turns out, they were screaming flight. I stepped on the gas so hard I nearly put the pedal through the floor.

Dalton's reflexes didn't even compare to mine. He tried to dodge but I clipped him anyway. He was fine, but the car fucked up his knee pretty bad.

He was on crutches for a couple of weeks. Like I said, it was his and Selena's fault."

"Mostly Selena's," Dalton reiterated Kat's earlier words.

"Not really. You were the idiot who believed her."

"Believed what?" Lili inquired. She looked thoroughly engrossed in our story as she munched on the chips and dip.

Kat answered for me, "Selena told him that she'd freeze up. Said she knew her sister better than anyone and knew how she'd react. She was wrong."

"Like I said, it's his fault too for believing that crap."

"Why do I feel like there are plenty more stories about the 'Three Amigas'." Tyler did air quotes too.

"We could write a book and three sequels and not cover all of our escapades," I joked, eating a chicken wing now.

"We're all ears." He smiled before sipping on his beer.

I quickly finished off my second beer.

"You asked for it. You better strap in. You're about to experience the ride of a lifetime."

* * *

"How were you able to sneak out of your house? Your parents are werewolves. They should have heard three teenagers leaving the house in the middle of the night," Tyler speculated.

"That's where I came into play. I had just learned the silencing spell," Kat explained to Tyler and Lili.

The silencing spell had been our best friend for a couple of months. It made all of our movements completely silent for everyone else, which allowed us to get out of the house unnoticed. We were always back before our parents could wake up.

It was perfect until the Head Enforcer caught us drinking and skinny dipping in the lake between our property and his. He had been out for a late-night run and accidentally stumbled upon us. The experience was horrifying and embarrassing for all parties involved.

Dad took extra precautions after that. He had Kat's mom cast a spell on our house so that we couldn't get out if we were under the silencing spell and had us grounded for three months. It ruined everything and sucked especially hard because we got caught a few weeks before summer, meaning we were grounded for the majority of the summer. Not to mention one of my dad's best friends was the first guy to see me naked.

"It only worked for a few months. We were caught eventually," I said evasively, choosing to leave out just exactly how we were caught.

"Yeah." Kat cringed, as did Matt. Tyler looked curious, but I started talking before he could ask, trying to distract him.

That was not a story I wanted to relive. The three of us promised to never speak of it ever again. No one ever knew why we were grounded. They knew about the silencing spell, but not how we got caught. My siblings did and our parents, but never our friends.

"Selena had just found out her boyfriend cheated on her with Carly Teller. She wasn't really upset. She didn't even like him that much. Of course, neither did Carly. It was just one of the many things they did to spite each other until their rivalry ended when they graduated. Anyway, she wanted revenge even though she didn't care about him. Everyone expected her to retaliate. So, we formed a plan."

I started laughing before I could even tell the story. I was feeling pretty buzzed. When I drank, I tended to laugh hysterically at the things my intoxicated mind deemed humorous. It made it hard to finish the story. Kat knew this and continued instead as I giggled along, sipping on my final beer of the night.

We had finished our food and were now drinking and talking. I had several beers already and decided after my seventh that I was done for the night.

I liked to feel buzzed, but I didn't like getting wasted. The thought of completely losing control of my actions never appealed to me. I used to get hammered when I first started drinking at fifteen but then quickly realized that not remembering what happened the night before wasn't my idea of a good time. Therefore, I always set a drink limit for myself and have never surpassed it since. I haven't gotten super wasted since I was seventeen.

"So, after I had cast the spell, we snuck out and drove over to Carly's house first. We parked half a mile away from her house and walked the rest of the way. We had somehow gotten ahold of this industrial-sized saran wrap; a bunch of them too. We completely wrapped her car. Like, it was completely covered from front to back. From what we heard, it took her hours to cut it all off."

"How did we even get that saran wrap?" I asked, still giggling.

"I don't even remember. Selena got it from somewhere. Who knows with her?" She turned her attention back to Tyler and Lili. "It took us forever to do it. I remember by the time we snuck back to the car, I was exhausted. I had kept up the silencing spell for the whole time. We couldn't get caught outside of Carly's house though, and we couldn't be quiet to save our lives, so I kept the spell going.

"I would have been fine, but we had to do Nate's truck as well. It took twice as long to do his since it was way bigger. He was so pissed. He was obsessed with that truck. He thought he'd punish Selena by ignoring her afterward, but she just thought the whole thing was funny."

"You girls caused a lot of trouble." Tyler shook his head but was still amused by our escapades.

We had been telling them stories the whole time we were here. I thought they'd get bored after just listening to us, but they continued to look thoroughly engrossed and entertained. We tried to ask them questions, but they said they didn't have any adventures like that. Our youths were drastically different. It seemed they were both living vicariously through our stories.

"Here's your check whenever you're ready." The waiter placed it on the pretty much-cleared table top. All that was left was our drinks.

"I got it," Tyler offered before anyone could say anything.

Matt argued with him but Tyler insisted on paying. We all thanked him and he gave the waiter his card.

"Well, this was fun," I said as I slid my jacket over my body. It was uncomfortable since I already was covered in a light sheen of sweat, but I knew I'd be grateful once we went outside.

"It was. We'll have to do it again soon."

"Definitely," Kat agreed with me.

"Thanks for coming. You all have a great night." The waiter returned and thanked us, bowing his head respectfully as he spoke.

"Thanks, you too," I replied.

Tyler stuffed the card back in his wallet and filled out the receipt. I couldn't help but notice the generous tip he left. With it included, the ticket came out to be over 600 dollars. It was really sweet of him to pay. I'll have to do something nice for him in return. I made a mental note.

We got up and walked outside. Just as I predicted, my heated body immediately cooled down to an uncomfortable level. I shivered as the cold wind blew my hair back, biting into my skin bitterly.

The sky was completely black, and the light from the stars and moon was obscured behind a wall of dark clouds. The air was filled with cold mugginess, hinting at the storm brewing above our heads.

We rushed to our respective cars. Once inside, we buckled up and cranked the heater up. I held my chilled fingers in front of the vent, letting the hot air warm them.

I turned up the radio and sang along as we drove. The drive was short, so I chatted with Tyler and Lili all the while singing along softly.

We returned to the castle in no time. As we pulled up, I couldn't help but marvel at the beautiful creation known as Cahill Castle. It was creepy and eerie but also marvelous and exquisite. Truly built for a king.

Tyler parked in the long garage and Matt pulled up next to him. We walked inside the castle together. Tyler led our group since we had only been this way once. He led us to the entrance of the guest quarters. He and Lili bid us goodnight and left us.

The four of us walked to our hallway. I stumbled a tiny bit as I walked. When we reached our hall, we said goodnight and went to our respective rooms. Once I was inside mine and finally alone, a strong sense of longing slammed into me.

I ignored it for a few minutes and changed into my sleepwear; a T-shirt and a pair of short cotton shorts. I washed off all my make-up and threw my hair into a messy bun.

I planned on getting into bed after that but I was suddenly filled with restless energy. I couldn't explain it. I didn't know if it was from the alcohol in my system or something else.

As I paced back and forth, I finally realized what I needed; I needed my mate.

I suppose the alcohol prompted my next actions because I sure as hell wouldn't have done it if I drank water instead of beer.

Like I said, I wasn't really drunk but I was buzzed. My inhibitions were dangerously low so I decided to get what I wanted, consequences be damned. My metaphorical balls had tripled in size.

With that thought process, I quietly, or as quietly as I could, slipped out of my room. In my haste, I didn't even think to cover myself up.

Goosebumps from the biting cold covered my bare arms and legs. I wasn't wearing a bra anymore; it was obvious through the thin material of my t-shirt. I didn't even have shoes on. All this didn't even seem to register to me because I kept walking.

I quickly located one of the secret passageways for the workers. It wasn't that far from my room so it wasn't hard to find. It was completely empty at this time of night. It was after midnight after all.

My feet lightly slapped against the cold stone of the stairs. I padded up them quickly, stumbling a couple times along the way. Luckily, I made it to the door of the sixth floor without getting caught.

I held my breath, hoping the door wasn't locked. I twisted and, to my surprise, it opened. I supposed it didn't really need to be locked; no one but me was stupid enough to venture up to the King's private quarters.

I opened the door just enough to slip through, then closed it lightly. I took in my new surroundings.

It seemed colder up here somehow . . . lonely even. The walls were bare except for the low lighting of the lantern-like lights on the walls, which were all over the castle. They left the otherwise dark hallway in a yellowish-hazy glow. There was no artwork or pictures on the walls or pieces of furniture anywhere. Just doors lining both sides of the walls.

I gulped and started walking. I didn't know where I was going. I wasn't particularly looking for King Finnian at this point since I was so focused on taking in my new location.

I turned down the hall and came into a large open area. It was like a study of sorts. It was huge and filled with furniture but looked completely unused. A sheen of dust covered every surface as if no one had stepped foot inside in years. I kept walking past it.

I went a ways in before I opened a door at random. It was an empty room.

I did that for several other rooms; all empty. I frowned as I turned another corner.

I didn't get far. Before I could even register what was happening, I was flattened against the cold stone wall, with something warm and hard pressing against my back. I groaned in surprise and turned my head to the side since my nose had been uncomfortably pushed against it.

"The hell . . ." I muttered, not realizing what was going on. My reflexes and senses were almost nonexistent. Whatever was behind me held me firmly but gently against the wall.

I suddenly felt warm air blowing into my ear. After a few seconds, I realized it was coming from a person. I inhaled a deep breath and opened my mouth, prepared to scream in alarm. Before I could, a large hand clamped over my mouth, muffling the noise efficiently.

"I wasn't expecting you tonight, mate." A voice rumbled in my ear, lips brushing against it. A shiver of excitement ran down my spine. "I suppose I underestimated your courage. Although, I'm sure the alcohol in your system played a part in that. Still, that doesn't change the fact that you shouldn't be up here. You broke the rules." He paused and nipped the skin under my ear. His next words were spoken in a low, deep whisper, "Looks like I'll have to punish you now."

My heart raced with both excitement and fear. I both regretted and was satisfied with my decision to come up here. No matter what happened, it was certainly bound to be interesting. My night just got more exciting.

CHAPTER EIGHT

I didn't even think my words over before they left my mouth. I didn't even know what I was saying until I heard them. I was as surprised as he was.

"Ooh, kinky. I love it when you talk dirty to me," I said with mirth in my voice.

He growled lowly in my ear, his body pressing further against mine, if that was even possible. In the process, I felt something hard poking against my lower back. It didn't take long to figure out what it was.

"If I were you, I'd choose my next words very carefully." His voice was low and gruff.

"Maybe I should make my words as dirty as you." Just to tease him further, I stood on my tiptoes and ground my ass into the manhood that he had threatened to show me on my first day here.

I was suddenly flipped around, my back now pressing against the cold, hard wall and my front pressed against his. His eyes were glowing golden. I knew I was dealing with his wolf right now, not him. Good. His wolf was the only one who seemed to like me.

I already knew what he would have said anyway. He would have threatened to act if I didn't stop. What he didn't seem to grasp is that I wanted him to act, but I didn't think he ever would.

So before he could say anything, I spoke again. "You're so beautiful," I mumbled. I knew my eyes were glazed over as I took in his handsome features. I stroked his cheek gently, feeling his dark stubble tickle my fingertips.

His hard eyes softened considerably. They stayed golden but were now smoldering and affectionate. He grabbed my hand from his cheek and intertwined our fingers, holding it softly against the wall above my head. His other hand was resting on my hip, stroking my skin through my t-shirt, which just seemed to be in the way at that point.

It seemed King Finnian was getting ready for bed as well. He was in a pair of boxers and nothing else. I wasn't sure how I didn't realize he was shirtless earlier, but now that I had, it was all I could focus on.

I couldn't see his abs, but I could feel how defined they were against my stomach. His tanned chest was strong with a light dusting of hair across it. His arms were thick and muscular, with thick veins running down the length of them. His hands were big and calloused but still warm and soft against my own. He was the epitome of perfection.

"Men don't appreciate being called beautiful," he informed me. He didn't seem too upset at my word choice though. Instead, he was taking me in.

"Does sexy work better for you?" I whispered in his ear and nibbled on his ear lobe gently.

He groaned and dropped his head so it was resting against my shoulder. His hand tightened against mine. "Why are you making this so hard for me?" he whispered. I barely heard him. I think he was talking to himself more than me. He didn't seem to expect a reply, but I gave him one anyway.

"I can tell I'm making something hard." I gave him a mischievous grin when he pulled his head from my shoulder and looked at me. He seemed surprised at first, but then he growled.

"You need to stop." He looked at me with hard eyes again. It didn't deter me.

"You need to take me to bed, King Finnian."

"I'm not joking. Stop. Now," he commanded. His commands didn't work on me like they did everyone else. My wolf saw him as our equal, not our superior.

"I'm not joking either." I started pressing kisses against his chest. He was now at his full height, so I couldn't reach his face like I wanted. I settled for what was right in front of me.

"Stop!" he half yelled, half growled harshly.

I pulled back in shock. I looked up at him with wide, unbelieving eyes. I wasn't sure how to feel. I was torn between rage that he would speak to me that way and hurt at his harsh tone. I wasn't usually an emotional person but alcohol always made me a little more susceptible to my emotions. This is the only reason why instead of yelling at him what an asshole he was, my wide green eyes started to well up with tears.

His hard gaze softened again as he took in my tearful eyes. I pulled my hand out of his hold and wiped it away angrily. I was angry at not only him but myself as well. I couldn't believe I let this shithead see my tears.

I was preparing for a confrontation. Instead, I suddenly felt drained. I was just tired of this. I was tired of the constant back and forth and the mixed signals. I wanted this to be easy. I'd never been more lonely and exhausted.

"Sorry . . ." I muttered, refusing to meet his eyes.

"No, I'm sorry." He tilted my chin up, forcing me to look at him. His eyes held remorse. "I shouldn't have yelled like that. But I refuse to be intimate with you when you're even the slightest bit inebriated."

"I just wanted to be around you." I wrapped my arms around his stomach and buried my face against his bare chest. I was disgusted by my own actions, but I'd rather deal with it tomorrow. For now, I just wanted to be with my mate. My wolf was howling in approval at my actions. It felt good to finally be on the same page as her for the first time all week.

He wrapped his arms around me tightly as well and buried his head in my hair. He sighed heavily. I didn't know if it was a good one or a bad one.

We stayed like this for several minutes. Not talking, just enjoying each other's embrace. All too soon, it came to an end. He kissed the top of my head, lingering for a few seconds, before pulling away.

"I'll walk you back to your room," he stated, his voice void of any emotion, not giving away what he was really feeling.

I immediately pouted and looked at him with wide, pleading eyes. "I want to stay with you for tonight . . . Just tonight. Please."

Ugh, I was so pathetic. I was practically begging him. Tomorrow's disgust grew.

He sighed again and looked away from me. He was silent for a while. When he turned back to me finally, I thought he was going to tell me to leave. He surprised me when he instead said, "Just for tonight."

He grabbed my hand again, lacing our fingers together. A grin lit up my face as I let him pull me behind him. I squeezed his hand in appreciation that he didn't reject me yet again. He squeezed mine back but didn't turn to look at me.

We walked down a couple of hallways before he stopped at a pair of wide wooden double doors. He twisted the brass handle on one of them and pulled the door open. He pulled me inside and shut the door behind me.

I was stunned by my surroundings. We were in a bedroom. His scent was overpowering, assuring me that it was his room. The walls and floor were stone, and the ceiling was domed. One wall had a huge stone fireplace, which was unlit. There were a couple of chairs facing the fireplace. One looked worn and used, the other looked brand new.

On the wall across from us was a big window and a glass door. It led out to a balcony, where I could see a table with a couple of chairs. Raindrops pounded against the windows, a strong wind blowing forcefully against them. There were deep red curtains, but they were pulled open. They were covered in dust, making me believe that they usually stayed open.

Across from the fireplace, there was a king-sized four-poster wooden bed. It was covered in dark red sheets, matching the curtains. There was a bedside table on either side, each with a lamp. The two lamps were turned on, lighting the room with a soft yellow glow. There were plush white rugs scattered around the room. There was a door on the wall across from the balcony and I assumed it led to the bathroom and closet.

The room was huge, but it seemed rather empty. It was lacking any personal touches. Other than the rumpled bed sheets and King Finnian's scent, it did not seem lived in. No books were lying around, save for the lone one on the table between the chairs in front of the fireplace. There were no pictures or knick-knacks. The floor was bare of clothes, which was weird to see since my and Selena's bedroom floor was always covered in dirty clothes.

"I love your room." I turned back to him after I finished my survey of the room.

His lips tugged up at the corner then quickly dropped back down. "Thanks," he said gruffly.

"What are you reading?" I rushed forward to grab the book off his table. He stopped me before I could reach it.

"None of your business. I didn't say you could touch anything," he snapped.

"You don't have to be rude," I said nonchalantly, not letting him get to me again.

"You don't have to be nosy," he countered. An amused chuckle escaped my lips.

"Coming from you, that's hilarious. You don't seem to know how to mind your own business. My phone conversation earlier can attest to that." My voice was teasing. It held no animosity.

His eyes lost their harsh edge. "It's not a book. It's for work."

"Information on a pack? Is it mine?" I asked curiously.

"Not werewolf work."

"What other kind of work is there?"

His eyes held an entertained glint. "My work in the human world."

"What do you do?"

"So inquisitive . . ." He paused. "I'm the CEO of Cahill Incorporated."

"What's that?"

"A financial services company. The second most profitable in the country."

"You run a multi-billion dollar company and you're King to an entire species? When do you sleep?" I asked incredulously.

"Right now. It's time for you to go to bed. Question time is over." He grabbed my elbow gently and pulled me over to the bed.

"I'm not tired yet," I whined, probably sounding incredibly annoying.

"It's after midnight. Get in the bed." He pushed me lightly.

I glared back at him but still did as he said. His bed was as comfortable as it looked. It was like lying on a cloud. A sigh of contentment left me as I snuggled deeper into the covers, trying to warm my frozen body.

I wanted to ask him to light the fireplace, but I didn't want to push it. King Finnian shut off both lamps and climbed into the bed as well. He left as much distance as he could between us.

The rain continued to beat against the windows, the relaxing sound starting to make my eyelids grow heavy. I was fighting sleep, trying to enjoy this time with him. He usually wasn't so open.

"When do you ever have time for yourself?" I asked, referring to the many duties that came with being King Finnian Cahill.

"I like to keep myself busy," he answered dryly, not even looking over at me. He was lying on his back, the sheets pulled up to his waist, leaving his bare upper body exposed to me. He had both arms tucked under his head. His eyes were closed, but I knew he was still fully awake.

"It's either that or you're scared of the loneliness you feel when you're not working?" I didn't know where my bold question came from but I felt the need to ask it.

His eyes shot open but he still didn't look my way. He didn't answer either. He just laid there, his body tense and his jaw clenched.

"It's okay to not be alone all the time. You don't have to numb yourself. It's okay to let yourself feel."

My eyelids were getting heavier and heavier. I scooted closer to him slowly like I was approaching a scared animal. I laid my head on his chest and draped my arm across his stomach. He didn't move to pull me closer but he also didn't push me away. My eyes drifted shut.

"We could be happy together or lonely apart. I don't want to be lonely anymore, Finn," I mumbled, barely conscious.

He still didn't talk as I felt sleep tugging on me, pulling me into a dark abyss. It wasn't until I was nearly completely unaware that I heard him speak. I was too far gone to do anything or to remember his words.

"I'd rather you be lonely than dead," he muttered lowly. He moved his arm so it was wrapped around my waist, pulling me tighter against him. I felt his lips brush against my forehead.

I barely registered his words as I drifted off, completely warm and content for the first time in a while . . . maybe ever.

* * *

When consciousness pulled me from sleep, the first thing I noticed was the rain. It was pattering softly against the windows. The sky was dark with heavy storm clouds but still light enough to illuminate the room, so the use of the lamps was not necessary.

The second thing I noticed was the smell. It smelled heavily of fresh rain, smokey oak, and King Finnian. A delicious combination.

As I took in my surroundings, I realized I was alone. His side of the bed was cold, making me wonder how long he had been gone. I bit my lip in dejection; I had hoped to wake up next to him.

I checked the clock next to the bed and realized it was only seven AM. Just how early had he gotten up?

I quickly sat up and stretched my arms over my head, causing a satisfying crack from my spine to echo throughout the large room.

I sat up and shuffled my way towards the door opposite the fireplace—which was now lit and saturating the room in a pleasant warmth.

As I walked through the doorway, I couldn't help but admire his amazing bathroom. It had a huge walk-in shower with shower heads on the sides and ceiling. It was big enough for several people to fit inside, and far enough back from the entrance that it didn't need a door.

The bathtub was equally as large. It was lifted from the rest of the room, two steps leading up to it. It made me want to take a bath, but I figured I should find King Finnian first.

There were his and her sinks with a large vanity area in between. Both the vanity and the left side of the sink were bare and unused. The toilet was in a little room by itself, which was where I headed first.

After relieving myself, I walked to his sink. I washed my hands and searched for a new toothbrush. I couldn't find one, so I just stuck to swishing some mouthwash around my mouth.

As I looked at my reflection, I cringed slightly. My hair was still in a messy bun but was loose and falling to one side; several pieces had fallen out and were frizzy, sticking out in random directions. I straightened my clothes and tried to smooth the wrinkles out of my T-shirt. I had a red mark on my cheek from where I had been sleeping.

I didn't look great, but I felt the opposite. I had slept better than I ever had. Lying next to Finnian, I had felt enveloped in a warmth that I never knew I was lacking before. I felt refreshed, rejuvenated even, and I didn't feel the least bit hungover.

After retying my bun, I deemed my appearance good enough and exited the bathroom, intent on tracking down King Finnian. I didn't have to travel far. He was standing with his back to me, looking out the window and at the drizzling sky. He was dressed in a black suit, which I thought was weird since it was Saturday. I figured he wouldn't be working today.

"Morning," I chirped happily as I walked over to him. I stopped in my tracks when he turned to look at me with cold, hard cerulean eyes.

"It's time for you to leave," he stated, not a hint of emotion in his voice.

"What?" I whispered in confusion.

"You heard me. I entertained this impertinence while you were under the influence, but now you need to go." He still sounded so callous.

"I don't understand . . . I thought we were making progress." I was so confused about where this was coming from.

"You were wrong. We'll only make progress if I want to, and I don't. I don't want this."

"You mean me . . . you don't want me," I stated, my voice empty. I wasn't going to show him the hurt he was causing me.

He paused for a minute, just staring at me with unreadable eyes. "No, I don't," he finally admitted it, causing my heart to shatter in my chest. I kept my face impassive but on the inside I was breaking.

"I understand. I won't come back up here again, Your Highness." My voice matched his now.

He didn't stop me when I turned to leave. He just allowed me to walk away, out of his room and out of his life. It was stupid of me to expect him to stop me. I expected him to say that he didn't mean that. But he didn't.

As I walked away, I let a cold feeling settle over me. I shut out the hurt I felt and let the anger and bitterness take over. I'd never let him get to me again. I'd never let myself feel the pain that I had just experienced again. Especially because of him. He didn't deserve my pain, nor did he deserve my love. From now on, all he would get from me was cold, bitter resentment.

*   *   *

"Are you alright, Kendall?" Niki asked at the breakfast table.

Currently, Kat, Niki, Lili, and I were sitting in the sunroom enjoying a simple breakfast of waffles and orange juice. Well, they were enjoying it. I was just stabbing at the waffle, a scowl settled firmly on my face.

I had made it back to my room unnoticed this morning. After a quick shower, I had dressed in a simple pair of torn jeans, a hoodie, and tennis shoes. I had no one to impress today, so I dressed for comfort. I braided my hair in two French braids with a grey knitted beanie pulled over it.

"I'm fine," I muttered, stabbing at another piece of waffle. I knew I was being rude to her but I couldn't bring myself to care.

I could feel three pairs of eyes on me. As I met each pair, they all gave me a worried look. Niki also looked knowing as well. It wouldn't surprise me if she knew where I spent the night. The damn witch seemed to know everything.

"I'm fine, really. I guess I just woke up in bad mood. I'm a little hungover too," I lied, trying to reassure them. Kat was the one to give me a knowing look now. She knew that I only got hungover when I drank hard liquor, which I hadn't last night. I knew I'd have to spill everything to her later.

Lili seemed to take my words as the truth because she looked away from me and back to her breakfast. Niki's gaze burned a hole through me for a few seconds but she too turned away and changed the topic of conversation.

"Are you ladies ready for Monday?" Niki looked at each of us as she spoke.

"What's happening on Monday?" I inquired, confused about what important thing was supposedly happening in two days.

"We're going with them to get a gown for the ball, remember?" Kat reminded me.

"Oh, yeah. I forgot."

"It should be fun. It'll be a nice girl's day out." Kat tried to make it sound exciting.

"Katerina is correct. It will be quite delightful," Niki added.

"Sounds great." I smiled tightly at them. It was fake but it was all I could muster.

"So, who exactly is going?" Kat turned her attention to Niki, which I was grateful for. I could tell that she realized that I wasn't in the mood to chat, so she was diverting Niki's attention away from me.

"The four of us, of course, and Emiliya as well."

I'm sure it would be a blast. How could a whole day with Emiliya not be? She was the life of the party after all. I held back from rolling my eyes.

I was tempted to just skip the mating ball altogether. For one, I had already found my mate and he didn't want me. I'd have to see him there, looking incredibly handsome of course, and stay away from him. Secondly, I was not looking forward to this so called girl's day out. The only girl's day out that I wanted right now was with Kat and Selena.

Lili wasn't the problem at all. I really liked her and already considered her a good friend. The problem was Niki and Emiliya. I liked Niki too, but she seemed to know anything and everything, especially about my mate and me, and it was really starting to grate on my nerves. I knew she was just trying to help, but nothing would help us at this point. It was done. And obviously, my reasoning for not wanting to spend the day with Emiliya was pretty self-explanatory.

As much as I wanted to skip it, I knew I couldn't. Dad would throw a fit if I did. He would look at it as me being disrespectful for not attending an event while I was staying here. It wasn't worth it to either face Dad's wrath or have to explain myself to him. Besides, my family would likely be there, and all I wanted in the world right now was to see them.

"I'm not really hungry," I said, pushing away my still full plate. "I think I'm just gonna go take a nap."

They nodded. I stood up and walked out. I made it to my room quickly. Luckily without bumping into anyone.

I didn't have to deal with Matt, Dalton, or Tyler this morning. Although it was Saturday and the castle was basically shut down for the weekend, other than a few necessary workers, they were still up bright and early, ready to work.

They were going to spend the morning training, then take the afternoon as well as tomorrow off. I knew Matt had plans to spend the day with Kat but I wasn't sure what Tyler and Dalton had planned.

I had just settled onto the couch, ready to watch a movie, when there was a knock at my door. I sighed in annoyance and threw the fuzzy throw blanket off me. I stormed my way to the door and threw it open. Niki stood there, not looking at all deterred by my behavior.

"May I have a moment of your time, Kendall?"

I sighed again. "Sure." I walked away, leaving the door open for her. I curled up on the couch again. I heard her shut the door behind her and walk over to sit on the other side of the couch. She had a knowing but saddened look on her face. I could tell what this conversation was going to be about and I already didn't like it. "Let me guess. You want to talk about the King." I refused to say his name.

"Yes, I would like to discuss Finn." She put emphasis on his name, trying to get me to say it instead of calling him the king.

"There is really nothing to discuss, Niki. Nothing is going on between the King and me," I stated.

"If that were true, then why did he have a visitor last night for the first time in years?" She raised a questioning eyebrow at me.

"How do you know it was me?" I tested her.

"Had it been anyone else, he would have killed them for entering his quarters without permission."

"Maybe he did. Maybe there's a dead body up there right now."

"I don't believe so. My spell wouldn't have been successful had it not been you."

I bristled at her words. "What spell?" I spoke slowly, trying to control my sudden rage.

"I had cast a spell on you during your first night here. If you tried to sneak up there, you wouldn't be caught. It came in handy this morning. Kieran would have caught you."

I ground my teeth together in irritation and clenched my fists. "You know, I'm really tired of you and the King thinking it's okay to cast spells on me without my permission."

My anger didn't seem to affect her whatsoever. "It was never my intention to offend you, Kendall. I've attempted to make it safe for you and Finn to be together. It wasn't Finn's intentions either. He has been struggling to stay away from you. He wants you to be safe."

"I don't think he's had much problem staying away from me. And what the hell do I need to be safe from?" I spat out.

"There are many dangers lurking in the shadows, dear girl. We're just trying to protect you from them."

"What does that even mean? Am I in danger?" I was kind of scared of what she's saying. What did they know that I didn't?

She hesitated slightly before she spoke, "No, dear. You're safe. But as the king's mate, you'll have many enemies. You can never be too careful."

"It doesn't really matter anymore. The King made it exceedingly clear that there is nothing between us. It's over, so you can lift all these spells now," I said bitterly.

"I wouldn't be so sure about that. He cares deeply for you, Kendall."

I suddenly reached the end of my rope for the day. I finally snapped. As I yelled, I could feel my claws and canines both extending.

"He doesn't give a shit about me," I sneered, "and I care even less for him. The only reason I'm still here is for my father. After the two months are up, we'll never have to see each other again. I would appreciate it if you would mind your own business until then, Royal Witch Nikolina."

She just looked at me sympathetically. Before she could say anything, another knock sounded throughout the room. I breathed deeply, trying to calm myself down.

I stood up and walked towards the door. Niki did the same as well. Before I could pull it open, she spoke to me.

"My intention was never to anger you, Kendall. You have my sincerest apologies for overstepping your boundaries. Finnian is my dearest and oldest friend. I want nothing more than for you and him to be happy and healthy together."

She didn't give me a chance to respond to her. She pulled open the door to reveal Kat.

"She's all yours, Katerina." She left before either of us could speak.

I didn't have much time to think over her words because Kat walked in, pulling the door shut behind her. I followed her over to the couch. Unlike Niki, Kat sat right next to me. We both turned to face each other.

"What's going on, Kendall?" she asked worriedly.

I gulped, trying to swallow the knot in my throat. I found myself debating whether or not I should tell her. If there was anyone I could share this with, it was her. Before I could think further, I was spilling everything to her. I needed to talk to her. I couldn't keep this completely to myself.

"He doesn't want me, Kat." I tried to sound uncaring but even I could hear the hurt in my voice.

"What happened?" she probed softly.

"I went up there last night. I thought we were making progress. He let me stay with him. Then this morning, it was like a flip switched. He kicked me out and told me he didn't want me."

"Did something happen to make him act like that?" Kat asked, seemingly as confused as I had been.

"I mean, I don't think so. Maybe, I don't really know. Am I really that bad to be with?" I asked, feeling more vulnerable and insecure than ever before.

"No, Kendall," she stated firmly. "You're amazing, and he'd be lucky to have you. Don't let that jackass make you feel bad about yourself. You're beautiful and strong. You deserve so much better than that. I've always admired how secure and confident you are in yourself. Don't let him take that from you."

That was why she's my best friend. She has always been there to pick up the pieces when I needed her to, and I knew she would never leave me. I would always do the same for her as well.

King Finnian may be my mate but Kat was my real other half. I could live without Finnian as long as I had my best friend.

"Thank you, Kat." I pulled her into a tight hug, which she returned. After a minute or so, we pulled away.

"Anytime. You know I'm always here for you." She smiled at me. For the first time all morning, I was able to give her a real smile in return.

"I know. Me too. I love you."

"I love you, too. Now, are you gonna play this movie or what?"

She knew me so well. She knew exactly what I needed to hear. She didn't try to make the situation sound better than it was. I didn't want that. I just wanted to sit here with someone that I knew had my back no matter what. We didn't need to do anymore talking.

The movie started playing and I felt so much better. I would survive King Finnian Cahill.

CHAPTER NINE

"Be safe. And call me if you need anything," Matt said to Kat for the hundredth time this morning.

She nodded and wrapped her arms around him tightly. He immediately returned the gesture and kissed her forehead then her lips. I withheld a gag and turned away.

Soon, they released each other and he turned his attention to me.

"Watch after her for me, little sis. I'll keep my mind-link open in case anything happens. Be careful and please, stay out of trouble."

"You worry too much. Nothing's gonna happen," I mumbled as he pulled me into a hug. I rolled my eyes but still hugged him back briefly before pushing him away. He chuckled slightly.

"You can't be too careful, Kenny."

I shot him one last glare at the nickname and slid into the car. We were riding in style. Apparently, royalty get fancy limos.

The outside was a shiny black while the inside was decked out in stark white leather. There were two seats towards the front, which were facing the back. Niki and Emiliya were already seated in them. At the back, there was a long seat for three. Lili was on one side and I was in the middle. Kat slid in beside me after hugging Matt once more.

There was a table in between us, which was covered in fancy snacks. There were mini-fridges on both sides between the seats. The doors were made of glass; I could see water, champagne, and orange juice inside it. Behind Niki and Emiliya was a small TV situated between their seats. A large sound system also seemed to be hooked up back here. No music was playing, though. Instead, awkward silence was filling the car.

We all buckled in and the driver, whom I hadn't seen, started driving away. The windows were incredibly dark, but I could see that we were taking the back way out, going through town. I had no doubt that no one would be able to see inside the vehicle, even with werewolf vision.

"So how far is it again?" I asked no one in particular.

Niki was the one to answer, "Our destination is approximately three hours away." Her voice held no animosity. Even though I blew up at her two days ago, she acted like it had never happened. We never got the chance to discuss it in private but she didn't seem upset with me at all. My anger to her had faded as well. Had she not caught me at such a low point, I probably wouldn't have been mad at her in the first place.

Speaking of my low point, I had yet to see King Finnian again. I had spent all of Saturday watching movies with Kat and pigging out on junk food. Matt was so pissed at me. He was supposed to spend the day with her, but she ditched him to hang out with me instead.

Had he known the truth, he wouldn't have been mad, but we didn't tell him. Instead, we stuck to every girl's excuse when they wanted a man to leave them alone; it was that time of the month and I was hormonal. No questions were asked after that.

I didn't get lucky enough to get Kat two days in a row. Matt had stolen her on Sunday. I still stayed in my room all day and, instead, spent the time with Dalton. He wasn't the best company in the world, but our bickering had successfully distracted me.

I had only left my room the last couple of days for food. I didn't eat dinner with everyone. I only got junk food from our kitchen. I hadn't had real food since our outing last Friday, so I was basically all ice cream and Cheetos by that point.

Having not left my room, I hadn't had much chance to run into my mate. He hadn't shown up in my room either. I guess deep down, I kind of hoped he would. It hurt that he hadn't, especially with how we ended things, but I guess it reinforced what he had already told me and what I already knew. He didn't want me.

Getting up this morning had been a chore. I was feeling bloated and lazy. I just wanted to spend the day in bed. Kat wouldn't allow it. She had woken me up bright and early and all but tossed me into the shower. I shot daggers at her all throughout the morning but got ready anyways.

Since I was feeling so lazy, I dressed that way as well. I was in a simple pair of black leggings, an over-sized sweater, my favorite Ugg boots, and a grey beanie pulled over my messy, wayward curls. Not a drop of make-up was on my face, which showed how tired I felt.

I sighed and leaned back, resting my head against the headrest.

"Have you ladies ever had the chance to wear a couture ball gown before?" Niki asked, making conversation to fill the deafening silence.

"Not really. Our pack doesn't really have a whole lot of fancy events like that," Kat answered her.

"I'm well and truly shocked," Emiliya commented, sarcasm dripping from her voice.

My eyes shot open and glared at her. She returned it by giving me one of her own. A growl rumbled through my chest at her disrespect. My wolf was trying to claw her way out, wanting to show this little witch bitch who was really Queen. I had to push her down and remind her that I wasn't, and never will be, a Queen.

"Emiliya, dear, sarcasm doesn't suit you in the slightest. It would behoove you to cease making yourself so exceedingly unlikeable," Niki scolded. Emiliya turned her glare to her older sister.

"I'm not the least bit interested in making myself likeable to such lowly creatures," she answered snootily.

My wolf raised her hackles again. I gritted my teeth so hard, I thought one might break.

"Perhaps if you didn't turn your nose up to everyone, you would have more acquaintances. As it is, the only person who actually does like you is your mate," Niki threw back at her, not missing a beat.

"I don't require the approval or friendship of anyone but Kieran. You wouldn't understand. You need to have someone love you first to be able to understand."

I suddenly felt the need to stand up for Niki. Emiliya's comment was completely uncalled for. It didn't get any lower than that. She said it with such malice as well. I could never imagine being so hateful to one of my sisters. Even Selena and I would never talk to each other that way.

"At least once Niki finds love, she'll know it's real, that they love her for her and not just because the mate bond paired them with some bitch they're forced to be with." My tone was light, like I was simply commenting on the weather, but my words were harsh.

Emiliya's head snapped back over to me. She looked like a woman possessed, but I didn't regret my words . . . At least I didn't, until I felt a burning sensation consume me from the inside. It felt like a fire raged inside every crevice of my body, the flames licking every inch of my skin. I cried out and collapsed into myself, my head falling between my knees.

The pain was unlike anything I'd ever felt before. I thought I was going to die. I could hear yelling around me but I couldn't make out the words. It sounded like I was listening from under a pool of liquid hot magma. I knew some of the yells were coming from me, painful cries leaving my lips, but I couldn't hear those either.

And suddenly, as quickly as it had begun, it stopped. I breathed heavily for a few seconds, waiting to see if it would return. When it didn't, I lifted my head and looked around me.

Niki had a look of rage that I had never seen before on her face. She had Emiliya's forearm gripped in her hand, the latter of whom now had a look of pain on her face. Lili looked over to me worriedly and Kat, after she saw that I was okay, turned her hateful glare to Emiliya. She looked ready to jump over the table between us and claw her eyes out.

After a few seconds, Niki released her hold on Emiliya, whose look of pain went away. It took a few seconds for me to realize what had happened. Emiliya was causing my pain. She had used her magic to make me feel like I was burning alive. *Bitch.*

"If you ever do that to her again, I swear I'll kill you," Kat declared. I had never heard her sound so lethal. She was usually the calm and collected one of the family.

"Like you could. I'm far more powerful than you ever could be. I'm a Petrova. You're nothing but a lowly Abara witch."

"I wouldn't be so sure about that, Emiliya." Niki, for once, didn't sound calm as she insulted someone. Her voice had a furious edge that was new for her but somewhat terrifying. I wouldn't want to face her wrath. "Katerina is far more powerful than you realize. I predict she will reach the Petrova power level eventually.

"You, on the other hand, may lose your powers completely. If you ever do something like that again, I will bind your powers quicker than you can even beg me not to. You may think Katerina is not more powerful than you, but you know I am. Don't make me take your powers because you're abusing them, Emiliya."

Emiliya glared at her but didn't say anything in return. Eventually she nodded at her and turned away, looking out the window. Niki turned her attention to me.

"Kendall, I sincerely apologize for my sister's behavior. I assure you on the Petrova name that this will never happen again."

"Yeah, it's fine," I mumbled. I wanted to make a bigger deal out of it but Niki handled it. It was done, no need to draw it out. Besides, Niki sounded like she felt bad enough as it was.

"I will inform King Finnian of her actions as soon as we return. She will be punished accordingly," she added.

"That's completely unnecessary, Niki. It's fine, really. It was a moment of anger that got out of control. Let's just forget it."

For some reason, I didn't want the King to know about it. I felt like he wouldn't react any differently if it had been any other wolf she had done that to. I couldn't handle seeing him care so little about my well-being.

"I insist, he must know."

"Please Niki. Let's just drop it. I'm fine, we're all fine. Let's just let it go. It never happened."

Niki looked like she wanted to argue some more but when I shot her a pleading look, she dropped it.

"Emiliya, don't you have something to say to Kendall? She is, after all, keeping you out of trouble, even after your abuse of power towards her." Niki looked at Emiliya expectantly.

"I'm terribly sorry about my actions, Miss Keating. I am incredibly grateful for your understanding and kindness. I surely don't deserve it." She looked as pained as I had. I smirked mockingly at her.

"You're forgiven, Emiliya."

She shot me one last glare before looking away again.

"Now, how about we try to enjoy the rest of our trip. Hopefully it can go a lot smoother than the last half hour," I suggested. This will surely be a long ass day.

* * *

I sighed heavily in annoyance and frustration. I was one ugly dress away from walking out the door and playing in traffic, leading to my not so tragic ending. It would assuredly be better than this torture I was currently enduring.

At any given time in werewolf history, there has always been some form of rebellion. It wasn't always a real threat but occasionally it would grow bigger than expected. I wasn't sure what the current status of the rebellion was, but I did know how to end it. All the King needed to do was send them with us for the day to suffer this agony. For the first time in history, we could end the rebel movement.

We have currently been here for two hours already and had only succeeded in finding Lili a dress. Niki, Kat, and I hadn't even tried any on yet.

I had certain expectations in mind when I was invited to this trip. I figured we would stop at some fancy dress store, try a few on, and all would be good after. I thought we would all find a gown we liked relatively easily and be out within an hour . . . two tops. My expectations weren't even in the same ballpark with reality.

Once we arrived, I quickly noted that the store was empty, aside from a few workers scattered around. One of them greeted us. Somehow, the willowy blonde had known who we were, calling us all by name once we entered, even Kat and me.

The store wasn't set up like I anticipated either. I had expected racks upon racks of ball gowns. Instead, all I saw were accessories and shoes dotted around the store. I had been confused at first about where the dresses were, but I was soon informed.

We had been ushered over to a seating area. It had stark white modern couches that were as uncomfortable as they were ugly. They were set up in front of a makeshift runway. At the back, there were mirrors surrounding the runway and a door that led to the changing rooms.

Somehow, I pictured this type of set up for someone picking out a wedding dress, not a ball gown. I guess my imagination is just too small to conjure up the extravagance that is ball gown shopping.

The girls helping us, Sarah, the willowy blonde who greeted us, and Penelope, who looked like a Victoria's Secret model, were bringing out racks of dresses in a timely manner. We were trying them on one at a time. Lili had gone first. She didn't seem to care what she got, but Niki and Emiliya did.

Emiliya had relaxed slightly, the incident in the car long forgotten. We both remained stiff and tense around each other at first but, eventually, we relaxed. She and Niki seemed to be quite the fashionistas, so they were guiding the choosing process.

Currently, Emiliya was trying on another dress. I had lost count of how many came before it. Lili had found hers after trying five different dresses; I stopped counting Emiliya's at ten. In a way, I was urging her to take her time. I had been informed that I was up next, and I was not at all pleased with that.

After seeing the dresses they had, I realized that they weren't the simple dresses that you could slip on and off no problem. No, not at all. That would be too easy. These were designer dresses, some of which I had never even heard of. The majority of them were difficult to get in and out of. Sarah and Penelope had to help with that.

The dress Emiliya just walked out in was the perfect example. It had a long, heavy looking train and an equally heavy looking cape. The monstrosity of a dress was adorned in feathers, pearls, and lace. Parts of it were see through, and it had a slit up the leg that was almost so high that it felt like we were sitting in a strip club, not a designer gown shop. It had an intricate series of buttons going up the back, which had to have taken forever to button up. It was a shame so much time was spent on it too, considering we had all denied it within five seconds flat.

She walked back to the rear of the room, Sarah and Penelope trailing behind her, guarding the train carefully. These dresses were worth a fortune, after all. I'm sure the merchandise in this store costs more than everything in my house. Dad would have a nice dent in his bank account after all was said and done, not that he couldn't afford it though.

After another mind numbing and soul crushing ten minutes, Emiliya managed to make her way back out. She stopped at the end of the runway and turned slowly for all to see. I had to begrudgingly admit that she looked beautiful. She was now decked out in a simple black dress, strapless with a sweetheart neckline. It was tight all the way down to her knees, where it slightly flared out to her feet. It had black sparkles all over it; it was tasteful, at least. Not atrocious like the last.

"That is the one, Emiliya," Niki commented, sipping on her complimentary sparkling water with lemon.

"I believe you are correct, sister," Emiliya admitted. She walked back over to the mirrors and looked at herself from all angles. After a few seconds, she turned to Sarah. "This is the one," she affirmed, repeating Niki's words.

Sarah nodded and followed her to the back, where she would change and take her measurements. We weren't actually getting the dresses today. They would be made in our exact sizes and delivered to the castle on a later date.

While Sarah helped Emiliya, Penelope ushered me up after another rack of dresses was brought out by an unfamiliar girl.

I groaned but stood up nonetheless.

"Kat, help me?" I asked rather pathetically, needing my best friend's help.

She rolled her eyes with a slight smile on her face but still stood up and walked over to me and the dresses. I started on one end of the rack and her on the other. I was knocking off dress after dress. The first was an ugly orange. Definitely not my color. The second was high and wrapped around the neck, which I knew would drive me crazy. The third had a huge, gaudy bow on the back. Not my style.

It went this way for the first eight dresses. Finally, I reached one that was somewhat decent. I pulled it off the rack and held it in front of me, looking it up and down.

"That might work. Try it on. I'll keep looking," Kat said to me as she continued down the row of dresses. She had already looked at half of her side of the rack.

I walked in the dressing room with the dress just as Emiliya was walking out. She surprised me by nodding in acceptance at my dress choice. I smiled tightly back at her, appreciating the gesture.

I quickly got out of my comfortable clothes, leaving my lacy black bra and purple boy shorts on.

The dress I picked out was simple. It was a deep plum color with thin off-the-shoulder straps. It showed a little cleavage but not too much to bother me. It was tight to around my mid-stomach, then fell loosely down to my feet.

After Penelope zipped up the back, I walked out and stood in front of the quartet of witches. I twirled around slowly, much like Lili and Emiliya had done.

"Pretty, but I think we can do better," Kat commented, still looking at the rack.

I nodded and walked back to the dressing room. Penelope helped me out of it. I stood in my underwear, waiting for the next one. After a few minutes, Sarah walked in, holding the dress Kat picked out for me.

A huge smile lit up my face. It was gorgeous. The two girls quickly helped me into it, careful not to rip the delicate fabric. Once I had it on, I pulled it up a little so I didn't trip as I walk back out.

As I modeled the dress for them, I felt slightly nervous this time. I already adored the dress and wanted them to love it too. As soon as I finished my spin, I received the most important opinion from the most important person. My best friend's.

"That's the one." A large smile lit up Kat's face, which I copied.

It was definitely the one.

* * *

After a few more hours, we finally finished. It hadn't taken more than ten minutes to find my dress, but the same couldn't be said for everyone else. It had taken three hours alone to find Kat and Niki's gowns; plus another hour or two to pick accessories.

Now that we were finished, we were having a late lunch / early dinner. My stomach had been demanding food for hours now. Thankfully, Kat and I had convinced them against the fancy French restaurant that they wanted to go to. Instead, we were sitting around a round table in a higher end steak house. It was a happy compromise, since all I wanted was a greasy fast food burger.

When we got to the restaurant, I tried to invite our driver to eat with us. I felt bad that he had been left alone all morning and afternoon while we shopped. I thought it was rude to ignore him. But he had declined, choosing instead to run a couple of errands, such as filling up the gas tank.

We got a table rather quickly. Due to the weird time we were eating, we were only surrounded by a few old couples having a four o'clock dinner.

After sitting down, they brought us a basket of sweet rolls with butter. I devoured half of them within minutes. Thankfully, I didn't have to feel guilty for not sharing, because the waitress soon brought out more.

We ordered our drinks and food fairly quickly. I wanted a beer more than anything, but I figured I should keep my wits about me if the ride here was anything to go by. My instincts were telling me not to let Emiliya have any kind of ammunition against me, even though we had got along the rest of the day. Either way, I decided to stick to iced tea.

"Well this has been a nice little outing, despite the bumpy beginning," Niki commented once our food was brought out. We quickly dug in.

"Yeah, it's been nice," I agreed halfheartedly.

"Perhaps you two will also join us for our trip to the spa the morning of the ball?"

"You have a whole spa day beforehand?" Kat asked after swallowing a bite of chicken.

"Indeed, we do. We begin our day with a facial and a massage. Then we get our nails done along with our hair. At the end of the day, we have our makeup applied before getting ready on our own for the night," she explained.

"Now that sounds like a proper girl's day. I'm in," Kat agreed.

As I chewed on my steak, they looked over at me. I quickly swallowed it before I answered, "Sure, why not."

I wasn't exactly a girly girl, so these types of things didn't excite me. Sure, a massage sounded alright, and I could surely use a professional doing my hair and makeup before a formal event, but other than that, it wasn't my cup of tea.

I was girly in my own way. I loved trying new hairstyles and makeup. I even liked clothes, although I didn't like shopping for them. I guess I just liked the result of that stuff, not the process.

"Please, try to contain your enthusiasm," Kat drawled out sarcastically. "Don't mind her. She's not into that kind of stuff. Selena and I have been trying for years to get her to a spa. Other than the occasional haircut, she doesn't do things like that."

"You're not alone. It's not my cup of tea either," Lili added, surprising me.

I noticed that Lili didn't seem to speak much in the presence of her sisters. She wasn't exactly a real chatterbox when they weren't around but she did talk if she had something to say. But around them, I don't think I've heard her talk unless spoken to. Her relationship with them seemed strained at best, despite Niki's maternal nature towards her.

"Finally, someone who understands. I'm the only girl in my family who thinks like this."

"It does seem quite frivolous to me."

"Exactly my thoughts. I think it's a waste of time and money. The massages are alright, but they also make me feel a little uncomfortable. Half of the things they do, you can just do at home if you really feel the need, which I don't. And waxing is horrendous. A razor works just fine for me."

"We are in complete agreement."

"You two are no fun." Kat pouted at us.

"And feeling uncomfortable and fussed over is fun?" I asked her teasingly. This is not a new argument.

"Yes," she answered.

I shook my head at her softly, knowing we'd always disagree about this.

"It will still be a nice time to bond. Maybe your sister can join us as well," Niki suggested to Kat and me.

"Selena would love that," Kat told her, since I was currently inhaling another roll. They were delicious. I was on my third basket already.

As they continued to discuss the spa day, with Lili and Emiliya commenting occasionally, I kept eating. I finished faster than the rest of them. I was now just sitting and listening to them talk, when something got my attention.

I subtly sniffed the air. I didn't know what I smelled but my wolf perked up in anticipation. After a few seconds, I caught the scent again, this time it was stronger. I noticed that it blew in when the door was open. It was the smell of a wolf. There shouldn't be any wolves in the city, and I had already been informed that a pack was not close by.

"Excuse me," I said to the witches and stood up. I walked to the front of the restaurant, where the restrooms were. I'm sure they assumed that was where I was headed for or else they would have joined me. I didn't want to freak them out unless there was really a threat though. I knew the scent wasn't our driver's so I was determined to find out who it was.

I snuck out the front door when I noticed they weren't looking. Since I barely caught a scent, I knew they wouldn't be able to sense the wolf. Witches had a natural detection instinct, but they had to be in somewhat close proximity. They would have sensed him if he was in the restaurant, but not when he was outside.

Once outside, I sniffed the air discreetly. It was stronger to the left. I called my wolf forward as much as I could without shifting and giving myself away to the humans. I let my nose guide me around to the back of the building.

Since we were on the outskirts of town, the woods were thick behind the steakhouse and other businesses along the street. As I scanned the area, I growled when something caught my eye. Thankfully, there were no humans around to hear me. The back of the building was completely deserted.

I saw someone trying to hide behind a tree. They were hiding from me, meaning that their intentions couldn't possibly be good.

I snarled again and ran into the woods. Sensing me coming, the coward took off running, but I was faster. I tackled the guy from behind. He quickly shifted positions, leaving him on top of me, but I pushed him back just as quickly. I dug my knee into his chest and let my fist fly to his face. I felt and heard his nose crack and saw blood starting to spurt out.

I punched him once more for good measure and pressed my forearm against his throat forcefully, effectively cutting off his air supply.

"Who the hell are you?" I growled out. I lifted my arm slightly, just enough so he could breathe and talk.

"I'm your worst nightmare, pup." He smiled, blood covering his crooked teeth.

I punched him again.

"Please. You're a pathetic excuse for a wolf. I'm almost offended that you thought you were a threat to me."

Despite my abhorrence to all things physically challenging, mainly exercise and training, I could still fight. My father made us train until we were twenty-one. Even now, at twenty-three, we still had to have a little refresher day a couple times a month so we wouldn't get rusty. Aside from the training, I also had Alpha blood in my veins, which gave me more natural strength than non-ranked wolves.

"Now, don't make me ask again, bitch," I ordered him, pressing my knee further into his sternum.

"The only bitch here is you."

Before I could reply, I heard movement behind me. I ducked off the wolf just in time, a foot narrowly missing my head. Before I could get my bearings, the wolf that had been under me was now on top. It was his turn to slam his fist into my face.

I groaned as my cheek split open from the gaudy oversized ring on his finger. My head whipped to the side and into the ground at the same time, causing an ache to start in the back of my skull. I pushed the pain away and focused on my two assailants.

I lifted my knee and got him in the spot that affected all males, no matter the species. I kneed him as hard as I could. He groaned in pain, his hands leaving my shoulders, where he had been holding me down, to cup his manhood instead. I easily pushed him off of me. He was down for the count at the moment, so I focused on the new guy.

He was slightly younger looking than the first man and slightly stronger as well. But just because someone is strong doesn't mean they're well trained.

Before I could assess him further, he ran at me. I barely managed to side step him. I used his momentum against him and threw him to the ground. I sat on his back and shoved his face into the ground trying to suffocate him with the dirt.

"Who are you?" I demanded again. I forcefully yanked his head up by his short hair.

"The King won't be able to protect little bitches like you once we kill him." He sneered.

I suddenly saw red; metaphorically, of course. I wasn't in control of my actions. All my instinctual wolf side knew was that he threatened our mate's life. The threat needed to be neutralized. Had

I been thinking clearly, I wouldn't have acted so rashly. He needed to be alive to be questioned, but all rationality left me.

I put one hand on his chin, the other on the back of his head. I twisted it to the side, a sickening crack resounding around me. I knew that noise would be stuck in my brain later. I've never killed anyone before.

I dropped the guy's head. I could see he died with his eyes open, the dull blue irises now glazed over as his head twisted unnaturally.

Before I could turn to look at the other guy, he was back on top of me. I slammed painfully into the ground, my shoulder taking the brunt of the fall. I hissed in pain.

He quickly pushed me onto my back fully. I tried to lift my knee again, but he blocked it this time. His fist landed on my face again. My nose now resembled his, blood pouring down my mouth and chin, soaking into my light grey sweater. My eyes watered at the hit, blurring my view of him.

He lifted my head while I was still disoriented and slammed it into the ground. Black dots danced across my vision and I saw two of him as he did it again and again. He paused briefly to punch me again, twice in a row, in my chest. Air whooshed from my body and didn't come back for what felt like eons, and I felt something crack under his fists. He grabbed my hair once more and continued his slamming.

By then, I knew it was over. I was barely conscious. Even if I could get the upper hand, I couldn't even see straight. Blood covered my face entirely. With the jerky movements, it was spilling in all different directions. I could feel the sticky warm substance filling my mouth and running down my chin. It slid down both sides of my neck and gathered in the hollow area between my collarbones.

The collar of my sweater was soaked, ruining the soft material. The blood from the cut on my cheek ran down my ear, puddling inside. My ribs ached and my lungs burned, refusing to inflate.

As he continued slamming my head into the ground, all I could think about was Finn. We'd never have a chance now. We'd never be happy together. Would he even miss me? I was going to die letting myself think that he would.

Before he could finish me off, he let go of my hair and stopped moving. Through my double vision, I could see him grabbing his head. His mouth was open like he was screaming but I couldn't hear anything.

I didn't know what was going on or why he stopped but I let my instinct take over.

I reached up blindly until I felt his skin under my palm. I couldn't twist his neck in this position, so I did the next best thing. I let my claws elongate and sunk them into his soft, fleshy neck and ripped out his carotid artery. His blood immediately spilled out, soaking my clothes completely. I barely managed to push his dead weight off my body.

I blinked heavily a few times, trying to stay conscious. I saw Niki, Kat, and Emiliya enter my line of vision. Kat's mouth was moving but I couldn't hear a thing. I wanted to reassure her as she knelt over me that I was okay but I couldn't form the words.

My eyes felt heavy. I couldn't keep them open any longer. Kat's worried expression was the last thing I saw as I drifted into darkness.

CHAPTER TEN

The first time I was pulled from under the darkness didn't last long.

The first thing I saw was Kat, my head on her lap. Her eyes were closed. She was speaking a foreign language. No, she was chanting.

Soon after my eyelids pried open, they met her dark green eyes. She smiled weakly at me and told me it was going to be okay; that she was healing me.

Once I let my eyes drift away from hers, I recognized the familiar interior of the limousine. I was laid across the back seat, my legs draped across what was supposed to be Lili's seat. I wanted to ask where she was but I couldn't talk.

Niki and Emiliya were sitting across from us, both witches on their phones. Niki looked at me and gave me a reassuring smile. Emiliya didn't spare me a glance.

My head was pounding. My face and chest ached and throbbed. My sweater clung to me, still soaked with blood. I wanted to peel it off, but if I couldn't talk, I sure as hell couldn't move.

When I looked back at Kat, she must have seen the pain and fear on my face. She quickly reassured me.

"You're gonna be okay, Kendall. I promise. I'm healing you. Your head was almost completely bashed in, and a rib punctured your lung. It's taking me a while, but you'll be fine. I'm gonna put you back to sleep now, okay? It's easier to heal you when you're unconscious."

I wanted to nod, but since I couldn't move I just laid still and let her work. Her hand, which had been running through my bloody, tangled curls, rested on my forehead. She closed her eyes again and started chanting. She was more effective than anesthesia because I was out within seconds.

The second time I came to, I saw the face of my brother.

He was carrying me through the castle, one of my arms thrown around his neck and the other hanging limply. It felt heavy; I couldn't lift it if I tried. My head had been hanging backward at an uncomfortable angle. Luckily, I managed to roll it just enough to rest against his chest.

I felt him press a chaste kiss on my forehead which was soon replaced by a hand. It wasn't his since he was carrying me.

Darkness greeted me once again.

That led me to the third and final time I woke up.

A groan of pain and discomfort escaped my lips before I could even open my eyes. My mouth was dry and felt like it was filled with cotton. My chest felt like it was on fire with every ragged breath I drew in. My head ached with an intensity far greater than any I've ever felt before.

As I lifted my arm to massage my temples, I was grateful to realize that I had full control of my limbs once again.

I wanted to fall back to sleep but my bladder screamed at me to get up. I groaned again and finally peeled my eyes open.

I was in my room in the castle. It was dark with no source of light, not even from the moon. From the window, I could tell it was the dead of night. Dark clouds obscured the dusky light from the night sky. It was quiet too. I couldn't hear anything, although that didn't say much because my senses seemed to be dull.

I sat up slowly, letting myself adjust to the movements as a wave of dizziness swept over me. Once it passed, I swung my legs over the side of the bed. I was thankful that instead of my blood-soaked clothes, I was now dressed in a t-shirt and shorts.

When I finally got my bearings, I made a move to stand up. Before I could though, a low growl vibrated the bed behind me, stopping me in my tracks.

What the hell?

I gulped, my back now ramrod straight. I took a deep breath and slowly turned around. I couldn't make out much but I could see the outline of a wolf . . . a freaking huge wolf at that. Whoever it was took up half of the king-sized bed. How did I not notice him before?

I sat there for a minute, waiting to see if he would make a move. When he didn't, I slowly reached for the lamp on the bedside table. He didn't try to attack me, so I turned it on.

Once the room was filled with a yellow glow of artificial light, I could take him in more clearly.

He was a dark-brown, almost black, colored wolf. He was bigger than any other wolf I'd ever seen, including my dad and brothers. As I looked into his glowing amber eyes, which were looking me up and down, seeming to survey my body, I realized that there was only one person this magnificent creature could be; King Finnian.

I rolled my eyes and shook my head. Why in the hell would he be in my bed? In wolf form, nonetheless? He didn't get to suddenly act like he cared just because I got hurt.

I sighed in irritation and stood up. He growled lowly at me, causing me to spin around and glare at him.

"I have to pee, you asshole. Back off. Better yet, leave," I snapped.

He growled again, but I ignored him and walked into the bathroom. After relieving my bladder and washing my hands, I was able to take in the damage.

Other than a few spots in my hair, all the blood was cleaned off my body. I needed to shower, but I'll do that in the morning after a few more hours of sleep.

My wounds weren't nearly as bad as they would have been if Kat had not healed me. My headache was dull, showing that she had focused most of her energy on the back of my head. My chest and shoulder ached, but at least my lungs seemed to be okay for the most part. My face and chest were stained with deep purple bruises and my cheek had a nasty gash that looked like it could start bleeding at any moment.

Although Kat was powerful she wasn't a miracle worker. Witches could heal people but the worse the injuries, the longer it took to heal. I was sure Kat had worked on me the whole drive home and possibly even after that. She did a damn good job in the time frame, considering my injuries. Had I not been healed, I could have died considering how many times my skull had been slammed into the ground and how my lung wouldn't take in any oxygen.

Kat was probably drained and sleeping soundly, but I made a mental note to do something special for her as thanks.

I flipped off the light and walked back into the bedroom. I expected it to be empty but was surprised to see King Finnian sitting on the edge of my bed in nothing but a pair of underwear. His elbows rested on his thighs and his head rested in his hands, obscuring his face from my vision. I forced my eyes to stay up and not linger on his naked chest. I held on to my anger to do this.

And lord knows I had plenty of that particular emotion.

I was angry at King Finnian for being such a colossal disappointment of a mate. I was angry at my dad for sending me here. I was angry at those assholes in the woods for threatening me and my mate and for getting the jump on me like they did. I was trained better than that. Hell, I was even angry at Selena for not being more mature so that she could have come instead of me.

Most of all though, I was angry at myself; angry for letting everything get to me; angry that I wasn't as strong as I always thought I was. I wasn't strong enough to handle this, and I hated myself for that. I let the bitter fury rush through my veins.

"What the fuck are you doing here, King Finnian? You rejected me. You don't have the right to just show up whenever you want." I crossed my arms over my chest and prepared for a verbal confrontation.

I didn't get that though. Instead, he stayed as he was, holding his head in his hands. After a few seconds, he ran his fingers through his hair roughly, tugging harshly at the dark strands. He still didn't look at me.

"What do you want from me?" My voice lacked any emotion except for maybe exhaustion. I was too tired for this.

Suddenly his face snapped up, finally meeting my gaze. His eyes burned golden as he looked at me intensely. I swallowed harshly at the emotions playing across his face. I was surprised by the one that stuck out the most. Fear.

"It was my fault that you were hurt," he rumbled out. His voice was low and gravelly like he was still on the verge of shifting.

"You weren't even there, Your Highness. I don't know why you think that," I said coldly.

If I was being honest with myself, I wanted nothing more than to run to him and comfort him. I hated seeing him look this way. But I couldn't make myself do it. I couldn't give in to him just so he could crush me all over again. So, I held on to my anger like it was a lifeline.

"I should have anticipated this. I should have sent guards," he mumbled, more to himself it seemed than me.

"I can take care of myself just fine."

His eyes, which had drifted over to the wall, snapped back to me, anger simmering in the gold depths. "Obviously, you can't."

My hackles raised, all thoughts of comforting him long gone.

"I killed them both, didn't I?" I asked rhetorically.

"After you were almost killed in the process," he said bitterly. He stood up and made his way towards me, like a predator stalking its prey. I was no prey though. "The only reason you weren't was because Niki realized that you foolishly pursued them alone and was able to save you in time."

"I didn't need her help. I would've been fine without her."

"Oh yeah? Was that before or after he finished smashing your skull in?"

"Maybe I should smash yours and see what you think?" I threatened although I could never physically hurt him. Not only would I never be able to get the jump on him, but my wolf side wouldn't allow it.

"Don't make threats you can't follow through on, mate."

"Who says I can't?" I said, fury shaking my body. He was making me sound like I was incompetent at defending myself. It was insulting.

"I'm sure the witch that healed you can attest to that."

I snapped. My inability to hurt him lifted and all I wanted was to punch his stupid, smug, asshole-ish face.

I let out a frustrated cry and ran at him. I tried to use my momentum to knock him over, but he didn't even look fazed. My need for his blood grew.

I raised my fist to smash against his face, but he grabbed it and twisted it behind my back before I could land it. His hold wasn't painful but it was firm.

I lifted my knee, aiming between his thighs. He also grabbed it and pinned it to his side, leaving me hopping around on one leg. I half groaned and half screamed in frustration.

I threw my weight backward, trying to release myself from his grasp. He let me go but only after he knew I wasn't going to tumble backwards onto the floor.

I ran at him again, faster this time.

Before I could do anything or even comprehend what had gone wrong, we were suddenly on the bed with him on top of me. His legs pinned mine down, and he held my arms above my head. I wiggled around, trying to get away from him, but he had me completely immobilized.

I tried the last thing I could think of. I slammed my head forward. He moved at the very last second, right before my forehead connected with his nose.

"Enough, Kendall!" he boomed.

My eyes widened in surprise. That was the first time he called me by my first name.

"You're going to hurt yourself. I'm not going to let you get hurt again." He glared down at me.

"Don't try to act like you care now. I can see right through your bullshit," I mumbled bitterly.

He sighed heavily and let me go. He got off the bed and looked down at me. "You can think whatever you want, but I promise I will never let anything like that happen again. Whether you can protect yourself or not is debatable, but I won't ever take any chances. Now get some rest," he said gruffly. "And take it easy, for God's sake. Don't make me come show you again how easily I can restrain you."

"Fuck you."

"Goodnight to you too, mate." He smirked as he walked away. He turned off the lamp on his way and stopped at the doorway. He looked like he wanted to say something else but decided against it. He sighed once more then left, leaving me in my room alone and pissed off.

I fought off the urge to sleep after he left. I was tired but still so angry at him that I wanted to defy him in any way I could. He told me to sleep so I tried as hard as I could not to. I was still healing, so it didn't take long for my defiance, like my consciousness, to slip away.

* * *

When I woke up again, I was alone. The sun shone brightly on my face, its rays streaming in through the window; bathing the room and me in its light.

I felt better than I did when I first woke up in my room. My head didn't ache as much as last night, and my face had stopped throbbing. I grazed the cut on my cheek with my fingers, feeling the scab forming on top of it.

I flung the thick blanket off of me and shivered when I felt a rush of cold air attack my exposed skin like tiny little needles. The sunshine had created a pretense of warmth but it was just that; a pretense. Deception. The room was freezing.

I glanced over at the clock as I ran my fingers through my hair. It was just after one o'clock. As my fingers caught in my hair, the dried blood making it tangled and ratty, I decided the first thing on my to-do list was a long, hot shower.

Once in the bathroom, I let the water warm up until steam started to fill the room. When it was hot enough to all but melt my skin off, I stepped in.

I didn't usually take such hot showers, even when I was cold, but for some reason, I felt the need to today. I had been covered in blood yesterday. To be more specific, I had been covered in the blood of the wolf that I killed. I knew it was kill or be killed but it still didn't sit right with me. The thought of taking someone's life . . . I gulped painfully at the thought. What about their families? Had I taken someone's son, mate, or father away?

I couldn't bear the thought, so instead I tried to scrub away all evidence of the harsh reality I was now living with. I was a killer.

I let the nearly boiling water purify my skin and scrubbed my body until it felt raw, my skin scarlet with the harshness of the strokes of my loofah.

I had to wash my hair three times to get all the blood out. Once I caused my own blood to mix in from how hard I was scratching and scrubbing at my scalp, I decided I was doing more harm than good. The conditioner burned against the cuts on my scalp, so I washed it out quicker than usual.

After about an hour, I finally deemed myself clean. I pushed away the thoughts of killing two people and instead focused on my growling stomach. I had been asleep for the majority of the last twenty-four hours. I hadn't eaten in nearly that long. I usually couldn't go more than five hours—if that, without eating—so I knew I needed to remedy the problem.

I dried off quickly and threw on a pair of pajama bottoms and a long-sleeved T-shirt. I braided my hair into two french braids and left the bathroom, intending to make my way to the kitchen but that wasn't necessary. Kat was sitting on the couch, a tray of food on the coffee table in front of her. I couldn't see what exactly was on it but when I inhaled deeply, I smelled the delicious scent of French toast and bacon.

Before I could reach it, Kat stood up and pulled me into a tight hug. I returned the gesture. When she pulled away, I could see dark circles hanging under her eyes, hinting at just how drained she had been from healing me. She looked well rested, just tired . . . if that made sense.

"You scared the shit out of me, Kendall. Out of everyone," she reprimanded. She looked me over again, inspecting her work.

"Sorry. I didn't mean to scare everyone."

"I'd lecture you about how stupid it was to go out there alone, but I know you'll get plenty of that from everyone else. You're in for quite the phone call after breakfast."

I groaned. I didn't feel like dealing with my family.

"You should really be eternally grateful to me. Matt wanted to come in here with me. I told him to give you a chance to eat before everyone jumped down your throat." She sounded slightly amused.

I looked at her seriously. "I am grateful, Kat. Thank you." She knew I didn't mean to keep Matt at bay. Her playful face sobered.

"Any time, Kendall. You're my best friend and sister. I'll always be there when you need me."

I pulled her into another quick hug before pulling away.

"Okay, I love you and all, but enough of this sappiness. Fill me in on everything that happened while I eat?"

She nodded. We both sat down. I tucked my cold feet under my thighs and pulled the food tray on my lap.

"Thanks for bringing this to me, by the way. You didn't have to do that." I told her as I cut into the French toast. I brought a piece of the delicious cinnamon and syrup-covered goodness to my mouth, nearly moaning in appreciation as my stomach all but verbally thanked me.

"I wanted to. I asked one of the castle chefs to make it for you and bring it to me when he was done."

"You want some?"

"No, thanks," she declined. "I ate with Matt a couple of hours ago."

"So, what went down after my spontaneous nap?" I asked between bites.

"I guess I'll start from the beginning. Well, a few minutes after you left the table, Niki and I noticed you weren't close to the restaurant. She told Lili to wait inside and pay so that we didn't cause a scene or draw attention to ourselves. Niki, Emiliya, and I went outside to look for you."

I gulped down the bacon in my mouth, remembering how they had found me. Next to a dead body with someone straddling me and beating my head into the ground.

"I freaked out as soon I saw you. Niki didn't even have time to react as fast as I did."

"You're the one who caused him pain," I stated. "I was so out of it, all I knew was that he stopped and then my instincts kicked in."

"I know. Don't feel bad about that, Ken . . . I know you will anyway, but try not to. Any werewolf would have reacted the exact same way. It's a natural instinct."

"I know that. It's just going to take some time."

She smiled weakly at me, but continued, "Anyways, you passed out after that. I could sense how injured you were. I thought you were going to die." Her voice cracked and a single tear rolled down her cheek.

I grabbed her hand, reassuring her that I was okay now.

"I should have let Niki heal you. She's stronger than me. But I guess my own instincts kicked in. I wouldn't let anyone else use magic on you. I was so scared and worried that I didn't trust anyone else. I started as soon as you passed out. We were in the woods for like an hour after that. I had to heal you enough so you wouldn't die when we moved you. Once we were on our way back, shit just about hit the fan."

I looked at her curiously, wondering what happened during the three-hour car ride.

"Okay, so when we were in the woods, we couldn't really call anyone to let them know what happened. We didn't know if there were more attackers, so Niki, Emiliya, and Lili guarded us while I healed you. They had to focus on that. When we were safe in the car, which Niki spelled so we could go undetected on the way back, we had to deal with all the angry phone calls. I couldn't really focus on that completely, but I did hear bits and pieces of it. If you had any doubts about whether King Finnian cared about you before . . . Well, you can stop."

My eyes widened. What the hell happened with Finnian? Did people know about us now? Kat seemed to read my mind because she answered my nonverbal questions.

"No, nobody knows about you two. If you didn't already know beforehand, you would have thought he was just furious about rebels attacking a she-wolf under his protection. Everyone knows he can lose his cool sometimes, so Emiliya didn't seem surprised at all."

"How exactly did he lose his cool?" I asked hesitantly.

"Well I didn't find out until Niki told me in private later, but apparently she had cast a spell on you so that if you were hurt or in trouble, King Finnian would know it. And it worked perfectly. Niki told Emiliya that she had spelled herself instead of you, so it wouldn't raise suspicions. He knew you were in trouble from the very beginning.

"To make matters worse, he had to wait until we were safe in the car before she could return his calls. He knew you were safe by then—hurt, but alive. He was livid. Niki didn't even get to finish explaining what happened before he shifted. The phone was still connected, and all we could hear was growling and furniture being smashed apart."

As she explained this to me, a seed of doubt seeped into my mind, ceasing all thoughts of him caring.

He had a short temper, and I'm sure it had more to do with what Emiliya assumed. He was angry about the rebels harming a wolf he was supposed to protect.

If he was worried about me as his mate, he would have told everyone about us. I kept my mouth shut about my doubts because I knew Kat wouldn't agree.

"It took a while for Niki to finally hang up. I asked her to call Matt next. He freaked out and wanted to talk to me, but I couldn't right then. He was so worried about both of us. I've never seen him as brotherly as he was when we got here. He wouldn't let anyone else carry you inside."

It warmed my heart that my big brother was so worried and protective of me. His brotherly protectiveness wasn't anything new to me, but it was usually about stupid stuff like boys. Between Brody, Matt, and Dad, Selena and I had a hard time keeping boyfriends when we were teenagers.

"Was . . ." I paused, not sure if I wanted to know the answer to my next question. I steeled myself and asked anyway, "Was the King there when we got back?"

Just by the look on her face, I knew he wasn't. "I'm sorry, Ken. I know he was worried about you though."

I nodded weakly, trying not to let it bother me and failing.

"It took me a while but I finally got you almost completely healed. It was around midnight I think. Jeff wanted to bring everyone here, he was so concerned about you. I think he feels guilty. Matt convinced him that you would be fine, that it would overwhelm you."

"Are they mad at me for killing those wolves instead of leaving them alive to be questioned?" She knew I meant the Royals, not my family.

"No, of course not. They knew you did what you had to. Tyler even said he wouldn't have reacted any differently. They're looking into it. They have scouts in the area, searching for more rebels," she explained.

"That's good." I looked down at my now empty plate before looking back at her. I sighed heavily. "I guess it's time to face the heat."

* * *

"Kendall Taylor Keating, what the hell were you thinking?" Dad growled lowly. I flinched at the use of my full name.

I was sitting on Matt and Kat's bed. Matt had already yelled at me for a good ten minutes before we called home. That was after he hugged me first of course. We now had his phone on speaker while our parents had us on speaker. Dad was the first to speak, but I somehow knew Mom, Selena, and Brody were sitting around the phone as well.

Matt was pacing in front of us, shooting daggers at me every once in a while. Kat was sitting next to me, providing support as I faced my biggest nightmare . . . my entire pissed-off family.

"I don't know . . ." I mumbled almost incoherently.

I usually wasn't so timid, but I didn't really know what to say in this situation.

"You don't know?" he said, clearly seething on the other end. "Do you know how stupid it was to go after a threat—of which you had no idea how many there were—by yourself? I raised you and trained you better than that, Kendall."

I flinched at his tone. He was furious, but most of all, he sounded disappointed. That stung worse than anger ever could.

"I realize that *now*," I said, emphasizing the "now".

"You should have realized that then. Now I'll ask again, what the hell were you thinking?"

"I didn't know if it was a threat or not. I smelled a werewolf nearby and I didn't want anyone to worry if it was nothing. I wasn't planning on fighting them alone, but the guy started running and my instincts kicked in. If I had gone back inside, I would have lost him," I tried to explain my reasoning.

"Better for you to worry about them unnecessarily than to be dead, dumbass," Selena threw in her opinion.

"Well, I'm not dead. I'm fine. I held my own, just like you taught me," I stated, mostly to Dad.

"Oh, yeah? Is that why Kat had to heal you for hours? Because you held your own?" Matt yelled in front of me, finally stopping his pacing.

His anger was probably greater than anyone else's. He wasn't just mad that I put myself in danger, but that his mate had to spend hours healing me. He hated seeing her drained after a big spell, so the fact that I caused it for reasons he deemed unnecessary made it worse for him.

I got defensive at his words.

"I did pretty damn good for taking on two fully grown male wolves. I even sensed Beta blood in one of them. They were strong. I managed to kill one of them before the other was able to get the jump on me."

"You're missing the point, Kendall. Yes, you did well in the fight. Not great but alright. But the point is that you shouldn't have gone after them alone. You were with the most powerful witch alive. She could have easily overpowered them. And yet, you still didn't inform her of your actions," Dad jumped back in.

I groaned in annoyance and frustration. "I'm sorry, okay? I don't know what else you want me to say. It was stupid of me, and it won't happen again."

"Oh, honey. Don't mind them. You scared them, that's all. You scared us all. We're just happy you're alright," Mom spoke for the first time, relief strong in her voice.

"Thank you, Mom." I was extremely grateful that I had her on my side. The males in my family were jumping down my throat enough as it was, I didn't need it from her too.

"No problem. Just . . . Please, don't scare us like that again. I couldn't handle it." Her voice broke at the end, and I could tell she was crying now. I always felt bad about making her cry, but now I also felt awkward.

"Always making Mom cry, Kendall. Shame on you," Selena taunted, officially ending the awkwardness.

"Shut up, Selena," several voices, mine included, said at once.

"Geez, did you guys rehearse that or something?" she murmured. She was ignored.

"Listen, I really am sorry. I won't do it again. I'll start training again. It's been a couple of months, and I'm getting a little rusty."

"Good," Brody added gruffly. He was a man of few words so I wasn't surprised that I hadn't heard anything from him until now. I had no doubts that he was there the whole time though.

"I'm still a little tired," I lied. "Can I call you guys later?"

"Sure sweetheart," Mom jumped in, speaking over Dad. "Get some rest. We love you. We'll talk to you later on."

"Thanks. I love you guys too." I hit the end button before anyone could object further. I turned to Matt and stood up. "I'm sorry, Matt. I'm sorry Kat got so drained from having to heal me. Forgive me?" I looked up at him with misty green eyes, willing him to let me off the hook.

I could see the resistance on his face. I knew he was going to scold me some more, but Kat stepped in before he could.

"Yes, he forgives you." She looked at him menacingly before turning back to me. "Go get some rest." She urged me with her eyes to leave, probably so she could convince him to let it go. I didn't plan on sticking around for that.

Just as I exited their room and pulled the door shut behind me, I saw Tyler turn to our hallway. He smiled at me and I returned the gesture as best as I could and waited for him to reach me. He pulled me into a brief hug.

"I'm glad you're alright. You worried everyone."

"I know. I already heard it all from my family. They scared me more than the rebels I fought."

He laughed but it sounded strained. "Mind if we talk for a few minutes?"

"Sure." I led him to my room, where we would have privacy from listening ears.

I plopped down on the sectional couch in my room and he sat on the other side.

"I just wanted to update you on the situation." I nodded for him to continue. "You did good work by noticing them. They had been stalking you for most of the day. We found their base camp about seventy miles from the castle. They happened to be on watch that day and saw the limo, and smelled the witches inside. They realized they were Royal Witches. The wolves at the base camp planned on ambushing the limo on the way back. Had you not noticed them, Niki wouldn't have known to shield the limo. You did good," he repeated, looking impressed. Finally, someone was acknowledging that I didn't royally screw up.

"They had a base camp? How many were there?"

"A little over one hundred. A small base camp, but they had to be since they were so close to the Royal Territory. If they were too big, we would have discovered them. They stayed under the radar by keeping their distance and sticking to the woods. They had been living out there for months."

"What'd you guys do?"

"We captured them. Some were killed in the process, but we managed to capture over half of them. Luckily, none of them got away. We've got them locked up in the dungeon on the other side of the territory. We're questioning them now. That's how we knew what their plans were.

"We've also found out that they were just a tiny fraction of the rebellion. We're trying to find out where their other base camps are and who their leader is, but most don't know. They just followed orders from their base's leaders, who were killed during the battle. We still have a lot of questioning left to do," Tyler explained.

I nodded. "Okay, well, I really appreciate you keeping me in the loop on all of this."

"Well, I don't think King Finnian would appreciate it, but you led us to them. I figured you have the right to know. I'm sure he's heard me telling you."

"Hmm, no he didn't," I said to him absentmindedly, distracted by the thoughts of the rebellion. Who knew how many there were. "Niki put a silencing spell on my room."

"Why would she do that?" My eyes, which had been staring into space, snapped back to his face. His eyebrows were furrowed in confusion. My mind blanked. "The only rooms she's done that to were for Finnian and herself. Why you?"

"Uhh . . . I asked her to. She didn't mind." I struggled to find a good explanation.

He looked skeptical but didn't comment further on the matter.

"Can I ask you something?" I asked, after we sat in silence for a couple of moments.

"Sure."

I hesitated slightly but decided to ask anyway. I felt more comfortable asking him this particular question than anyone else. I couldn't ask my family.

"Have you ever had to . . . kill someone?"

He looked at me seriously. "*Sí*. I have."

"How do you live with it? I mean . . . does it get easier?" I bit the inside of my cheek, trying to word my question right.

This had been sitting with me since I had been conscious. I felt guilty. I didn't know how to deal with this.

He looked at me, understanding shining in his eyes.

"It does. It's never easy to end someone's life, but it has to be done. You can either let the guilt consume you or you can let yourself off the hook. It's all about perspective. I like to look at it like if I hadn't killed the people I've killed, they could have harmed someone I loved. I've done the things I've done to protect my loved ones."

"I don't know how to not let the guilt consume me," I admitted.

"Life is about choices, Kendall. They made the choice to rebel against the kingdom. They made the choice to stalk you. They made the choice to try and kill you. Now you need to make a choice.

"You can decide to let the guilt go. You can decide to be proud of yourself, not just for protecting yourself, but your family as well. They were after Kat yesterday as well. They wanted to kill you, her, and the Petrova sisters. They deserved what they got because of the choices they made. Don't let their choices consume you. They don't deserve your guilt. Now decide not to give it to them."

I nodded at him, mulling over his words. It made sense but it seemed easier said than done. I'd have to work on it.

He stood up and made his way to the door. "I'll keep you updated. I'm here if you need to talk."

I nodded at him again and smiled weakly. He left, and I was all alone with my thoughts, which were haunted with the sickening sound of a neck being snapped.

CHAPTER ELEVEN

I woke with a gasp, my breathing heavy and labored. The sound of a snapping neck and the gush of blood pouring from a clawed carotid still echoed through my mind. My body was drenched in a warm liquid. My panic increased at the thought of being covered in someone's blood again. Looking down at my chest, I realized it was sweat. Despite the chill in the air, my body was saturated with it.

I tried to calm myself, taking deep, slow breaths. My sweltering body was cocooned in a sea of blankets. I sat up and kicked my legs out, trying to disentangle myself from the mass of material.

I sighed in relief as I was able to breathe a little easier once the blankets were off me and the chilly air was able to caress my skin, cooling it immediately.

It had been five days since the incident, and I couldn't relieve myself of the guilt I felt for taking the lives of two men. I had been able to distract myself easily enough during the day. The first morning I woke up, I was surrounded by a plethora of people. The second day, I spent training with the Head Enforcer, Harrison Trager. Tyler was happy to set it up for me, and Harrison was pleased to have me join. He had certainly kept me busy.

It was, unfortunately, during the night that I couldn't distract myself. My dreams were filled with the incident. Sometimes, I would even get glances at people sobbing for the loss of their loved ones.

Their faces were all a blur, but I could feel the grief coming from them in waves. It made me sick with shame.

I shut my eyes tight, pushing the nightmare away. I was trying to take Tyler's advice about choosing to accept what I had done without guilt but that was easier said than done. As much as logic told me I had done what I had to do, my morality painted a different picture. Hopefully, time would help heal this wound.

Once I had calmed myself down, I turned on the lamp by the bed and looked at the clock. It was barely four in the morning, but I knew trying to sleep again was pointless.

As I stood up, I finally was able to catch the lingering scent in the air. King Finnian had been in here.

I wasn't surprised. He had been in my room every night since the incident. The only problem was, he only came when I was asleep. I had only caught him that first night when I tried to attack him. The only evidence I had been left with of his visits was his scent that clung to the air. It was barely detectable, others wouldn't have caught it. As his mate though, his scent was stronger to me than others.

I didn't really know how to feel about his visits. I was completely confused with our relationship; I didn't know what to make of it. Half of the time, I thought that he cared; but the other half of the time, it seemed he wanted nothing to do with me.

Deciding to leave the empty stillness of my room, I swung my legs off my bed and made my way to the bathroom. I quickly got ready for a workout, not bothering to shower first since I'd just sweat again in a few minutes. I put on a pair of black Nike shorts, a sports bra, and a loose racerback tank top, along with my favorite tennis shoes. I left my hair in the French braids from the day before.

I stopped by the kitchen on the way to the gym and grabbed a bottle of water. I walked quietly through the halls, careful not to wake anyone since it was still too early. I didn't see a single soul in the hallways until I was out of the residential wing. After that, I saw workers arriving for and beginning their shifts. I sent them polite smiles when they greeted me but didn't stop until I reached the gym.

It was completely empty, like I expected. I decided to start my workout with a run. I hopped on the treadmill and turned it up high. It was probably stupid of me not to start out slow. I didn't exactly work out regularly. Me and exercise never got along. Aside from training, I have never hit the gym like some of my family did. I was in good fighting shape in both forms and good running shape in my wolf form, but running as a human? Not so much. But the exertion helped take my mind off other things, so I pushed my body as far as it could go.

I pushed and I pushed, endlessly for two hours. I pushed until the only sound in my head was the heavy thumping of my heart and the slapping of my feet against the treadmill. My breathing was heavy and labored, and my sides ached with the effort, but I kept going. I kept going until sweat covered my whole body, dripping off me disgustingly.

I kept going until I could hardly breathe. Black dots started dancing in front of my vision. Then I stopped. When the treadmill came to a stop, I quickly collapsed to the ground next to it. I gulped down water between my ragged breaths. Eventually, my breathing and heart rate slowed to a normal pace. I took another sip of water before I stood up again.

I made my way to another room in the gym. I stopped in front of a punching bag, needing to release some of my pent-up aggression. I didn't bother wrapping my hands or putting on gloves. I wanted to feel the pain.

Once I threw my first punch, I couldn't stop. I threw punch after punch, kick after kick. I felt like I was in a blind rage. The pain didn't even register in my mind as a red haze took over my vision, guiding my actions.

I wasn't sure how long I went for; could have been minutes, could have been hours. I let out a scream of frustration as I slammed my fist into the bag as hard as I could. My last hit did in both the bag and my wrist. The bag snapped off the hook, sand slipping out. My wrist throbbed painfully. I wondered briefly if I had broken it.

As the haze lifted, I surveyed the damage to my hands; my knuckles were raw and bloody. I was feeling the pain now that the adrenaline was wearing off. I hissed as I wiped the blood against my tank top, staining the grey material with crimson. More blood seeped from the wounds but not as much. My hands were swollen and bruised. I shook my wrists out. They hurt like hell but didn't feel broken. All in all, the damage should heal within a day or two.

"You should consider wearing gloves next time, Miss Keating," a voice spoke up from behind me.

I whirled around in surprise. I hadn't even heard anyone approaching me. My defenses were up, but once I saw the owner of the voice, they lowered.

Royal Beta Kieran was standing in front of me, looking every bit the Royal he was. He was in a fancy dark blue suit, not a wrinkle in sight. He wore an expensive-looking gold watch, and his hair was neatly combed back, not one strand out of place. His cerulean eyes were fixed on me. They looked so much like his brother's that it hurt.

"You scared me." I put my battered and bleeding hand against my chest, willing my heart to slow down.

He looked amused, his lips curling upwards ever so slightly. "My apologies, Miss Keating. That wasn't my intention."

"Don't worry about it. It was my fault. I should have heard you." I smiled slightly at him.

"Are you in need of medical assistance?" His eyes looked down at my hands and then back to my face.

"No, no. I'm fine. It looks worse than it actually is. I'll be sure to wear gloves next time."

"Perhaps try a little restraint to not obliterate the bag as well."

I would have thought he was angry by his words, but his voice held a teasing edge that told me otherwise. I hadn't talked to Kieran much, or at all really, but he didn't seem as intimidating as I once believed.

"I'll do what I can."

"I do not doubt that the gym manager will appreciate that."

I nodded in response, not sure what else to say. He spoke again so I didn't have to.

"King Finnian sent me to retrieve you. He would like a word in his meeting room," he informed me.

My nerves skyrocketed. What could he possibly want to see me for? And why couldn't he come get me himself?

"The king wants to see me? Why?" I asked, sounding anxious.

He didn't say anything about my nervousness. He must have assumed it was because I was intimidated by the king, not because he was my mate.

"He has given you a few days to rest, but now he needs to question you about the events that took place during the attack."

I nodded slowly. I didn't know what more I could tell him. The guys refused to answer questions that day but I'd go along with this. He gestured for me to follow him. I walked next to him, leaving a couple of feet between us. We walked in silence for a few minutes—with me still trying to stop the bleeding from my knuckles—before he spoke up.

He cleared his throat hesitantly. I looked up at him. "I would just like to extend my gratitude for your actions that day. I loathe to think about what might have happened to my Emiliya had you not sensed the wolves when you did."

I was surprised. I hadn't expected that from him. I guess I assumed he was like the male version of Emiliya but maybe he wasn't like her. "Yeah, well, I'm glad I sensed them in time. Had they been smarter, they would have kept a greater distance. I got lucky, I guess."

"I wouldn't call it luck. You have good instincts. Accept that with pride. It is, after all, something to be quite proud of."

I nodded at him in appreciation. "Thank you. That means a lot coming from you, Royal Beta."

"I give credit where credit is due, Miss Keating. You earned that credit."

We stopped in front of a familiar door. The same room King Finnian interviewed me in last time. He opened the door and allowed me to walk inside.

"Please wait here. King Finnian will be with you shortly."

I nodded to him. When he shut the door, leaving me alone, I took a seat and faced the exit.

I waited for about five minutes before King Finnian decided to make his appearance. When he fully shut the door, leaving us in complete isolation from everyone else due to Niki's silencing spell on the room, he turned his gaze towards me. His eyes were golden and filled with fury. I quickly racked my mind, trying to figure out what I had done to piss him off, but I came up blank.

He must have noticed my look of confusion because he growled lowly and strode over to me, his long legs reaching me in just three steps. He ripped my rolling chair out from under the table and grabbed my arm, his hold gentle despite his aggressive actions.

He pulled me to my feet and brought me close to his body. His musky scent made me dizzy in the best way possible. I was so enraptured with it, that I didn't even feel self-conscious about my sweaty body.

After a few seconds, I got my bearings and rage filled me, matching his to a tee.

"What the hell is wrong with you? You can't just manhandle me whenever you want to." I tried to jerk my arm out of his firm grasp but he wasn't having it. In fact, he just pulled me closer.

"No, what the hell is wrong with *you*?" He glowered down at me.

"I don't know what you're talking about."

"Your hands," he gritted out. He looked like he was on the verge of shifting, trying desperately not to.

I glanced down at my hands and finally realized what his problem was. My knuckles had stopped bleeding but were still cut up. My fingers and wrists were tender and hurt to move. He was pissed because I had abused my hands, but why? Why would he care?

He released his grip on my upper arm and grabbed my hands in his much bigger ones. His touch was gentle, his thumbs massaging my aching wrists. He lifted them to his lips, kissing every cut tenderly. My eyes fluttered at the feeling of his lips on my skin. All pain disappeared when he touched me.

His lips lingered for a few moments before he pulled back. My eyes snapped open at his words. "If you ever do something like this again, I'll make sure you never step foot in another gym."

I pulled away from him harshly, his words infuriating me. "You have no right to tell me what to do!" I yelled at him.

"I have every right. I'm your king," he spoke calmly, but his eyes gave away his real feelings. They were practically glowing with anger.

"You may be my king but it's my body. I can do whatever I want to with it, including abusing it. Back the hell off."

"No one is going to hurt you, including yourself. Not while I'm alive." He lowered his voice, trying to sound menacing, and intimidating. It didn't work for me.

"Oh, yeah?" I asked challengingly. He just raised an eyebrow at my defiance. Had I been any other wolf, a challenge would have resulted in my death.

My next move was stupid, so incredibly stupid. My temper got the best of me, forcing me to do things I wouldn't normally do. I guess between the guilt I was feeling, the hatred and the fury, I wasn't exactly myself. Which was why I slammed my fist into the stone wall as hard as I could, effectively shattering the bones in my hand.

As we were talking, I had slowly been putting distance between us. He hadn't bothered to stop me but he should have. He tried to grab my hand before it could hit the wall but he was too far away. Despite his crazy fast reflexes, I somehow managed to beat him based on the pure fact that I was closer to the wall than he was to me.

It took a second to comprehend the pain, but once I did, it hit full force. A cry of pain left my lips as tears built up in my eyes. I cradled my throbbing, bloody hand against my chest, feeling like an idiot.

I had no idea why I broke my hand like that, but I felt the need to defy him. I wanted to go against everything he said. It wasn't reasonable or mature, but it was what I wanted. So I went for it, not thinking over the consequences first. Now those consequences were kicking me in the ass.

King Finnian swore under his breath and grabbed my hand, pulling it away from my chest. He held it gently, kissing my knuckles once again. He pulled one hand away from me to grab his cell phone out of his pocket. He typed in it for a moment before putting it back and grabbing my hand in both of his once again.

I blinked away the tears, trying not to cry. I focused on him instead. I focused on his eyes, his scent, and the softness of his lips against my fingers.

I finally calmed down enough to speak, to try and explain my actions. Before I could, the door opened and Niki strolled in. She was wearing a long dress that was trailing behind her. It was modern but had the style of something you'd see in a movie set before the 1900s. Her long black hair was down, hanging to her waist, half of it pulled back.

"What are you doing here?" I asked as she closed the door behind her.

"I asked her to come to heal you," King Finnian growled out.

His brief attention on his phone made sense now.

Niki walked over to us, stopping in front of me. She gave King Finnian an expectant look when he didn't release my hand. He pressed a few more kisses on my knuckles before reluctantly extending it to Niki, laying my hand in between hers. She examined it closely.

"Oh, dear girl. You are too recalcitrant for your own good." She shook her head slightly.

"Okay, Merriam-Webster. Are you sure you're a witch and not an SAT tutor?"

Her lips twitched upward.

"You are also quite droll."

I rolled my eyes but didn't reply. She closed her eyes and started chanting. I felt the pain in my hand fade to a numb tingling. Within a few minutes, it was as good as new.

"Thanks, Niki," I said to her once she was done.

"You're welcome, Kendall. Please, do be more circumspect next time."

I blushed, feeling embarrassed for my actions. I nodded and she left us alone. I almost begged her to stay, not wanting to deal with King Finnian, but I knew she wouldn't so I kept my mouth shut.

As soon as the door clicked shut, King Finnian had me pressed against the wall, his body pressed against mine. He dipped his head, letting his lips skim against my ear.

"If you ever do something like that again, I'll have you locked in a padded room," he whispered against my ear.

At his words, all enjoyment of his actions left and I pushed him away. It didn't do much, but he willingly stepped away from me.

"I don't like threats, and I don't like being ordered around. Hence why Niki needed to come to heal me in the first place. Perhaps try asking, King Finnian. Politeness can go a long way." I crossed my arms over my chest and glared at him.

He gritted his teeth and sighed through his nose. "Fine," he spat out. "Please, don't harm yourself again."

He looked pained like he never had to ask instead of demand something. I got a twisted sense of amusement from his displeasure. I wasn't planning on hurting myself again, but I still wanted him to ask instead of threatening me and bossing me around.

"Fine," I agreed.

I sat down in satisfaction. He took a seat in the chair across from me. I tucked my legs underneath me and leaned my elbows on the table, my chin resting against my now-healed fists. He sat up straight, his posture screaming confidence and dominance.

"So, what did you want to know?" I inquired, looking him directly in his now cerulean eyes.

"I need you to tell me exactly what happened and what was said. Word for word, Miss Keating." All emotions had been wiped from his face.

I rolled my eyes. If I was never called Miss Keating again, it would be too soon.

"I caught one of their scents while we were in the restaurant. I didn't know if he was a threat, and I didn't want to alert Niki and everyone until I was sure."

He cut in, a hint of anger settling on his face, "You should have alerted her."

I waved him off. "Yeah, yeah. Don't even start. You and my entire family have already succeeded in making me feel like a five-year-old with all the scolding I've received. I get it. I was dumb. Let's move on."

He glared at me but kept his mouth shut.

"So anyways, when I got outside, I followed his scent. He was hiding in the woods. When he ran off somewhere, I followed him. I was able to subdue him pretty easily. I questioned him for a few minutes, he deflected, then another—"

"Word for word, Miss Keating," he reminded, interrupting me.

"Are you serious? It was just a bunch of insults and unanswered questions."

"I'm always serious."

I snorted unattractively. "Yeah, I realized that the second you tried to kill my pack's future Beta."

He gave me an unimpressed look. I sighed.

"Fine. I asked him who he was. He said something along the lines of my worst nightmare. I told him I was insulted that he even considered himself a threat to me and to not make me ask again. He called me a bitch or something. Before I could say anything else, someone came up behind me. I moved before he could kick me in the head, but the first guy was able to push me down."

"Did he do anything to you?" he asked through gritted teeth.

"Not really. I think he managed to punch me then, but I kneed him in the crotch and he got off me. The second guy ran at me. I was able to move just in time. I had him on the ground and asked him again who they were . . ." I paused, not sure I wanted to disclose my next actions. I didn't want to give him the upper hand in our screwed-up relationship.

"What did he say?" he demanded.

I sighed and told him, knowing I wouldn't leave this room until he had the truth. "He said, and I quote, 'The king won't be able to protect little bitches like you once we kill him.' I wasn't planning on killing them. I was going to restrain them so that you guys could question him. But when he said that, my wolf instincts told me to kill him before he could hurt you. I always follow my instincts."

Once I finished, I moved my gaze from the tabletop to him, looking at him through my lashes. He had a thoughtful look on his face. I didn't know how to interpret it.

"Did he say anything else before you killed him?"

"No . . ."

"What happened next?"

I narrowed my eyes in frustration. "Don't you have anything to say about why I killed him?"

I wanted him to feel something. I wanted him to open up somehow. I mean, damn. I tell him I killed someone, ended their life because they threatened him. A threat they never would have been able to achieve, by the way. And he has nothing to say? Screw that.

"What is there to say? You did what any wolf would have done if their mate was threatened," he said it like it was common sense like he didn't know what my problem was.

"I doubt you would have," I mumbled bitterly. I crossed my arms over my chest in anger. Was it that difficult to give me some kind of reaction?

He had a look of exasperation on his face, which irritated me more. He sighed like I was some petulant child who he was tired of talking to.

"I don't have the time nor the energy to ease your doubts and insecurities all day. I would have reacted similarly. That is all I have to say on the issue."

"You're an ass," I added, wanting to get the last word at least.

"Wrap this up, Miss Keating." He ignored my insult.

"Fine. After I snapped his neck, the first guy managed to tackle me to the ground. He disoriented me before I could fight back by slamming my head multiple times into the ground. Before he could kill me, he stopped. I didn't realize it was Kat at the time. I took the opportunity while he was vulnerable to attack and ripped his throat out. I passed out after that."

"He didn't say anything else?" he questioned.

"Nope," I said absentmindedly.

Guilt ate at me, gnawing at my stomach painfully. I looked down at my hands. All I could see were weapons—weapons that ripped out the throat of one man and snapped the neck of another. I had to blink hard to get the image of blood saturating them out of my head.

"You feel guilty, don't you?" It wasn't a question. His voice was softer than I was used to. I blinked a few times, trying to focus on what was happening now and not on the events of a few days ago.

I hesitated but finally nodded once.

"They don't deserve your guilt," he stated simply.

"I know they don't, but it's not that easy."

"I know. It'll get easier."

I chewed on my lower lip, thinking over my next words. "Who was the first person you had to kill?" I finally asked.

He didn't answer for a while, and that gave me my answer.

"It's none of my business. I guess I forgot my place again," I said bitterly, remembering what he said to me the last time we were in this room. I stood up, intending to leave now that he knew the whole story, but I didn't make it out of my seat.

"His name was Levi Redford. He was the Alpha of the Redford Pack and a member of my father's Royal Council. He was a trusted friend and ally. At least, that's what my father thought at the time."

He looked thoughtful. He stared at the wall, not looking at me. I stayed silent, not wanting to ruin this moment. This was the first time he had ever opened up to me. My heart swelled at the thought of him trusting me enough to share this story.

"Redford had it in his head that he would make a better King than my father. There is always someone who thinks they would do a better job. My father was far too trusting. That was his biggest mistake."

His eyes moved from the wall to meet mine. They were a stormy swirl of midnight blue and gold. They were mesmerizing, and I couldn't look away if I tried. I wanted to comfort him but I was too scared to move even an inch.

"My mother was pregnant when she died. There are only six people who are still alive who know that—seven now including you. She couldn't shift due to her pregnancy. Redford used this to his advantage. He was here for a party. It was a small get-together to celebrate my parents's anniversary. Mother had slipped away to freshen up. Redford snuck out and followed her. Father had been drinking; his senses were slower than usual. Had he been sober, things might have ended differently."

His eyes left mine again. He seemed more thoughtful than upset.

"Redford shifted. My mother didn't stand a chance. Due to her inability to shift and the element of surprise, it didn't take Redford long. He killed her quickly. That was the only bright side to the situation. At least she didn't have to suffer. My father was fueled by his drunken grief. He was sloppy. Redford killed him."

He paused for a few minutes, just staring into space. My need to get up and comfort him was growing, but I could sense that he wasn't finished, so I stayed seated.

"I've never been able to figure out what he thought would happen after that. I guess he figured taking out the King meant the throne automatically went to him. I had been the first one in the room that day. The first one to see my parent's mangled bodies. Kieran and Tyler weren't far behind. They killed Redford's men. Once he saw his men being taken out, he tried to run. He didn't even make it to the hallway. I chased him. He was my only focus. I didn't stop until his head and limbs were completely severed from his body. He died a coward."

"Did you feel guilty?" I whispered after a few moments of silence. His eyes snapped to mine.

"Not even a little bit. And neither should you. Redford doesn't deserve your guilt and neither did those wolves you killed. I wish I could have been there to protect you. I'll always regret not being there to end them myself. You did them a favor."

"Why is that?" I asked, feeling confused and weirdly vulnerable.

"You ended them quickly. They didn't have to suffer. Had they killed you instead, I can promise you I wouldn't have granted them the same courtesy. Even if they hadn't killed you, they still hurt you. I'll keep to myself exactly what I would have done to them, but just know that you did them a favor by saving them from having to deal with me." His eyes darkened, just like his tone.

I gulped and tried to lighten the subject. "Is that your twisted way of making me feel better?"

"Did it?"

"Maybe a little."

His lips tugged up in the corner, the closest I had gotten to a smile from him. He soon dropped it and got serious again.

"Let the guilt go, Kendall." I stared at him in shock. He called me by my first name twice now. "You shouldn't feel guilty about protecting yourself. I'm glad you did. I don't know what I would have done if I lost you . . ." he trailed off and looked at me with a tenderness I haven't seen before. I nearly melted in my seat and he didn't even have to touch me.

I nodded at his words. I couldn't say that the remorse was completely gone, but I certainly felt lighter than I had in days. King Finnian had gotten through to me in ways no one else could. All it took was him opening up to me.

He nodded back and stood up.

"I appreciate your time, Miss Keating. I have some work to do now."

I nodded and stood up as well. I walked over to him. He was about to pull the door open but I stopped him, surprising both him and myself. I wrapped my arms tightly around his waist and rested my cheek on his warm, strong chest.

"Thank you . . ." I mumbled into him. It was thanks with many meanings.

Thank you for being honest with me; thank you for opening up to me; thank you for easing my sorrows. Thank you for just being here.

He stood still for a few seconds before pushing me back gently. He swallowed hard and nodded to me. I gave him a weak smile and left the room, finally starting to feel like myself again.

CHAPTER TWELVE

"Watch the body language, Kendall. The body language can give its owner's next move away," Harrison Trager, the Head of the Royal Army, instructed me.

I nodded and watched my sparring partner, Nathan's, movements. I scrutinized him, trying to take in everything he did. He had his fists raised, and he bounced on the balls of his feet, waiting to strike.

When I saw him tighten his right fist and cock his shoulder back a bit, I knew what was coming. I ducked my head just as his fist came flying towards my jaw. He hit nothing but air, so I used his momentum against him.

With his shift in weight, I was able to push him forward. Once I had him on the ground, I dug my knee into his back, twisted his arm around, and pushed his face into the mat. I smiled victoriously once I had him pinned, but I spoke too soon.

Nathan managed to throw me backward and pin me into the ground before I could even blink. The air left my lungs briefly as my back was slammed against the mat. Now it was his turn to smile smugly down at me.

He bent my arm at an awkward angle and dug his knee into my chest painfully. I struggled for a few moments, but begrudgingly submitted and tapped out.

He immediately released me, his knee leaving my chest making it easier to breathe. As I sat up, I rubbed my throbbing shoulder and looked at Harrison, waiting for his feedback.

I had been training with Harrison since my chat with King Finnian for over a week now. I hadn't seen much of him, although he still came to my room while I was sleeping like a creeper.

I had fallen into a routine. I would start my morning in Tyler's office, answering the phone. After lunch, I would spend the afternoon training with Harrison. I also made a friend out of Nathan, who had become my unofficial sparring partner.

Nathan was of Alpha blood. He, like me, was the youngest of the alpha children. He decided to join the Royal Army instead of staying with his pack. He was a strong wolf and an excellent warrior. He was no doubt stronger and more skilled than me, but I had learned a lot between him and Harrison.

I was lucky to be training with two amazing warriors. Most of the Royal Army trained under lower-ranked warriors, who in turn trained under Harrison. The Royal Army was huge, so it would be impossible for him to train each soldier individually. I was the exception.

Since I was labeled as King Finnian's guest, it got me certain benefits, such as training with the best. Harrison had been taking the time to teach me in ways even my father hadn't. Although he wasn't of Alpha blood, it didn't matter. He was the biggest badass I'd ever met, even for an old guy. He wasn't all that old, about the werewolf equivalent of middle age, but I still liked messing with him about it.

Nathan, on the other hand, was fairly young. He was about fifty, which was the werewolf equivalent to the early twenties. He had bright red hair and freckles covering his pale skin. He had a baby face, which I thought was the perfect disguise. He looked sweet and innocent but could secretly kill you in at least a hundred different ways using nothing but his hands. He was tall and muscular and was ranked as the Second in Command of the Royal Army. It was quite an accomplishment for his age.

"You didn't twist his arm hard enough. He was able to break out of your hold. You got too smug and loosened your grip. You never let up until the enemy is dead, or in this case, they tap out," Harrison explained. I groaned but nodded nonetheless.

Nathan held his hand out for me, which I accepted gratefully, and hoisted me to my feet. We both got in a fighting position once again. I continued to carefully observe his body language, waiting for him to give away his next move.

I never attacked first. I always waited for him to make the first move and go from there. Harrison taught me not to become complacent in doing that, for the simple matter that in a real-life situation, you might have to attack first. But for now, he was allowing it.

Nathan tightened his fist and dropped his shoulder just a bit. I was about to duck, preparing for a punch, but his slight weight shift let me know that the punch was a fake out. I was proved correct when he kicked his leg, trying to catch my knee and knock me off balance.

I moved just in time. I knocked his leg out from under him. He fell onto his back. I got on top of him before he could move. I was able to neutralize his hands, just in time to avoid an elbow to the face. When his hands weren't a threat, I put pressure on his throat with my forearm. I held tightly, not letting my hold budge even an inch. After a few minutes, he reluctantly tapped out.

I jumped off of him and got on my feet, letting out a girly, excited squeal. That was the first time I forced Nathan to tap out. I felt accomplished.

Nathan had kicked my ass all week. I had been reluctant to give it my all at first. I didn't want to really hurt him. Their training was way more hands-on than our training back home. I quickly got over my fear.

Nathan hadn't taken it easy on me whatsoever. I was usually pretty bruised up by the end of the day. Since Nathan wasn't holding back, I stopped and gave it my all. While it was intense and usually painful, although we could tap out if we needed to, it was certainly beneficial. I felt stronger in the last week than I had in all my twenty-three years of living.

Nathan grumbled unhappily but seemed proud deep down.

"What was that, Red? Was that a congratulations, I'm sorry it was so easy for you?" I mimicked his voice for the words he hadn't spoken and held my hand to my ear mockingly.

"If it was so easy then, how come it took you so long?" he objected.

"I was scared you were going to steal my soul. My bad." The ginger jokes had certainly not been in short supply.

"I'm glad you can finally admit that you were scared."

"Of your gingerness? Of course, always," I teased.

"I'll keep that in mind, Simba." He looked up at my hair and smirked.

"It's humid," I defended myself while trying to smooth out my frizzy locks. I gave up and tied it up in a messy bun with the rubber band on my wrist.

"Thanks, now you won't be able to suffocate me with it." He full on chuckled now.

I spun around before he could see me coming and slammed my fist into his stomach. It wasn't hard enough to really hurt, but it was enough to surprise him since he didn't see it coming.

"Don't anger the beast," I warned, pointing at him threateningly.

"I like how you refer to your hair as the beast but not your wolf."

I shook my head at him and turned my attention to Harrison, who looked mildly amused at our bickering.

"What's my feedback, old man?" I joked with him.

"Your feedback is that you're a little shit and I'm not old."

"Someone's mighty sensitive."

"Someone can and will kick your ass, little girl." His voice held nothing but affection, letting me know he wasn't serious.

"Anytime, grandpa."

He chuckled, but then got serious. "That was good. That's really all the feedback I have. You did good."

I smiled brightly at him, proud of myself for his lack of feedback. "Thanks, Harrison."

"No problem. Now, why don't you two take a break."

We nodded and collapsed onto the training mat. Harrison walked off, moving on to another sparring couple.

We were on the training field. It was on the opposite side of the Royal Territory than the castle. It was basically just a wide open field covered with training mats. People were all over the place, either sparring or watching someone spar while instructors gave feedback. Nathan and I were on the edge of the field, away from everyone else. We both grabbed our water bottles and took long sips.

"So, you going to that brunch tomorrow?" I asked him after I finished drinking. Despite the temperature being almost below freezing, I was sweating so hard that had to I wipe my forehead with a towel.

"Yeah, you?"

I nodded. Tyler had told us about it earlier in the week. Apparently, they held a brunch on the first Saturday of every month. It wasn't open to the public like the Mating Ball was. It was more for the high ranking members of the Royal Pack to meet with the Royals and talk with them. Council members were also free to attend but weren't required.

Since Matt and Dalton were making good progress with securing my dad a seat on the Council, we were invited to attend. I never turned down free breakfast.

"Who usually goes to those things?" I wondered.

He shrugged. "Not many people, actually. The Royals, of course. The high ranking members of the Royal Army and the Royal Trackers. A few other important people who help run the castle. Council members will sometimes show up."

I nodded and took another sip from my water bottle. I was going to ask him more questions but was interrupted. Tyler, Matt, and Dalton walked out of the woods and onto the training field. Harrison met them halfway, leaving them all stopped in front of our training mat.

"What are you guys doing here?" I asked them.

Tyler answered me first, "King Finnian likes to come observe training every once in a while. He decided to come today. He should be here with Kieran soon. We finished our work early today and decided to come and watch as well."

I nodded and suddenly grew nervous. I hadn't spent a lot of time, or any really, with King Finnian since last week. He told me about his past, willingly, and I ended our time together with a hug. Butterflies started fluttering around my stomach at the idea of seeing him.

They disappeared when Harrison spoke, "You heard Royal Gamma Tyler. The King is coming. Back to work. Don't want him to see anyone slacking."

Nathan and I both nodded and got back on our feet. Although Harrison had become a mentor of sorts to me rather quickly and we had a friendship where we could joke around, he was still in charge. And he didn't take it easy on me in the slightest. Not because I was a girl or because I wasn't a member of the Royal Army. He trained me just like he would anyone else, and he had my respect because of that.

"This should be good." Dalton snickered. Matt and Tyler both looked over at him and raised an eyebrow, but they didn't say anything.

I paused as I pulled my sparring gloves back on. I glared at him then looked back at Nathan. "You know what, Red, you look tired still. Sit back down." He smirked and shook his head but walked off, muttering something under his breath. I turned my icy stare back to Dalton. "Collins. You and me. Now."

He smirked arrogantly. I wanted to punch him so hard that he wouldn't have control over his facial features.

"This should be easy enough." He sounded so sure of himself, it fueled the fire simmering in my belly.

It was true, Dalton was a good fighter. Perhaps even better than me. I always refused to spar with him though, so I wouldn't really know. I had always trained with Selena. It was always a good way to take our anger out on one another, so we never argued on the arrangements.

Now that I had spent some time training with two of the best warriors, I felt more secure about my skills.

I finished securing my gloves while he did the same. He was already in workout clothes, probably with the intentions of training while he was here. Matt and Tyler were dressed similarly.

"Whenever you two are ready," Harrison informed us from the side of the mat.

We both nodded and got prepared. He was cocky, so he came at me quickly. He threw a right hook to start, and I dodged it flawlessly. His left fist moved quickly, trying to catch me in the stomach before I could move upright after I ducked. I jumped back just in time.

I faked aiming for his face next, finally going on the offense. He lowered his head just in time, setting me up perfectly for the move I planned from the beginning.

As he ducked, I grabbed the back of his and slammed it against my knee, effectively cracking his nose. Blood started gushing out. He lost his cocky attitude and finally got serious, ignoring his injury.

He ran at me next, trying to throw me to the ground. I maneuvered my body at the last second, so instead of him knocking me over, I was able to flip him over. He landed with a hard thud on his back.

I made my move before he could even sit up. I was on top of him, similar to how I was on top of Nathan earlier. I bent his arm painfully and dug my knee into his chest. He fought back, trying to free himself. I just twisted his arm hard, as far as it would go without breaking.

It took a lot of struggling, but he finally conceded and tapped the mat harshly. I got off of him with a grin.

"You're right. That was easy enough," I told him.

He glared up at me as he stood up. He walked back over to Matt, spitting out blood along the way. Nathan threw him a towel so he could wipe his nose.

"You've gotten good. I'm impressed," Matt told me.

I beamed at him. His words meant a lot. I sometimes acted like my family's opinion didn't matter to me, but in all honesty, it meant everything. So to get Matt's approval on something that the men in my family dominated was refreshing. It was good to finally be on their level physically.

"Wait until you see her fight Nathan. He's damn near one of the best I've ever seen. And I've been doing this for a while," Harrison told Matt.

"Let's see it then."

My attention snapped towards the woods. I hadn't even heard him coming, the sneaky bastard. Apparently, no one else had either, because we all looked surprised.

King Finnian stepped out of the tree line with Royal Beta Kieran right next to him. All at once, it seemed the entire field noticed his presence, his power, and dominance radiated over everyone. Everyone bowed to him. I didn't at first but then did the same if only to keep up appearances.

"As you were," he commanded everyone. He wasn't overly loud, but everyone heard him, returning to what they were doing.

His blue eyes turned to our group. They raked over me briefly but not long enough for anyone to notice.

"King Finnian, it is always a pleasure." Harrison bowed again once they were next to us.

"You know I like to check on things regularly, Harrison," King Finnian told him, his voice calm and cool.

I'd come to realize, he used that voice with everyone. It was very rare that he would openly show emotion. I guess he usually liked to save all his anger for me.

"Yes, sir." Harrison turned back to us. "Well, you heard King Finnian. He wants to see you two spar, so get to it."

We nodded and got into position. I didn't look back over at King Finnian. One reason was because I knew I wouldn't be able to look away. The second was because I was nervous.

I wasn't sure what his game was here. He had been adamant that I should not get hurt. So why did he want to watch me fight, where I could very well get hurt?

I pushed away my nerves and focused. I had to get away as unscathed as possible. Finnian may not want me, but his wolf sure as hell did. Meaning, that seeing me get hurt could end badly for Nathan. He didn't deserve that. As strong and as skilled as he was, he was no match for the King of all werewolves.

I was walking a thin line because I also didn't want to appear weak to him. I wanted to prove to him that I could hold my own in a fight. The only way to do that would be to go all in on the fight. I couldn't tap out unless he was really hurting me. The only solution would be to not let him hurt me . . . easier said than done.

I exhaled slowly and watched his movements, letting them guide me.

The fight moved slowly for a while, with not much happening. He'd throw a punch or kick, I'd dodge. I'd do the same, he'd dodge. For the first five minutes or so, that was all it was. Missed hits and a lot of dodging. The only thing it showed was I had gotten better at defense.

After a while, Nathan finally managed to land a hit. It wasn't where he intended, but it still got me. He was aiming for my cheek but caught the edge of my chin and lip. I felt my lower lip split open, but I ignored the blood.

I didn't hear growling, and no one came after Nathan, so that was a good sign. I didn't look over to see if he was angry. I kept my eyes trained on Nathan. Harrison's number one rule and the rule he drilled into my head, to begin with: Never take your eyes off the enemy. Keep your senses open and alert, but never let your eyes stray. So I didn't.

I decided it was time for a secret move Selena and I had come up with. Male werewolves were ridiculously tall and Selena and I are stuck with the short gene. We had found a way to use that to our advantage.

Nathan's legs were shoulder-width apart, which was good since his shoulders were so wide. I dove down quickly before he could stop me. I also had the element of surprise on my side. He had never seen me do this move.

I twisted my body on the way down so that I landed on my back. Once I was on the ground, my hips touching his feet, I hit the backs of his knees as hard as I could. They buckled, and he fell on them. I pushed him forward and pulled myself out from under him at the same time.

I jumped on his back before he could get up. I dug my knee into the back of his neck and twisted his arms behind his back. I didn't let my hold on him slacken like I had earlier.

"Tap out, Red," I ordered him as I twisted his arms higher.

He fought and struggled for a few minutes, but I kept my grip on him. Finally, I noticed his hand awkwardly tap against my arm. It was hard for him to do with his arms at the angle they were, but he had to make do with that.

I immediately released him and jumped up. I fought the urge to squeal again, not wanting to look immature in front of King Finnian.

To show my good sportsmanship, I reached my hand down and helped pull Nathan to his feet. He patted me on the shoulder to congratulate me and beamed with pride. I suppose he didn't mind losing to me twice since he won so many times already that it was just sad.

I looked away from him and turned my attention back to the guys. I took in all of their facial expressions. Dalton looked happy, probably that I had not just defeated him but Nathan as well. Matt couldn't look any prouder if he tried, Harrison too. Kieran looked impressed. I hesitated briefly before I turned to look at King Finnian last.

His face remained blank but I could see the emotions in his eyes. Once he saw I was alright, pride lit up his eyes. Elation filled my heart at the look.

It didn't last. His eyes soon left mine and turned impassive again, but it didn't matter. I saw how he really felt, and that meant everything.

I waited with bated breath, waiting to see if King Finnian would say anything. After a moment of silence, he finally did.

"It is unfortunate you couldn't have done that when you were under a real attack, Miss Keating," he said evenly.

"I don't know. I rather enjoyed having my head bashed in," I drawled sarcastically. Based on the gasps around me, I should have bit my tongue and nodded submissively.

"Kendall," Matt hissed as he glared hatefully at me. I winced uncomfortably under his scrutiny.

"That's quite alright, Matthew."

Really? Matthew? He called my brother by his first name, but I constantly got Miss Keating? What kind of shit was that?

"I apologize for my sister, Your Highness. She lacks functioning brain cells," he continued.

"Like I said, it's quite alright. Her sarcasm is refreshing," he repeated to my brother.

"My sarcasm detector is usually spot on, but apparently you broke it, King Finnian. Are you being sarcastic or not?"

His eyes lit with humor, his lip barely tugged up in the corner. "I'm never sarcastic, Miss Keating."

"I'll keep that in mind, Your Highness," I said, not sure how to answer back.

He looked like he was going to smile, but he just shook his head and walked away to the next mat. Harrison gave me one last good job before dismissing me for the day.

Tyler, Matt, Dalton, and Nathan remained surrounding me. Matt turned to give me a dirty look.

"Really, Kendall?" He looked at me expectantly.

"What?" I feigned innocence.

"Don't give me the puppy dog eyes. Those don't work on anyone anymore. You know that."

I sighed and dropped the act. "Sorry, it just slipped out. You know I have no filter."

"Well you better get one," he snapped.

"I think he is rather fond of you," Tyler commented.

I blanched, but tried to hide it. Matt caught it, but kept silent. Dalton looked at me knowingly. I shrugged off Tyler's comment and played nonchalant.

"He'd have to know me to be fond of me. We've barely spoke three words to each other, and those were during interviews," I told him.

"I suppose you're right," he said, but he still looked at me disbelievingly.

"Well I could use a run before dinner. Anyone care to join me?" I changed the subject.

"I think I'll take a rain check. I'd like to train a bit today," Tyler answered first.

Matt and Dalton both agreed with him.

"What about you, Red?" I asked Nathan.

"As much as I so enjoy your smartass insults, I'm going to have to pass this time."

"Okay, well I'll see you at brunch tomorrow anyway," I told him.

"Yeah, see you. Goodnight." He walked off the training field and into the woods.

"I'll see you all at dinner. Have fun."

With that, I walked deep into the woods, stripped once I was a good distance away, and shifted into my wolf form and took off. I ran for two hours, letting out any pent-up energy that remained.

As much as training helped me release that energy, somehow Finnian always managed to bring it back. He has a way of managing to rile my wolf up. It was getting harder to ignore my need to mark and mate with him. My instincts were screaming at me too, and I never ignored my instincts.

I could only hope that we could work things out soon. I was trying to stay positive considering we'd seemed to be making progress, but you never knew with him. At the very least, I hoped I could find out what he was hiding. Because I knew, without a shadow of a doubt, that he was hiding something.

CHAPTER THIRTEEN

I just finished coating my lips in a soft nude lipstick when I heard a knock on my bedroom door.

I recapped the lipstick and smoothed out my modest blush pink lace dress. I matched it with a pair of white open-toed heels, which were sitting by my bed. I ran and slipped them on before opening the door to reveal Kat, Matt, and Dalton.

We greeted each other and walked together towards the banquet hall where the brunch was being held. Tyler told us that it was usually outside, but since it was cold and drizzling right now, they moved it to one of the banquet halls instead. It didn't take us too long to reach the big, well-lit room. One of the walls was made completely of windows, giving it a sunroom type of feel.

There were tables along the wall opposite the windows, food and beverages on display like a buffet. There was a coffee bar which had any kind of hot beverage you could think of. Hot chocolate, tea, espresso. They even had the makings of iced coffee.

Next to that, there was a waffle bar with all kinds of toppings and sauces. Anything you could think to put on a waffle, and even things you'd never think to, they had. I also saw an assortment of bagels, croissants, and scones.

There were tables scattered around the room, covered in fancy white table cloth and colorful ornaments. Some people were seated but most of them were standing around in groups, talking and catching up.

My eyes unconsciously scanned the room for King Finnian, but I couldn't find him. The only people around the room that I recognized were Nathan, Harrison, Tyler, and Lili. Lili and Nathan were talking to each other, both holding a cup of coffee. Harrison was sitting at a table, booming laughter coming from him. He was sitting with a group of older men; they were probably close to his age.

Waiters were walking around, carrying trays, and offering people food and drinks. They had mimosas and plain orange juice in champagne flutes. When a young girl, probably close to my age, walked in front of us and offered us a drink, I took a mimosa. Matt and Dalton declined, choosing to go get coffee instead. Kat took an orange juice.

We thanked her, and she walked off to serve someone else. I saw some of the other trays. They all had things that could be eaten standing up. I saw colorful fruit skewers, mini pancakes on a stick, mini quiches, cucumber sandwiches, mini yogurt parfaits in shot glasses, and several other finger foods that I didn't recognize. I grabbed a mini pancake skewer when another girl walked by.

"Come on, I want to introduce you to Nathan. He's my sparring partner," I told Kat after I took a sip of my mimosa.

I held my now empty toothpick from my pancakes in the same hand as my glass and linked my arm with Kat. The guys were still getting their coffee and were now talking with a couple of other guys.

We made our way across the room, to where Nathan and Lili were standing. They smiled when they saw us heading over. Nathan pulled me into a hug and I did the same to Lili.

"Kat, this is Nathan. Nate, this is my best friend and sister, Kat," I introduced them to each other.

"Nice to meet you." Kat smiled politely and held her hand out to shake his.

"You too. I've heard a lot about you." He shook her hand.

"All good things I hope." Kat laughed lightly.

"Fortunately, yes. Your other sister, Selena, wasn't so lucky."

Kat lost her polite laugh and laughed for real. "Doesn't surprise me. They have a love-hate relationship, emphasis on the hate," she joked.

"If she's anything like this one, I can understand." He pointedly glanced over at me.

"What is that supposed to mean?" I asked, not sure if I should feel insulted or not.

"It means you're kind of a pain in the ass. Kind of easy to hate." His eyes twinkled with humor as he looked at me.

I gaped at him. "Don't make me kick your ass again, Red. You know I can. I proved that twice yesterday."

"And I proved that you couldn't a countless number of times."

"I guess we'll find out Monday. You better be ready. Have a paramedic on stand-by," I warned playfully.

"I'll have them waiting for you, Medusa."

"Your insult is sad and irrelevant."

"Just like you."

Kat snickered and sipped on her orange juice. She held up her hand to Nathan, giving him a high five. I gave her an incredulous look. She was supposed to be on my side. Lili said nothing, but she did giggle under her breath at the three of us.

"I wish your kind had gone extinct before you were born."

"Harsh." He grinned down at me. "You're a never-ending supply of ginger jokes. I'm sure you'll run out soon."

"Challenge accepted, Strawberry Shortcake."

"You do realize I'm like a foot taller than you." He raised an eyebrow down at me. "Even with your hooker heels." He glanced down at my feet.

"They're just shy of receiving hooker status."

"Good to know. Thanks so much for that stimulating piece of information."

"You two are like the same rude, sarcastic person." Kat chuckled.

"I take offense to that," I told her.

"What do you know, I finally agree with you for once."

I rolled my eyes at him and swallowed the last of my mimosa.

"As riveting as this conversation is, I need food. I'm going to go see what all there is."

They all nodded. I looked at Kat, curious if she wanted to come with me or stay there. She said she was going to talk to Lili for a few minutes and would catch up to me later.

I left the little group and made my way to the buffet. I grabbed another mimosa off a tray on my way and sipped as I walked. Once I reached the table, I glanced over my options.

After a few minutes of indecisiveness, I decided to start with a croissant. I spread some butter on the warm bread and it melted quickly. I nearly moaned in delight as it hit my taste buds. I had never been to Paris, but it was what I guessed their croissants tasted like. It was delicious.

I walked away as I munched on my treat, promising myself to come back later for a waffle. I glanced around to see if anyone else had arrived that I knew. Before my eyes had time to scan the room, I heard a booming voice call my name.

My eyes snapped to the left and I saw Harrison waving me over, still at the same table as before. I took another bite of my croissant and made my way over to him. I smiled at him once I reached the table and sat down next to him. He was surrounded by three other men, all middle aged.

"Fellas, this is Kendall Keating, my new student. Quite the fighter, this one," he bragged.

"You sound like a proud dad, old man." I giggled.

"As you can tell, her attitude is a work in progress." He chuckled. "But she's got a hell of a right hook. Knocked Nathan on his ass twice yesterday."

"This little thing managed to take out Nathan?" one of them asked disbelievingly. I withheld a cringe at the sexist old fuck referring to me as "this little thing."

"She sure as shit did. Tougher than she looks. Took a beating for over a week before she managed to take him out. Didn't complain once."

"Impressive," another man added.

"That's what I said." He looked over at me and then realized I had no idea who these men were. "Oh, damn. Sorry, I forgot to introduce you. Keating, this is Carl Francis. He's the Head Tracker."

"Nice to meet you, kid. I've heard nothing but good things about you. You did a hell of a job leading us to that group of rebels in the woods," Carl told me.

"You're the one who found them?"

"Me and my men, yes. Wasn't hard once we knew to actually look in the area."

I nodded and Harrison continued his introductions, motioning to the second man. "This is Ian Johnson. He's my third-in-command."

He was the one who called me "this little thing". I smiled at him politely. He nodded at me.

"And this is Alpha Jim Evers. He's a member of the Royal Council. He's also my oldest friend. We grew up together. And before you even say it, the dinosaurs didn't roam the earth with us."

I grinned. "You know me so well, Harrison."

"Well, between your old man jokes and your ginger jokes, you're not hard to predict."

"I just tell it like it is," I said cheekily.

"You're a little shit is what it is."

I just grinned again and turned to the men across from me. "It's really nice to meet you all. I've heard great things about all of you."

It was true too. I knew of Alpha Jim because of my father and Carl and Ian from Harrison and Nathan.

"Likewise. I actually met you once, when you were just a little girl. I went to your territory for a meeting with your father. He's a good man, I have nothing but respect for him," Alpha Jim said.

"That he is. He's a great alpha," I agreed with him and I appreciated his kind words towards my dad.

It didn't surprise me that he had been to our territory before. Dad liked to be on good terms with other packs, friendly even. It wasn't an uncommon occurrence for him to invite alphas to our territory and go visit theirs. He had a lot of allies and made many alliances. He didn't have any enemies.

"He is. That's why I recommended him to join the Council. A couple of us did actually."

"That is really nice. He definitely appreciates it."

"He earned it. One of the most honest, respectable alpha I've ever met."

"I'll let him know you said that. He'll be happy that he has such a good reputation amongst his peers."

"Please do. Tell him I look forward to him joining the Council."

"I will, sir."

"He gets sir and I get old man? How is that fair?" Harrison butted in.

"He doesn't have one of his strongest men beat the crap out of me." I rolled my eyes.

"If I didn't think you could take it, I wouldn't have done it."

"Well thanks for the compliment, old man," I joked.

I swallowed the last of the buttery croissant then washed it down with the last of my mimosa.

Before anyone else could say anything, the room got quiet, and everyone who was seated stood up. I felt his power emanating, filling the room and washing over every person here. Everyone looked in his direction, bowed their head, and tilted it to the side, exposing their necks submissively. I did the same. After a few seconds, he continued into the room and everyone went back to their conversations.

As I sat back down, I finally let my eyes land on my mate. He was wearing a black suit, black shoes and tie, and a white button up. His hair was pushed neatly to the side, and his beard was short and trimmed. He looked mouthwatering.

His eyes meet mine after a few moments. They didn't stay on me for a second but it was enough time for his eyes to flash golden briefly. I smiled to myself and looked away after he did.

"So, do you gentlemen have mates or kids?" I turned my attention back to the men, who hadn't even noticed it had left them.

I accepted another mimosa from the waitress beside me as she took my empty glass. I sipped slowly while they spoke.

I continued to talk to the guys for a while, but I eventually got hungry again and decided to get more food. I told them all that I'd see them later and left their discussion about whose mate was a better cook.

I made a detour to the buffet when I saw one of the trays a familiar waitress was carrying. They had mini lemon pound cakes with an iced glaze drizzled over the top. I grabbed one and took a bite, the dense, moist cake filling my taste buds. I finished it in a few bites and washed it down with the last of my mimosa.

Once I finally made it to the waffle bar, I filled a plate with a waffle and topped it with cream cheese and powdered sugar. I grabbed a fork and knife and turned around, looking around the room to decide where to sit.

The room was getting fuller than it had been earlier. More chairs were being occupied now, so there were more people standing around in groups.

My eyes finally landed on a table in front of the windows. Kat, Nathan, Lili, Matt, Dalton, and Tyler were all sitting around it. I made my way over to them, grabbing another mimosa on the way and plopping down between Kat and Nathan.

I cut into my waffle and lifted a piece of it to my mouth, chewing slowly. Kat and Lili were talking together, discussing some spell I couldn't understand. The guys were talking about food of all things. I decided their conversation was way more in my league than witchcraft, so I focused on them.

"I'm just saying, who in their right mind eats their waffles with chicken and gravy?" Nathan said incredulously, looking over at Matt.

My face scrunched up in disgust when I looked down at his plate. It had a waffle, but instead of normal toppings like syrup or whipped cream, his was covered in fried chicken strips topped with brown gravy.

I nearly gagged when I saw the ruined waffle. I saw those toppings at the waffle bar, but I assumed no one would be stupid enough to add them for the simple fact that they just didn't belong on a waffle. I knew Matt was known to eat almost anything but this was insanity.

"It's good," Matt insisted as he cut into it and took a bite.

"That is disgusting," I told him. "Waffles are supposed to be sweet, you freak."

"Agreed," Nathan added.

"It's savory. Just as good as sweet." He took another bite.

"Chicken, I might comprehend. But gravy? Gross."

"Coming from the human vacuum?" He snorted.

"You're the only human vacuum I know, Matthew." I rolled my eyes and turned my attention back to my own waffle.

"I disagree."

"You do that. Have you called home lately?" I asked him, changing the subject. I called this morning, and my mom told me Selena had been working with Brody for the last week. She and Dad were impressed with her and were even leaving her as back up to Brody over the weekend while they had a romantic getaway trip.

"Not in a few days. Why?"

"Did anyone tell you about Selena?" I asked.

"No, what about her?" He continued to eat the monstrosity of a waffle.

"She's been going to work with Brody. She's trying to get more involved."

"Well, it's about damn time she grew up."

"She'd punch you in the throat if she heard you say that," Kat said with a snicker, joining in on our conversation.

"Probably." He shrugged. "I'm glad to hear that though."

"Yeah, me too. She's even staying in tonight. Mom and Dad are going out of town for the weekend and she's staying at home."

"Wow. Never thought I'd see the day."

"Is that significant?" Tyler asked. He was cutting into his normal waffle, covered in nothing but maple syrup.

"Very. Selena Keating staying home on a Saturday night? It's like a miracle. I doubt it will ever happen again," Matt said.

"I don't know," I mumbled to my brother. "I think she's really trying to change."

"Well, I hope you're right." Matt took another bite of the monster waffle.

"I'm always right," I corrected him.

"That's debatable," Dalton added.

"Shut up, Collins. Don't make me knock you on your ass again." I smirked smugly at him.

He shot me a nasty glare but didn't reply.

"So, what's everyone doing for the rest of the day?" I asked, looking around the table.

"We all decided to go for a run after this. You want to go?" Tyler asked me.

"Hmm, maybe. Kat, Lili, what are you two doing?" I turned my attention to them.

"We're going to get in some practice with Niki later. We just started working with wind. I want to master my first wind spell before Monday," Kat said.

I nodded and turned back to Tyler. "I'll probably go with you guys then. Either that, or I'll be so full from all this food that I'll need a nap," I joked.

"Full or drunk?" Kat teased as I sipped on my mimosa.

"It's only my fourth," I said in defense. Truth be told though, I was starting to feel just slightly buzzed. I wasn't planning on getting drunk but a little buzz was fine.

"Whatever you say, boozy." Nathan laughed at me. I rolled my eyes.

Nathan turned to Tyler, starting another discussion. I couldn't hear what they were saying. My attention was suddenly drawn to King Finnian, my entire focus on him. He was standing around, a coffee cup in his hands. I looked at him in admiration at first, but then my thoughts took a nasty turn.

Standing in front of him was some blonde bombshell. She was everything I wasn't. She was tall, where I was short. She had big breasts and a shapely ass, whereas mine were seriously lacking. Her blonde hair was long and full of voluminous waves, not a hair out of place; my dark brown curls were frizzy and wild. She looked like a Victoria's Secret model, I looked like troll doll.

A shot of unfamiliar insecurity ran through me. I was usually full of confidence in myself and my appearance, but taking in the beautiful she-wolf he was talking to, I couldn't help but doubt myself.

She looked up at him through her mile long eyelashes and bit her lip. Even from a distance, I could see the expression in her blue eyes. She was giving him a *take-me-to-bed* look. I balled my hands into a fist, my nails digging into my palms; they would have broken the skin had I not cut them short recently.

Kat distracted me before I could try to listen in on their conversation.

"Hey, you okay?" she whispered in my ear, shaking my shoulder to get my attention.

My eyes left my mate and the bombshell he was talking to and met my best friend's emerald gaze.

I nodded and swallowed the last of my mimosa. "I'm fine. I'm going to go get another drink."

She looked unsure, but I stood up and walked away before she could argue. I grabbed another champagne flute on my way over.

I was about ten feet away from them, but I didn't make it any further. Niki was suddenly standing in front of me, blocking my way. I nearly stumbled in surprise. I hadn't even seen her nearby. My drink sloshed in my glass, but luckily didn't spill as I came to a standstill. Niki gave me an understanding but firm look. Her eyes said what her mouth didn't. Not here.

I bit my lip in frustration, trying to hold my tongue. I wanted nothing more than to push her out of the way, march up to them, beat the hell out of the blondie, and mark my territory in front of her, letting her and everyone else know Finnian was mine.

I respected Niki though, so I pushed those urges away and nodded slightly at her.

"Kendall, dear. Come, I want to introduce you to some people."

She grabbed my arm lightly and pulled me away. I gave one last fleeting look to my mate, downed the rest of my mimosa, and followed Niki, putting on a fake, polite smile. Time to put on an act and let everyone think I was fine.

*　　*　　*

I stuffed my face with another mini pound cake, following it with a chug of iced coffee. I was feeling more than buzzed and had cut myself off about twenty minutes ago. I just swallowed my third pound cake, which was helping soak up the alcohol a bit.

I have been in this brunch for over four hours now, and I was getting tired of it. I was beyond full but I ate when I was annoyed, so I continued to stuff my face.

I didn't really have much reason to be annoyed anymore but I still was. My good mood from the morning was long gone.

King Finnian hadn't talked to the blonde girl long, much to my appreciation. That made me happy, but it sucked to see him talk to everyone but me.

Niki had been steering me around, making me talk to more people than I cared to count. She wouldn't let me get near King Finnian. If my eyes even strayed to him for too long, she would distract me. It confused me, since I thought she was on team Findall, but I suppose I was wrong.

Despite my foul mood, I tried to be polite and engage everyone in good conversation. I didn't want to get a reputation of being a bitch when I'm the daughter of a future Council member. So, I put on a smile, tried to remember everyone's names, and let my Keating charm out while keeping my Keating temper at bay.

Niki had assured me that this brunch would be coming to an end soon, for which I was extremely grateful for. Everyone pretty much finished eating, and some of the attendees have already left.

No one was sitting anymore; they were all just standing around, sipping mimosas or coffee and munching on the finger foods that the waiters were still carrying around.

"You're Jefferson's daughter, correct?" the man in front of me asked.

I think his name was Rylan, but it was hard to remember.

"I am. Do you know him?"

"I'm a member of the Council. I have never met him personally but I did hear he is next in line to receive a seat."

"That's the hope. It would be such an honor to him and our pack." I smiled courteously, repeating the same line that I had told every other Council member that I'd met.

Before he could answer, our attention was drawn to the front of the room. King Finnian was standing on a small stage and was waiting to give a short speech. Once all eyes were on him and all voices silenced, he spoke.

"I want to thank everyone for attending our monthly brunch. I have enjoyed speaking with everyone and discussing matters important to the kingdom. I will take all suggestions given today into serious consideration. I look forward to seeing you all again next time. Thank you again for your attendance and please, drive safe."

Everyone bowed to him and exposed their necks one last time. He stepped down gracefully and exited the room through a side door at the back that I hadn't noticed earlier.

"It was so nice to meet you." I smiled at him and shook his hand one last time.

"You as well, Kendall. Maybe I'll see you again before you leave the castle."

I nodded and smiled a tight smile. I was beyond ready to get out of here. I already decided what I was going to do next. I was going to see my mate. Maybe it was the alcohol again or the fact that I was insecure and jealous, but I was going to see him and nothing was going to stop me.

I said goodbye to Niki. She returned it and gave me a knowing look. I liked to think that she knew my next move and was going to make it safe for me to go to him.

I mindlinked Matt that I was going to take a nap instead of running with them. I grabbed one last mimosa from a waiter next to me on my way out, downed it in one long gulp, and gave it back with a tight smile.

I found the same hidden stairwell that I had used last time. I walked quickly and quietly, keeping a look out for people that may see me. I made it to the sixth floor in record time, not passing by a single soul.

I slipped into the door of the sixth floor, leaving my heels outside so I didn't make too much noise. Goosebumps welled up on my skin. I forgot how cold it was up here. It wasn't just the temperature . . . it felt lonely, abandoned, as weird as that sounded. That made it feel colder.

I rubbed my arms as I walked. My bare feet slapped against the cold stone floor, my toes freezing. I didn't look around like last time, my mind fully focused on finding Finnian again. I had a few things I wanted to say to him. I wasn't leaving until I did.

I wasn't slammed into a wall this time. I was able to make it to his bedroom. I remembered the way, but I followed his scent as well, breathing it in as I went.

Once I reached the wooden double doors, I pushed one open and walked in like I owned the place, not feeling the least bit shy or doubtful.

He was sitting on one of the chairs, the one that was worn from use, in front of the unlit fireplace.

He didn't turn around; he just continued to sit there, staring into the cold fireplace. I cleared my throat impatiently, but he still ignored me.

I groaned in annoyance and walked around him, stopping in his line of sight. His eyes moved up and finally landed on mine. His expression was blank, empty. I had an expectant look and put my hands on my hips, which were cocked to the side dramatically.

"I thought I told you not to come up here," he said coldly.

"I don't really give a shit what you told me. Who the hell was that blonde bitch earlier?" I sneered.

He returned my sneer, finally showing some emotion. "None of your damn business. How many times do I have to tell you to remember your place?"

"How many times do I have to tell you how much of an ass you are before you stop being one?" I countered.

"That's not how that works. I'm your king. You listen to me."

"Well guess fucking what. I'm your mate, which makes me your queen. And I'm tired of your attitude. Get over yourself."

"You're not my queen. You will never be my queen," he spat out to me.

His words hurt, but I tried not to let it show.

"And what? That blonde girl will?" My voice dripped with jealousy.

"That doesn't concern you."

"Actually, it does. I'm a werewolf and you're the Werewolf King. Your queen concerns everyone, but especially me. I can promise you, another woman will never be my queen." My voice was filled with spite and hate.

"And you'll never be mine."

"Why are you such a fucking coward? When are you ever going to admit how you feel about me? Whatever is holding you back, just tell me. We can work it out, together."

His eyes glowed golden now and an enraged growl rumbled from his chest. I was suddenly backed against the wall. He was looming over me, trying to use his size to intimidate me. I wouldn't let it work. I wouldn't show him fear.

"When are you going to understand? You're so convinced that I am hiding something that you missed what I've been trying to tell you this whole time. You're just too stubborn to listen. So listen now and listen closely, because this is the last time I'm saying it."

He paused to make sure I was listening. I couldn't muster up any words so I remained silent.

"There is no big secret that is holding me back. There is nothing we need to work out. I'm not a coward, I just don't want you. It's as simple as that. I don't want you. I'll never want you. My wolf may be pushing me towards you but I'm not. There is no hidden reason why. Get that through your head and move on."

I pushed back the tears that threatened to fill my eyes, which I knew were glowing gold to match his. My emotions were raging through me, but I focused on the fury I felt. I pushed him back with all the strength I had. He went back willingly to put a few feet of distance between us.

"You're a bastard. I hate you," I spat out between gritted teeth. "I'm done with this shit. If you let me walk out of this room right now, then I'm done trying. You won't get to change your mind later. If you let me leave, then this is through," I warned him as I took a step away from the wall.

He paused for a moment, letting my words sink in before completely shattering what was left of my heart. "It's about damn time." He looked me directly in the eyes, not showing any signs of hesitation or regret.

I nodded slowly, looking at him with unfocused eyes, not really seeing him. "Goodbye, King Finnian." My voice was devoid of emotion.

I walked past him, not once looking back. I thought he might stop me, but he didn't. I made it out of his room and his floor, not once with him stopping me.

I made my way back to my room, pacing back and forth. I growled in rage and frustration, pausing in front of the couch. I used my werewolf strength to lift the end of it and flip it across the room. It landed harshly on the ground. I grabbed the table next to it and threw it as well. It smashed into the wall and shattered, splinters of wood raining down everywhere.

I continued to destroy the room before I made a decision. I growled again and fought off a shift, needing to stay human.

I left everything behind, including my cell phone. I didn't need anything. I'd get it all later, or hell, I'd even replace it.

I stormed out of my room and into Matt's. I looked around, searching the area before my eyes landed on the object I needed. I grabbed it off his bedside table and stomped out.

I made my way through the castle to where I needed to go. I came across people, no one I knew, but still people. No one stopped me or dared to even talk to me. I think they were scared.

It took a few minutes, but I finally reached my destination. I got in Matt's SUV and cranked it as hard as I could without breaking it. I pressed the garage door open before I got in, so I backed out as soon as I buckled my seat belt.

I was still buzzed but it didn't matter. Even with alcohol in my system, my reflexes were still faster, stronger, and better than a human's.

I slammed my foot on the gas after I threw it in reverse. I threw it into drive before it even had time to stop completely. As I drove around the side of the castle, the valet looked at me weirdly, but no one stopped me. Gates opened for me and everyone let me through. Which was good, because they did not want to tell me no right now.

Once I had made it through security, I entered the address into the GPS. It guided me to the freeway.

It was time to go home.

CHAPTER FOURTEEN

The drive home didn't take nearly as long as I thought it would. My hate filled thoughts occupied my time and made it seem to pass quickly. My thoughts only proved one thing; I had a slight anger problem and I could conjure up some pretty sadistic images when I was pissed.

I was a little ashamed to admit how gruesome my cognitive processes became when I was in such a rage. I thought up at least a hundred different ways I wanted to torture King Finnian.

It worried me a little at first, but I soon just went with it. I knew my fury was a cover for the heartbreak I was currently feeling. Anger I could deal with. Anger was easy, I had someone to blame—King Finnian.

If I let myself feel the pain and sorrow that I buried deep inside, I didn't know what I would do. I'd have no one to blame but myself, since I was apparently the problem. I couldn't face that yet, so I focused my energy on hating him.

The music made it easier. The first two hours of my drive were made in silence. The only time any noise was emitted in the SUV was when another driver pissed me off and I screamed insults at them. My insults had gotten very creative and a lot more frequent.

After silently stewing for two hours, I felt the need to blare the radio as loud as it could go. Unfortunately, I had left my phone behind, so I was stuck with nothing but the radio. Fortunately, fate seemed on my side for once, because I found a heavy metal station that matched my mood perfectly.

After three hours doing nothing but screaming angry lyrics nonstop, I finally reached the Keating Pack Territory. I had yet to talk to any members of my family. I felt Matt and Dalton pushing against my mental barriers, trying to mindlink with me, but I blocked them out.

Surprisingly enough, I hadn't heard from anyone else, letting me know that Matt hadn't called home to let them know I had left the castle. My only guess was that Kat managed to convince him to let me be for a while; see what I did next before he got me in trouble with Dad. I was extremely grateful to her. I wasn't ready to deal with my parents or brothers. Meaning my next move would have to be sneaky.

I pulled the car over on the territory line. I waited for a few seconds for someone to greet me. Humans would just drive right through. That didn't happen often, since our little town was out of the way and away from any major roads. But werewolves could sense the boundary line and would stop for inspection.

Dad had men doing rounds, so there were always at least five wolves hiding in the woods, guarding the road where our territory started. Not to mention a patrol around the entire outer edge of the boundary line in case someone tried to come in through the forest instead of the road.

The car idled, and I turned the radio down low, waiting for someone to come over. I was keeping my fingers crossed that it was someone I knew; who wouldn't mindlink Brody that I was here. I got lucky when I saw an old friend walk out of the woods and around the front of my car to stop by my window.

I rolled my window down, letting the fresh, cool air blow in. It was considerably warmer here than the castle but since twilight had set in, the air had a slight chill to it.

I smiled brightly, not letting my foul mood show, as I took in the face of Theo Anderson, my ex-boyfriend from high school.

"Kendall? What are you doing here? No one told us you were coming back." He sounded surprised, which was warranted.

"It was a last minute trip. I was homesick." I put on my best smile and looked at him through my eyelashes flirtatiously. "I actually didn't tell them I was coming home. I wanted to surprise them in the morning. Could you maybe keep it between us?"

He hesitated. "I really want to, but you know how Alpha Jefferson is. He wants us to notify him or Brody of anyone who enters the territory."

I pouted my lips and widened my eyes. I stuck my hand out the window and rested it on his bicep. "Please, Theo? For me? I'll take all the blame, I promise. You know they only have that rule to make sure no one can cause trouble, and that's the last thing I want to do. You know you can trust me."

He finally relented, giving me a charming smile. "Fine, only for you. If Brody asks me if anyone came through though, I'm not going to lie," he warned me.

"Okay, that's fine. Thanks." I leaned out and kissed his cheek, lingering for a few seconds. I pulled back with a smile, wiggled my fingers at him, rolled up my window, and continued down the road.

I made it to my house in record time. I pulled the SUV into the garage, which was empty besides my car and now Matt's, and shut the garage door behind me so no one could see I was here.

I was pretty sure Selena was the only one home since her car was the only one parked in the driveway, but I couldn't be positive. The vehicles here were never a good indicator of who was home since we ran a lot.

Our town had no humans, so we could run in wolf form wherever we wanted. It wasn't uncommon for one of us to leave our car somewhere and run home. I just hoped that what Mom had told me before was still valid.

After the garage door was completely shut, I exited the SUV and walked in through the side door that led into our kitchen.

The kitchen, living room, and dining rooms were just as it was when I had left. There was a covered glass jar that was filled with an assortment of cookies. Mom always kept it stocked with homemade cookies for us kids and for guests. The kitchen was clean, like always, with only a pizza box on the center island.

The TV was off for once and the couches were unoccupied. There was no one standing in front of the fridge or pantry, or sitting at the bar eating something. I wasn't used to seeing the house so empty and quiet. The only thing I could hear was a lone TV upstairs.

Growing up as an alpha's daughter and with three siblings, our house was usually filled with people. I couldn't remember a time where I was ever really alone in the house. Even if all my siblings were gone, we usually had other pack members hanging around. Whether it was someone's friend, someone here to see Dad, or a pack member who was helping Mom or vice versa. It was always someone.

I didn't like the quiet stillness. It felt wrong; it felt like change, and I was sick of change.

I frowned and walked out of the room and towards the stairs. I barely made it to the top before Selena burst out of our bedroom door. She looked ready to shift and fight but relaxed once she saw it was just me.

"What the hell are you doing here?" she asked demandingly. She sniffed the air, her face scrunching up in confusion. "And what is that smell?"

"I live here. And what smell?"

She sniffed the air once again then ignored my question. She promptly forgot about the smell.

"You're supposed to be at the castle. Why are you here?" She crossed her arms over her chest and gave me a pointed stare, her eyebrow tilted upwards.

"Because I wanted to come home," I answered vaguely.

"Does Dad know you're here?" She followed me into our room when I walked around her to get inside.

It was just like I left it. The walls were still lavender. My bed was still pushed into one corner, parallel to hers. It was still a wooden queen-sized four-poster bed with cheetah sheets and comforter. It was still messy, unmade, and covered in clothes. The TV was turned on, with a movie on Netflix being played. Clothes were still haphazardly flung everywhere, and our desk and bedside tables were still littered with dust and other crap that probably needed to be thrown away.

I breathed a sigh of relief. At least my room still felt lived in, especially with Selena nagging in my ear like usual.

I turned to her as I finished taking in our bedroom. I matched her stance as I crossed my arms over my chest and cocked my hip to the side. "No, he doesn't. And you're not going to tell him." I narrowed my eyes at her threateningly.

"He's going to find out, Kendall. He's only gone for the night. He'll be back in the morning."

"Well, that's when he'll find out then. But he sure as shit isn't going to find out tonight; not from you."

"Fine, but only if you tell me why you're here." She relented and walked past me to plop down on her bed, still facing me. I did the same on my bed and looked at her as well.

I groaned in frustration, not wanting to confess everything.

"Things didn't work out, now I'm home," I grumbled bitterly.

"Gee, what a detailed story. Now care to expand a bit?" she said dryly.

I glared daggers at her. "No, actually, I don't. You'll find out when I'm damn good and ready for you to." I stood up. "Now, we're going out. I need to have some fun tonight and get wasted."

My earlier mimosa buzz had long since worn off, and I needed a drink more than anything. I needed to have a crazy night where I could drink and dance my pain away; a night like I used to have before I went to that castle.

"You want to get wasted? That's not like you anymore," she mumbled.

"What are you, my mom?" I looked at her in annoyance.

"No, I'm not. I'm your sister, and I'm kind of worried about you," she admitted.

"Get over yourself. All you do is party so don't give me shit, because I need a night of fun. Now, you can either get ready and go with me, or you can sit down and shut the hell up so I can go alone. Your choice," I snapped.

I knew deep down I was being a bitch, and she didn't deserve my hateful attitude, but I couldn't stop myself. She was the only one around, and I couldn't keep my anger in. She glared up at me but stood up anyways.

"I'm only going because someone needs to watch your dumbass tonight. And why don't you take the bitchiness down a few notches."

"Why don't you quit being so sensitive?" I suggested sarcastically.

I walked into our walk-in closet before she could respond. She followed behind me, looking through her side of the closet. Luckily, I still had plenty of things to wear despite leaving all my clothes at the castle.

I had packed all the nice looking ones, so they were all still there, but all my party clothes were here. When I had packed my bags, I didn't think I'd have any use for them. I wasn't planning on partying while I was at the castle, and I needed to look presentable to help my dad get in the Council. Maybe I should have shown more skin?

I shook my head and pushed my insecure thoughts away. I didn't want to think about him tonight, and I was certainly done feeling insecure about myself.

I rifled through my clothes, frowning as I went. Nothing was right; nothing until the last outfit.

I picked it up with a smile, pulling out a new bra and underwear from my drawer and stripped out of my clothes, not caring that Selena was still in the closet with me.

I got dressed quickly and walked over to our full-length mirror hanging from the door. I looked myself over from all angles and smiled happily.

Selena's jaw dropped when she turned around after putting on a pair of black shorts and a loose olive-green V-neck with black combat boots.

"You look like you're getting dressed to work the corner, not going to a house party."

"You're just jealous that I'm hotter than you."

Truth be told, I was showing way too much skin, but that's what I was going for. I had a pair of torn, high-waisted blue jean shorts on. They were short, with my ass cheeks peeking out of the hem. I also wore a tight, lacy black crop top. It was low cut and was paired with a lacy black pushup bra. It made my boobs look bigger than they really were and showed way more than was appropriate. I matched it with a pair of black sandals since heels would be too hard to dance in.

I had the outfit for a few years now but had never actually worn it before. I bought it without actually trying it on first. I didn't realize it showed so much skin until I got home and put it on. I always meant to return it but just kept forgetting to. It had been hanging in my closet unworn, since I usually liked to keep something to the imagination. Not tonight.

"If anyone asks you how much for an hour, tell them you're off the clock."

"Ha ha," I mumbled dryly. I walked past her and into our bathroom. I added dark eyeshadows and winged black eyeliner to my eyelids, making my mossy green eyes look darker. I put on a few coats of mascara, touched up a few other spots on my face, and painted my lips with matte burgundy lipstick.

As I took in my overall final look, I was pleased. I looked hot.

Selena had already finished and was waiting for me in our room.

"Are you sure you don't want to at least add a cardigan?"

"It will get hot with a cardigan." I shrugged off her request.

"Maybe at least a different shirt? Your boobs look like they're about to fall out."

"Stop nagging me," I said dismissively. "You sound like a prude."

She rolled her eyes. "Whatever. Let's just get this over with."

We left our room and the house. We didn't bother to lock the door when we left; we never did. Even if someone was stupid enough to break into the alpha's house, a lock wouldn't keep a werewolf out anyways, so it would be pointless.

We decided to take Selena's red Mustang. It was filled with trash and clothes; I had to throw a ton of shit to the backseat before I could actually get in.

She started her car, and I immediately took over her radio. I sent a silent thanks to whoever controlled the songs playing because "Nightmare" by Avenged Sevenfold started playing. I turned it up as loud as it would go, or as loud as a werewolf could tolerate anyways. The bass thumped against my leg as the angry music blared around us as I screamed along to the lyrics.

After the first chorus, Selena turned it down and looked at me strangely.

"What?" I snapped in annoyance.

"You sound so mad . . . and bitter. What happened?" She seemed legitimately worried now.

"I told you, I don't want to talk about it. Back off."

I cut off any further attempts of conversation as I turned the music back up and started singing along. I didn't ask where we were going and didn't really care to know. As long as they had booze and people, it didn't matter to me. I knew Selena would know of a party going on, which is why I even included her to begin with. She always knew of the best parties.

By the time the song was finished, she was pulling down a dead end street. It was secluded from other houses, so no one had to worry about noise complaints. I could hear the music thumping from down the block. I dulled my senses as much as I could. I knew a couple drinks would also help with that.

Selena maneuvered into an open spot. Cars were littered up and down the street, with the driveway filled with even more cars.

She shut off the car, and we both got out and walked towards the house. The house was vaguely familiar, but I wasn't sure who it belonged to. I knew most people around our age, and by that I meant within twenty years of us, but I didn't know everyone.

The front yard had several stragglers. A couple people were throwing up in the rose bushes already—lightweights—and a few people were sitting on the porch railings, passing a joint around.

We walked through their cloud of smoke. They recognized us, even though I didn't know them, and bowed respectfully. Even when they were high, they could still sense someone of Alpha blood.

We nodded and continued to the front door. Selena opened it and let us in without knocking. The house was of decent size, but it was packed to the brim with people.

Some rap song I didn't know was playing, the bass pounding in my eardrums. The living room and kitchen were in front of us. The living room was full of people dancing, some of them dry humping the person nearest to them. The kitchen was full of people standing around talking, making drinks, even a couple of people laid across the counter tops doing body shots.

I grabbed Selena's wrist and pulled her towards the kitchen so we could get a drink. She followed behind me, although she seemed reluctant.

Once we made it further inside, I could see through the windows into the backyard. There were even more partygoers outside than in the house, but there was more room to move around since the backyard was spacious.

Some people were dancing and some were surrounding a keg. There was a beer pong table set up on the big patio, which had drawn a large crowd. People started cheering when one of the guys made the ping pong ball go in a red plastic cup. The other guy picked up the cup and chugged.

When we made it to the kitchen, Selena was pulled into a hug by a girl who was already drunk. I dropped her wrist, rolled my eyes, and grabbed my own cup and filled it with Crown and Coke, adding way more Crown than I usually would. By the time I finished making my drink and took my first large gulp, the girl released Selena and turned towards me.

"Who is this?" She sipped from her cup.

I rolled my eyes again. She was either really drunk or really stupid. How could she not tell I was her sister? Not only should she be able to sense my Alpha blood and put two and two together, but she should also see the resemblance. Selena and I shared more features than we didn't.

Selena began introducing us, "This is my sister, Kendall. Kendall, this is my friend Sarah. This is her house."

Sarah's grey eyes widened in excitement. "Oh, it's so nice to meet you. I've heard so much about you," she practically yelled, causing me to flinch at her shrill voice.

"Yeah, you too," I mumbled, not even trying to sound convincing.

"I can't believe it's taken so long for us to meet," she continued with her shrill voice.

I quickly chugged the rest of my drink before answering and poured another, leaving out the Coke this time.

"What a shame," I muttered insincerely.

"Kendall, don't be so rude," Selena scolded me.

"Selena, back the fuck off." I rolled my eyes at her.

Before she could say anything else, I refilled my cup again—after downing its contents first—and walked off, leaving her behind. She didn't try to stop me, probably so she could apologize for my rude behavior.

I took big gulps from my cup as I walked out of the house and into the backyard. I scanned the yard, looking for a familiar face. I got lucky when I saw a group of people standing around talking. I went to school with all of them.

I made my way in their direction and received a hug from one of the girls when she saw me.

"Kendall! What are you doing here? I thought you were gone until next month?" The girl pulled back to look at me.

Her name is Meredith. We were friends in high school but had drifted apart a bit after we graduated. We still hung out sometimes, but we were usually busy with our own lives and didn't get to see each other often.

Around her were people I was also friends with, but not as much as her.

"Hey, Mere. I just got back today. Guess I missed home."

She nodded and accepted my answer. I was glad she didn't probe any further, because I didn't want to have to be rude to her.

"Well I'm glad you're here. It's been months since we hung out. Is Kat back too?" She led me into the circle they had formed, and we both sipped from our cups.

"Nope, just me. Kat, Matt, and Dalton are still at the castle. Selena came with me tonight. She's still inside."

I inspected the faces around me closer. I smiled tightly at all of them. Once I reached the last guy in the group, my smile turned flirty. I didn't know how I had missed him before. This was perfect.

Standing on the other side of Meredith was none other than Theo, who had let me into pack territory earlier. When we dated back in high school it was never serious, but we used to fool around. That was basically our entire relationship; going to parties together, getting shitfaced, and doing everything besides fucking.

I hadn't been paying close attention earlier but now that I was, I realized he was just as handsome as I remembered. A nagging voice in the back of my mind told me that the look I was giving him was wrong; that he wasn't handsome and that I shouldn't think he was. My need for retribution silenced that voice.

He was the opposite of *him* in every way possible. He had shaggy blonde hair that was always messy. He always looked disheveled but it worked for him. He had a surfer type of look. His warm brown eyes always had a mischievous twinkle, and he always had a grin on his face, showing off his deep dimples which were easy to see on his clean-shaven face. He was almost always happy and always had a smile on his face. His face was one of the most expressive I had ever seen.

He had a sexy body to match his pretty face. He wasn't the tallest wolf I had ever seen, but he was a good five inches taller than me so it didn't matter. He was leaner and not as obviously muscled as some wolves, but his body was still hard and well defined. I had spent enough time in the past exploring it, so I knew that for sure. He always dressed casually; he was wearing a pair of ripped, worn blue jeans, a faded old t-shirt, and a pair of tennis shoes. A lot more casual than a suit.

He gave me a flirty look as well once his eyes landed back on my face. "You look beautiful as always Kendall. It's good to see you again."

"Thanks, Theo," I said in the sultriest voice I could muster and looked at him through my lashes. "I don't know how I forgot how handsome you are. I'm glad I ran into you again."

I sipped at my drink and looked at him over the rim. When I pulled it away, I slowly licked the whiskey from my top lip, careful to not mess up my lipstick. His expressive face showed desire, and I smiled at him again.

"So how was your time at the castle?" Meredith asked, drawing my attention away from Theo.

"Uneventful," I muttered.

With the moment ruined, I tipped my cup back and swallowed the rest of the Crown inside.

"You need another drink?" Theo asked, ever the gentleman.

"Yes, please." My flirty smile was back. "I'm drinking Crown. Thanks, Theo."

I handed him my empty cup, brushing my fingers against his; lingering for a few seconds.

"No problem, beautiful." He grinned down at me then walked back towards the house.

"You and Theo seem to be picking up right where you left off," Meredith said suggestively, wiggling her dark eyebrows.

"If all goes according to plan." I giggled.

"Well, you two are certainly a cute couple. And he's always been super into you."

"As long as he's *into* me tonight."

Meredith and the other girl, Tara, barked a laugh. The other two guys who were standing with us had been called away, so it was just the three of us now. Tara and I were acquaintances but never really friends.

"You seem different," Meredith commented after her laughter died down. She looked at me, scrutinizing.

"Still the same Kendall." I smiled at her, trying to be convincing.

"No, something is different about you. Even the way you're dressing." She glanced down at my outfit.

"Just trying something new. I've been locked up in the castle for weeks. I just wanted to have some fun tonight and let loose."

She nodded but looked like she still didn't believe me. It didn't matter what she believed so long as she kept her mouth shut.

"I'm gonna go find Theo. It was good seeing you Meredith. Let's get together soon, yeah?"

She nodded and we hugged again. "Good seeing you too, Tara." I wiggled my fingers at her in a wave goodbye. She did the same, and I turned and walked away.

I met Theo halfway in the backyard and put the flirty smile back on. He handed me my cup and our fingers brushed again.

"Thanks, handsome." I batted my lashes and took another gulp from my cup, swallowing the burning liquor like a champ. My stomach burned, but in the best way.

"Anything for you." He winked at me. "I brought the bottle." He grinned and held up the half empty bottle of Crown.

"You're the best." I pulled him into a hug, molding my body against his and even rubbing against him slightly.

I pulled back after a few seconds and grabbed his hand, intertwining our fingers.

"Let's go sit."

I pulled him over to the empty swing further in the yard. We both sat down, and I sat as close to him as I could get. I crossed my legs slowly and let the bare skin of my calf rub against his. He placed the bottle of Crown on the ground and rested his cup on the arm rest of the swing. I rested mine against my thigh.

Our hands were still intertwined, and the back of his hand was also pressed against my bare thigh, higher than my cup.

"I missed you, you know," I told him before I lifted my drink to my lips, taking a long gulp.

"I missed you, too. It's not the same around here without you." He bumped his shoulder against mine playfully.

"Good thing I'm back for good then, huh?"

"A great thing." He took a drink of his beer.

"So, tell me . . ." I said seductively, "are you seeing anyone right now?"

"Absolutely not. Are you?" He beamed down at me.

"I wasn't. I am now."

I chugged the last of my drink and threw my cup carelessly to the ground as I let go of his hand. I uncrossed my legs and slung one over his lap, straddling him. He grabbed my hips to hold me in place. I leaned into him, letting my breasts rub against his chest. My lips skimmed his jaw, up to his ear. I teasingly bit his ear lobe before whispering softly in his ear.

"I'll always be drawn back to you, Theo Anderson."

His hands skimmed up my bare stomach until they rested right under my ribs, his palms warm against my cold skin. Deep down, his hands on me felt wrong. His body underneath mine felt wrong. But I pushed those thoughts away and focused on the familiarity of his face and body.

"Dance with me," I told him when I pulled away from his ear.

He nodded and kissed my cheek. I got off him slowly and grabbed his hand, pulling him up as well. I grabbed the bottle off the ground and twisted the lid off. I threw it down and took a long sip straight from the bottle. I walked towards the makeshift dance floor with him right behind me, his hands on my hips.

Once we reached the mass of dancing bodies, we stopped. I turned around and wrapped my arms around his neck, the bottle hanging from my hand loosely, his arms wrapped around my waist, resting right above my ass.

It was dark outside now; the only source of light was from the moon and the bright porch light. The grass was short and covered in a layer of dew. It soaked my feet, making my toes colder.

I didn't recognize the song playing but it was good to dance to since it had a fast beat. We moved our bodies sensually together. My chest was completely pressed against his, not an inch of space between us. I ran my free hand over his shoulder and down his chest, raking my nails against his shirt lightly.

I turned around and started grinding my ass against him. I threw my head back against his shoulder as I chugged from the bottle. His hands wrapped around my waist, drawing me even closer. His hands splayed out against my stomach, his thumbs caressing the skin under my breasts.

I continued to take long gulps from the bottle as I moved. I felt his erection pressing against my ass, causing a small smile to pull at my lips. His lips pressed against my neck, peppering kisses on my skin as my head rested on his shoulder.

The song ended after a few minutes but another one started up right after. I continued to move my body with him, letting my eyes flutter open and closed and losing myself in the moment. I continued to drink, letting the alcohol numb me of everything.

It didn't last nearly long enough. I suppose all good things must come to an end. I heard my name being called and the music shutting off abruptly. Through my alcohol induced haze, I managed to open my eyes and scan the yard for the source of the noise.

My eyes widened in surprise when I saw Tyler storming towards me, Selena right behind him. I blinked hard, making sure the whiskey wasn't causing me to see him when he wasn't really there. When I opened my eyes, he was even closer. Guess he was real.

I vaguely felt Theo move away from me, but it was hard to tell. My mind was wasted and confused. He could have completely disappeared into thin air right then and I probably wouldn't have noticed.

Tyler stopped a couple feet in front of me, and Selena stopped right by his side. Had I been sober, I probably would have questioned why she stopped so close to him but my mind was occupied with finding out why he was here.

"Tyler?" I muttered in confusion.

"Kendall, you're making a mistake," he told me seriously. His eyes left mine and looked over my shoulder. I turned to see him looking at Theo.

"What?" I continued to question, feeling disoriented.

"You don't want to do this. I know you're angry and hurt, but you'll regret this even more." His eyes shone with honesty.

"Are you talking about Theo?" I managed to say without slurring.

"Yes, that's what I'm talking about."

I snorted unattractively. "At least he wants me," I spat out. The fog in my brain cleared, just slightly, as the familiar feeling of rejection and heartbreak churned in my gut.

"He wouldn't have sent me if he didn't want you." His voice lost its hard edge.

"What are you two talking about?" Selena asked, looking between us in confusion.

"It's not my place to tell you that, mi alma." He looked down at her adoringly. He grabbed her hand, holding it in his, and brought it to his lips; placing a soft kiss on her knuckles. My brows knitted together. "Ask your sister."

Both their eyes turned back to me. A shot of jealousy ran through me. Not because of Tyler but more because he could openly show Selena his affection. King Finnian would never do that to me. It left a bitter taste in my mouth, so I lifted the bottle again to wash it away.

Only it never made it to my mouth. Selena slapped it out of my hand, and it tumbled to the ground, landing sideways and spilling out. I looked down at it, my mouth gaping open, then back up to her.

"What the hell was that for?" I shouted to her.

"You've had enough. You're practically dry humping Theo in front of half the pack."

"You're exaggerating! And you're not my parent," I yelled at her in frustration.

"No, I'm your older sister and I'm looking out for you," she yelled back. "Now what the fuck is going on?"

"None of your business." I glared at her.

"It is my damn business, now tell me."

Before I could argue back, another familiar face stormed over to us. Brody, his eyes narrowed murderously at me.

I gulped at his expression.

"Everyone go home, now!" Brody boomed, causing everyone to immediately disperse. The backyard emptied in record time.

Theo tried to walk away, but I grabbed his hand, not ready to let him leave.

"Kendall, so help me, you better let him go. Now is not the time for games," Brody said in menacing tone.

I pouted but still let him go. He practically ran away.

"Explain why you're here. Now," he continued with his no nonsense, no arguments tone.

"I had to get away," I muttered defensively. I crossed my arms over my chest.

"From what?" he growled.

I stubbornly kept my mouth shut.

"Kendall . . ." he warned.

I finally exploded, the rage I had been feeling all day finally being released.

"It's none of your fucking business! I don't have to tell you shit!" I screamed to him, my voice taking a shrill tone.

He growled at me but before he could speak, Selena stepped forward, away from Tyler and right in front of me. Before I could speak, her palm landed hard against my cheek, knocking my head to the side. Pain exploded from where her hand made contact. I stared at her with glassy wide eyes as I held my heated cheek.

"Wake the hell up, you bitch. We're your family and we love you. Stop being so selfish. I just met my mate, and instead of getting to know him, we're both too focused on your drunken ass. Stop being such an attention seeking little drama queen and tell us what happened so that we can help fix it." She ended her rant with another slap that I, again, didn't see coming.

What I did next couldn't be stopped even if I tried. I let out a noise, that was half war cry, half scream of frustration.

I ran at her and tackled her to the ground like a football player.

CHAPTER FIFTEEN

TYLER

I stepped behind the tree that had my clothes and focused on my human form. I felt my bones reshaping and my fur receding as I shifted back from four legs to two.

Once I was back in my human form, I rolled my neck around to get rid of the tension and stood up. I grabbed my clothes off the ground and put on my black slacks, dark-blue shirt, and black shoes. I left the tie off and the top two buttons undone since I would be heading straight to my room.

I rolled up my sleeves to my elbows as I stepped from behind the tree. Soon, Nathan, Matt, and Dalton stepped out from behind their tree as well, now in human forms instead of the wolves I had just run with.

It was nice to have people to run with. I knew it was only temporary, but I enjoyed it while I could. I felt a kinship with the Keating's that I didn't usually feel. I couldn't explain why, but they felt like good friends already, even though I had only known them for less than a month. I would almost go as far to say they felt like family. It was a weird sentiment, but it was true.

It was something I wasn't used to. My own family—which had dwindled down to just my sister, brother-in-law, and mother—didn't live anywhere near the castle. I had friends here, but Finn usually kept me so busy that I didn't have time to go out much. I was enjoying having some companionship again.

Speaking of Finn, I felt him pushing on my mental shield, so I dropped it before he could force his way in. As the king, he could break down anyone's mental shield but he usually didn't unless it was an emergency.

As soon as I let my shield down, his voice boomed in my head, a slight panicky edge in his tone that was completely unfamiliar coming from him.

"Tyler, I need you in my meeting room. Now!"

Hearing the panic and worry in his voice caused my hackles to rise. Something was wrong.

"I've got to go," I called back to the guys, already running towards the castle.

I ran as fast as I could in my human form. I didn't stop until I reached Finn's meeting room. I didn't bother to knock, instead barging straight inside. I was surprised to see the room destroyed.

The table had been thrown against the wall and now laid upside down, full of cracks. The chairs also had signs of being flung against the wall as well, its plastic scattered everywhere.

He was pacing along the opposite side of the room. He didn't look normal. He was usually so put together; now, he was a mess. His hair was disheveled and sticking out in different directions, like he had been running his hands through it repeatedly. His shirt was wrinkled and torn in a few places, only half of it still tucked into his slacks. His eyes glowed golden, and his canines were extended.

"Took you fucking long enough," he growled out, sounding more animal than human. He stopped his pacing and looked over to me, his fists clenching at his sides.

I didn't reply. I didn't feel that his words needed a reply. I had gotten here as fast as I could, faster than most other wolves would have. He was just taking his frustrations out on me because whatever or whoever had caused it wasn't here.

"She's gone." If I thought he sounded animalistic before, it was nothing compared to those two words. His normal cold and detached tone was now thick with emotion.

"Who's gone?" I asked, my eyebrows drawing together. I had to handle this situation delicately. He was like a landmine, ready to explode if I made a wrong move. I had to make sure not to provoke him.

He started pacing along the wall again, not looking at me now. "I let her go. I told them to let her go. I couldn't keep her here after what I did," he mumbled under his breath, more to himself than me. He ran his hands roughly through his hair, tugging at the ends in frustration.

"You let who go?" I kept my voice even and calm.

His pacing suddenly stopped and he looked back at me. "You have to go after her, keep her safe. I don't trust anyone else to," he commanded.

Despite the fact that he had been my best friend since we were five, his command still affected me like it would any other wolf. He had enough respect for me to not command me often, and I had enough respect for him to do what he asked without a fuss. When he needed to command me though, I couldn't refuse. The only time he had really commanded me before was in emergency situations where his wolf took over and it would slip out unintentionally.

"Of course, King Finnian." I used his title since he was in full king mode now. "Who do I need to keep safe?" I questioned lightly, trying to respectfully pry information from him.

He paused slightly and took a deep breath, trying to pull himself together. It didn't seem to work.

He hesitated before he finally gave me a name. "Kendall." His eyes squeezed shut like he was in pain.

Suddenly everything clicked for me. I had suspected something was going on between them but this confirmed it. I noticed little things about them, like how their eyes always seemed to be on each other when they thought no one was looking. I doubt anyone else had noticed, since they seemed to be careful.

But I had been paying close attention since the day he accused me of flirting with her and interviewed her himself, something he would almost never do for that type of interview.

My thoughts weren't completely correct though. I thought that they were just seeing each other and sleeping together, but now I knew I was wrong. As I took in the almost feral look in his eyes, I knew the truth. She was his mate. He wouldn't look like this—like he was on the verge of a breakdown, if his wolf wasn't invested in her.

Our human side could develop feelings for someone who wasn't our mate, though I was told it didn't even compare to the mate bond, but our wolf sides couldn't feel anything for anyone but our true other halves. They didn't want anyone but the soul made for them.

"She's your mate," I stated.

He stared me down for a moment, gritting his teeth, causing his jaw to pop. Finally, he nodded once.

"Can I ask why she left?" I asked cautiously, not wanting to push him too far.

"I can't be with her. I had to push her away." He had a faraway look in his eyes. I didn't question him further. I knew he wouldn't tell me what his reason was.

"Where is she going?"

"I assume she's going home. Go to Niki's workroom. She can help you track her. Then pack a bag, take one of the SUVs, and get to her as quickly as possible."

"I will, King Finnian."

I turned to walk away, but he stopped me.

"Tyler . . ." He paused. "Please, take care of her." His eyes were pleading.

"I'll protect her with my life, Finn." I dropped the formality and promised him as his friend, not his Gamma.

I spoke nothing but the truth to him. I already considered Kendall a good friend before this and would have protected her, but now I would risk my life to keep her safe. She was not only my friend and my best friend's mate but my queen as well. As her Gamma, it's my job to keep her safe.

He cleared his throat and nodded. I returned the gesture and turned around, only pausing briefly at the door.

"I don't know what is keeping you from her, but I can see how much you care for her. I know she cares about you too. I've seen the way she looks at you. You both deserve to be happy. Just tell her what's going on. It will be a lot better if it came from you than if she finds out on her own."

He didn't say anything back to me, so I continued my way out the door. I made the short walk to Niki's workroom. I knocked twice and walked in when I heard a muffled come in.

Niki was sitting at her round table in the middle of the room. She had a spell book in front of her, her eyes scanning it quickly, not once looking up at me. She motioned me over with her hand, and I sat down in the chair next to her. She finally looked away from the ancient looking book and turned herself towards me.

"This spell will guide you to Kendall. It will feel like a GPS in your mind. You won't hear anything, but you will instinctively know where to go."

I nodded after she explained the spell. She grabbed my hand and said a few words. The candles on the table suddenly lit up. It didn't surprise me. Niki liked to work with fire. Every witch had a certain elemental preference, an element that they had an easier time working with. Niki could no doubt harness every element successfully, but she preferred fire.

Her grip on my hand tightened as she held it between both of hers. She started chanting and the flames grew larger. I didn't try to understand her words, just stayed silent and let her work.

It took a few minutes, but she finally stopped and pulled away. I felt the same, except I had this nagging feeling in my brain pulling me towards the door. Once Niki gave me the all clear, I followed through on that feeling. I made my way to my room, packed a small bag just in case I would be away overnight, and left the castle.

I got into the first SUV in the garage and backed out. I mindlinked the head guard on duty today and let him know I was coming through. All the gates were open for me before I even reached them.

Before I knew it, I was on the highway, following the GPS in my mind to bring the Queen back home.

*   *   *

I had an inkling the entire way that she was going back to her pack, but it wasn't confirmed until I felt the unmarked Keating Territory boundary line.

After five hours of driving, I pulled over at the edge of the boundary line. As the Royal Gamma, I had the right to just drive in, but I didn't want to get off on a bad foot with the Keating Pack. So, I waited for someone to come over.

Within thirty seconds, a young wolf, probably around Kendall's age, walked in front of my car. I already had my window down before he reached me. He looked confident before, but once he sensed my power and royalty, his nerves kicked in and he started fidgeting in front of me. His mouth opened and closed a few times, unable to form words. I was in a hurry, so I spoke up before he could muster up the courage.

"I'm Royal Gamma Tyler Guzman. I'm here in search of Kendall Keating," I spoke in a no-nonsense tone.

"Umm, she just passed through about, uh, forty-five minutes ago," he stuttered.

"Did she say where she was going?"

"Uhh, I'm not sure . . ." He scratched his head. I fought the urge to growl at him.

"Did she or not?" I finally snapped.

"I don't know, sir. It was Theo Anderson that she talked to. He left a few minutes after she came through," he said in a rush.

"Alert your alpha and let him know I'm in your territory. I don't want him to be surprised to find me wandering around later. I'm going to go find her."

"But, sir, you don't know where she lives," he said in a rush when my window was halfway up. I paused.

"I can find her, don't worry. Just alert your alpha."

I finished rolling up my window before he could argue and drove off. I followed my instincts, which lead me to a middle-class neighborhood. The houses thinned out as I kept driving before I finally reached a dead end street.

It was filled with cars, and I could hear the music pounding from a block away. I winced at the thought of going inside with my sensitive hearing.

I managed to find a parking spot at the end of the street. I walked down the block, passing by drunken wolves along the way. Most didn't spare me a second glance, too busy trying to walk without falling.

The house was a medium-sized two-story brick house, nothing special. I walked past a cloud of smoke on the front porch, not breathing until I was through it. I walked inside without knocking, and my senses were immediately overwhelmed.

The bass from the music pounded against my eardrums painfully, my olfactory senses were flooded with the scent of alcohol, sweat, vomit, and something else that I couldn't quite detect. That unknown scent was actually pleasant unlike the rest. The only sense that had a break was my advanced eyesight, since the room was dark except for a few lights from the kitchen and out in the backyard.

I scanned the dark room, looking for any signs of Kendall. I didn't see her in the mass of bodies in the living room, so I pushed through the crowd toward the kitchen. Some people stopped and stared at me in shock or fear, but I ignored them. Once more people noticed my presence, the room started thinning out with people leaving.

I finally made it to the kitchen, where the unknown scent grew stronger. It was sweet and overpowered all the unpleasant smells. I breathed it in greedily and looked for the source. It didn't take long to find, and the thoughts of finding Kendall were pushed to the back of my mind.

Her eyes landed on me the same time mine landed on hers. She was by far the most beautiful she-wolf I had ever laid my eyes on. Her light ashy-brown hair fell down her shoulders in loose waves, stopping at the bottom of her ribcage. It looked smooth and silky as it cascaded around her figure, and I had the urge to run my fingers through it. Her oval shaped face had delicate features, with a small, dainty nose and full pink lips that begged to be kissed. Her almond-shaped eyes were a warm hazel, and her cheeks were flushed, turning a beautiful shade of pink.

Her body was enclosed in a green t-shirt, which hinted at her figure underneath without revealing too much. Her smooth tan legs were on display as she wore a pair of black shorts. She was at least a foot shorter than me, but I knew her body would fit perfectly against mine. I felt a surge of pride run through me at the thought of this exquisite creature belonging with me.

Without thinking about it, my legs carried me over to her. I hadn't planned on walking over but my legs wouldn't stop until she was right in front of me. She stayed still, waiting me for to reach her.

Within three steps, I was less than six inches in front of her. I breathed in her scent again now that I was so close. The sweet scent overwhelmed me, but I continued to take in lungfuls of it, unable to get enough.

I lifted my hand to stroke her rosy cheek. Her skin was hot and felt like silk under my fingers. I leaned forward and rested my forehead against her's. My other hand found her hip and one of hers landed on top of my hand on her cheek, holding it there. The other flattened against my chest.

"*He estado esperando tanto tiempo por ti,*" I breathed out.

Her lips pulled up into a sweet smile, revealing straight white teeth. My breath got caught in my throat at the sight of her smile. I wanted to do everything in my power to make her happy so she would always smile at me like that.

I moved my forehead away from hers and replaced it with my lips. I pressed a lingering kiss on her forehead, enjoying the feeling of her skin underneath them. I hugged her for a second, just enjoying having her in my arms before I reluctantly pulled away.

I took a small step back but stayed close enough for my hands to rest on her hips. As I took her in again, I finally realized who she was.

I had been so consumed with her at first that I hadn't realized. I hadn't sensed the Alpha blood in her. I hadn't noticed how similar her features were to the girl I came her looking for. This was Kendall's sister.

"Selena . . ." I whispered, testing out her name. It rolled off my tongue like I was meant to say it.

Her face scrunched up cutely, her nose wrinkling and her eyebrows drawing together. "How do you know my name?" she asked in a confused manner. Her voice was hypnotizing and smooth, like honey.

"You're Kendall's sister. She's told me about you." I felt my eyes glaze over as I looked at her; a dopey smile appeared on my lips.

She didn't return the sentiment though. The next thing I knew, she was pulling away from me as far as she could, pressing herself against the counter. She didn't get far, but it did put a few more inches between us. My smile turned into a deep frown.

"How do you know Kendall and what the hell did she say about me?" She crossed her arms over her chest and raised her eyebrow at me.

I barked out a laugh at her attitude, which she didn't appreciate. She tried to push me away but I didn't go far.

"Did you do something with my sister?" she asked gruffly, shooting me a glare.

I knew that despite the anger she was showing she was feeling insecure, so I didn't laugh again. I looked at her seriously. "I've never been with your sister. We're friends, that's it. I only have eyes for you, mi alma."

"Mi alma?" she asked, her anger fading away.

My gaze softened. "It means my soul."

Her cheeks heated again, and she bit her lip, looking away shyly. "What's your name?"

"Tyler. Tyler Guzman."

"The Royal Gamma?" she asked in surprise.

"Mhm," I mumbled as I pulled her closer to me again. She didn't fight me. Instead, her hands flattened against my chest, and mine wrapped around her waist.

"So why are you here anyways?"

Her question brought me back to my original mission. I was supposed to find Kendall, protect her, and bring her back. I groaned as I pulled away from her again. I had a job to do.

"King Finnian sent me to bring Kendall back. I need to find her."

"Why? Is she in some kind of trouble?" Her eyes widened with worry for her sister.

"Nothing like that. I'll explain later but for now, I need to find her."

She nodded. "She went to the backyard earlier."

I grabbed her hand and pulled her behind me, towards the backdoor. She stopped along the way, next to a girl who she asked to turn the music off and get everyone out. She let her Alpha voice out when she asked. The girl agreed, and we continued outside.

My eyes scanned the yard, not taking long to find her. She had her back pressed against some pup, grinding her ass against him. I knew if Finn were here, that pup would be dead.

Kendall was drunk. I could tell even before she lifted the bottle of Crown to her lips, taking a long swig. Her eyes were closed, and her head leaned back against his shoulder. He was kissing her neck. I knew I had to stop this. She was pissed off and hurt, but I knew she would regret her actions.

"Kendall!" I yelled from across the yard just as the music shut off. I stormed over to her, ready to pull the pup off of her if he didn't go willingly.

She opened her eyes and looked around in confusion. They were glazed over with intoxication. She blinked hard as her eyes finally landed on me. When she opened them back up, I was standing a few feet from her.

I glared at the pup, and he backed away. Selena stopped next to me, looking between all of us. Now that I was closer to Kendall, I could smell the alcohol practically seeping out of her pores.

"Tyler?" she asked with a slight slur in her words.

"Kendall, you're making a mistake." I glanced over at the pup behind her. He backed up another couple of steps, looking at the ground in fear and discomfort.

"What?" she asked, not quite catching on to what I was talking about.

"You don't want to do this. I know you're angry and hurt, but you'll regret this even more." I tried to sound understanding.

I could tell when it finally clicked for her. "Are you talking about Theo?"

"Yes, that's what I'm talking about."

She snorted in derision. "At least he wants me," she spat out harshly.

"He wouldn't have sent me if he didn't want you." My words softened when I realized how sad she was deep down. If only she had seen how worried Finn had been about her earlier.

"What are you two talking about?" Selena's smooth, sultry voice captured my attention right away. I looked away from Kendall towards my mate.

"It's not my place to tell you that, mi alma." I wanted to tell her. I didn't want any secrets between us, but it wasn't my secret to tell. It should come from Kendall. I grabbed my beautiful mates soft, dainty hand and kissed her knuckles. Kendall looked at me with confusion clear on her face. "Ask your sister."

Selena looked back to her sister and my eyes followed. She clenched her jaw and looked at us bitterly. She lifted the bottle to her lips again, but Selena didn't let her drink from it. She slapped it out of her hand, stunning her for a moment as she watched it spill.

"What the hell was that for?" Kendall yelled when she looked back up at her. Fury lit her eyes, lessening the drunken glaze that had been in them.

"You've had enough. You're practically dry-humping Theo in front of half the pack," Selena told her sternly.

"You're exaggerating! And you're not my parent!" Kendall's voice got shrill as it rose in volume.

"No, I'm your older sister and I'm looking out for you," Selena yelled back, but her voice didn't sound shrill to me like Kendall's. "Now what the fuck is going on?"

"None of your business."

"It is my damn business. Now tell me," Selena argued back.

Kendall didn't have a chance to reply before someone else joined our group. He looked pissed. I subconsciously took a step closer to Selena in case I needed to protect her, but I soon sensed his Alpha blood and knew it was her other brother, Brody.

He yelled for everyone to go home. Most of them had already left, but a few brave wolves were still standing around, watching the scene unfold. They all left now that Brody had commanded them to. When the pup tried to walk away, Kendall grabbed his arm.

"Kendall, so help me, you better let him go. Now is not the time for games," Brody warned her threateningly.

She pouted but then released his arm. The pup ran off so fast he practically left a hole in the ground.

"Explain why you're here. Now." I stayed silent for the moment, letting him interrogate her. He was her brother; it wasn't my place to interrupt.

"I had to get away." She sounded defensive now.

"From what?" Brody growled at her. She kept her mouth shut. "Kendall . . ." His voice held a warning.

"It's none of your fucking business! I don't have to tell you shit!" she yelled again with that shrill voice.

Brody growled again but didn't get to say anything else when Selena walked away from me and stopped in front of her sister. My jaw dropped when she slapped her sister. Kendall's head whipped to the side harshly, her cheek turning bright red.

"Wake the hell up, you bitch. We're your family and we love you. Stop being so selfish. I just met my mate, and instead of getting to know him, we're both too focused on your drunken ass. Stop being such an attention seeking little drama queen and tell us what happened so that we can help fix it." She ended her rant with another slap to the face.

Her actions weren't the only surprising ones. Kendall let out a strangled scream and tackled Selena to the ground.

My protective mate instincts kicked in when I saw Selena splayed out on the grass with her sister hovering over her. I growled and made a move to protect my mate but a hand on my chest stopped me.

"With all due respect, Royal Gamma, you need to let them handle this. I know you feel the need to protect your mate right now, but it will just piss her off. This isn't the first time they've fought, and it won't be the last. They're not going to seriously hurt each other. So, just let them work it out," Brody coaxed me into not intervening.

After a few seconds of internal debating, I knew he was right. Even though I have only known Selena for less than an hour, I knew without a doubt that if I intervened in her sisterly business I'd never hear the end of it. I didn't want to start out on a bad foot with her.

And besides, from the looks of it, she'd have no problems taking on an extremely drunk Kendall.

Selena was underneath Kendall but it didn't take her long to switch their positions. Kendall flung her hands around wildly, trying to land a slap on Selena but none did. Selena grabbed her hands and pinned them over her head with one hand and used her other to slap her again, though not as harsh as before.

"Tell me," she ordered roughly, giving her cheek another hard tap.

"Fuck you." Kendall snarled up at her.

When Selena went to hit her cheek again, Kendall snapped her head to the side and bit Selena's arm. Selena cursed and released her grip on her hands so she could push her away. Kendall switched positions with her and slapped her twice. I tried to push my wolf down so I wouldn't interfere.

"Why are you such a bitch? Can't you just be happy I'm home and not question it?" Kendall yelled.

Somehow, Selena got out from under her and pushed her face down into the dewy grass. Kendall tried to throw her head back and hit Selena in the face. She missed but managed to roll over and get free. Selena jumped on her again and put her in a headlock.

Kendall's arms and legs flung in every which direction, trying to escape Selena's hold on her. Selena used her legs to hold down Kendall's.

"I'd be happy if you didn't show up acting like such a cunt. Now tell me!" Selena yelled back at her.

"I'd rather be a cunt than be the laughingstock of our family!"

"No one is laughing at you!"

"Only because you don't know!"

Kendall threw her elbow back and hit Selena in the gut. Her headlock loosened just enough for Kendall to worm her way out of it. She pushed Selena on her back and climbed back on top of her. She raised her hand to slap her but paused it midair.

She suddenly didn't look so good. Her face was pale but with a slight green hue. Her cheeks puffed out slightly, and she gagged a little. She scrambled off Selena, who helped by pushing her off. She only managed to crawl a couple feet away before she emptied the contents of her stomach.

Brody walked over to her and pulled her hair back. Her arms barely managed to hold herself up and away from her growing pool of vomit. She continued to puke until she started dry heaving with nothing left to come out. I breathed through my mouth to avoid the acidic stench.

Once finished heaving, her arms finally gave out. Brody grabbed her before she could land face first in her own vomit. He gathered her in his arms and stood up. Her head rolled pathetically onto his shoulder, her eyes half closed.

"Please don't make me go back," she whimpered, half conscious now.

I grabbed Selena's hand and pulled her from the ground. As I checked her over for any injuries, she was looking at her sister, a mixture of disgust and worry on her face. I pulled her into me and wrapped my arm around her waist.

"We'll talk about it tomorrow." Brody tried to sound comforting.

Kendall's hands fisted around his t-shirt and her eyes squeezed shut. "Please, Brody! I can't go back," she begged.

"Okay . . ." He finally relented. She relaxed in his hold. "One of you has a car here, right?" He turned his attention to us as we all started walking.

"We can take mine," I said firmly, not wanting to part from Selena for even a few minutes.

He nodded in response. We walked towards my SUV, Kendall already asleep by the time we got there.

*   *   *

Once we made it back to the Keating house, Brody left me and Selena in the living room. He took Kendall upstairs and Selena collapsed on the couch. I sat next to her and pulled her close to me. She snuggled into my arms and smiled. I breathed in her scent.

"Mom and Dad are on their way home," Brody stated when he walked back in the room a few minutes later.

Selena's head left my shoulder and looked over to her brother, who sat in the chair across the couch. "Why would you do that?" she asked in a demanding tone, sounding angry now.

"They needed to know." He shrugged.

"It could have waited until tomorrow. You know how excited Mom was for a night away." She glared at him.

"And you know that it'd be worse for everyone if we waited. They'd be pissed."

She continued to glare at him but didn't argue back. Her head found my shoulder again, and Brody turned his attention to me.

"Royal Gamma, can you please explain what is going on?"

"It's just Tyler. And I think it would be best coming from Kendall."

"I can appreciate you respecting her privacy, but I need to know what's going on *now*. I need to know if she's in some kind of trouble."

I struggled with trying to decide how much to tell him. On one hand, it should come from Kendall; it was her business. But on the other hand, her family should know. They were worrying about the wrong things, thinking she was in trouble somehow. She refused to tell them, but did that mean I should?

"She's not in any trouble," I finally told him, deciding that was the most important information they should know.

"Did someone hurt her?" He looked furious now.

I hesitated. Finn did hurt her, but not in the way he thought. I didn't know Finn's reasons, but I knew him. I knew he wouldn't hurt her like this without a valid reason. He's wanted his mate since he was fifteen. There had to be a damn good reason for his actions.

"No, no one hurt her." Physically, that is.

Brody sighed heavily. He leaned forward in his seat. "Please, Tyler, tell us. My mind is thinking of all the worst possible scenarios. She's my baby sister. It's my job to protect her. I have never seen her act like she did tonight. Something is wrong with her. She needs her family, even if she doesn't realize it. Tell me, please, so I can help her."

I didn't have a chance to decide whether to answer him or not, because the side door to the garage opened. An older couple rushed in; the woman had tears filling her red rimmed eyes, and the man looked alert and ready to shift.

"Where's my baby?" The woman sounded near hysterical.

"In her room—" Brody didn't have time to finish his sentence before she was out of the room, rushing up the stairs.

The Alpha walked into the room. I stood up when he stopped in front of the couch. "Royal Gamma." He bowed his head respectfully.

"Your daughter is my mate, I think we can drop the formalities. It's Tyler, sir." I held my hand out to shake his.

"Jefferson Keating. That was my mate, Abby." He gestured towards the stairs after he shook my hand firmly.

"It's a pleasure."

We both sat down, him on the chair across from Brody and me on the couch, next to Selena. She curled up closer to me again. I smiled and wrapped my arm around her, pulling her in my embrace.

"So, what's going on? Why is Kendall here?" he inquired, looking mainly at Brody.

"I was hoping Tyler would explain that, since Kendall refuses to." All eyes looked back over to me.

As I looked in Jefferson's eyes, I saw the worry and panic in them. I tried to put myself in his shoes. I pictured having a little girl, one who resembled my beautiful mate. If she had come home like that, I would set the world on fire to figure out what was wrong so that I could make it right. As I looked at him, scared for his little girl, I finally gave in and hoped that Kendall could forgive me.

"I don't know the whole story," I warned before I finally gave them answers. "All I know is that she's . . ." I paused for few seconds, trying to decide if I really wanted to tell them. With a bit of hesitation, I finally said, "She's King Finnian's mate."

Selena pulled away from me and looked up at me, hurt filling her eyes. "What? Why didn't she tell me?"

"I don't know, mi alma. I didn't know until today either." I ran my fingers through her silky hair.

"You don't know what happened between them?" Jefferson asked, bringing my attention back to him.

"All I know is something happened after the brunch this morning. She had a few too many mimosas and said she was going to take a nap. Matt, Dalton, and I went for a run and once we were finished, King Finnian called for me. He was . . . upset, to say the least. Told me she left and to follow her, keep her safe. That's all I know."

He nodded slowly, deep in thought. Finally, after a few minutes, he spoke. "Selena, what happened when she got home? Did she say anything?"

"She was just being super rude. Kept saying it was none of my business. She wanted to go out. I didn't want to, but I was worried about her and didn't want her to go alone." She sounded defensive, like she was worried they would blame her for going out. I clenched my jaw and hoped they answered in a way that didn't rile up my wolf.

He examined her closely, searching her face for any dishonesty. Finally, he nodded. "I believe you. I'm proud of you for not drinking, too."

She beamed up at him, thrilled at how he praised her. "Anyways, she was acting really crazy. She had her ass and boobs practically hanging out of her clothes. I tried to get her to change, but she wouldn't. She was also super rude to my friend who was hosting the party. She started drinking whiskey straight. If that wasn't bad enough, she ran into Theo Anderson. When we found them, they were pretty much dry humping. I'm convinced that she would have screwed him if we hadn't found her and stopped her."

Jefferson shook his head in irritation. "I never liked that pup. He was always a bad influence on her."

"Yeah, he's a douche. You should have seen what a pussy he looked like tonight once Tyler and Brody showed up. I thought he was gonna shit his pants." She snickered adorably.

"Language, Selena," he warned halfheartedly. "It's late. We should all get some sleep. We'll figure all of this out tomorrow."

We all said our goodnights and dispersed. Brody left down a hall on the first story. Jefferson followed us upstairs, pulling his crying mate away from Kendall's room then went back downstairs. Selena pulled me in the direction opposite to them, down one hall then another.

She pulled us into a room that looked unlived in. Selena's scent wasn't present, letting me know it wasn't her room. It looked like a guest room. My eyebrows furrowed together at the thought of her leaving me.

"This isn't your room," I pointed out.

"I share a room with Kendall. I wanted us to have some privacy. The bathroom's across the hall. I'm gonna go change really quick."

I nodded. Luckily, I thought to bring my overnight bag with me, so I didn't have to go out and get it.

I went across the hall and brushed my teeth. I went back to the room and stripped down to my boxers and crawled into bed.

Selena returned a few minutes later, wearing a t-shirt and a pair of pink pajama shorts with yellow ducks on them. Her face was bare of any makeup, allowing me to see what a natural beauty she was without it. Her hair was in a messy bun on top of the head, a few strands falling out.

"Cute pajamas. You look beautiful before bed."

"And you look so damn sexy. I want to lick your abs." She looked down at my bare chest and stomach.

Desire filled me, and I growled lowly at her as a warning. "Don't say things like that unless you want to follow through with them."

She got a cheeky, thoughtful expression on her face. "Hmm, maybe I do."

She walked over to me slowly, adding an extra sway in her hips. Once she got close enough, I grabbed her and pulled her on top of me before she could blink. A yelp of surprise left her plump lips, and she smiled at me as she straddled my body.

"Your abs aren't the only thing I want to lick," she whispered seductively in my ear.

"You're a little tease," I growled playfully and flipped us over so her body was underneath mine.

"Only for you, baby," she whispered.

"Better be," I growled out, then I pressed my lips against hers.

Everything I had been told about mates before paled in comparison to actually experiencing it. Her lips fit mine perfectly. The kiss was full of passion, and desire. She returned it as soon as my lips landed on hers.

She wrapped her arms around my neck, pulling me down closer and closer, one hand tangled in my hair. I used one arm to hold myself up so I didn't crush her under my weight, and my free hand to run up and down her side, stopping on her hip. I pulled her shirt up, and her skin was soft and warm under my fingers.

I licked her bottom lip, needing to taste her. She opened her mouth, and my tongue dove inside. She tasted as sweet as her scent smelled, which was mixed with mint from her toothpaste. My tongue massaged hers, and she moaned into my mouth.

I kissed her for a few more seconds, then finally pulled away. I fell down beside her and pulled her body against mine.

"Why'd you stop?" she whined. I chuckled in amusement.

"I had to stop or else I wouldn't be able to control myself," I told her seriously.

"Who says I wanted you to?" she questioned sassily.

"When we mate for the first time, it won't be in the same house that your parents and siblings are in. I want to be able to make you scream without worrying who hears," I whispered huskily in her ear. She shivered against me, and I knew it wasn't from the cold.

"I look forward to it," she finally whispered back.

I smiled down at her. "Go to sleep. It's late, and I'm sure there will be a lot going on tomorrow." I kissed her forehead gently.

She nodded. I watched her, waiting for her to fall asleep before I did. It didn't take long. Within minutes, her breathing was slow and even. She was out like a light.

Before I could do the same, I felt King Finnian pushing against my mental barriers. I cursed internally. I had forgotten to contact him. He had contacted me a few times on the drive here, but I finally told him I would mind link him when I could. Finding Selena distracted me.

I opened the link to him.

"How is she?" His voice sounded worried, and anxious.

"She's okay. Drunk, but okay."

"Did you kill the wolf that had his paws on her?" I could hear the growl in his voice.

"What?" I questioned in confusion. Did he know about the pup? How?

"Nikolina cast a spell on her to let me know if another male put his hands on her. Did she sleep with him? Did you kill him?" He sounded jealous and enraged, a dangerous combination.

"She didn't sleep with anyone. She got wasted at a party and was dancing with some pup. I stopped her from doing more. And no, I didn't kill the pup." I rolled my eyes at the fact that he expected me to.

"She's safe?"

"Very. She's sleeping down the hall."

"Why the hell did it take you so long to let me know how she was then?" he asked roughly.

"Sorry about that, Finn. I met my mate. It's her sister, Selena. I guess I got a little distracted."

I expected for him to be pissed, to yell at me for getting distracted, but he didn't.

"I understand how that can be distracting. Just . . . please don't let it distract you from keeping her safe."

"Of course," I agreed wholeheartedly with him.

"Contact me in the morning with her condition."

"Okay."

"Oh, and congratulations Tyler. I'm happy for you," he added before I put my barrier back up.

"Gracias, Finn."

He closed me off after that, not saying another word. I closed my eyes and drifted into unconsciousness, holding my mate tightly to my chest.

CHAPTER SIXTEEN

KENDALL

I felt like death warmed over. I may be immune to human diseases and illnesses, but certainly not hangovers. And unfortunately, I remembered every detail of last night. Every shameful, mortifying detail of my actions.

I groaned as I pried my eyes open. They were full of crust and gunk in the corners. I rubbed them so harshly that they may burst in my skull. When I blinked them open again, a ray of blinding sunlight was streaming right in my face. My mouth felt like cotton, and it tasted like I had swallowed ammonia. My lips were dry, crusty, and in desperate need of chapstick.

I groaned again as I lifted my hand to block the light. My head pounded like a drum, beating in time with my heart. I sealed my eyes shut again and massaged my temples.

I sat up after a few minutes and took myself in. Someone had changed me out of my clothes last night. I was now dressed in a t-shirt and shorts. Even my bra was gone. I should feel violated at the thought of someone seeing me naked while I was passed out, but I was just thankful that I was in something comfortable.

I pushed my cheetah print comforter off my legs and swung them over the side of the bed. I groaned for the third time as a wave of dizziness swept over me, so I stayed seated for a few seconds until it passed.

In those few seconds, I was finally able to smell myself. I nearly gagged at the lingering scent of vomit that clung to me like a second skin. There was even some dried up at the ends of my hair.

I breathed through my mouth as I walked into my bathroom to take a much-needed shower. I grabbed a few pain relievers from the medicine cabinet and downed them along with two full glasses of water before getting in.

After a nearly hour long shower, I finally felt human again . . . or, well, werewolf. I got dressed in another pair of cotton shorts and a t-shirt, with a sports bra underneath since a real bra just wasn't in the cards for the day.

I brushed through my hair and pulled it into a messy bun. To feel and smell even better, I lathered my body in lotion, leaving my skin soft and smelling like honeysuckle. I brushed my teeth three times and rinsed thoroughly with mouthwash.

I sighed again once I was done, not at all prepared mentally to go downstairs. I focused my hearing and almost groaned again when I heard my parents downstairs. I wouldn't be surprised if they got in late last night after everything that had happened. The thought of them coming home from their night away together because of me piled on the guilt.

I felt so ashamed of my actions now. I was in a dark place yesterday and had taken it out on the people who loved me most. They didn't deserve that. I just couldn't bring myself to tell them.

Deep down, I knew they wouldn't judge me, but I was judging myself. Obviously, something was wrong with me if my own mate didn't want me. I didn't want my family to know that and look at me differently.

I wondered if they already knew though. I also wondered how much Tyler actually knew. He was blissfully ignorant before I left yesterday, so the King must have told him after. I didn't let myself get my hopes up that he may care. He made it perfectly clear that he didn't.

I mustered up all the courage I could and left my room, making my way downstairs slowly. My pace was about as fast as a turtle stuck in peanut butter. Finally, after what seemed like an eternity, I reached the open living room, kitchen, and dining room area.

Dad, Brody, and Tyler were sitting in the living room, while Mom and Selena were in the kitchen. Mom was stirring a big pot of something, and Selena was pulling another thing out of the oven. It smelled like chicken noodle soup and cookies, but I couldn't be positive since I couldn't see.

I felt five pairs of eyes all land on me, but I couldn't make eye contact with any of them. I fidgeted nervously and looked at the carpet in front of my feet. Before anyone could say anything, Mom rushed over to me, pulling me into a hug.

Her arms around me felt comforting. I usually didn't like hugs that much; I'd give them but wasn't touchy feely like Mom was. But I suppose I needed comfort more than I realized; because I wrapped my arms around her and leaned into her, accepting the support she was offering.

She held me tightly, rubbing my back soothingly. I buried my face in her shoulder so I didn't have to look at anyone else and inhaled her familiar, soothing scent. She always smelled of cookies since she was always baking. It had never comforted me more than it did now. It smelled like home.

"I'm sorry," I whispered into her shoulder.

"Oh, sweetheart, it's okay. No one's mad at you." She pulled back and grabbed my face in her warm hands. "We can talk later. For now, we need to get you hydrated and fed. Come on, lunch is ready."

I nodded at her words. She pulled me into the kitchen. I still didn't look up to meet anyone's eyes. Mom all but pushed me into one of the bar seats. Luckily, my back was now facing the guys but that left Selena right in front of me, the person who deserved an apology the most.

Before I could muster one up, Mom placed a bowl of steaming chicken noodle soup and a big bottle of blue Gatorade in front of me. It smelled delicious, which made my stomach rumble. I pushed the thoughts of apologies to the back burner. Selena left the kitchen when I started eating. I took big sips of the Gatorade between mouthfuls of soup, letting it hydrate me.

Once I finished the soup and Gatorade, I felt a thousand times better. My headache was now just a dull thumping in my head, the stomach cramps had let up, and my dry mouth and throat felt quenched. I always knew Mom's cooking could work miracles.

Mom took my empty bowl and filled it with water in the sink after I declined another serving. I wanted it, but I needed to face my family. I stood up and made my way into the living room, carrying my almost empty bottle to keep my hands busy.

I collapsed down on the edge of the couch. Dad and Brody were both in the chairs while Selena and Tyler were curled up together on the other end of the couch. They had been sitting in silence since I came into the room, so I didn't have to talk over them or the TV.

I crossed my leg underneath my body and toyed with my fingers. I stared at the ground and cleared my throat awkwardly, trying to dislodge the lump that was stuck there.

"I owe all of you an apology. I'm so sorry for the way I acted."

Selena moved away from Tyler and over to me. I didn't know what to expect, but it certainly wasn't a punch in the arm. "Ow!" I glared at her, finally meeting her eyes. She had a mischievous look on her face. I rubbed my arm up and down.

"You're forgiven. Just don't be such a colossal bitch next time."

I nodded and looked down again. "Sorry," I mumbled. She punched me again. "Ow!" I yelled as I scowled at her again.

"Stop apologizing, it's so unlike you. I just want my sister back."

"Fine, I'm back." Before my words were even finished, I balled my fist and punched her in the arm as well.

She winced and rubbed her arm, but I could tell she was pleased by the slight smile on her lips. Mine mirrored hers, glad that I was forgiven, but it immediately turned into a frown at my father's words.

"We know about you and King Finnian, Kendall." He tried to make his voice smoothing, but I still tensed up.

"What about us?" I spoke slowly, trying to figure out exactly how much they knew before I confessed anything. I shot Tyler a glance, or more like glare, out of the corner of my eye.

I saw him mouth, "Sorry." He rubbed the back of his neck, a look of guilt on his face. I looked away, not sure how I felt about him telling my secret when he seemed adamant not to last night. I turned my attention back to my father.

"We know he's your mate."

I started shaking my head before he could even finish his sentence. I bounced my leg but that wasn't enough to get rid of the nervous energy in me. I stood up and started pacing in front of the TV, in front of all of them. "I don't want to talk about it," I mumbled as I continued pacing.

"Kenny, sweetheart, I know something is bothering you. Let us help you," Dad continued the attempt to console me.

"You know I don't like to be called that," I growled at him, trying to change the subject.

"Kendall, just tell us. No one here is judging you," Selena added in.

I shook my head and continued pacing while chewing on my thumb nail. They continued trying to coax the truth out of me, and I continued to refuse. I could tell they were getting frustrated, but so was I.

Getting rejected by your mate was a big deal in the werewolf world. It almost never happened. When it did, it would bring shame upon the rejected wolf. They were looked down on as being defective somehow. If my family knew the truth, I would feel the full force of that shame.

"Did you two have a fight?" Dad continued, trying to fill in the blanks himself.

"No," I snapped.

He finally stood up from his chair and stopped in front of me, halting my pacing. I looked up at his frustrated face. In return, he looked down at my annoyed face.

"Enough of this Kendall! Tell us now!" he yelled with the authority of an alpha.

The command didn't work on my wolf, but his words and angry tone did make the dam finally break. I had held it together until now. I had let my rage numb me of all other emotions. But now, standing in front of my dad, who looked at me with exasperation and fear, the rage finally faded and allowed in everything else.

My lips trembled, making it hard to speak. "He doesn't want me." A harsh sob tore from my throat at my last word.

Once I started, I couldn't stop. Loud, guttural cries escaped my throat as tears poured down my face like a never-ending river. My legs gave out, and Dad was there to catch me. He wrapped his strong arms around me, holding me upright. I clenched his shirt tightly and buried my face in his chest. He held me against him tightly, shushing me and rubbing my back up and down.

I didn't have it in me to focus on anyone else. I didn't know what their reactions to my break down would be but by that point I didn't really care.

I couldn't hold it in anymore. Everything that had happened with Finnian finally hit me, full force, in front of the majority of my family. Every uncaring word he'd spoken to me; every moment he tricked me into believing we had a chance, just to crush it in the next; every time he rejected me and pushed me away. It was all coming out.

I couldn't be sure how long I stood there. All I knew was that the room was completely silent except for my loud sobbing. I wasn't even completely sure they were still in the room.

I was having trouble breathing after a while, the air not making it to my lungs. My whole body shook, and a cold sweat broke out across my skin. My heart was racing, beating painfully against my ribcage.

Dad finally pulled my face away from his chest once I started getting lightheaded from lack of oxygen. He cupped my face in his hands. I grabbed on to his wrists to steady myself. I looked at him with a panicked face.

"Take slow, deep breaths, sweetheart. Try to calm down." He demonstrated what he was instructing me to do. He took in long, deep breaths through his nose and released them through his mouth.

I tried to do the same. Tears still spilled down my cheeks, but eventually my sobs quietened and my breathing slowed. I continued to take in deep breaths, letting the oxygen fill my lungs.

Once my breathing returned back to normal and my sobbing stopped, I collapsed into him again in exhaustion. My eyes felt heavy and raw from tears, and my throat was sore from sobbing for so long. I let my eyelids shut completely and my breathing slow even further.

I felt my feet leave the ground and my body being cradled to Dad's chest, but I still didn't open my eyes. He walked for a while before I was lowered onto a soft surface. A warm blanket was pulled tight around my chilled body. The last thing I felt before I completely drifted off into oblivion was Dad kissing my forehead and mumbling that he loved me.

* * *

When I woke up for the second time that day, I felt like crap, although not as crappy as the first time. My temples throbbed in sync with my heartbeat, and my eyes were dry and scratchy. I rubbed them with the heel of my palm and sat up.

I was disoriented for a few minutes, but once I got my bearings I was surprised to see Selena sitting on her bed, gazing at me. I would have called her a creep for staring had she not looked so upset.

"What time is it?" I mumbled.

"It's just after two. You've been asleep for about two hours."

I nodded and sat up completely, letting my comforter and sheets pool in my lap.

"Why didn't you tell me?" she whispered after a few minutes of silence.

I sighed. "I was ashamed. I didn't want to admit that there was something so wrong with me that my own mate wouldn't want me."

"There's not a damn thing wrong with you. The only person who should feel ashamed is King Dickwad. He's the problem; not you," she told me fiercely.

I smiled weakly at her. "Thanks, Sel. That means a lot to me."

"Do you want to talk about it?" she asked hesitantly.

"Not really, but I feel like I owe you an explanation for how I acted yesterday."

"You don't owe me anything, Kendall. You were hurting, I understand."

"That's not an excuse," I argued, "I was horrible. I practically forced you to go out. I knew you were trying to change, show Dad that you could be trusted. I was so selfish. What I did was unforgivable."

"I do forgive you though. I'm letting you off the hook. Now let yourself off the hook."

"I don't know if I can. I was horrible to the people who really love me just because of some asshole who doesn't."

"You can. I'm sure I'll do something crappy in the future, probably sooner rather than later. I'll get a free pass and we'll be even," she joked.

I laughed lightly. "Okay." I finally agreed. "So, you and Tyler, huh?"

A light blush covered her cheeks and I fought back a laugh. "He's pretty great. Although I still want to know what you told him about me. He kept his lips shut." She glared at me now.

I tried to think back and then finally remembered our conversation in the pool . . . We had talked about the King that day . . . I shook my head and pushed all thoughts of him away, instead focusing on my sister.

"I didn't say anything *too* bad."

"Expand," she stated, practically demanding the truth.

"I just told him that me, you, and Kat had been causing Mom and Dad trouble for years."

"What else?" She continued to glare at me.

I grinned when I thought back to our night out a couple weeks ago. "I might have told him a few stories about you."

"Which ones?"

"I told him how you got me to run over Dalton." I giggled.

"Kendall! I did no such thing! That was entirely on you and him. You should have been smarter to realize it was him and he should have moved faster. Werewolf speed, my ass," she grumbled, crossing her arms defensively.

My giggle turned into a full-on laugh.

"Did you mention Kat's silencing spell?"

"Yeah, I had to tell that story.

"Did you tell him how we got caught doing it?" Her voice rose like ten notches, turning shrill.

"No, geez. You sound more like a banshee than a werewolf when you talk like that. We all promised we'd never speak of it again. It was just as embarrassing for me as it was for you."

"Now I have to hear this story." Tyler sauntered into the room and took a seat next to Selena.

"You will literally have to have a witch pry that memory from our brains if you want to know, because none of us are ever telling." I crossed my arms over my chest.

He looked at Selena pleadingly, but she just raised an eyebrow and agreed with me.

"So why are you here anyways?" I finally asked him, addressing the elephant in the room. Now that I was calmed down a little and had released some of my pent-up emotions, I was able to finally talk about it without crying or wanting to punch someone.

"After you left, Finn called me into his meeting room. He seemed . . . really upset."

I glared at the ground. "Good, he should be. I hope he still is," I said spitefully.

"Anyways, he wanted me to go after you; to keep you safe."

"Why?" I stared at him imploringly.

"Is it really that surprising after what happened the last time you left the castle?"

"Yes, actually. Because I know he doesn't give a shit."

"I can promise you, Kendall, he gives plenty of shits." I looked at him in amusement at his word choice, despite the meaning behind them.

"If he was so worried, then how come he let me leave? How did I manage to make it past all the guards?"

"He told them to let you through. He felt guilty for what happened, whatever that was, so he wanted you to be able to get away for a few days, but he also wanted you safe."

"He didn't tell you what happened?" I asked meekly.

"No, and I didn't pry for information. If one of you wants to tell me, you will." Tyler starts rubbing his neck nervously. "I do want to apologize to you, by the way. I'm sorry for telling your family. I should have let you do it, but they were so concerned that I couldn't say no."

I shook my head at him. "Don't apologize, Tyler. You didn't do anything wrong. I'm sorry for how I acted."

I wanted to ask him if he had talked to the King, but I couldn't bring myself to. I didn't want to know if he asked about me or not. It would just hurt if he hadn't. It would also get my hopes up if he had, which would hurt worse later.

"I understand, Kendall. No one is mad at you." I smiled at him gratefully.

I was feeling better now that I apologized to two of the five people who were affected by my actions last night. And that was only the people here. I'm sure Matt was pissed at me too, which made me wonder if anyone had called him to let him know I was okay.

"Thanks, Tyler. By the way, has anyone talked to Matt?"

"I called Kat on the way back from the party yesterday, so they know you're safe," Selena answered.

"Does he know anything?"

"As far as I know, he doesn't. You'll have to ask Mom, Dad, and Brody if they told him though."

"I guess it's time to face the music anyways."

I stood up from my bed and walked out of the room, Selena and Tyler following behind me. They didn't really need to be present, but I knew Selena just liked to be in everyone's business. She would still eavesdrop even if she wasn't in the room, so it didn't really matter either way.

Once I made it downstairs, it was a similar sight to this morning. Dad and Brody were both sitting in their favorite chairs. Mom rushed up to me, pulling me into a tight hug. She didn't pull away until a few minutes later.

"Are you feeling better? Do you want something to eat? I was so worried about you." She looked me over frantically.

"I'm feeling better, Mom, really. You don't need to worry. And maybe later, okay?" I smiled weakly at her.

She nodded hesitantly and released me. I walked over to the couch and sat down. Selena sat in the middle and Tyler on the other side of her.

"So, I guess it's time to tell you everything," I started before anyone else could talk. Mom walked over and sat down on the arm of Dad's chair. All eyes turned to me.

"Only when you're ready, Kenny," Dad said carefully.

"I'll never be ready, but I need to get it out in the open."

He nodded. Everyone sat silently, waiting for me to begin. I struggled with where to start, but decided that the beginning was the best.

"Okay, so I realized the King and I were mates on my first night there. I guess he sensed me and was listening to what I was doing in my room. Dalton was also in there. We were arguing, or at least I thought we were. But then the King stormed in, choked Dalton, and told him to never flirt with me again."

"You didn't realize he was flirting?" Selena snickered, interrupting me.

"How was I supposed to know that he had a thing for me? Kat was the only one who knew. He wasn't exactly obvious about it."

"Uhh, wrong. Everyone knew, and he made it very obvious," Selena snapped back.

"Did he tell you? Who else knew about it?"

Every single person in the room then informed me that they were aware of his feelings, even Tyler. I gawked at all of them.

"Whatever, can I finish my story now? Anyways, he commanded Dalton not to tell anyone he was there. He seemed into me at first, but then he got all cold and distant. He then tried to command me not to tell anyone either. His commands don't have an effect on me, but I was embarrassed, so I didn't tell anyone but Kat."

"Kat knew and I didn't?" Selena whined.

"Selena, be quiet and let your sister talk," Mom chided.

I continued the story, giving them details that I never thought I would share. They stayed quiet, absorbing the story of my misfortune.

"So, that leads me to yesterday. We were at that stupid freaking brunch. I got jealous when I saw him talking to some other girl. Niki wouldn't let me confront him there, but once it was finished, I went up to his room and he . . ."

"What happened up there, Kendall?" Dad lightly coaxed me after I stayed silent for a little too long.

I sighed heavily, not really wanting to tell them what happened but knowing I had to. "He said I'd never be his queen and that he didn't want me. That he'd never want me. I told him if he let me leave, then I was done." I took a deep breath. "He didn't try to stop me. So, I left. I'm sorry, Dad. I know this is important to you, but I can't be there anymore. Please don't make me go back."

A few tears leaked out of my eyes as I begged my Dad not to push the issue, not to force me back there where I was unwanted.

"Of course, sweetheart. You don't have to—"

"No," Mom interrupted, sounding firm and unrelenting, which was unusual for her. My jaw dropped slightly. "You promised your Dad two months, you'll finish those two months."

My jaw dropped even further. I suspected Dad might try to force me back, but never Mom.

"Abby, it's fine—"

"Don't you Abby me, Jefferson. She is going back and that's final."

"Mom, I don't understand. Selena will be there with Tyler, she can just take over for me." I tried to change her mind, but my words were breathy and unconvincing as confusion and panic took over my mind.

Mom stood up and walked over to me, sitting down between me and Selena. I turned to face her, and she grabbed my hands.

"I love you, Kendall. You're my pup. As much as I want to give in and let you stay, I can't do that. I didn't raise you kids to back down from a challenge. I didn't raise quitters. I know this is hard for you, and I'm so sorry you're going through this. But you promised your father two months and you're going to fulfill that commitment and finish those two months." She explained. More tears leaked from my eyes.

"Mom," I choked out, past the lump in my throat. "I can't be near him. It hurts too much."

"Oh, sweetie." Her hand rested on my cheek. "You're so strong. You're a fighter, Kendall. I'm not going to let you stop fighting just because you're hurting. He's your mate; your destiny. You two are meant to be, and I know you'll find a way back together. And if you don't, at the very least you'll be able to say you gave it your all. Don't give up just yet, baby girl."

I released a shaky breath. My hands were trembling slightly. I thought over her words for a few minutes, mulling them over, before I finally decided she was right. This wasn't me. Running away from my problems. I've always faced my problems head on with my head held high.

I wasn't so sure about the part about the King and me making it, but I was sure that I wasn't going to lose myself because of him. I deserved better than that, and I wasn't going to let him take anything else from me. I was going to walk back into that castle like I owned the place, with my head held high and full of the confidence that I always had before him. I let him break me down, now it was time to build myself back up.

"Okay," I finally breathed out.

I was ready to show him what a fighter Kendall Keating really was.

CHAPTER SEVENTEEN

"I can't believe I'm losing another baby." Mom sniffled into Selena's neck, before pulling back and smothering her face with kisses, causing her to scrunch up her nose in discomfort.

I tried not to laugh at Selena, knowing it would bring Mom's attention back on me. She had already spent five minutes hugging, kissing, and crying into my shoulder. Despite her stern demand yesterday about me returning to the castle, she didn't seem as sure about her decision today. I was, though. I woke up feeling brave, ready to face the world, or more specifically, my mate.

After two days away, I was seeing things more clearly. I was pissed at Finnian, no doubt, and still incredibly hurt, but I also knew he was keeping something from me. His treatment of me didn't add up. I was determined to figure out what it was. I didn't suspect we had a chance in hell of making it, but I at least wanted to know what was keeping us apart.

Although the first half of my trip wasn't exactly great, the second half was. I was able to spend the night with my family. After confessing everything, it was like a weight was lifted off my shoulders. I figured that my family would look at me differently, treat me differently but they didn't.

We decided to have a family game night. We played Monopoly, which ended with Selena knocking the board to the ground. See? Just like old times.

After the failed attempt at a board game, we switched to movie night instead. Due to our competitive nature, it wasn't the first time this had happened. We had spent the rest of the night eating pizza and ice cream. It made me sad that Matt and Kat were missing, but I was glad Tyler was there to fill that void. He fit in perfectly with our family. Mom adored him, and he had a lot in common with Dad and Brody. They were already buddying up, which made Dad more comfortable with letting Selena leave with him.

We had spent the morning packing up Selena's things. She packed more than I had, since she would be moving to the castle permanently, not just for a couple of months. She did leave a few things behind, saying she planned on visiting often and wanted to have stuff here.

I was a little surprised that she was going with Tyler so willingly. He didn't even really ask her to, she just wanted to. My guess was that she was okay with it because Kat, Matt, Dalton, and I would all be there. I had a feeling she would be a lot more reluctant to go if we were not there despite how much she already cared for Tyler.

Selena and I were similar in that family was the most important thing. It was all we knew, really. It was a difficult shift, making your mate the most important thing in your life; more important than your family. I just hope she'll be able to adjust completely by the time we leave. I wanted her to be happy.

I was a little nervous to face Matt once we returned. I found out yesterday that no one told him about my situation. We had all agreed that it was best that he didn't know for now. Matt had always been the most protective of the guys in my family, especially with me and Selena. It wasn't safe to tell him while he was there. If he knew, he would no doubt confront King Finnian and probably challenge him. That wouldn't end well for Matt.

When a wolf challenged a king, it was a fight to the death. He would have no choice but to kill Matt. I knew he would be able to, too. Despite how strong Matt was, King Finnian was the king of werewolves. No one would be able to take him out on their own, not even Matt. So, for now, it was the safest option to keep him in the dark.

I felt guilty that he was the only one who didn't know about the reason for my disappearance but I had to protect my brother. He'd have to understand. And I would tell him as soon as we got home.

Dad made a bold declaration while he was still pissed yesterday about not wanting to be on the King's Council when the King himself could treat me so poorly, but I put those thoughts to an end as soon as they begun.

The Council position wasn't about me, or even King Finnian for that matter. It was for our Pack and for werewolves in general. Dad would have a say in how things in the werewolf world were handled, and that was bigger than my problems.

So, after some convincing, he agreed to continue. He would just have to leave his personal problems with the King at the door once he was initiated into the Council.

"You're not losing anyone, Mom. I'll call and visit all the time," Selena said, trying to convince Mom. It didn't seem to work because she just squeezed her tighter.

"It's not the same. I'm down to having one baby at home. I started with four. How did it whittle down to one?" Mom cried out in dismay.

"You'll get to see me on Saturday, Mom. That's something to look forward to," Selena said enthusiastically.

Her words were true. The Mating Ball was on Saturday, and Dad had finally decided to attend. Brody would be staying at home to run things, but Mom and Dad were both going.

Selena had to go; she was the new Royal Gamma Female now, after all. She was expected to attend these events. I still chose to attend the event as well, for a couple of reasons. One was that my family would be there and I wasn't going to pass up a chance to spend time with them. The second reason was because I already had a dress.

I was going to look hot. I also didn't want to pass up a chance to show King Finnian what he was missing.

"I suppose you're right . . ." A sniffling Mom pulled away, her cheeks still wet and eyes rimmed red.

Once she released Selena, Dad was quick to swoop in and pull her tight into his embrace, trying to distract her so she wouldn't grab one of us again. She'd spent over ten minutes hugging the both of us and even hugged Tyler for a few minutes. He seemed surprised at first but then hugged her back awkwardly. He would have to get used to it.

"Call me when you get there. Don't be like your siblings." Mom shot me a glare, still upset that I hadn't called her to let her know we made it that first night. I rolled my eyes when she looked away.

"I promise. Can we go now? We really need to get on the road . . ." Selena trailed off.

"Okay, go. I love you all and I'll miss you."

We returned the sentiment and walked over to Tyler's SUV. I should be driving Matt's back, since I did steal it after all, but I didn't want to drive back on my own. Tyler said it was fine, that we could use his car whenever and that when we were ready to go home, he would drive us. I was extremely grateful that I would have some company on the way back.

We left with one last goodbye, and I silently prayed that I wouldn't get my heart broken again for my last month at the castle.

* * *

We had been driving for over five hours. We'd stopped for lunch and for gas twice, plus pee breaks, which Selena and I could never sync up, so we'd stopped twice as much for that. I could tell Tyler was glad to finally be back after being alone in a car with Selena and me for so long.

Once we reached the Royal Territory, we had to stop a few times like we did on the way here the first night. They mainly searched the car for any kind of explosive material, such as bombs, and weapons that could be used against a werewolf, which was basically just wolfsbane.

Wolfsbane was the deadliest weapon to use against a werewolf. It stops us from shifting and weakens our strength, speed, and senses. It could be fatal in large doses. Every car had to be searched for it. Even though they trusted us, they never knew if someone planted it inside without us knowing, since the scent was difficult for werewolves to pick up. After a thorough search of the SUV, they deemed us clean. We made it to the front of the castle.

Tyler stopped to have our doors opened for us. Tyler handed his keys to the guy who opened his door. We all stepped out after that and the guy drove off. I assumed he would bring Selena's bags up to Tyler's room.

As I looked up at the beautiful, medieval castle, I squared my shoulders and lifted my head high, ready to take on anything. As we walked inside, it was just like I remembered. I didn't see anyone I knew waiting for us.

As we walked, I could feel him. He wasn't near me, but I could feel that I was in close proximity of him. I briefly wondered where he was and if he could feel me too. I pushed those thoughts away.

Tyler gave a small tour to Selena as we made our way up. Well, it was less a tour and more him pointing and explaining things to her; dinner was in twenty minutes, so he told her he would give her a better tour tomorrow. Once we reached the second floor, Tyler left Selena with me. I had to face Matt before dinner, and I didn't want to do that alone.

Tyler kissed her goodbye. We walked down the hall to my room. I pointed out which rooms were Dalton's and Matt and Kat's. The latter two weren't actually in their room, they were in mine.

We walked in and saw Kat sitting on my couch, telling Matt to calm down as he paces back and forth. He stopped when we walked in and glared at me. I sighed through my nose, ready to get this over with.

"You better have a damn good reason for leaving like you did, Kendall." He nearly growled at me.

"Get your panties out of a twist and sit down. I'll tell you."

He actually growled now but did as I asked. Selena hugged both him and Kat. We all sat on the sectional couch, which had been replaced since I broke the old one. The entire room had been cleaned actually.

"Explain." Matt turned his attention back to me.

"I got homesick." I shrugged like it was no big deal.

"You got homesick? You trashed your room, took off without a word, left your cell phone and purse, and put up a mental barrier the size of Russia . . . all because you were homesick?" he said in disbelief.

"I was drunk, pissed off that Dad shipped me off here in the first place, and acted impulsively. It was irresponsible and immature. I don't know what I can say except I'm sorry—sorry that I did it and sorry that I worried you."

"You did all that because you were mad that Dad made you come here and you missed home?" I nodded. "Wow, Kendall, I'm impressed. You took irresponsible and immature to a whole new level. Not to mention selfish. Well done," he quipped sarcastically.

Anger pricked at me. I wanted to tell him the truth, make him feel bad for being so rude, but I had to protect him. I couldn't let him go after King Finnian. I had to fight my own battles and leave my brother out of it.

"I'm sorry, okay? I know it was wrong. It will never happen again." Frustration coated my words.

He looked like he was going to attack me some more, but Kat touched his arm and gave him a meaningful look. He met her gaze for a few seconds then sighed and looked away.

"Just don't let it happen again," he grumbled.

"I won't, I promise."

"Get ready for dinner." He stood up and walked out, not saying another word to me. I knew he just needed time; he would move on. Matt wasn't one to hold grudges.

"Are you okay?" Kat asked as soon as Matt pulled the door shut behind him.

"I'm better now. I just needed a few days away."

"What happened to set you off?"

"I'll tell you while we get ready."

Kat was already dressed, but Selena and I were in sweats. Selena decided to just borrow something of mine instead of walking up to the fifth floor, which was where her new room with Tyler was.

Kat perched herself on my bathroom sink as Selena and I picked out our clothes. She sat quietly and listened as I explained what happened in King Finnian's room. She didn't say anything, but her facial expressions gave away her true feelings. She looked disgusted that he could treat me, his mate, like that.

"I just needed to get away after that. I couldn't be around him. I wasn't even going to come back but Mom convinced me," I explained to her as I slipped out of my sweats and pulled on a burgundy sweater dress and black knee-high boots.

"I don't blame you. I would have left too."

"I acted crazy though. I was right when I told Matt I was immature and irresponsible."

I then dove into the events of the last two days as I applied makeup to my bare face. I didn't have time for much, so I kept it light.

"Theo Anderson? Really? You could have at least done better than him," she said after I finished my story.

"Right?" Selena agreed as she pulled the mascara wand away from her lashes.

"What's wrong with Theo?"

"What isn't wrong with him? He's a tool," Selena stated nonchalantly.

"He's not that bad. I dated him on and off for years."

"Yeah, because you're a tool too."

"Don't listen to her." Kat rolled her eyes and lightly pushed Selena once she finished with her mascara. "He is a tool, but you're not. You just weren't ever great at picking guys."

"I guess not much has changed then." I laughed ironically.

Kat gave me a sad smile.

"Forget about him, you can do so much better. I'm gonna find you a nice guy while you're still here. The best way to get over a guy is to get under another," Selena tried to cheer me up, although I was feeling fine right now.

"I can find my own man, Selena." I rolled my eyes at her.

"Sure you can." She waved me off. "Now, how do I look?"

I shot her a thumbs up. We walked out of my bathroom. Kat and I led the way to the dining hall. I pointed out more things along the way to Selena, though not as much as Tyler could.

We were the last ones to enter the dining hall. King Finnian's chair was empty, no surprise there. On the opposite side of us was Kieran, Emiliya, Niki, and Lili. On our side, it was Tyler, three empty chairs for us, Matt, then Dalton. Selena waved cheerfully to Dalton and ruffled up his hair as she walked past him. Selena sat next to Tyler and Kat sat next to Matt, I sat in between them and across from Niki.

Immediately, salad was brought out and wine was poured. I decided to stay away from the wine tonight and stick to water. I had enough alcohol that Saturday to last me a while.

Once the waiters were gone, the introductions started, thankfully before I could be questioned.

"You must be Selena. It is quite a pleasure. I am the Head Royal Witch, Nikolina Petrova. You may call me Niki."

"It's nice to meet you. Kat told me a lot about you."

"Katerina is a dear and a pleasure to teach." She looked over at Kat fondly, who smiled in return. She then turned back to Selena and continued her introductions, gesturing to everyone. "This is my youngest sister, Liliya; my middle sister, Emiliya; and her mate and the Royal Beta, Kieran."

"It's nice to meet you all," she spoke confidently but a slight blush creeped up her cheeks.

"I'm truly thrilled for you and Tyler. You make a lovely couple."

"Thanks, Niki." Tyler smiled down at Selena, gazing at her affectionately. She returned the look and her cheeks grew redder.

"Kendall, I'm sure you are thrilled at having your sister here." Niki turned her gaze to me.

"Yeah, it's great."

"Thank goodness you decided to take a trip to visit your family," she continued.

Emiliya snorted lightly. "You speak as if her trip were planned, dear sister. She destroyed her room, which was so generously given to her, and left the castle without alerting anyone. Tyler owes finding his mate to Miss Keating acting like a petulant child."

"Emiliya, mind your manners," Niki countered with a warning in her voice. "Kendall is free to leave as she pleases, and werewolves are known to be temperamental. It is not the first time furniture has been ruined and it won't be the last."

"Her temperament played no part in her behavior," Emiliya continued, ignoring her sisters warning.

"No, my impulsivity did. Which, by the way, was the reason I went after those wolves that day. Which saved us from being ambushed. Just in case you forgot," I informed her calmly.

"I am more than capable of protecting myself, Miss Keating," she sneered at me. "Need I remind you how easily I subdued you in the limo?"

I growled lowly at her, but Kieran cut in before I could lose my temper. "Enough, Emiliya. You're very powerful, but the five of you could not have defeated one hundred wolves alone. Give credit where credit is due," he told her sternly.

She glared at him hatefully, her eyes full of a surprising amount of malice. He fidgeted slightly before clearing his throat and turning away from her.

"I am curious, why did you go after Miss Keating?" Kieran asked Tyler, his adam's apple bobbing until Emiliya looked away from him.

"She's my friend and I was worried for her safety," he lied smoothly, not revealing that King Finnian had sent him. "I'm more than happy I did, or else I might not have met my mate."

"How did you know where she was going? Did she tell you before she left?" Kieran continued his questioning.

"I cast a tracking spell on him to be able to locate her," Niki told him.

"I see."

After that, the conversation was light. No one else questioned me. Emiliya ate in silence while Niki kept the conversation flowing, asking Selena questions about herself and getting to know her.

After dessert was finished, we all got up to leave. Kieran and Emiliya left the room quickly, as did Niki after she told us goodnight. Lili hung back to ask if I was alright. I appreciated her concern and assured her that I was fine and had just been homesick.

She left to go back to her room. The rest of us walked out. Selena and Tyler parted from us, going up a floor while we went down a couple. Once we reached our hall, we all went to our separate rooms.

I went into the bathroom and turned on the faucets in the bathtub, letting it fill with soothing hot water before submerging myself. I soaked for a while, letting my eyes shut in relaxation but they soon shot open.

"Shit," I mumbled to myself. I had forgotten to call Mom. Again.

"Did you call Mom?" I asked Selena through mindlink after she dropped her barrier.

"Yes, because I'm a good daughter," she answered back, her tone filled with humor.

I ignored her after that and raised my own shield back up. I let out a sigh of relief that she remembered and relaxed once again.

After a while, I got out, the water gurgling as it swirled down the drain. I got ready for bed and left the bathroom.

As I stepped out, a wave of déjà vu hit me. Sitting on my bed was none other than King Finnian. I was in nothing but a t-shirt and panties. I had just taken a bath after dinner. It was just like my first night here all over again.

Why was he here? What could he possibly want now? Why does he insist on leading me on all the time? My endless questions were exhausting, and I was done with it.

I stayed silent and crossed my arms over my chest, glaring daggers at him, but still giving him the silent treatment.

"You're back," he stated, his blue gaze meeting mine. I noticed dark bags hanging under his eyes. Good.

My silent treatment didn't last long, more for the simple fact that my mouth ran without my permission and my sarcasm was never ending. "Great observation."

"Are you okay?" He ignored my sarcasm. He sounded sincere, worried even, but I wasn't buying it. I wouldn't let him get my hopes up again.

"I was great until I saw you on my bed like the creepy stalker you are."

He clenched his jaw. "You really test me sometimes, Miss Keating."

"Yeah, well—"

My clever remark was cut off by my door slamming open and someone storming in.

"I don't appreciate you pushing me out of your mind," Selena snapped at me.

King Finnian, who was sitting on my bed, was on his feet in front of me as soon as the door opened. He stood between us protectively and growled at Selena threateningly. She stopped in her tracks and gaped at him for a few seconds.

"Shut the hell up." I snarled at him and pushed him away. "She's my sister. Do *not* growl at her."

He relaxed but still shot me another glare. I pushed him again. He finally moved a few feet away from me, which allowed Selena to walk over to me. It was now her turn to stand in front of me protectively.

"You must be the idiot who doesn't want my sister. Now that I've seen you in person, I can see you're doing her a favor. She's so far out of your league, it's not even funny. She could do so much better," she sneered at him.

"I'll let you off with a warning since you are new to the castle and my Gamma's mate, but I won't tolerate being spoken to that way."

"Oh, shut up, you mouth breather. Why don't you cry me a fucking river, get in your douche canoe, and row the fuck away. Or better yet, drown in it."

I smiled at the appalled expression on his face but stopped once he sneered at her and took a threatening step towards her. I pushed her behind me and growled at him as well.

"Stay the hell away from my sister," I warned him.

"She's being disrespectful. She needs to learn her place," he said sternly.

"I do know my place. It's with my sister. You may be my king but my loyalty will always lie with her," Selena retorted defiantly.

I ignored her and continued, "I think it's you who needs to learn his place, King Finnian. You can't just come and go as you please. You may get some sick pleasure from getting my hopes up just to tear me down but that's over. My hopes are nonexistent when it comes to you, so just stay away from me. Your game is over. You won, now leave me alone."

He stared at me for a few seconds, his expression blank. "It was never a game to me, Miss Keating."

With that, he turned and walked away, closing the door softly behind him.

CHAPTER EIGHTEEN

I had spent most of Tuesday and Wednesday helping Selena get settled and familiar with the castle. She didn't just want to hang up her clothes in Tyler's room. No, she wanted to make it her room as well and add some personal touches.

I found out that the Royal floor was different from the guest floors. Instead of rooms, they had suites. They had a living room with a kitchenette and a breakfast nook. Next to that was the bedroom, which had a bathroom. Tyler's suite in particular had one bedroom, but some suites had multiple bedrooms depending on if they had children.

We had spent the day hanging up family pictures and changing a few other things. Selena didn't really appreciate Tyler's decorating skills, or lack thereof. She changed everything from the sheets on the bed to the curtains hanging from the windows. Tyler didn't seem to mind the changes. In fact, he seemed to be happy that she was making herself at home. I could tell Tyler already adored her.

It took a long time to get her settled, but I didn't mind. I was glad to get to spend some quality time with her. We caught up on everything that had happened with each other for the last few weeks. We even had a game night with Matt, Dalton, Kat, Tyler, and Lili.

Now it was Thursday morning, and I was ready to get back to training after nearly a week off. Selena agreed to go with me, so we were traipsing through the woods in wolf form; heading towards the training field.

Once we were close, I whined, letting Selena know to stop. We both shifted and put our clothes back on, which we had been carrying in our mouths. We walked the last half mile or so, arguing playfully along the way.

After a while, we finally broke through the tree line, our vision filled with wolves training and watching. I passed by all of them and walked over to the edge of the field, where Nathan was waiting and stretching out on the blue mat.

"Well, well. Look who finally decided to grace us with her presence. I was wondering when your lazy ass would come back." Nathan chuckled, his orange hair practically glowing in the sunlight.

"I learned a new fact while I was gone, Red." I grinned at him and dropped down to start stretching as well. "Do you want to hear it?"

"I'd say no but I know you wouldn't listen. So, go ahead, enlighten me."

"Gingers earn a freckle for every soul they steal. You must have set some kind of record." Selena grinned at my words and dropped down next to me.

His freckled face pulled up into a grin, his eyes crinkling in the corners. "That's a new one, I must admit. Better be careful though, I might just steal yours next."

"You'd have to actually beat me first. By the way, this is my sister Selena. She's Tyler's mate." I pointed my thumb over to my sister.

"Nice to meet you, Royal Gamma Female." He held his hand out for her to shake and bowed his head slightly.

"Oh, just call me Selena." She seemed surprised at the title as she shook his hand.

"Sure," he said with a kind smile.

"How come you're so nice and polite to her?" I asked incredulously. "When I first met you, you put me in a headlock and told me to try and get away."

He grinned widely. "In my defense, it was a part of your training."

"She's here to train too."

"Maybe I just like her better." He shrugged.

"I am the more likeable sister." Selena agreed.

"You're the more ugly sister but definitely not the more likeable," I grumbled.

"More ugly? You're definitely the illiterate sister."

Nathan stood up and reached down to pull Selena up, but ignored me. They both gave me cheeky grins while I glared and stood up myself.

"I have to agree with you," Nathan added.

I was appalled at this turn of events. I never thought they would join together and team up against me. I didn't like it at all.

"You two look like Cinderella's ugly stepsisters when you're all buddy buddy like this," I muttered.

"You're more like Ursula if you want to bring Disney into this." Selena cackled like a hyena at her own joke.

"Let's just get started," I mumbled and rolled my eyes at her.

"I have no doubt in my mind that she must be your sister," Harrison cut in with a chuckle as he walked up to our training mat.

"Unfortunately. Selena, this is Harrison. He's the head of the Royal Army. Harrison, this is Selena."

"It's a pleasure, Selena. I look forward to training you."

"Let's get this show on the road. I feel out of practice." I rolled my neck side to side and shook my body out, getting ready to spar.

"If you'd actually showed up to practice, maybe you wouldn't feel that way, kid." He chuckled heartily.

"I like to keep everyone on their toes." I grinned at him cheekily.

"I believe that. Now, I want the two of you to spar first." He pointed at me and Selena.

We both nodded and walked to the center of the mat, facing each other. We lost our immature bantering and got serious. This wasn't the first time we had sparred. We knew when it was time for joking and when to get serious.

We began slowly, circling each other and watching the other's movement. Selena struck first, throwing her fist towards my face. I easily dodged it and sent my fist into her gut, causing her breath to catch slightly.

She backed up. We circled each other again. Neither one of us were particularly patient people but she was more impatient than me. Which is why she struck first again. She aimed her fist towards my face again but when I dodged that she kicked me in the side of the knee. It buckled a little but I managed to stay upright. Until she tackled me.

My back hit the mat, her full body weight on top of me, knocking the air from my lungs. She threw a right hook, nailing me in the eye, before I got my bearings.

I drove my forearm into her ribs, knocking her off of me and switching our positions. I returned the punch to the eye. She reached up and punched me in the gut. I countered with a gut punch of my own, which knocked the wind out of her since she was flat on the ground.

She managed to maneuver her leg up between mine and sent her foot into my stomach, throwing me backwards. She jumped on me and twisted one arm painfully while wrapping the other around my neck. I tried to lift my other arm to push her off, but she fell to the side, trapping my free arm under her body, but still keeping me restrained.

I struggled to break free, while she kept urging me to tap out. I refused. This fight wasn't over until I was unconscious or victorious.

I've been training with Selena for years and I had only beaten her a handful of times. As much as I hated to admit it, she was stronger than me during those times. I was faster, but that only did so much when she overpowered me. I wouldn't let that happen now. I was stronger now, smarter. I've been training with the best of the best. I was able to beat Nathan. I won't let her win.

With that new burst of inspiration, I wiggled my arm out of her death grip and elbowed her in the temple. It wasn't hard enough to knock her out but enough for her to loosen her hold on my neck so I could slip out.

Since she was already on her side, it was easy to flip her onto her stomach. I sat on her back and forced both of her arms around her back and up towards her neck, pushing as far as they would go without pulling her shoulders out of its socket.

Her legs flailed, trying to kick me. She only managed to kick me in the butt a few times but not enough to hurt. She continued to fight, but I didn't let up. I moved her hands up the slightest bit, making the hold more painful.

Finally, her hand tapped lightly against my arm. I released her from my hold. We both stood up and faced each other. Her eye was already starting to bruise, as I knew mine was as well. Her nose was trickling blood. She looked at me begrudgingly, but I could tell she was impressed; not that she'd ever admit it.

"Your dad taught you two well. You're already in pretty good shape, Selena. There are a few things we need to work on, for both of you, but you're both natural fighters." Harrison drew our attention to him. "Now, let's get to work."

* * *

"You've reached the Royal Office, how can I direct your call?" I asked into the phone receiver.

My legs were propped up on the desk, my left ankle crossed over my right, as I leaned back in the rolling chair. It was Friday morning, and I was back to answering phones in Tyler's office. Selena was supposed to be helping. Instead, she was sitting on Tyler's desk, being nosy and distracting. Not that he seemed to mind.

We were planning on spending the morning in here then head out to train after lunch. After that, Selena, Dalton, and I were going to Harrison's place for dinner. Tyler, Kieran, and King Finnian were heading out of town for the night at one o' clock, so Selena had no choice but to hang out with me.

Matt and Kat were going on a date tonight, then Kat would be joining me and Selena for a much needed girls's night. The guys wouldn't be back until early in the morning, so we had plenty of girl time before Tyler stole Selena back from us.

She hadn't been very happy when she found out about his overnight trip since they just found each other, but Tyler had to go. Apparently, King Finnian had some kind of business he needed to attend to in the human world.

Tyler and Kieran not only helped him with werewolf matters but also with his company. He had a human that he trusted acting as the CEO. He couldn't really publicly act as the CEO since he didn't age. That was something he couldn't let humans notice. So, he had a human who knew the truth as the face of the company while he did all the work from the castle. It worked out great because he was anonymous and stayed away from any radars but still made plenty of money, which was needed to rule an entire species.

He liked to go every few months, just to check on things personally. Tyler, Kieran, and several guards always went with him.

"I need to speak to King Finnian, please." A deep voice grunted into the phone.

"He's not taking any calls this morning, can I take a message?"

It didn't surprise me that the call was for him. He had gotten a ridiculous amount of calls; most weren't important. I would usually transfer them to Tyler or Kieran, who would determine if they were of importance.

Although sometimes, I could tell that they weren't and handled it myself. But today, Tyler told me to only take messages since Finnian wasn't going to talk to anyone today; he was preparing to leave, after all.

I had, unfortunately, seen him twice this morning since he decided to work out of his public office today. I'd gotten used to not seeing him regularly while I was in Tyler's office; I had actually only seen him in his public office three times.

But he was here today, just down the hall. I could feel his presence. His scent clung to the air, thoroughly distracting me. I ignored him both times, which I could do easily since Tyler and Selena were the only people around, and they both knew the truth.

Selena had sent him glares both times and tried to mouth off to him, but Tyler stopped her. If looks could kill though, Finnian would be dead a hundred times over.

I refused to even look at him, even though I felt his eyes on me both times.

"This is important. Tell him it's Alpha Rylan Covington. He'll want to take the call."

I was going to tell him no but something in his voice told me that it *was* important. I glanced over at Tyler to see what he wanted me to do but he wasn't paying any attention. Instead, he was distracted by Selena's shrill laughter.

I sighed heavily. "Okay, hang on."

I pressed the hold button and walked out of the office, still unnoticed by the lovebirds. I swallowed thickly, gathering my courage, and walked to the end of the hall. Once I reached the thick wooden door, I raised my fist and knocked gently twice.

"Come in." I heard him grunt.

I twisted the knob and walked in. As I laid eyes on him again, I made sure to keep a straight face, acting completely unaffected by his presence. His eyes swept over me, from head to toe. His eyes were soft and glazed over as he took me in, but I didn't let it fool me.

"There is an Alpha Rylan Covington on the phone, Your Highness. I was going to take a message but he insisted that it's important. Do you want me to tell him you're unavailable?" I mumbled formally.

He cleared his throat, his eyes meeting mine again. I couldn't handle his piercing cerulean eyes but I didn't want him to feel superior, so I held his gaze, refusing to look away.

"I'll take the call. Thank you, Miss Keating."

I gritted my teeth. "He's on line one."

I turned and walked away, closing his door softly behind me before he could say anything else. I was tempted to enhance my hearing and listen to his conversation since his public office wasn't spelled to be soundproof, but I didn't care. Or, I didn't want to care anyways. I shouldn't be concerned about him or what he's doing. So, I walked away and let my hearing stay human.

"Who was that?" Tyler asked when I walked back in his office, finally noticing my disappearance.

"Alpha Rylan Covington."

"Rylan called? Did he say why?"

"Nope," I answered shortly. "Why? Is he important?" I asked as an afterthought.

"He's a Council member. King Finnian ordered him to look into the rebellion."

He didn't give any more information and I didn't ask for it.

The rest of the morning after that went by quickly. I split away from Tyler and Selena after a quick lunch to go to my room to change into workout clothes. After throwing on a pair of shorts and a t-shirt, I walked out of my bathroom.

When I saw Finnian leaning against my bedpost, I let out a disgruntled groan and threw my hands up in exasperation.

"What could you possibly want now?" I grumbled in irritation.

"I just wanted to tell you I'll be away from the castle overnight."

"Yeah, I already know that." I rolled my eyes.

His lips tugged up in the corners. "If you have any problems, Niki will be available to you. If you get in any trouble, she will keep you safe. I'll be back around seven in the morning."

"I can take care of myself," I retorted.

"I know you can; but she's here, just in case."

"Whatever. Is that all? I have better things to do today than talk to you."

He smiled a tight smile at me but it looked more sad than anything. "That's all, Miss Keating. I'll see you at the ball tomorrow."

"There will be a lot of people there, King Finnian. Hopefully, I can avoid being in your general vicinity. If I'm lucky, that is."

He ignored my comment. "Have a good night. Stay safe."

With that, he walked out, leaving me alone once again.

* * *

The rest of the day passed by quickly. Training went well, and dinner went even better. Harrison's mate, Winnie, was a sweetheart and a damn good cook. She reminded me of my mom. She told us we were welcome back anytime. I knew I'd take her up on that offer soon.

Tyler, Kieran, and Finnian left soon after Finnian left my room. Selena went to go see Tyler off, but I chose not to be in attendance for that. They were taking Finnian's private plane to New York, where his headquarters were located.

Selena had gone upstairs after we got back to take a shower before meeting up in my room. I was going to do the same, as was Kat. I already had movies and snacks spread out on the coffee table for our girls's night.

Before I could go to the bathroom, a knock on my door stopped me. My eyebrows scrunched together, perplexed at who it could be. Selena and Kat would just walk in, Tyler was gone, and

Matt and Dalton were at a poker night that Nathan was having at his house.

I walked over and pulled the door open, surprised to see Niki. I stepped aside and allowed her to walk inside, before shutting the door behind her. We walked over to my couch and took a seat.

"To what do I owe this visit tonight?" I started.

"I know how confused you have been, dear girl."

"What do you mean?" I mumbled.

"Finnian has kept you in the dark. I didn't want to get involved. My hopes were high that he would have told you on his own, when he was ready, but I fear that day may never come. He's stubborn, that one . . ." Niki trailed off.

"You're going to tell me?" I asked hopefully, perking up slightly.

"Of course not, I could never betray his confidence like that." My hope deflated again.

"But he *is* hiding something?"

"He is. You will have to discover what it is yourself, I'm afraid."

"No offense, Niki, but why did you come here if you weren't going to tell me?"

"I have excellent news to share with you," Niki said cheerfully.

"What's that?" I raised an eyebrow, half in question and half in annoyance.

"Katerina mastered a very important spell recently." Her eyes gleamed knowingly.

"Oh yeah?" I asked, uninterested.

It wasn't that I didn't care about Kat's training; I did. I was just feeling disappointed and let down. I felt like Niki dangled a hook in front of me only to snatch it away before I could actually reach it.

"Yes. It is a spell to view someone's memories."

"I already knew about that. She already spelled us so that no one could do it to us. She mastered it like, at least a week ago."

"Oh, good, I'm so glad you already know how the spell works," she stated joyfully.

I just continued to give her a dry, annoyed look but it didn't seem to bother her. She stood up.

"I hope you have a wonderful night, Kendall." She walked towards the door and I followed behind her. She stopped before she could open it and turned to face me. "I assume Kat informed you that Finnian's mind is also shielded from prying witches?"

I nodded.

"His mind is open to Kat but only until he gets back tomorrow morning. I suggest you tell Kat to search for the vision I showed him to narrow down her search. Goodnight, Kendall."

With that, she left. I did nothing but stare at her retreating figure, my mouth hanging open in shock. I walked to my bathroom and showered, my movements entirely on autopilot.

I thought over Niki's words. She was giving me the opportunity to find out the truth, to find out what Finnian had been hiding from me . . . What was keeping him from me.

If Finnian and I were making any kind of progress, I wouldn't do it. I would wait until he was ready to tell me. It was an invasion of privacy and trust. I knew if he did it to me, I'd be pissed. But I really had no choice. He would never tell me, and I wanted to know; needed to know. I needed to know what was so bad that we couldn't be together.

With that in mind and my decision made, I got dressed and waited on the couch for Kat.

Looks like our girls's night was going to go a little differently than expected.

CHAPTER NINETEEN

After I got tired of sitting, I started pacing around my room, chewing on my thumb nail nervously. I wasn't sure about this; I wasn't sure about anything. But I did know that I needed to know. I couldn't live in the dark anymore.

As I paced, I thought of all the things that could go wrong. Would he know what we were doing? Would he feel us riffling through his head? Would he be mad at me or would he be relieved that I finally knew?

More importantly, I thought about what I might find. Would *I* end up mad or relieved? Would he do something in the future or had he already done something in the past? Or was it something I would do, or maybe someone else.

I let out a rugged sigh and raked my fingers through my dark brown curls roughly. I pulled my hands out of my tangled locks and rubbed my face harshly, anxiety filling me to my core. *What would I find?*

After a few minutes, my door finally opened. Selena walked through first, with Kat right behind her. They shut the door, leaving the three of us alone and away from prying ears. Kat noticed my tension filled state right away and glanced worriedly at me, but Selena took a minute.

"Finally, a room with some freaking heat. I almost froze my tits off walking down here," she complained dramatically. Normally I would agree; the castle was always cold, which was why I turned the heater in my room on earlier. But, right now, it could have been freezing and I probably wouldn't notice. "What's up with you?" she asked, finally noticing my anxiousness.

"I need you to do a spell," I blurted out, looking at Kat.

"Of course, what's going on? What do you need me to do?" Kat agreed immediately.

"I need you to search through King Finnian's memories."

Her dark eyebrows knitted together. "I can't, Kendall. I wish I could, but Niki spelled his mind to keep people out."

"She did, but she said you have access to it until he gets back."

Her eyebrows unfurrowed and rose in surprise, her eyes widening. "What? She told you that?"

"Yeah, like fifteen minutes ago. She said she couldn't tell me what he was hiding from me but his mind was open and unblocked. She told me to tell you to search for the memory of the vision she showed him."

After a few seconds of thinking, Kat asked, "Kendall, are you sure about this?"

"Of course, she's sure. Let's see what that lying asshole is hiding," Selena interrupted.

"I'm sure, Kat," I reassured her, "I need to know. I understand if you don't want to do it; he might consider it treason. If you don't want to get mixed up in that, you don't have to."

"I'm with you, Kendall. If you go down, I go down. I just wanted to make sure that this is really what you want. You can't unsee or unknow what I show you," she clarified.

"I know. I'm sure," I repeated.

"Okay, let's do it then." Kat looked like she was ready to perform the spell.

"So, how will it work? You can do it without him here, right?" Selena asked.

"Yeah, I can. He won't even feel me in his mind. Niki taught me how to do it without alerting the target. I'll need to harness water.

I've had an easier time doing this spell with that element. I'll hold your hand and you'll be able to see what I see. It will be from his eyes, so we'll see whatever he saw," she told me.

I nodded and Kat walked out of the room to gather her supplies.

"You can show us both, right?" Selena asked when Kat returned.

Kat and I shared a knowing look and both rolled our eyes at her nosiness. "Yes, Sel, I can show you both."

We cleared the coffee table of all the junk food so Kat can put a bowl full of water in the center. She sat on one side and Selena and I sat across from her.

"This will probably take a while; at least an hour. It will take me some time to get into his head and track the memory down. Once the memory is over, I'll leave his head and we'll be done," she explained. We nodded. "Are you ready? I won't be able to stop once I start." We nodded again.

She held her hands out for us, on either side of the bowl. I grabbed her right hand, Selena grabbed her left. I crossed my legs, getting comfortable. Kat closed her eyes and we did the same. She took a deep breath and started chanting lowly.

I could hear the water sloshing around in the bowl and her chanting slowly got louder and louder. Nothing happened for a while; nothing appeared behind my closed eyes.

And finally, after what had to have been over half an hour, I finally saw something. One second I was staring at the blackness of my eyelids; then the next, I was staring down at a legal document.

My eyesight was hazy, like I was in the middle of a dream. I saw colors but they were muted and dull.

A pen moved in front of me, but I could tell I wasn't the one writing when I saw a large hand scribbling on the paper.

It was weird to be in his head. I couldn't feel what he was feeling but I could see and hear everything that he did.

He signed the bottom of the document and dropped the pen. He leaned back in his chair and looked up. I saw the inside of his office for a few seconds before it was obscured from my vision when he rubbed his hands over his face, his eyes closed as he sighed in exhaustion. I wasn't sure where he was, but I could tell it wasn't his public office. It still looked like an office though, so I figured it must be his private office on the sixth floor.

He kept his relaxed posture, his eyes closing for a few seconds, showing us only darkness. After a few minutes, he heard someone walking down the hall. He smelled that it was Niki before she even knocked. When she did, he grunted out his permission to enter.

Niki's willowy frame entered the room. She looked a few years younger but still had that knowing, powerful glint in her eyes, though they held a heaviness I hadn't seen before.

Finnian sat up straight once he saw her and gestured to the chair across from him. She sat down gracefully, tucking her dress under her as she lowered onto the chair. Her raven hair was pushed back, showing her sharp, regal features.

"What do I owe this pleasure, Nikolina?" he asked slowly. Even in this dream like vision where I couldn't see him, his voice still gave me chills in the best way possible.

"I'm afraid I come bearing troubling news, King Finnian." Her voice was sympathetic, and her lips pulled down in a frown.

"What?" He sat up straighter and spoke tightly, his voice thick with apprehension.

"I had a rather disturbing vision this morning."

"Of what?"

"I believe it would be more beneficial if I show you, Your Highness. I don't believe I dare to describe it in great detail."

His vision moved up and down twice, like he was nodding to her. She held out her hand across his desk. He hesitantly reached over and grabbed it.

Niki closed her eyes and started chanting. Finnian closed his as well. My mind went dark until Niki's vision started playing in his mind.

It felt weird, the sensation of the vision was odd. It was Niki's vision, who was showing it to Finnian, who Kat was seeing it from him, who was showing it to us. It felt like a game of telephone but with visions instead of phrases. Despite that, I knew the vision wasn't distorted or altered in any way. What we were seeing was what Niki had originally seen, however long ago it was.

The vision wasn't completely clear. Faces were blurred and half of the vision was just feelings and not images. It started with Finnian running in wolf form. Trees blurred past him as he ran faster than I've ever seen any wolf run. After a few minutes, he finally slowed. He shifted back while he was still jogging.

He fell down to the ground, an overwhelming sense of loss and despair sweeping over him. Nothing was in front of him at first, but suddenly it appeared. *She* appeared. Her face was a blur, and her body was mangled and bloody. Death surrounded her, seeping out of her pores. She laid still, unmoving and unbreathing. He cradled her to his chest as her arms hung limply. His vision blurred with tears before they fell.

It took me a minute, but I finally realized who the girl was. The face was still blurred but those dark curls hanging over her shoulders were ones I'd recognize anywhere, even when they were covered in blood.

It was me.

He continued to hold me, crying over my lifeless body. He ran his hand over my hazy face and muttered apologies, over and over again.

After what felt like a lifetime, his sorrow mixed with something else. As he looked up, I felt it clear as day, deep in my bones. The person in front of him was blurred and distorted, but whoever he saw caused one feeling.

Betrayal.

The betrayal ran deep, as deep as the sorrow he felt for his fallen mate. Whoever was in front of him was someone he trusted. Whoever was in front of him was my killer.

The vision faded away, and I was suddenly back in his office, looking at Niki. He snatched his hand from hers and she opened her eyes. She gave him a sad, sympathetic look.

He looked away from her and turned to stare out the window instead. It overlooked the backyard, the forest, and the mountain behind the castle. Niki stayed silent, giving him a moment to collect himself.

I heard him swallow harshly. His gaze left the window and looked down at his hands. They were clenched so hard that his knuckles were as white as paper. He relaxed them. Blood flowed down his fingers from the puncture wounds in his palms. His claws had extended and dug into his skin relentlessly.

After a few minutes, he turned back to Niki. "You don't know who my mate or her killer was?" His voice was cold, unattached now. But I could hear grief if I listened closely.

"I'm sorry, Finnian. I don't. Faces are often blurred in my visions."

"I understand." He looked back down to his papers. "You may leave. Thank you, Nikolina," he said emotionlessly.

She stood up and walked away, but not before stopping by the door briefly. "I know you're scared, Finn. Even if you won't admit it. But visions aren't always set in stone."

He didn't respond, so she continued her way out, closing his door with a soft click.

He got back to work.

A loud gasp escaped my throat when I was pulled back to the present. I drew in ragged breaths, my heart thundering in my chest. I closed my eyes tightly again, trying to calm down.

When I opened them back up, I saw Kat and Selena both looking at me with tears streaking down their cheeks. As I reached up to touch my face, I realized the same was happening to me. I didn't even realize I was crying.

I wiped my cheeks of all moisture with the palm of my hand then rubbed my hands over my cotton shorts.

I didn't know how to feel about what I saw. I suddenly understood Finnian and why he's done what he's done. Whoever killed me in that vision had done it because I was his mate. *He had been trying to protect me.*

In a way, I understood that. But I also resented it. He let whoever that was keep us apart—keep us from happiness. I certainly didn't want to die, but we were letting this douchebag win by staying apart. I didn't want that either.

Before I could think about it some more, Selena launched herself at me, squeezing me tightly. She buried her face in my shoulder and started sobbing. It was shocking considering she wasn't a crier, but I wasn't either and had cried too.

I wrapped my arms around her. Kat joined in and we added her into our hug, all of us holding each other and crying together.

I couldn't get the image of my dead, mangled body from my mind. I was scared and I hated that.

We sat there on the floor for God knows how long. They were my best friends and sisters. We held each other like I would die tomorrow.

Eventually, our tears stopped and we pulled away, all of us sniffling.

"No more crying. You heard Niki at the end; not all visions are set in stone," I instructed them sternly.

"You're right." Selena agreed, wiping her tears away. "No one is going to hurt you without going through me first," she insisted fiercely.

"Me too. We'll protect you." Kat agreed.

"That's all the protection I need right there," I teased, making light of the situation.

"Damn straight," Selena joked back, but it was weak since I could tell she was still shaken up.

"I'm gonna be fine," I promised them. I grabbed both of their hands and squeezed. "Why don't we get some sleep?" I suggested when I looked over at Kat. "You look exhausted. We can figure all this out in the morning."

When I looked at my phone, I realized it was only eleven o'clock. I knew that Kat was drained from such a big spell. She nodded gratefully and we all stood up.

We pulled the comforter and sheets on my king-sized bed down and climbed in. Kat and I were on the edges while Selena laid down in the middle. I grabbed the remote and turned the TV on, turning it down low. I usually didn't sleep with it on, but Kat did, so I always left it going when she was in the room.

Kat and I both switched off the lamps, leaving the room to only be lit by the dull glow of the TV across the room. I handed her the remote, letting her put on whatever channel she wanted, but she left it on the sitcom that was already playing.

The three of us snuggled deeper under the blankets. Selena stuck her cold toes on my bare leg, and I kicked them away. She moved them over to Kat, who did the same thing.

"Tyler lets me put my feet on him," she whined, a pout on her face.

"Tyler's also whipped like cream," I mumbled.

She didn't reply right away, but when she did, it wasn't about my comment. "I love you, Kenny, you know that, right?"

I turned on to my side to face her. "I know. I love you too, Sel. You too, Kat."

"I love you guys too," Kat added.

"Alright, enough of this mushiness. Let's go to sleep. Goodnight."

"Night," they both mumbled in return.

We all closed our eyes and drifted off into unconsciousness.

* * *

My sleep didn't last long.

A couple of hours at most.

I tossed and turned, my dreams filled with images of my dead body. I woke with a silent gasp, which thankfully didn't wake Kat or Selena since they both slept like the dead. I didn't try to sleep again after that; instead, I lay awake, staring at the canopy over the bed.

After a while of that, I finally gave up on sleep.

I swung my legs over the side of the bed, staying as quiet as possible. I slowly tiptoed out of my room, pulling the door gently behind me. The cold air of the hallway bit at my exposed skin, causing goosebumps to erupt across my flesh.

I wrapped my arms around myself. I hadn't changed out of my short pajama shorts and thin t-shirt before I left and was regretting it. I hadn't even bothered to put on shoes either. It helped to remain quiet, stealthy, but my toes were freezing against the cold, hard stone floor.

I tiptoed my way through the castle and walked up the hidden staircase and into the sixth floor. I slipped through the door and made my way towards King Finnian's bedroom. He wasn't there, but I would wait for him. I wasn't one hundred percent sure what I wanted to say to him, but I knew we needed to talk.

His bedroom looked just like when I left it last time, save for the fact that he wasn't inside, watching me walk away. It was dark, illuminated by only the moonlight through the window. The first thing I did was start a fire in the fireplace, which not only lit the room in a dull orange glow but also warmed it considerably.

I sat back in his chair, watching the fire crackle and burn. I stayed away from the unused, pristine armchair, instead choosing to sit in his. Not only was it worn but it was covered with his scent, which clung to the air. I breathed it in deeply, greedily; letting it wash over me and calm me.

I sat there for hours. The fire eventually died down, and the room lit up little by little as the sun rose. I should've been tired but I wasn't. I was keyed up and full of energy; ready for this confrontation. It could quite possibly be our last.

I heard him coming down the hall. His steps were quick, full of purpose. When he threw his door open, I didn't look at him. I stayed still, my eyes staring blankly at the dim glowing embers. It felt just like the last time I was here, except our positions were switched.

"What are you doing here?" he murmured lowly after a few beats of silence. I could feel his eyes burning a hole in the back of my head.

I stayed silent, not ready to answer him yet.

"Miss Keating, I suggest you answer my question."

I still stayed silent. His demanding tone and words didn't even seem to register in my mind, my thoughts still running wild.

"Are you okay?" He walked around the chair and stopped front of me, his voice taking on a worried edge.

He was staring down at me, but my eyes didn't move from the fireplace.

He moved closer and kneeled down in front of me. His hand held my cheek, and he tilted my face over to finally meet his eyes. They were glowing a deep amber. "Kendall, what's wrong?" he asked gently, concern clear in his voice.

Hearing my name come from his lips was a shock, to say the least. I had only heard him say it once, and that was out of anger. Now, his eyes shone with worry, and his voice held a desperation for me to tell him what was bothering me.

"I know," I whispered.

His hand left my cheek and he stood up. He tried to put on a blank face, but I could see apprehension in his eyes when I looked closely. "You know, what exactly?"

"I know . . . everything." I stood up slowly, crossing my arms over my chest. "About Niki's vision. About why you won't be with me."

His face paled for a split second, but then a deep growl rumbled deep in his chest. "Nikolina told you?" he demanded through his growls.

"No, she didn't."

"Then how the hell do you know?" He hissed at me.

"Is that really what's important right now?" I spat out, finally losing my temper. "Why didn't you tell me?"

"You didn't need to know."

"The hell I didn't. I had every right to know!" I yelled at him.

"I'm trying to protect you. I've always tried to protect you," he said with a snarl.

"No, you're just a coward," I snapped, standing up and poking him in the chest roughly.

"If you had actually seen the vision, you would understand." He glared down at my finger.

"I did see the vision. I know exactly what happened in it." I returned his glare and pulled my finger away when he grabbed it.

"How could you possibly call me a coward if you saw it? You died."

"You're a coward because you refuse to try and change things."

"That vision is our fate if I accept you. It showed us our fate. I would rather live in a world where you're safe, even if you hate me, than in a world where you don't exist. I can't live in that world. I need you safe."

"It's our fate? That's bullshit!"

"It is!" he insisted. "Visions almost always come true. That vision showed us our fate if we give in."

"So, you change it!" I finally exploded. "We change it! We change fate. We fight fate. We make our own damn fate. Stop letting your fear control you. If you want me, fight for me. Fight for us and our future."

"It's not that easy." He pinched the bridge of his nose.

"It is that easy. We're all going to die someday. That's inevitable. Does that mean we should live in fear of that happening? Hell no."

"If it were my life at risk, I wouldn't give being with you a second thought. But I can't risk your life."

"Do you want to be with me?"

He hesitated for a few seconds, but he finally answered, his eyes softening considerably. "Of course I do. How could I not want to be with you?"

"Then fight. Let's fight together."

I started to get hopeful when he had a thoughtful look on his face, like he was considering it. I grabbed his hands in mine and laced our fingers together, giving his hands a gentle squeeze.

Finally, he sighed deeply. "I can't. I'm sorr—"

I dropped his hands like they had burned me and took a few steps away from him. He didn't finish his sentence. It took a second for me to push the tears away and gather my thoughts.

"I'm disappointed in you, Finnian. I thought you were better than this. I thought you were stronger than this, more courageous. I guess I was wrong." He winced at my words, like they physically pained him. "I can't keep fighting for you when I'm not being fought for in return." I turned away from him and walked towards the door.

"Kendall . . ." he whispered, a hint of desperation in his voice.

I paused for a second before I walked out. "Whoever the traitor is, they're still going to betray you. We'd be stronger together, united. As a team. But if you want to do this on your own, be my guest. Just don't expect me to be waiting for you when it's over. Goodbye, Finnian," I concluded softly. I didn't turn around to look at him.

With that, I continued out of his room and back down to mine. I had a ball to get ready for.

CHAPTER TWENTY

I had hoped that Selena and Kat would still be asleep by the time I got back so I wouldn't have to explain my absence, but I guess my luck had run out.

Selena was pacing in front of the bed then stopped when she saw me walk in. Kat was perched on the side of the bed speaking to Selena but her words trailed off when I entered.

"Where'd you go? I woke up hours ago, and you were just gone," Selena asked angrily.

"Are you serious? You always sleep until at least lunchtime, but the one time I needed you to stay asleep, you wake up early? Really?" I deadpanned.

She gave me a dry look. "You can't just disappear like that after what we saw last night," she hissed in annoyance.

My irritation deflated. "Sorry, I didn't mean to scare you guys. I just needed to talk to him," I admitted.

"Oh." Selena's face softened. "What happened?"

"There's really not a lot to tell. Everything is still exactly the same. He still doesn't want to try and make things work."

"I'm sorry, Kendall," Kat said to me sympathetically.

"It's fine." I shrugged. "I'm used to it. It's disappointing, but I'll get over it."

"I mean, it's kind of understandable now, right?" Selena added.

"I understand it completely, but I don't agree with it. He's being a coward." I crossed my arms, somewhat defensively.

"He doesn't want to lose you. I'd probably do the same with Tyler if I were in his position."

"Well then, you're a coward too," I retorted, my tone harsh.

"So, you consider wanting to protect your mate cowardly?" She mimicked my stance, stopping a few feet in front of me.

"If you refuse to be with your mate because you're scared? Yes."

"I don't think you really understand, Kendall. You died. And based on that vision, you died young. He's trying to protect you from that. Give him a break."

I let out a sarcastic laugh. "That's great coming from you, really. You want me to give him a break? You, of all people? Didn't you just tell him the other day to drown in his river of tears?"

"That was before I knew the whole story," she snapped.

"I thought you were supposed to be on my side?"

"I am on your side. As annoying as you are, I'm always on your side. But now, you're being too harsh on him."

"How about you don't talk to me like you know what I'm going through. Your mate adores you. When he doesn't care and wants nothing to do with you, then you can come talk to me about this."

"Why are you so damn stubborn?" She threw her hands up in exasperation.

"Okay, okay. Why don't we all just take a breath and calm down," Kat instructed, coming to stand between us.

We both continued to glare at each other but did as she said.

"Okay, good. Now, you two need to stop fighting with each other. There's no point in it. Selena, she's right. You don't know how she feels, and you should be happy about that. If being pissed off at King Finnian helps her, then by all means, let her be pissed." I smirked at Selena but dropped it when Kat turned her attention to me. "And Kendall, don't get so defensive. Selena loves you and just wants the best for you. You need to keep that in mind."

I sighed. We both grumbled apologies to each other. Kat was right on both counts, but neither of us liked it.

"Good, now no more fighting today. Let's just have a nice day. We get to spend the morning getting pampered at the spa, and then we get to see your parents again. So let's focus on the good."

"Okay, yeah, you're right. I'm gonna take a shower. I'll meet you two in the dining room for breakfast?" I resigned myself to her demands.

"Yeah, sounds good," Selena agreed. She sauntered out of the room in a hurry, probably wanting to see Tyler now that he was back.

"Thanks for diffusing that. I didn't want to fight with her. She just knows how to get under my skin," I told Kat when we were alone.

"Yeah, of course. I could tell that would have ended badly. The last thing we need right now, with everything else, is you two fighting. If we're going to fight this together, we need to be on the same page. Now, take a shower. I'll see you in a little bit."

I nodded as she walked away. As I made my way to the bathroom, all I could think about was how Kat was willing to fight for me but my own mate wasn't.

*   *   *

Spa days weren't exactly my cup of tea but I couldn't say it was completely awful either. It was actually kind of relaxing.

We started the day with massages. It helped release tension that I didn't even realize I had. That made me feel a million times better. After our massages, we got facials. I didn't think I would like it—and I didn't, really—but the results were amazing. My skin looked clearer, healthier, and was practically glowing once they were finished with me.

In the process of getting the facials, we also had our nails done. I wasn't one for fake nails so I had mine painted. It was a shimmery gold color which matched my dress. They did my toenails in the same color.

After all that, it was time for the not so fun part of the trip; getting our hair and make-up done. I went for a soft gold eyeshadow and winged black eyeliner. The mascara they used made my eyelashes look longer than normal. They painted a light coverage foundation on my face and blended in bronzer, blush, and concealer to perfection. We finished the look off with a nude lipstick and highlighter on my cheekbones.

After that, it was time for my hair. They trimmed off all the dead ends first and then dried my curls with a diffuser. I requested an updo, so they braided it back into a low bun with curls left out around my face.

Now that we're all finished, it was time to return to the castle. We had a little over an hour before we had to be there. We still needed to put on our gowns and add any final touches.

I thanked the ladies who helped me get ready and got into the limo with the girls. We had surprisingly gotten along well today, even Emiliya. She seemed friendlier today, nice even. Apparently, she loved spa days; it always put her in a good mood. She even complimented my hair and makeup, which was shocking, to say the least, coming from her.

Once we returned to the castle, we all went our separate ways. I walked into my closet and stripped off everything but my panties. I grabbed my dress from where it was hanging. I pulled the cover off and threw it carelessly to the floor. It took some maneuvering to pull it over my head without messing up my hair, but I finally got it settled over my body and pulled the snug material down over my hips.

My dress for the evening was a shimmery gold gown. It fell to the floor, a little too long without shoes, but I knew once I stepped into my strappy gold open toed heels, it would be perfect. It was backless with thin straps that crossed over each other in between my shoulder blades and connected to the front of the dress.

The back started a few inches above my ass and was tight over my hips but then flared out slightly around my legs. The front had a V-neck design with built in support, so my breasts were pushed up. It revealed a good bit of cleavage, but not too much.

It was revealing, for sure; especially with my whole back on display, but I loved it. The gold paired perfectly with my skin tone. It made my naturally tan skin glow and my eyes look greener.

Since the dress was shimmery and flashy, I tried to keep everything else simple. I put on a pair of dangly gold earrings and a thin gold bracelet with diamonds encrusted all the way around it. The bracelet was a gift from Niki. It had to have been expensive since it was made with real gold and diamonds, but she insisted that I take it. She said that it matched with my dress perfectly; it absolutely did.

I touched up my lipstick and slipped on my heels, making me four inches taller than I really was. I flicked off the light and left my bathroom. I immediately saw Kat sitting on the couch, already dressed in her gown.

"You look beautiful, Kendall. That is definitely your color."

"Thanks. So do you."

Kat was wearing a peony pink gown that matched the color of the rose quartz resting on her chest. The color complimented her cocoa skin beautifully and contrasted perfectly with her long and wavy walnut-colored locks.

"I imagine Finnian will be ready to fight for you when he sees you in that dress," she said knowingly.

I shook my head and rolled my eyes. He had already seen me half naked and still didn't want me, but I didn't say that out loud.

"How are you holding up? You seemed sad all day."

"Honestly? Not that great." After hearing me, she patted the couch next to her. I eased down, trying not to mess up my dress. "I'm just tired, I guess. I feel like I'm the only one fighting for us. I guess I'm not worth fighting for." I swallowed the lump in my throat.

She didn't jump in to inform me that it wasn't true, which I appreciated. Some people thought that was helpful, to try and make me feel better about myself, but that didn't help. I didn't need other people to tell me that. I needed to get my feelings out and figure it out myself.

"I've tried to make it work with him, Kat. Even when he gave me nothing to work with, I tried. But he just doesn't want that. He's scared, and I get it. But where does that leave me? Alone.

"I might eventually find another rejected wolf to be with, but I don't think I can actually be with someone after Finnian. No one else will be able to compare to him. I'll never be able to have a family with anyone else. I never thought it was that important to me until I realized I might never have it."

I hadn't really considered having a family at first, but after running away last weekend, I started thinking about it more and more. Werewolves weren't able to have pups with someone who wasn't their mate. There was an orphanage in the Royal Territory for pups who lost both parents, but there were never many kids there.

Werewolves typically had big families, so there was usually someone to take the kids in, but the few who didn't have any relatives would go to the orphanage. I suppose I could always adopt a pup there, but it wouldn't be the same without my mate.

"I don't know what to do next, but I feel like I'm finally done. It's scary. I always had my life planned out. I would meet my mate, have a few pups, and that would be that. I'd live happily ever after. But now that I don't have that, I really don't know what to do. I guess I'm going to have to figure it out, because I can't do it anymore. He keeps getting my hopes up and then letting me down at every turn. I can't do that anymore. Does that make me a bad person? That I'm giving up on my mate?"

"Of course not. You can't help how you feel. You have to do what's right for you, and only you will know what that is. Don't let anyone else help sway your decision about this. If you can't do it anymore, then don't do it. That's your decision and no one else's.

But it's okay if you want to keep fighting too. Whatever you feel is right in your heart is what you should do." She squeezed my hand supportively.

"How do you listen to your heart when it's too shattered to even talk to you?" I asked helplessly.

She gave me a sad smile. "Maybe the sound of it shattering is your answer."

That answer was vague, at best. If the sound of it shattering was my answer, then I was screwed; I had no idea what it meant. I wish I had a less ambiguous answer.

"I guess you're right. But I don't really want to talk about it anymore. If I do, I'll start crying and mess up my makeup. I'll never get it to look this good again if that happens."

She giggled. "We don't want that to happen," she teased.

"Thank you, Kat, for checking on me; for supporting me through all of this."

"You're my best friend. I'll always support you."

I gave her a weak smile before taking a deep breath and changing the subject. "What do you think? Do I need anything else?"

"Nope, it's perfect. You don't want to over-accessorize with that dress."

"That's what I was thinking. Come on, let's go get Matt and head over to the ball."

She nodded and followed behind me. Matt opened the door just as we walked up to his bedroom door, already dressed in his black tux. His curly shoulder-length hair was slicked back, looking neat for once instead of his usual unruly look.

We knocked on Dalton's door so he could join us on the walk to the ball. He was dressed in a similar tux as Matt. He complimented all of us on our appearances.

I noticed how his eyes were on me for a second longer than they should have. I wouldn't have noticed it before but now that I knew he was into me, it was hard not to. I didn't say anything but hoped he could move on soon. I didn't really know what he saw in me; our personalities clashed horribly. But I kept my fingers crossed that maybe he would find his mate tonight.

The castle was crowded with people, and that was just the hallways. Half of the people we encountered were dressed in gowns and tuxedos, the other half were workers dressed in black slacks, white button downs, and black vests. They were speed walking around, trying to make sure everything was running smoothly. The rest of the people were walking slowly, admiring the artwork on the walls and the architecture of the castle.

Once we finally reached the ballroom, it was already crowded. Half of the room was filled with round tables with silky white tablecloths covering them and fancy floral centerpieces on every one. The other half of the room was the dance floor, which was already being used.

The band in the corner of the room was playing classical music loudly, but not loud enough to overwhelm our sensitive hearing. Waiters were walking around, offering drinks and hors d'oeuvres.

There was a large and elegant staircase directly across the room from us, which I knew the Royals, Selena being one of them, would descend from once everyone arrived. Two of the tables in the center were empty, leading me to believe that those tables were for them as well.

As we walked further in, a waiter stopped in front of us to offer us drinks. He had a variety of beverages on his tray, letting us have our pick. Matt and Dalton both grabbed bourbon, and Kat grabbed water.

I hesitated between grabbing a champagne or water, but finally decided that it probably wasn't a great idea for me to drink tonight. It didn't go so well last time, after all. I picked up a champagne flute filled with lemon water and gave the young werewolf a grateful smile before he walked off.

I did a quick sweep of the room, searching for anyone familiar. I didn't see anyone at first, but when my eyes landed on a familiar mop of bright red hair, I knew immediately who it was.

"I'm going to look for Mom and Dad. Do you guys want to come?" Matt told us just as I looked back over to them.

"Sure," Kat agreed, and Dalton followed suit.

"I'm going to go say hi to Nathan first. I'll find you guys later."

They nodded to me and went their own way. I weaved through the crowd, gracefully dodging anyone who was in my path. Finally, I made it over to Nathan. He was standing with a couple of guys I was unfamiliar with.

"You clean up nice, Red."

He glanced over at me. " 'Fraid I can't say the same about you." He smirked.

"Whatever, I look hot." I waved him off playfully.

"Are you going to introduce us to the beautiful lady, Nathan?" one of the guys in front of him asked, looking me up and down. He was older than me; probably by about fifteen or twenty years. His hair was slicked back, and his eyes were a dull, beady brown. I couldn't put my finger on what it was, but there was something I didn't like about him already. Something . . . disturbing.

"This is Kendall Keating. Kendall, this is Derek Chandler," Nathan introduced us.

Derek grabbed my hand and brought it to his lips, pressing a soft kiss to the back of my hand. "It's a pleasure to meet you, sweetheart."

I withheld a cringe and gave him a tight smile, pulling my hand away from his lips when he held on to it a little too long.

"You too. How do you two know each other?" I asked as I looked between Nathan and Derek.

What I really wanted to ask was how Nathan, a really good guy, knew someone as creepy as Derek.

"Derek attends the ball every year," Nathan informed me.

"Ah, okay," I gave a noncommittal reply.

"Is your family here?" Nathan asked, changing the subject away from Derek.

"Yeah. My parents should be around here somewhere. I'll have to introduce you to them later."

"Sounds good." He sipped on his bourbon slowly.

"Tell me, Kendall. Do you have a mate?" I turned my attention back to Derek when he asked that. He was glancing down at my chest while licking his lips.

"I don't . . ." I trailed off awkwardly.

"Me neither. How fortunate for us both." His eyes met mine again.

"Yes, I feel so lucky," I drawled sarcastically, which Derek didn't seem to catch.

"I'm staying at a hotel in town tonight. Perhaps you'd like to come back with me after this. I'd love to get better acquainted with you."

"I'm sure you would, perv. I hate to inform you, but this—" I gestured down at my body with my free hand. "—Isn't open for business."

He growled deeply, desire clear in his eyes. "I love a good challenge."

"Okay, I think that's enough for now. Come on, Kendall, let's go find your family," Nathan butted in.

He gave Derek a scathing look, one he didn't see because his eyes were back on my chest. Nathan grabbed me by my elbow lightly to lead me away, which I allowed so I could get away from the creepy Alpha.

"I'll see you later, beautiful." His voice held a promise. I couldn't help but shiver as Nathan pulled me away.

"You're friends with that creep?" I asked once we were far enough away that he couldn't hear us.

"Hardly. I hate the guy. He just came up to me and started talking."

"He seems like an abusive Alpha," I whispered to him.

"It wouldn't surprise me."

"Have you talked to Tyler about him?"

"No, but that's probably a good idea." He paused, a thoughtful look on his face. "Anyways, where's your family?"

I looked away from him and started scanning the room. After a few minutes, I finally found them. Before I could walk over, a voice coming from the speakers halted me. Everyone froze and looked up at the staircase. An elderly man stood at the top and over to the side.

"It is time to introduce the Royal Family. First, we have the Royal Gamma and the Royal Gamma Female; Tyler Guzman and Selena Keating."

The man paused, and Tyler and Selena came into view at the top of the staircase, a spotlight shining on them. They looked every bit the Royal couple that they were.

Tyler was wearing a black tuxedo with a red bow-tie and pocket square, which matched Selena's red gown perfectly. His onyx hair was slicked back, while Selena's was pulled back into a sleek ponytail. She gripped on to his arm that he held out to her and they walked down the stairs together. She was smiling and waving as people cheered, enjoying the attention.

When they made it to the bottom, the man spoke again. "Next, we have the Royal Betas; Kieran Cahill and Emiliya Petrova Cahill."

They came down the stairs next, both with stoic expressions on their faces. They were dressed in all black, which I thought matched Emiliya's personality perfectly. They made it to the bottom quickly.

"Now presenting the Head Royal Witch, Nikolina Petrova."

Niki walked out next, all by herself. She didn't look lonely standing by herself. Instead, she looked comfortable and relaxed. She smiled as people cheered. She looked elegant in her silver dress, which was trailing behind her as she walked down the stairs. Her hair was pulled into a classy chignon, and she wore matching silver accessories adorned with diamonds.

"And now, it is my absolute pleasure to present His Highness, King Finnian Cahill."

If I thought the amount of applause the others received was impressive, it was nothing compared to the amount Finnian received. Everyone went crazy, cheering wildly for him. It was obvious that his people adored him.

As he walked down the steps, I couldn't help but admire him. His hair was combed to the side, every strand perfectly in place. His tall and muscular body was encased in a black tuxedo which, coincidentally enough, had been paired with a gold tie and pocket square. It matched my dress perfectly; as if we had planned it.

He looked every inch the king he was. He exuded power and strength. You could feel it in your bones, and it made everyone bow to him, me included. He kept his face expressionless as he walked down, but his eyes found mine, however briefly. I couldn't look away.

Finally, he reached the bottom of the steps and was immediately swarmed by people wanting his attention. He was blocked from my view after that.

I sighed silently and turned back to Nathan. "They're over there." I pointed to my family. We walked over together. I gave my parents quick hugs before turning back to Nathan.

"Guys, this is Nathan. He's my training partner. Nate, these are my parents, Jefferson and Abby," I introduced him to my family, and they all shook hands.

"How's Kenny doing?" Dad asked, referring to my training. I groaned at the nickname.

Nathan grinned at me, catching on that I hated the name. "Kenny here is doing great," he teased me. "Harrison has nothing but good things to say about her. I'm sure he'd love to meet you as well. He should be around here somewhere."

"Harrison is the Commander of the Royal Army, correct?"

"Yes, sir. Your daughters are in good hands with him. Kendall has already greatly improved and it's only been, what? Three weeks?" He turned to me.

"Three or four, something like that." I shrugged.

"Well, I'm thrilled to hear that. Don't let her slack off," Dad instructed.

"Dad," I whined in annoyance at him talking about me like I was a child. He was giving Nathan way too much ammunition.

"Oh, don't worry, sir. I'll keep her in line."

"Good, she needs it." Selena snickered, butting her way into our conversation and circle.

She almost knocked me over squeezing between me and Matt. Nathan steadied me, and Selena started doling out hugs. She didn't even notice how hard I was glaring at her.

"You did such a good job, sweetheart. I'm so proud of you," Mom gushed to her.

"Yes, she walked down the stairs without falling. We should all be so proud," I muttered dryly.

Selena shot a glare at me, Mom gave me a disapproving look, and Nathan hid his grin away from my family, trying not to laugh. Tyler walked over and stepped between me and Matt and behind Selena.

"Girls, don't start tonight," Dad interjected, stopping Selena before she could say anything else.

"Fine, I wanted to dance anyways." She grabbed Tyler's hand and pulled him away from us and over to the dance floor.

Everyone else followed suit after that. First Matt and Kat, then Mom and Dad, though she hesitated until I pushed her to go. She didn't need to babysit me. So, in the end, I was left with Dalton and Nathan.

"So, you two think you might find your mates tonight?" I asked, striking up a conversation.

"It could happen. You?" Nathan replied.

I fidgeted a bit, but he didn't seem to notice. Dalton did though and he frowned over at me.

"Maybe . . ." I answered unenthusiastically.

"Try not to sound so excited." He smirked down at me.

"You know, maybe you'll get lucky and your mate will be ginger too. Then you could go around stealing souls together. You'll be the redheaded version of Bonnie and Clyde."

"You think you're so clever, don't you?"

I shrugged. "Only on days that end with y."

"I think I'll have to disagree on that one." Nathan chuckled.

"You do that. Do you know when they're going to feed us? I'm starving," I complained. We ate breakfast before we left for the spa, but I hadn't had the chance to eat after that.

"Whenever you want. Just pick a table to sit at and a server will bring you dinner."

"Are you two hungry?" I looked between the two.

"I could eat." Dalton shrugged.

"Yeah, me too," Nathan agreed.

With that, we found an empty table in the corner. A waiter came over immediately to our table, asking whether we wanted chicken or steak. Once we ordered, it only took him five minutes to return with our meals and fresh drinks. We dug in as soon as the food was in front of us.

"So, how was your poker night, by the way?" I asked before taking a bite.

"It was great until your brother took all my money," Nathan grumbled.

I let out a laugh at his sullen tone. "I guess I should have warned you he was good."

"Would've been nice," Nathan replied, cutting in to his steak.

"But not nearly as fun for me. How about you, Dalton?" I turned to him.

"Eh, I pretty much broke even, so could have been better, could have been worse," Dalton answered before taking a bite.

I nodded to him and took a bite of my steak.

"What about you? How was girls's night?" Dalton questioned while chewing on his meal.

I froze briefly but tried to act normal after that. "It was fine. Selena and I fought over what movie to watch."

"Well that's nothing new." Dalton chuckled lightly, although he eyed me warily at first, obviously catching my momentary hesitation.

He didn't say anything though, and we continued eating, making light conversation. After we finished eating, Nathan left us when he saw a few people he knew, leaving me and Dalton alone.

"You want to dance?" he asked after a few minutes.

I hesitated for a few seconds. I didn't want to get his hopes up by saying yes, but I finally decided it should be fine. He knew I wasn't interested in him; I made that very clear. So if he took this as something more than a friendly dance, that was his problem. I finally agreed, and we walked over to the dance floor together.

I wasn't exactly an expert on dancing to classical music—and neither was he—but we managed to not make it obvious by mimicking the movements of others. He rested his hand on my waist, surprising me by being respectful enough to keep his hand against my dress and not the bare skin of my back. I rested one hand on his shoulder and clasped the other in his. He twirled us around slowly, slower than the others so we could avoid each other's toes.

"I think we're getting the hang of this," he told me after a few minutes.

"I think so." I grinned at him as we started moving faster.

"So, what's up with you? Did something happen last night?" he questioned in a low voice, leaning in slightly closer to me.

"It was . . . not what I expected. I can't really talk about it in front of all these people."

"Okay, later?"

I nodded, although I wasn't entirely sure if I was being honest. I trusted Dalton. He got on my nerves, but at the end of the day, I knew he was on my side, which made him trustworthy. But the thing was, whoever had betrayed Finnian was someone he trusted. So, could anyone really be trusted?

That, I wasn't sure of.

I knew without a doubt I trusted my family, and that was about it.

That left a pretty short list of people.

Dalton didn't ask any questions after that. We continued dancing and talking. It was a rare occurrence, the two of us getting along, but we just enjoyed it instead of questioning it.

After a while, I got thirsty. I left to go get a drink. Selena filled my position, leaving Tyler to dance with her best friend instead. He walked off the dance floor with me, but when he saw Lili standing by herself, he went to her and asked her to dance.

I was left by myself and tracked down a waitress. I grabbed a glass of water from her tray and thanked her before she walked away. I stood at the edge of the room, watching everything that was going on while I sipped my water.

All around me, people seemed to be having a great time. Newly discovered mates were dancing and getting to know each other. I even saw two mates meet for the first time, a look of adoration filling their eyes as they embraced each other.

After seeing that, my eyes subconsciously searched the room for my own mate. I saw just about everyone else before him. My family was still dancing and having a great time. Mom was dancing with Matt and Dad was dancing with Kat. I even saw Niki dancing with an older werewolf.

Finally, my eyes found the King. He was standing on the other side of the room, still near the stairs, surrounded by a group of people. He had his hands shoved in his pockets as he listened to some elder gentleman talk. He was trying to look interested, but I could see boredom on his face that no one else seemed to notice.

When his eyes shot over to mine, he looked me up and down briefly. I held his gaze for a few beats before blushing slightly and looking away. I felt his eyes leave me after that.

"You got a thing for the King?" an obnoxious voice asked from behind me.

I whirled around and came face to face with none of than the pervy Alpha, Derek Chandler.

"I'm afraid you're mistaken," I told him formally.

"Are you sure? He seems to have a thing for you." He grinned creepily at me.

"I'm positive. We don't have a *thing* for each other."

"Well, that makes me a very happy man, darlin'."

"It's Kendall," I retorted, "and I don't know why it would."

"Why wouldn't it? It means you're up for grabs still." He moved closer to me, causing me to take a couple steps back, which didn't seem to deter him. He somehow managed to back me into a wall.

"I'm not '*up for grabs*', Alpha Chandler," I spat out.

"Ooh, feisty. I love it when you call me Alpha."

"You're going to be calling me Alpha when I kick your ass," I sneered.

"Mm, foreplay. I'm getting harder with every word that leaves that beautiful mouth of yours," he muttered lustfully.

"You're a disgusting prick."

He leaned in closer, whispering in my ear, his breath on my skin making me shiver in disgust. "You won't be calling my prick disgusting when it's buried deep inside of you."

I grimaced in revulsion. I was getting ready to knee him, to show him just what I wanted to do to his "prick", but he was off of me before I could follow through.

"I suggest you leave her be, Chandler," a voice growled from beside me. I glanced over to him. He seemed familiar, but I couldn't place him.

"Fuck off, Covington," Chandler replied. It was all talk because he turned and walked away, not once looking back.

"Thanks for that," I mumbled, turning to face the man in front of me. He radiated power—an Alpha. He was a little shorter than most alphas, but he was stockier than the others as well, his shoulders wide and his arms ripped. He had thick espresso locks and even thicker eyebrows, sitting over cerulean eyes. The lower half of his face had hair just as dense and dark, his lips pulled into a kind smile underneath his beard hair.

"No problem. I'm Rylan Covington," he introduced himself while holding his hand out to me, which I accepted.

"Kendall Keating. You seem familiar. Have we met before?"

"Briefly. At the brunch a couple of weeks ago. Niki introduced us."

Oh, right. I was wasted when we met. "Yeah, yeah. I remember now."

His grin grew even larger, revealing straight white teeth. "Good, I thought the champagne may have obscured your memory."

I snorted unattractively. "Yeah, you caught me. Was I that obvious?"

"A little."

"So, I hear you're on the Council. I answered the phone when you called a few days ago. Tyler told me who you are."

"I am. For about four years now. I hear your father is our next member?"

"Hopefully. That's why I'm here."

"I remember the process well. It's tedious but well worth it. I look forward to working with you and your family more closely."

I opened my mouth to reply but was cut off by the man who introduced the Royals earlier. He was back at the top of the stairs. "I am honored to welcome King Finnian as he gives his annual speech."

The music stopped, and everyone stopped talking. All attention turned to the stairs, where King Finnian was walking up. Rylan stayed next to me, both of us giving Finnian our attention.

Once Finnian reached the top and turned to face the room, he didn't need the microphone to be heard by everyone. His deep voice was so powerful it filled every crevice of the room; even someone with human hearing would be able to hear him.

"I would like to thank everyone for coming tonight. The Mating Ball is something that my mother, the late Queen Raina, started during her first year as queen. It is my honor to continue it, to keep her legacy alive."

He paused and his eyes found mine. Surprisingly, they stayed there.

"She believed that a mate was the most important thing to a werewolf. It gave her such great pleasure to bring two souls together, to watch them meet and connect. She lived for that, for the magic that is the mate bond. Which is why, if she were still with us today, she would be ecstatic for my next announcement."

He paused to let the anticipation build. I froze, not sure where he was going with this.

"It is my absolute honor to introduce to you your next queen," he announced, his eyes unreadable as they stared into mine.

My breathing quickened, and my heart began to shatter in my chest. He'd mentioned finding another queen, but I figured after I found out the truth that he'd just said that to hurt me. I didn't think he meant it, and I certainly didn't think he'd introduce her in front of me.

I turned to walk away, my eyes blurring with tears that I refused to let fall. I held my head high, but I had to get out of here. I couldn't bear to see him standing up there with someone else. The sight of me walking away didn't seem to bother him, because he kept going.

"I couldn't have asked for a better queen. She's beautiful, strong, kind, and a fierce warrior. She is perfect, and she will be an excellent leader. Please, help me welcome your new queen, Kendall Keating."

I froze when he said my name. My tears dried up and my mouth fell open in surprise. I could vaguely hear applause but it didn't seem to register to me over the whooshing in my ears. I slowly turned away from the door, which I nearly made it out of.

Every pair of eyes in the room were on me, but I only saw one person. His face remained stoic, but I could see something in his eyes; a softness that I couldn't quite decipher.

The crowd parted right down the middle, urging me forward. I walked slowly, almost in a trance. A few people hugged me on my way up; mostly family. I didn't look at any of them; I didn't want to see Matt, Nathan, Harrison, or any of the others who didn't know. I had no doubt that Matt was going to be pissed and hurt about this.

Once I made it to the front of the crowd, I reluctantly walked up the stairs. I gave Finnian a questioning look, but he just gave me a ghost of a smile and pulled me into his side.

He leaned in close to me. "I'm ready to fight," he muttered so quietly, I knew no one else would have been able to hear. I shivered when his warm breath hit my skin, but in a good way; unlike with Derek.

I wasn't sure what to feel when he uttered those words. I should have been happy. This was what I wanted all along, but I wasn't. If he'd done this weeks ago, I would have been nothing but thrilled, but I guess he was just a little too late.

I wanted this to work, but he was going to have to fight damn hard if he wanted to repair and win over my shattered heart. He had done nothing but hurt me, and that was going to take more than this grand gesture to fix.

I couldn't think of that right now because I was in the spotlight, in front of at least five hundred werewolves. I gulped nervously and turned to face the crowd. King Finnian pulled me closer.

"Your queen, ladies and gentlemen," he added again, pulling away briefly to gesture at me.

The applause picked up again, along with cheering and excited yells. I smiled at everyone and waved like Selena had done earlier. I pushed my apprehension away and focused on the moment. I pulled my wolf forward slightly. She felt more confident and comfortable in this role than me. My wolf half had felt like a queen since she had met the King, so it was easier to let my animal instincts take over.

Eventually, the clapping and cheering died down and I was able to speak.

"I am so honored and humbled to receive such a warm welcome from everyone. I'm new to this queen business, but I promise to always keep the werewolf population's best interests at heart for everything I do. Please bear with me as I navigate these unfamiliar waters, and please don't be afraid to come to me with your questions, comments, and suggestions. The late Queen Raina certainly left big shoes to fill, but I will work every day to be half the Queen that she was."

I finished, and the applause rose up again. My gaze found my parents. They looked at me with pride. Both of them seemed to be tearing up a little. They gave me a thumbs up, letting me know I had done a good job.

I glanced over to Finnian, who looked just as proud. He had the same look that he did the day he watched me train for the first and only time. His smile lifted only a fraction of a centimeter, but it was better than nothing.

"Thank you again for coming, and we hope you enjoy the remainder of your night."

At that, he tightened his arm around my waist, his forearm warm against my bare back, and guided me down the stairs. We were swarmed by people as soon as we reached the bottom. Everyone seemed to want to talk to me, if only to shake my hand. I was so overwhelmed by the sheer amount of people that I couldn't give them all the attention that I wanted to, so instead I just let people talk to me, hug me, and shake my hand excitedly.

It took about thirty minutes of this, and Finnian pulling me away from the crowd to finally get a moment of peace.

"You look stunning, by the way," he whispered into my ear again once we were alone.

"Thank you," I replied evenly. I wanted to question him but now wasn't the time nor the place.

"Dance with me."

I wanted to say no, just to be difficult, but I let it go for now and nodded once. He laced our fingers together and pulled me to the dance floor.

He held me much closer than Dalton had. The front of my body was pressed against his, hip to hip, chest to chest. He kept our fingers intertwined and held out next to us. He wrapped his other arm around my waist, his big hand splayed out against my bare back; his warm flesh against mine causing me to break out in goosebumps. I rested my hand at the back of his neck, twirling the ends of his hair absentmindedly.

"Do you want me to kill him?" he murmured lowly as we swayed.

I nearly choked on my saliva. "What the hell are you talking about?" I sputtered quietly.

"Chandler," he clarified.

"Why would I want you to kill him?"

He clenched his jaw, fury filling his eyes as they turned a shade of gold that matched my dress and his tie. "Because of how he spoke to you."

"No, I don't want you to kill him." I rolled my eyes. "He's a creep, but he didn't actually touch me or anything." Although he got close.

"He disrespected his queen," he argued.

"He didn't know I was his queen. Just let it go. How were you able to even hear him? It was completely across the room, which was very loud by the way."

"I hear everything that happens with you."

I pulled back slightly, or tried to, but he wouldn't let me. I was going to ask what he meant by that but he changed the subject.

"I'll let it go just this once since you asked me to, but I won't hesitate to take out anyone who I deem a threat to you," he warned.

"Fine."

We swayed in silence for a few minutes after that. No one interrupted us, and it was nice to be in his arms in front of people for once. He held me tightly, securely, like I was a delicacy that he had to protect from anyone around me. My heart swelled at being so close to him, at him holding me so tenderly. I couldn't help but lean in closer even though I was still upset with him.

"Was the tie a coincidence or did you know the color of my dress?" I wondered after a couple of songs, just swaying in silence.

"Nothing is a coincidence," he muttered.

"How'd you know what my dress looked like? Wait, don't even answer that. Let me guess. Niki?"

"I can't get anything past you, can I?" He gazed down at me adoringly.

"I'm glad you're finally figuring that out. Try not to forget again, King Finnian."

"Just Finnian. Or Finn. You're my equal; you don't have to call me King."

I nodded, but I would probably still do it for a while. Calling him King had never been about respect, just like him calling me Miss Keating hadn't been about being polite. It was a way for us to distance ourselves from one another. I needed to keep that distance for now, at least until I knew he wasn't going to change his mind.

"I hope you realize how much trouble I'm going to be in with my brother after this little surprise of yours," I said to change the subject.

"That certainly wasn't my intention." Mirth filled his eyes, his voice teasing.

"It's not funny," I mumbled and purposely stepped on his toes, which he didn't seem to notice.

"Why didn't you tell him? You told everyone else in your family."

"Oh, wait a minute. Let me take in this moment. I want to remember it."

"Remember what?"

"The day the great King Finnian Cahill didn't know something," I teased.

"In that case, you should remember it, because it will never happen again."

I giggled, then decided to answer him. "He's protective. If he knew everything . . ." I trailed off, not wanting to go into details right now about how he had treated me. He already knew anyways. "He would have challenged you to protect me, so I had to protect him by not telling him."

His eyes lost their mirth and turned sad. "You were protecting him from me," he stated.

I shrugged. "You know the rules of a challenge as well as I do."

"Just for future reference, I wouldn't kill your brother or any of your family. Even if challenged, I would never do that to you."

"So, you weren't planning on attacking Selena in my room the other day?" I raised my eyebrow at him.

"Of course not. My wolf was pushing me forward as a response to the way she disrespected me, but I never would have attacked her. Not only would I never do that to Tyler, but I certainly wouldn't do that to you and your family members. She does have quite the attitude though, I must admit."

"She's protective too." I smirked. "I hope you're prepared for the hate my family will have for you for a while."

"I'll win them over. I'll win *you* over."

"Hmm, can't wait to see what you come up with."

I laid my cheek against his chest, and he rested his chin on top of my head. His arms tightened around me.

"I know I don't deserve you, not after everything I've done. But I'm going to spend the rest of our lives making it up to you."

I didn't reply, just continued to snuggle up against him and sway slowly to the classical song the band was playing.

"If you're ready to leave, let me know. We can go whenever you want."

"We?" I lifted my head to look at him again.

"I need you with me." He gave me a meaningful look, and I understood what he really meant by that.

He needed to keep me close. It was the only way for him to ensure my safety against the traitor.

I was reluctant but still nodded. "I need to say goodbye to my family, then we can go."

He released me but still kept my hand firmly in his. He led me through the crowd and to my family.

They were sitting at one of the tables. Everyone except for Matt and Kat was there. I didn't see them anywhere. I pulled out one of the empty chairs and sat down, with Finnian taking the seat next to me.

"Where's Matt?" I asked warily.

"He needed to step out," Mom answered, since Dad was staring heatedly at my mate.

My gut churned with guilt. Matt was upset that I hadn't told him.

"Oh," I mumbled.

"He'll be okay, Kenny. He's just surprised. You know Matt doesn't stay angry for long," she said in an encouraging tone.

"No, but I do. This little romantic gesture doesn't make up for anything, asshole."

Everyone looked at Selena in horror that she would talk to the King that way. Tyler even looked a little fearful for her safety. I glanced over at Finnian. He looked annoyed but he didn't look ready to attack her.

Her words were a little contradictory to what she said to me this morning, but it wasn't hard to figure out why. She wanted me to give him another chance and to be understanding of the reason for his actions, but that didn't mean that she was going to give him a free pass or that she wanted me to give him a free pass for how he had hurt me in the past.

We were on the same page.

"Your growing list of insults never cease to astound me," Finnian grunted.

"Good, 'cause you're going to hear plenty of them."

He growled lowly but didn't do anything else.

"We're gonna leave now. I just wanted to say goodbye to you guys."

Before they could say anything else, a nervous looking waiter came up to our table. He bowed to Finnian and waited for permission to talk, which he gave.

"Can I get anything for either of you, Your Highnesses?" he whispered in a shaky voice.

"Do you want anything?" He turned to me. He stroked my back with his thumb as he spoke. His hand had been resting there since we sat down. It didn't slip my notice that he kept touching me in some way since I reached his side.

"No, thank you," I told the waiter and gave him a friendly smile so he'd relax. He did, but only a little bit.

"You sure you don't want anything to eat before we go?"

"I'm sure. I ate already."

"Okay." He turned back to the waiter. "We're good, thanks."

"Will I see you guys tomorrow before you head home?" I turned back to them. They were staying at a hotel for the night, but I wanted to see them again in the morning.

"If King Finnian doesn't mind, then yes, we'd love to see you again tomorrow," Mom said, directing her words mainly at Finnian.

"You don't need his permission to see me, Mom," I told her. I glanced over at him, daring him to disagree with me. He didn't.

"You're more than welcome to stay here at the castle for the night. We have plenty of room. You can have breakfast with Kendall in the morning before you leave. We have amazing chefs that work here. And please, call me Finnian."

"Thank you, Finnian. That's incredibly generous. We graciously accept your offer."

"It's no trouble at all. You're always welcome here."

I rested my hand on his leg, right above his knee, under the table and gave it a gentle squeeze, trying to show him my appreciation. My family meant everything to me, so it meant a lot that he was being so accepting of them and trying to make them feel welcome. It was a good step in the right direction in my eyes.

He added slight pressure to my back, which told me that it was no problem.

"Tyler, would you mind showing them to their rooms?" He looked away from me and over to his best friend and Gamma.

"Of course," Tyler agreed.

"Okay, well, I'll see you all in the morning." I stood up and made my way around the table, giving everyone a quick hug.

After that, Finnian pulled me back into his side and led me up the stairs and out of the ball room, up towards the sixth floor.

Where we would be completely alone and away from prying ears.

This would either get really interesting or be really anticlimactic. Either way, at least I'd finally be welcome in his room for once.

CHAPTER TWENTY-ONE

King Finnian and I walked in silence. I thought it was awkward but if he did too, he didn't let on. He kept me close to his side, his hand resting on the small of my back. He led us through a part of the castle that I hadn't seen before. We didn't pass any guests or workers, so I assumed this part of the castle was strictly for Royals.

The staircase we took led us to the west wing of the sixth floor, which I had yet to see. I was only able to see the east wing, which was his private residence. I assumed that this side housed his private office.

The air in the hallways was cold and musty, hinting at how deserted it really was. No one but Finnian had been up here in years, and it was obvious.

"I'll show you more of the place tomorrow. There are a lot of spare rooms up here; you can use them for whatever you'd like," he told me after what seemed like hours of silence.

"Mm," I mumbled a fake agreement.

I wasn't making myself at home until I knew if things would work out with us or not. I didn't want to get into that right now though.

He gave me a weird look, like he knew what I was thinking, but he didn't comment. Instead, he changed the subject.

"Are you cold?" he asked after he caught me rubbing my arm up and down.

"A little."

He pulled me closer, his hand replacing mine on my arm. He was warm despite the chill in the air. "I'll light a fire in our room."

It didn't escape my notice that he referred to it as our room. He seemed to be getting a little ahead of himself. I just nodded.

"Don't you have a heating system up here?" I asked as an afterthought.

"No," he informed me, and I looked at him weirdly. How could he not have a heater up here? "Why? Do you want one installed?" he asked when he noticed the look I was giving him.

I looked away from him, staring down the long and dark corridor instead. "It's your castle. That's your decision," I mumbled.

"*Our* castle," he corrected me, frowning deeply.

I didn't reply.

"Do you want anything to eat or drink?" he inquired a few minutes later, just as we were coming up to the kitchen.

"No, thanks."

"Okay . . ." he trailed off.

He didn't talk again after that, and we kept walking all the way to the end of the east wing, where his room was. He pushed open one of the oak double doors and let me in first. He closed the door behind himself, sealing us in for the night.

"Make yourself comfortable," he told me.

He walked past me, over to the fireplace. He got a fire going quickly and, eventually, warmth started filling the room. I stood there uncomfortably, fidgeting with my bracelet, despite what he told me.

After he had the fire roaring and burning strong, he stood up and turned to face me again.

"Are you going to stand there all night?" His voice was filled with amusement.

I shrugged and crossed my arms over my chest in discomfort.

"Why don't you go change out of that dress?" he suggested.

"What do you expect me to do? Walk around naked? I don't have any clothes up here," I snapped.

"As much as I would enjoy that, you can wear one of my shirts for tonight. We'll bring your things up tomorrow."

I bristled. "And if I'm not ready to live with you after everything that's happened between us?"

He sighed dejectedly. "Then you can take the room next door until you're ready. But I need you close so I can protect you. You can't stay on the guest floor anymore."

I softened slightly. I was grateful that he was giving me an option. I nodded thankfully at him.

"There are t-shirts in the middle dresser drawer of my closet. Take whichever one you want."

I raised an amused eyebrow at him. "You own something besides dress shirts?"

"Believe it or not, I do. I typically prefer not to wear a suit in the privacy of my own bedroom." He smirked at me.

"I guess we learn something new every day."

I turned and walked into his bathroom before he could reply. I grabbed a plain black t-shirt from his dresser and slipped off my dress. I hung it up with one of his spare hangers and slipped into the shirt. It was big, the bottom ending halfway down my thighs.

I let my hair down, pulling it loose from the uncomfortable braid it was in. I searched through his drawers and found an unused toothbrush, so I brushed my teeth and washed off my makeup.

I gave myself one last once-over before I left the bathroom. I didn't look as good, but I felt a hell of a lot better.

When I walked out, Finnian was laying his jacket across the back of the worn chair. He had stripped it off along with his tie and had undone the first few buttons of his shirt. He paused all movements once he saw me. As he took me in, his eyes burned into me, a mixture of dark, stormy blue and molten gold. His gaze caused a slow burn to start deep in my belly, but I pushed the feeling away, holding on to my anger instead.

"What?"

He shook his head and closed his eyes, taking in deep, shuttering breaths. After a few minutes, he slowly peeled his eyes open again, which now lacked his wolf's gold.

"Sorry, my wolf was pushing me to mark you."

I blushed at his confession. Marking took place during mating, which was something I wasn't the least bit ready for after everything.

"Well, keep the mutt in check," I murmured defensively.

"I will. You look so stunning right now."

"I guess one of us has to be the attractive one," I joked, trying to stomp out the butterflies that had taken up residence in my stomach.

He chuckled, a deep and throaty laugh that made me want to join in. I've never seen him show so much emotion that wasn't anger or indifference.

"I'll give you that one; you're definitely the looks in this relationship."

"I'm the brains too," I added.

"What does that make me? The brawn?"

"The ass," I corrected.

He laughed again.

"I'll accept that. Hopefully, I can change your opinion soon."

He started unbuttoning his shirt again. I gulped nervously and walked over to the bed, out of eyesight. No way in hell was I going to let him catch me staring. I wasn't giving him that ammunition.

"You, like, live in the stone ages up here. No heating, no TV, no computer. I'm surprised you have running water."

"I'll be sure to modernize it for you tomorrow." He laughed.

He disappeared into the bathroom, and I let out the breath I was holding. I plopped down on the edge of the bed. He reemerged a minute later. His lower half was covered by just his boxers, but he was thankfully wearing a t-shirt so it didn't feel too uncomfortable for me. I had a feeling that the t-shirt was purely for my benefit. The first night I snuck up here, he hadn't been wearing one.

I appreciated his efforts to make me more at ease. It wasn't that I didn't appreciate his naked torso. It was actually the opposite. I enjoyed it; a little too much, in fact.

"So, what made you change your mind?" I asked the question that had been lingering in my mind since his impromptu announcement.

"Everything you said earlier was completely right. I was scared. You deserved better than that. When I heard you talking to your sister before the ball, I realized that you really were done. I knew if I wanted you, I had to man up and fight for you. I had to stop living in fear. That's what I'm doing now."

I only caught one part of his confession.

"Which sister are you talking about exactly?" My voice was low, deadly. He plopped down on the other side of the bed. My back was turned to him; I didn't want him to see the scowl forming on my face.

"Katerina."

I turned around so fast, I almost gave myself whiplash. My eyes glowed amber, and I bared my teeth at him in a snarl.

"That conversation took place in my room, which has a soundproofing spell cast on it. How the hell were you able to hear that?"

"Nikolina obviously didn't include me in that spell." He frowned, like he didn't know why I was pissed.

"How much have you heard?" I demanded.

"Everything."

I growled again, not only at his statement, but at his casual tone. My anger didn't even faze him.

"Those conversations were supposed to be private."

Everything suddenly made sense to me. He always came into my room when I was in the bathroom. I always thought that was just a coincidence, but I was starting to learn there really was no such thing as that with him.

What he had done was such an invasion of privacy. It was the werewolf equivalent to a human hacking their significant other's social media account. I'd said so many things in there that he was never supposed to hear. I bitched and complained about him, but I didn't even care about that. What I did care about was everything that didn't involve him.

I had talked to Dalton about his feelings for me in there. I had told Kat about my lapse of judgment with Theo in there. He heard that I was planning on screwing him before Tyler showed up. I discussed private family stuff that he didn't need to know.

I was so fucking pissed.

"It was necessary." He shrugged.

That was the last straw. I lunged forward and attacked him. I was aiming to knock him off the bed but it didn't work in my favor. He didn't even move an inch backwards. Instead, he actually moved forward and slammed me onto the bed, holding my wrists above my head.

I bucked and twisted, trying to get him off me. At first, I was wildly flailing around in pure rage, but then I started to think more strategically. What would Harrison do to get out of this situation?

My answer was he wouldn't be in this situation, because he wouldn't be stupid enough to attack the King, who no one could beat; not even me. Eventually, I grew tired of struggling. My body went limp, my anger deflating.

"Are you done?" he asked quietly.

I growled at him but still nodded. He released me, and I sat on the very edge of the bed, as far from him as I could get.

"I'm sorry you're angry at me, but I'm not sorry for doing what I had to do. Everything I have done has been to protect you. If someone tried to attack you in your room and it was soundproofed, I wouldn't have been able to help you. I never did it to invade your privacy."

"So, you're telling me you've never listened in on anything for your own selfish reasons?" I pressed.

"If I said no, I'd be lying. There were times that I shouldn't have listened, but I was curious about you. I wanted to know you, even though I couldn't actually get to know you. I'm sorry for that. I hope you can forgive me."

"I'll think about it," I mumbled.

"I know you're tired. Get some sleep; we'll talk more tomorrow."

I wanted argue for the sake of arguing, but he was right. I was exhausted. My lack of sleep the night before was wearing on me. So, I nodded and slid in under the covers.

I stuck to the very edge of the bed, as far as I could get from him without falling off. He switched off the lamp on his side of the bed, leaving the room dark except for the burning embers of the fire and the moonlight streaming in from the balcony door windows. He hesitated before lying down. He didn't attempt pull me closer.

"Goodnight, Kendall," he whispered.

"Night . . ."

I drifted off within minutes.

* * *

"I can go get my own clothes," I argued, rolling my eyes.

"Not wearing that, you can't."

"It's practically to my knees. I have shorts shorter than this. Don't be such a drama queen."

He clenched his jaw and glowered at me. I informed him after I woke up that I needed to go down to my room to get ready for the day. He insisted that he would go down to get my things, but he didn't understand that I needed much more than a pair of clothes. I needed to shower, fix my hair, do my makeup, and then get dressed.

I was meeting my family for breakfast in an hour, and he was holding me up. I wanted to look nice this morning.

He glared daggers at me. "Must you always test my patience?"

"I must. Now, if you'll excuse me, I need to get ready."

I started walking out—again—but he blocked me—again.

"I'm seriously going to shove a cactus up your ass if you don't move."

"At least put a pair of my pants on."

"They're not going to fit me. Now let me go."

"Fine, but I'm going with you."

"Fine."

I stomped past him and threw his door open. I stormed out, and he matched my steps perfectly, staying right by my side. I shot him another glare just because I felt like it. Not only had he annoyed me with his demanding attitude, but I also woke up with him practically on top of me. He had a nice wakeup call; me pushing him onto the floor.

We weren't getting off to such a great start.

His dramatic attitude was for nothing, because we didn't run into anyone on the way to my room. It was just like I left it. I picked up my phone from my bed.

I was surprised when I had over fifty texts, all from different people. Most of them were from people in my pack, who had found out that I was Finnian's mate. Some were from numbers I didn't recognize, but they were all nice, or at least the couple I read were.

I made a mental note to reply to them later and left my phone to go shower. Finnian stayed in the room.

I got ready quickly. I French braided my hair over to the side, letting it fall over one shoulder. I threw on an oversized cream-colored sweater and a pair of black leggings, along with knee-high black leather boots.

Once I was ready, I exited the bathroom with ten minutes to spare. Finnian was laid out across my bed. He'd gotten dressed in a black suit this morning, so he was already good to go. He stood up once he saw me.

"You look beautiful. Your splendor never fails to amaze me," he said, his voice gravelly and rough.

"Okay, Shakespeare. Thanks, I guess. Are you ready?"

"It's too early."

"So?" I questioned.

"So? The King and Queen are never early."

"No, you're always late; which is rude and not something I will be participating in. My parents raised me better than that."

"It's a royal custom. You'll have to get used to it."

"Um, no I won't. Maybe you haven't figured this out about me yet, but I'm not one for politics, which is why I didn't want to be here in the first place. So, you can shove your rude customs up your royal ass. I'll do things my way."

"You didn't want to be here?" He looked and sounded a little hurt, if I wasn't mistaken.

"Of course not. I just graduated college. I was supposed to take over my pack's finances, not come here to kiss your ass for my dad for two months."

"Why'd you come then?"

"Dad told me to. I had no choice. He wanted to show you his commitment by sending two of his pups, three including Kat," I explained.

"I'm glad you came."

"Your life would be easier if I hadn't," I argued.

"It would, but it would also be empty."

My heart warmed at his words, but I kept my face blank.

"Are you ready?" I asked again, changing the subject.

He sighed, realizing I wasn't going to be following his customs. "Yes, let's go," he finally agreed.

He laced his fingers between mine and squeezed my hand gently. I couldn't make myself pull away like my brain told me to, so I didn't. He guided us out of my room, through the castle, and towards the room breakfast would be served in.

It was too cold to have breakfast outside like we did when I first got here, so we had been using a sunroom on the first floor. It was a more casual environment for breakfast—a nice contrast to the formal dining room our dinners were normally held in.

Once we arrived, half of my family was already there. Mom and Dad were sitting on one side, and Selena and Tyler were seated across from them. Matt and Kat weren't there yet. My shoulders slumped at the absence of my brother, who seemed to be avoiding me for as long as possible. He was perpetually early for everything, so his tardiness spoke volumes.

Finnian pulled me towards the head of the table, which was wide enough for both of us to be seated at. Two chairs were placed there instead of the usual one. He pulled my chair out for me to sit after I hugged my parents. He surprised me by shaking their hands as well. Dad hesitated but reluctantly gave in.

Once we were all seated, a waiter came with orange juice, which thankfully was champagne free this time. I sipped on it as we waited for the others. We still technically had five minutes until breakfast started. The atmosphere was tense and awkward, but Mom did her best to diffuse it.

"How was your night?" She looked between Finnian and me, not actually meeting his eyes.

"Great, thanks."

"Terrible, yours?" Finnian and I both answered at the same time, giving vastly different answers. I shot him a glare because he actually seemed to believe it was great.

She looked deterred for a few seconds but continued her best to make this breakfast a nice one. "Our night was great. You have a beautiful castle, King Finnian. Our room was lovely. We appreciate your hospitality."

"Call me Finnian, and it was no problem. You're all welcome anytime."

"That's very kind of you, Finnian," Mom replied gently.

Another awkward silence filled the table.

"Did he behave last night, or should I kick his ass?" Selena said, breaking the silence.

"I can do that on my own, thank you very much." I wish I could say that with confidence, but he made me question my fighting skills after what happened last night.

"You couldn't kick his ass if he was in a coma." She rolled her eyes.

"And you could?" I countered.

"Hell yeah, I could."

He growled quietly at her, but we both ignored him.

"I have no doubt you could kick his ass in a battle of wits, but physically? You'd be dead quicker than you caused Freddy to be."

Now it was Tyler's turn to growl at the mention of his mate dying. Men. They were so primal and annoying.

"*You* were one hundred percent to blame for Freddy's tragic passing. Don't try to pin that on me," she hissed.

"No, no," I denied fiercely, pointing my finger at her. "It was all you. And to make matters worse, I had to find him myself. I had to see his poor, dead body floating in the water. And it was *your* fault."

"Woah, woah! Time out! Who was Freddy?" Tyler silenced Selena and looked at her worriedly, like she had gone through some traumatic experience.

"Freddy was their pet fish," Matt grunted out as he finally entered the room with Kat. He refused to look at me, which stung. "Don't let their dramatics fool you; they had Freddy for two days and gave him half a bottle of fish food even after they were told not to feed him too much."

"*Selena* fed him too much," I corrected.

We continued to argue as the waiters brought out breakfast. We all dug into our crepes and fresh fruit immediately.

"I'm just saying, the first time was a fluke. A freak accident, if you will. I think we should have been given another shot as pet owners," Selena told our parents passionately while waving around a piece of cantaloupe on a fork.

"I agree. We missed out on a childhood rite of passage—no, a privilege. That's practically child abuse," I added.

"Yes, you girls had such a rough childhood in your big and fancy house. You always had food on the table and your closet resembles a shopping mall. It was downright horrendous how we treated you both. My sincerest apologies," Dad said dryly.

"Your sarcasm isn't appreciated, father." Selena rolled her eyes at him.

He shrugged at her, uncaring.

"And people wonder where we get it from," I mumbled with a smirk.

"No one wonders that. Everyone already knows." Kat laughed.

"Everyone knows where you get your dishonesty from too," Matt added. He glared at me, meeting my eyes for the first time. My smile dropped as guilt filled me.

"Matt . . . I never wanted to lie to you," I whispered past the lump in my throat.

"Yeah, well, that didn't stop you, did it, Kendall? Oh, I'm sorry, Queen Kendall. It didn't stop any of you," he growled out.

I saw Finnian tense up, but he wisely stayed silent.

"I was trying to protect you," I pleaded with him to understand.

"I'm your older brother; it's my job to protect you, not the other way around," he sneered. "It was a bitch move, lying like that. And it was even worse having my mate lie to me."

"Don't be mad at Kat; she was just—"

He slammed his hands down on the table, causing a crack to run down it, and stood up angrily. His chair clattered to the floor behind him. "Don't tell me what to fucking do."

Finnian interjected into our argument after seeing Matt's threatening stance. He stood up calmly and put himself between us.

"Don't speak to her that way," he told him evenly, although he didn't put a command in his voice.

"Stay out of this. This is between me and my sister. You're just her prick mate that has done nothing but hurt her. I should kill your sorry ass right now for how you've treated her."

Fear crawled up my throat, choking me and making it hard to breathe. This was what I had been trying to avoid. I didn't want Matt to get hurt. I couldn't let him get hurt.

I was on the verge of standing and putting myself in between them, a physical barrier between their pissed off wolves, but Finnian held his hand out behind him to stop me.

"You don't want to do this. Calm down," he instructed.

That just made Matt closer to shifting, if that was even possible. His body was shaking, and his eyes were completely golden. "I don't fucking think so, you son of a bitch. You deserve to suffer for what you put her through." With that, he drew his fist back and swung it forward, hitting his mark; which was Finnian's jaw.

I stood up to get between them, but Finnian still held me back. I gripped his arm hard, desperately trying to hold him back. Tears streamed down my cheeks at the thought of what he could do to my brother.

I didn't understand why Finnian wasn't just commanding him to stop and why he didn't try to stop Matt from hitting him in the first place. Even I saw that Matt was going to hit him seconds before he actually pulled his fist back, so I know Finnian noticed too. Why did he let Matt's fist actually reach his face?

"Walk away, Matt," Finnian told him firmly, still without a command in his voice.

He just threw another punch, catching Finnian in the eye this time.

"Walk away." His voice was stronger and firmer. "I don't want to hurt you. You're my mate's brother. Walk away before this gets even worse."

"Matt, please," Kat pleaded from behind him. She grabbed his arm, and he instantly relaxed.

He shook his head and scoffed angrily, "Fuck this."

With that, he turned and stomped out of the room. I took a step to follow him, but Finnian grabbed my arm to stop me. I glared down at his hand, then up at his face.

"Let me go. I need to go talk to him," I said, demanding to be let go.

"He's angry. He could hurt you. Let him calm down."

"Don't get me wrong, King Finnian, I appreciate how you reacted just now, but you don't know what you're talking about. You don't know him or our relationship. He would never hurt me, no matter how pissed off he is. Now, let go so I can speak to my brother."

I yanked my arm away from him and he let go. The second I was free, I ran out of the room and followed Matt's scent since he had already left. His scent led me out to the woods, where he'd shifted.

I quickly stripped and did the same. I put my muzzle to the dirt, sniffing him out again. I ran as quickly as I could to find him. It took some time to catch up, but I finally did after a while. He had stopped next to a small stream, just lying next to it.

I lied down next to him. He didn't move or acknowledge me in any way. He must have known I was following him. I whimpered and nudged his paw with mine, trying to urge him to shift back and talk to me, or at the very least drop his mental shield.

He didn't, he just continued to lay there and ignore me. I did the same and waited until he was ready.

After a while, he finally stood up, and I did the same. He indicated with his head for me to follow him. We trotted through the forest, back to where our clothes lay haphazardly. We shifted back and dressed quickly.

"I'm so freaking sorry, Matthew." I started before he could say anything.

He plopped down on the ground, his back to a tree. I sat right across from him.

"You know, when Kat explained last night why you didn't want me to know, I thought it was bullshit. I thought it was crazy, that I would never react like that. I guess I just proved you right though."

"Anyone else would have reacted the same. I was just trying to protect you."

"I hate that. I hate that you felt like you had to protect me. I should have been the one protecting you." He shook his head dejectedly.

"I love you for that, but I don't need that anymore. I'm a big girl now. You, Dad, and Brody have taught me well; taught me how to stand up for myself; how to never accept less than I deserve. I'll always need you, Matt, but I don't need protection anymore. I just need you to support me, because I'm scared shitless. I have no idea what it means to be a queen."

"You'll make a great queen, Kenny. And I'll always be here to protect you, no matter what. You're my baby sister, even though you're not a baby anymore."

"Did Kat tell you everything?" I questioned cautiously.

"I thought so, but hell, who knows?"

"Did she tell you about Niki's vision?" I switched to mindlink so no one could listen to what we were saying. We couldn't let the traitor know that we knew. We needed the element of surprise on our side.

"No?"

I sighed heavily and filled him in on everything, finally getting it all out in the open. He paled at first, horror on his face, then anger and fierce determination took over.

"That will never happen to you, Kendall. I'll protect you. Always."

"I know you will, Matthew. I hope you can see things from Finnian's perspective now. I have my issues with him, but I don't want all of you to hate him."

"I do. I suppose I owe him an apology."

"Nah, he deserved that." I smiled at him as I spoke out loud again, letting him know there were no hard feelings for his behavior.

He chuckled slightly. "I guess we should get back to tell everyone goodbye."

"I guess we should." I stood up and dusted off the back of my leggings. He did the same.

He pulled me into a hug before we could walk back. I returned it and buried my head in his t-shirt.

"I love you, Kenny."

"I love you too, Matthew."

And just like that, we were good again.

CHAPTER TWENTY-TWO

I took about an hour to say goodbye to my parents and actually get them on the road. It took a lot of consoling for Mom and multiple promises from all of us to visit soon; like within a couple of weeks soon.

Finnian stayed by my side the whole time, refusing to let me out of his sight. Which made my next task extra challenging.

"I'm gonna go find Dalton. I need to talk to him," I announced once we were back inside.

I had been wanting to talk to him since this morning. I was worried, since he didn't show up for breakfast. He already knew Finnian and I were mates, but knowing and actually seeing it were different things. I may not return his feelings, or even particularly like him as a person, but I wasn't heartless. Besides, we were friends; in a weird, hateful way.

Finnian reacted like I had asked him for his permission rather than told him what I was going to do. He growled deeply and told me no, like it was no big deal.

I pulled away from him and gave him a look that dared him to say no to me again. Tyler, Matt, and Kat all looked between us anxiously, but Selena was cheering me on.

"I wasn't asking, King Finnian," I growled back.

"I wasn't either. And stop calling me that."

"Fine, Your Highness. Does King Asshole suit you better?" I said bitterly, sending him a glare.

"That has a nice ring to it," Selena added.

"If you want to talk to him, it will be in my office, where I am present," he argued back, ignoring mine and Selena's comments.

"Fuck that. You can't dictate who I talk to and where I talk . Like I've been saying since day one, you're either my king or my mate. You chose what you wanted to be last night. My king may get to boss me around, but my mate doesn't. So back off."

"I've been telling you since the beginning, I'm both," he retorted.

"You're not doing such a great job getting back in my good graces. I thought you wanted to make things right between us?"

That got him. He hesitated briefly, then finally gave in. "Fine, but I'm only giving you thirty minutes. I'll bring your stuff to our room, then I'm coming to find you."

"Fine," I agreed just to appease him, but I planned on going with him when I was good and ready, whether my thirty minutes were up or not.

Since my room and Dalton's were on the same hallway, we walked together. He tried to lace our fingers together, but I pulled away and scowled at him to let him know I was not in the mood to be touched. He returned the nasty look but left me alone.

"Thirty minutes," he reminded as I stopped in front of Dalton's door.

"Fuck off."

He glared at me again but walked away in silence, leaving me to smile triumphantly when he couldn't see me anymore.

I raised my hand and knocked on Dalton's door twice. He must have heard me outside before I knocked, because the door opened not two seconds later.

"I wasn't expecting you, Queen Kendall." He smirked at me, but I could see past it.

I scoffed and pushed past him. He shut the door behind me, leaving us alone but definitely not unheard.

"Why weren't you there for breakfast?" I asked, demanding to know.

"Wasn't hungry." He shrugged casually.

"Don't bullshit me. He's not going to do anything to you. You can be honest."

He pondered my words for a few seconds before exhaling heavily. "I knew this was coming. I knew he wasn't going to be able to deny you forever. Not even an idiot would reject you, and he doesn't exactly strike me as an idiot . . ."

"So what's the problem?" I pressed when he trailed off.

"The problem is knowing it is different from actually seeing it. It's just going to take some time to get used to."

I chewed on the inside of my cheek in contemplation. "Would it be easier if you went home?" I finally asked after a few beats of silence.

"What?" he asked, his bushy eyebrows shooting up.

"Do you want to go home?"

"I can't just leave. Your dad needs me here . . . unless we're done with the vetting process?"

"No, we're not. Dad specifically said that he doesn't want any special treatment just because I'm the queen. He wants to earn his spot, just like everyone else. But that's beside the point. We're halfway through anyways. You've done a good job, but we can finish without you if you're not comfortable here."

He thought it over briefly, but ultimately shook his head. "No, I want to stay. My alpha gave me a job and I intend to see it through. I'll get over this; I just need a little space, at least for a few days."

"If that's what you want. I hope we can eventually be friends. Or as close to friends as we can get since I still hate you and all," I teased, trying to lighten mood.

It worked, since he threw his head back and chuckled. "I'll take that. And we will be, just not yet."

"I can accept that."

"Good." He smiled at me.

"Well, I suppose I should go make sure the King isn't jerking off on my underwear," I joked. I started walking towards the door, but stopped before I made it. "By the way, if you ever call me Queen Kendall again, I'll rip your nuts off. Anyone who has made mud pies with me while I was still in a diaper doesn't need to call me queen."

"Yes, ma'am." He saluted me sarcastically, but he had a smile on his face.

I nodded in appreciation and continued out of his room. I made the short walk down to my room and found Finnian in my closet. He had one of my suitcases open and was throwing my clothes inside, not even bothering to fold them. I glared at him and yanked away the shirt he was holding, folding it neatly and putting it inside. I did the same to the clothes he had already thrown inside.

"I would appreciate it if in any future dialogue you partake in, you not mention what I may or may not 'jerk off' to."

I couldn't help it. I burst into laughter. The crying while holding your sides in pain laughter. He sounded so uncomfortable and disgusted when he said jerk off; like it was a vile thing to do, much less discuss. As if he never did it, which I knew there was no way he didn't. His sex drive was even higher since he was the king. His primal urges were stronger. I didn't even need to ask him if he had gotten laid recently, because I knew the answer would be a hard no.

"Does it make you uncomfortable when I talk about your dick?" I tried and failed to contain my snickers.

"When you discuss it with someone who isn't me, yes, very," he growled out.

"In the future, I'll be sure to only talk to you about your masturbation habits."

His stare was colder than the tundra. "How about we just not discuss those at all?" he asked rhetorically.

"I don't know. I kind of like seeing you squirm a bit."

"I'm not squirming. I don't squirm," he insisted fiercely.

"Did I hit a nerve, King Finnian?" I raised a mocking eyebrow and folded another pair of jeans.

"No," he answered shortly, clenching his jaw. Redness was creeping up his neck and into his cheeks.

"Whatever you say," I replied in a singsong voice. "Can you put my toiletries in this?" I changed the subject and handed him a smaller bag.

He nodded and left me alone to pack. I finished quickly and rolled my bags out of the closet. He just finished as well.

"I think I have everything. Let me check my bedroom before we go."

Once I had my laptop, purse, phone, and charger, I was ready to go.

"I'll get those." He insisted gruffly when I started pulling my suitcases behind me.

He grabbed them from my hands and started walking, not noticing that he had just thawed through another chunk of my frozen heart. It was a small gesture but it meant a lot to me.

I followed behind him, carrying nothing but my purse and laptop. He was far more graceful walking up the steps with all my luggage than I would have ever been. He didn't even act like he was carrying it.

Once we got to the sixth floor, he stopped in front of the door next to his. I remembered him mentioning that I could stay there. Now that I had the opportunity right in front of me, I felt a strong urge not to take it.

Finnian and I had a lot to work through, that was the only thing I was sure of, but would we be able to do that if we weren't actually together to do it?

I wasn't ready for a lot with him. I didn't want to get physical yet, and I wasn't completely ready to hand my heart over to him on a silver platter, but I still felt like I had to try somehow. I had to make some kind of effort, even if it was something small.

Which is why I found myself grabbing his hand before it could reach the knob.

"I'll stay in your room. For now. But that doesn't mean I forgive you yet," I added sternly.

He gave me an intense look that I couldn't quite decipher, then nodded and continued to his room. I was surprised to notice a TV box sitting on the floor next to his bed.

"Where'd that come from? Did you let someone up here?" I asked in astonishment.

"Of course not. No one but you and I can even enter this floor. I had someone leave it on the stairs, then I brought it up while you were talking to Matt. I didn't have time to install it yet, but I thought you might enjoy it," he said it so casually, like it was no big deal.

It *was* a big deal.

It hasn't even been twenty four hours after I mentioned it, and he had already gotten me something. It wasn't the TV itself that was important, it was the fact that he went out of his way for me for no other reason than to make me happy.

My heart melted a little more.

"I'll hang my clothes up while you work on that?" I asked softly.

"Sure," he agreed and wheeled my bags into his closet first.

We worked quickly after that. His closet was even bigger than mine, so I was able to fit everything despite his overabundance of suits. I still had room to spare too, which was good considering over half of my wardrobe was still back at home. I'd have to get it at some point. He even emptied one of his dressers, which I filled with underwear, pajamas, workout clothes, and old t-shirts and shorts.

In the bathroom, I quickly filled the bare half of the sinks. There was a little built-in vanity on one end, so I set up my makeup and hair products there. I filled the shower with everything, from body wash and shaving cream to shampoo and conditioner. There was more than enough room on the built-in shelves of the stone walk-in shower, considering all he had inside was a bar of soap and a single bottle of shampoo.

I would never be able to figure out how men needed so few products to shower.

When I walked back out, he was just finishing up. He'd managed to mount the TV to the wall, despite the fact that it was made of stone, and hung it directly across from the bed. He even angled the two chairs slightly to be able to see the TV. He hooked up Netflix too and somehow knew my account information.

"You work fast," I said, impressed.

"It doesn't exactly take a rocket scientist to hang a TV and connect it to Netflix," he mumbled.

"Well thank you. This is really sweet, I appreciate it."

He rubbed the back of his neck. "It was nothing," he murmured.

"So, what are your plans for the rest of the day?" I asked after I jumped onto the bed.

"Spending the day with you."

My eyes widened at his announcement. "What? Don't you have work to do?"

"I always have work to do, but you're more important."

"I feel like I've entered an alternate universe where you're a super nice person. Like that episode of Boy Meets World where Topanga finds the portal in the back of her closet."

"I'm not familiar with that reference."

"You're missing out. You could learn a thing or two from Cory and Topanga's relationship. They're definitely my aspirational couple," I told him seriously.

"What kind of name is Topanga?" he questioned, his tone just as serious as mine.

I laughed. "Don't hate on her, she was my childhood role model."

"I suppose I'll have to look into this Cory and Topanga then if they're so important to you," he answered. He sounded like he was ready to go out and conduct extensive research into the inner workings of the fictional couple instead of just watching a few episodes.

I shook my head at him in disbelief. "How about we just watch a movie for now?"

"We'll do whatever you want." He joined me on the bed, and I cautiously allowed him to pull me into his side as I searched for a movie.

It wasn't so bad.

* * *

Our third episode of Boy Meets World ended just before dinner. Finnian hadn't even really watched what I had put on, other than a little bit of the first movie. Instead, he started glancing at me not so subtly but then fell asleep soon after that. I let him sleep since I knew he didn't get as much rest as he should.

After the last episode, I decided to wake him up. I was starving and I was sure he was too. And despite his beliefs, I didn't like being late for things.

"Hey, wake up. It's time for dinner," I told him as I shook his shoulder softly.

Before I could do much else, he switched our positions, pulling me under him before I could blink. He smirked down at me, a mischievous glint in his eyes.

"I'm not hungry for food," he whispered in a low, rough voice.

I was turned on for sure, but I hid it well with an eye roll. "Get off of me, you horny bastard. The only thing you'll be eating tonight is whatever the chefs cooked. Now let's go, I'm starving."

He kissed my cheek softly, rolling off of me. "You're always starving," he added once he stood up.

"Maybe you just don't feed me enough," I countered.

"How do you figure that? You get three preplanned meals a day; plus, you can have the chefs make whatever you want at any time of the day or night. You have twenty-four-hour access to any kind of food you can think of. How could that possibly not be enough?" he asked, deadpan.

For once, I had no response. He had me there.

"Shut up," I muttered immaturely, not wanting to admit defeat.

He looked amused but otherwise dropped it. He threaded our fingers together and walked us down to the dining room. We were right on time; everyone was already there. Just like this morning, another place setting and chair had been added next to his, so I took the seat next to Tyler while he took the seat next to his brother.

Everyone except for my sister bowed to us as soon as we walked in. It made me uncomfortable, especially seeing my brother and best friend partake in it. As much as I enjoyed undermining Finnian, I didn't want to do it in front of his people. My people were fine, but I didn't want to embarrass him. I made a mental note to talk to him about it later.

"Hey, guys," I greeted everyone rather awkwardly.

"Good evening, my queen," Niki replied. She had an accomplished smile on her face, like she was finally getting her way after an extended period of being told no.

"Please, Niki. Don't call me that. It's weird," I asked while grimacing.

"A good queen accepts her title with pride," Emiliya added, sneering slightly at her subtle dig.

"I don't see it that way, Emiliya. I think it's a sign of a humble queen."

"It is Royal Beta Female Emiliya, Miss Keating," she hissed her entire title.

"Fine, then it's Queen Kendall to you, Royal Beta Female," I returned her hostility.

Kieran shot her a nasty glare before turning his attention to me. "Please ignore her, Your Highness. I speak for both of us when I say we are thrilled that you are my brother's mate. You're a strong she-wolf, and you'll be an amazing queen. Please accept my sincerest apologies for my mate's behavior and my heartfelt congratulations. I am elated that you are not only my queen but also my sister-in-law. Welcome to the family, Kendall."

"Thank you, Kieran," I replied to him sincerely, feeling touched at his kind words. "Your acceptance means a lot to me. I look forward to getting to know you better."

"I look forward to that as well." He shot me a small grin, which was a first that I had seen from him. Emiliya had turned her glare to him. He tried his best to ignore it, but I could see his eyes darting to hers nervously.

The waiters brought out salads and filled our glasses. They seemed nervous that they were in Finnian's presence, so it took a little longer than normal. I thanked them before they left.

"I do have one question, if I may?" Kieran spoke to me again once they were gone and once Emiliya had turned away from him.

"Sure," I answered before I took a bite of my salad.

"You've been here well over a month. Why is it just being announced that you two are mates?"

Finnian's leg was touching mine under the table, and I felt him tense slightly at his question, although his face didn't show it.

"I wasn't ready for a mate," I lied skillfully. "I asked him to give me some time to adjust before we told anyone. I'm sorry for asking him to lie to you and everyone else."

"If it helps, I didn't know until last night either," Matt added.

I gave him a weak, thankful smile. He returned it with a wink.

"Don't worry. I'm not upset. I understand that discovering you are the queen can be quite the adjustment."

I nodded at him thankfully and continued eating.

"So, Kendall, have you thought about when your coronation may take place?" Niki inquired a few minutes later.

I looked between her and Finnian. "I'm not sure. We haven't really talked about it yet," I answered, sounding uncertain.

"Soon," Finnian added.

I shot him a questioning look, wanting him to expand on his comment, but he didn't. We didn't speak of it again, instead making small talk the remainder of dinner. Everyone acted normal around me after a while, and the conversation went a lot smoother.

After dinner, Finnian and I walked back upstairs. He started loosening his tie as soon as he shut the door behind us. He tugged it off completely and bent down to start a fire. I plopped down on the bed and watched him.

"Coronation?" I asked after he finished and was standing again. He turned to face me.

"What about it?"

"You said soon. How soon? And what exactly is it? Like, I know to humans it's crowning a king or queen, but what is it to werewolves? Do you even have a crown?"

"Soon is soon, within the next month. It's just a ceremony. There aren't any crowns involved but I suppose I could get you one if you want. It takes place outside, in the Coronation Arena. You'll enter from the tunnels in front of all the alphas. They will bow to you and pledge their loyalty to serve and protect you. You will make a pledge to them as their queen. That's about it."

"No crown necessary," I whispered lowly and gulped nervously.

He was walking towards me slowly, like a predator stalking its prey. He had this look in his eyes, like he wanted to devour me. I scooted back on the bed, trying to put space between us. He didn't let me get far.

He leaned down and slowly crawled over my body until his face hovered right over mine. He was so close that his nose brushed against mine. His body was pressed firmly against me, only being held up enough so he didn't crush me.

I held my breath for a while but finally released in a whoosh when my lungs started burning. Nervousness and desire crawled through me, flooding my veins and lighting them on fire. His eyes burned into mine, showing more emotion than I had ever seen.

"You're so beautiful," he murmured, brushing back a loose strand of hair from my forehead.

I suddenly felt vulnerable. More vulnerable than I ever had in my life. I didn't push him off, I didn't move closer. I just laid there, watching his every move.

"You're scared." He pulled back just slightly, but not by much. "You don't have to be. I know I'm far from a perfect mate. I know I've treated you horribly. But if there is one thing you need to know, it's how much I care about you; how important you are to me. You're *everything.* Please, don't be scared of me, Kendall. I will never hurt you again."

I couldn't stop the tears that sprang to my eyes at the conviction, the promise, in his tone. I realized then how well he knew me. He knew that I was scared, and even the exact reason why. He may not know every single detail about me, like my likes and dislikes, but he knew me. He knew me past the superficial level. He knew my heart and my soul. He intertwined himself around both.

"I know these are just words, but I will spend every day proving how true they are." With that, he brushed away my fallen tears with his calloused thumb, pressed a sweet lingering kiss to my forehead, and lifted himself off of me.

"I'm going to take a shower."

I nodded absentmindedly. He walked away, leaving me alone with my thoughts. My thoughts that were telling me that he was slowly chipping away the ice around my heart.

CHAPTER TWENTY-THREE

"I'm surprised he's even letting you train still," Selena gave me her unwanted opinion as we traipsed through the woods.

We usually ran in our wolf forms to the training field, but we decided to walk this morning after breakfast. The weather was nicer than it had been in weeks. Rain clouds were nowhere in sight, leaving us with a beautiful view of a clear blue sky filled with fluffy white clouds. A slight warm front had blown through the night before, leaving the air chilly but tolerable.

It was warm enough that we only needed a light jacket over our workout clothes. It would likely be the last remnants of warmth before the cold fingers of winter grasped the royal territory.

"Mind your own business," I commanded.

What she said was true, much to my annoyance. Finnian had bickered all afternoon the day before and all morning as well. We had a few nice days, just spending time together, but as soon as I informed him I would be returning to training, he flipped out.

I honestly had no clue what his problem was. Training was a good thing. I would have a much better chance of defending myself against my possible future killer if I were properly trained.

But he didn't see it that way. He saw it as an opportunity for me to get hurt, which was unnecessary because apparently he could and would defend me.

It was crap, and I had no problem telling him that. I finally had to put my foot down this morning and tell him I was going no matter what he said. He finally relented, but informed me that he would be watching closely since, apparently, he had cameras out there that had been watching me the whole time.

I was completely unaware of them.

Finnian and I were doing decidedly better after only a few days, but we were still discovering each other's boundaries. One thing he had been respectful of was my need for space. He touched me a little, but never tried to kiss me or push it further than cuddling. I was grateful for that.

"No can do, baby sister. Your life is like a soap opera; I can't look away."

I elbowed her in the gut. "First off, I'm literally a year younger than you. I don't think that constitutes me as your 'baby sister.' " I made air quotes at her term of endearment. "And second, you've had your fair share of drama in your life."

"Yes, and you've made that drama your business, so we're even."

I rolled my eyes but didn't comment, changing the subject instead. "So, you have any plans for tonight?"

"Tyler and I are having dinner with Matt and Kat," she told me.

I gaped at her. "Wow, really? Thanks for the invite."

"Sorry, I didn't think about it. We planned it as a double date before you and Finnian went public. You two should totally come. We'll triple. We're going bowling after dinner."

"Gee, how can I turn down such a heartfelt invitation?" I said sarcastically.

"Don't be such a titty baby. You know we want you there. I just forgot. I forgot that we were even going until last night. Kat too. You know how busy she's been with Niki lately. Tyler and Matt were the only ones who remembered."

"Shouldn't that be reversed?"

"That's sexist, Kendall. Now, are you going or what?" she asked demandingly.

"Why not? King Finnian should get out at least once every decade."

"Don't get me wrong, I love how much it pisses him off, but are you ever going to call him Finnian?" she asked, probing me for answers.

I shrugged. "Eventually. I like pissing him off too." I grinned at her.

"Then by all means, keep it up," she commented just as the training field came into view.

Before we could say anything else, we had the attention of the entire training field. Everyone bent down on one knee and bowed their heads. Simultaneously, everyone spoke loud and proud, "All hail Queen Kendall."

"This is like the part in the Spongebob movie where everyone starts chanting 'All hail Plankton.' " Selena leaned over, murmuring softly in my ear.

I was shocked silent, so I didn't respond to her. I felt touched that I had the support of the Royal Army behind me. Before I could say anything, Harrison came to the forefront of the men, standing about five feet in front of me. He kneeled as well, mimicking the other's positions.

"My queen, on behalf of the Royal Army, I would like to pledge our loyalty and protection to you. Any one of us would be proud to die protecting you."

"Thank you, Harrison. That means so much to me," I choked out. "I want to thank all of you. I promise to be the best queen I can be and to advocate for every one of you. I cherish your loyalty, and I promise to always return it in full."

At the end of my little speech, they repeated their first phrase, then went back to normal.

"You gave us all quite the surprise, my queen," Harrison told me as we walked over to our usual mat.

"No, none of that nonsense. You're my trainer, my mentor, and my friend. It's just Kendall," I lectured him sternly, which earned me a smile and a nod.

"My quee—" Nathan started once we were in hearing distance.

"You too, Red."

"Whatever you say." He smirked and held his hands up in submission.

"Good. I don't want to be treated any differently."

"Alright. I think I can do that. You ready to get your ass handed to you?" He grinned at me, humor lighting his eyes.

"Oh, yeah. He can definitely do that." Selena chuckled from behind me.

"Let's do it." I began stretching quickly to loosen up.

"Actually, we'll be doing things a little differently today," Harrison said from behind us.

I nodded and turned to give him my attention as I continued to stretch.

"You've mastered pinning your opponent. Now you need to learn how to execute the kill."

I shot him a look of horror.

"No, you won't be killing Nathan or Selena." He chuckled. "You just have to get a hand on their throat. The fastest and easiest way to kill your opponent in a fight is to strike there. It's the easiest to access and the quickest way to end things. Always go for the throat if possible.

"What you'll start practicing today is getting your hand on your opponent's throat. You have to hold on long enough that, in a real life situation, you would be able to elongate your claws, bury them into their flesh, and pull it out. I'll be the judge of what is considered long enough."

Selena and I nodded in understanding. Nathan didn't, since he apparently already knew what we were going to do.

Harrison made us wear special gloves so that our claws couldn't poke through. None of us would intentionally try to kill each other, but if we got angry enough—which was always a possibility for werewolves when training—they may come out subconsciously. That could end badly, so it was best to take precautions.

Selena and I went first. Nathan seemed hesitant to fight me. My guess was it had less to do with me as an opponent and more to do with the fact that he was now aware of who my mate was. Finnian would be watching, and if Nathan did something he didn't like, it could get ugly. I wouldn't let him do anything of course, but to Nathan, he seemed to not want to take that chance.

"Ready?" Harrison asked once we were in position.

We both nodded.

"Go."

We lunged at each other.

*   *   *

"I'm just saying, a throat punch was a low blow. Like, I know we were aiming for the throats and all, but did you really have to punch me there?" I whined and rubbed my sore neck.

I felt especially beat up after today's training. Selena and I never took it easy on each other, but today was even worse. I had a feeling it was because of Niki's vision. Selena was probably trying to get me in the best fighting shape she could, and that meant that she came at me with everything she had so I could get better.

"Like Harrison said, your real-life opponents will throw low blows. You have to be ready for them."

I rolled my eyes. That was fine and dandy, but my throat still hurt like a bitch, causing my voice to sound far raspier than normal.

"Whatever. I'll be sure to return the favor tomorrow."

"I'm sure you will."

"I'll meet you guys downstairs at seven. I need to take a shower and actually tell King Finnian we're going out."

"Good luck with that." She snickered.

"Thanks, I'm sure I'll need it."

With that, we parted ways. I went to go search for Finnian. I found him right where I left him that morning; his private office. It was the same office he had been in when Niki showed him her vision.

He used to allow other Royals and some staff up on the sixth floor, but apparently, after seeing that vision, he had made the entire floor off limits to anyone—period. No one knew why except for Niki and now me.

He couldn't trust anyone, so he distanced himself from everyone he cared about, kept them at arm's length. Close enough to watch, but far enough so he couldn't be blindsided.

He was on the phone when I walked in, seemingly talking to an alpha. I plopped down on the chair across from his desk and waited for him to finish. He shot me a small smile in acknowledgement, which I returned with a similar smile and a short wave.

"Okay, thanks Rylan. I appreciate it. I'll see you in a couple of weeks."

With that, he hung up the phone and gave me his full attention.

"You going somewhere?" I asked him.

"Rylan managed to capture one of the higher ups of the rebellion. We're going there in a few weeks so I can question him," he explained.

"We?"

"Yes, we. There is no way in hell I'm leaving you here without my protection. Not when I'll be four hours away," he growled out.

"Okay," I agreed.

His stern look softened. "Okay? I was expecting more of a fight." He leaned back in his chair, eyeing me suspiciously.

"I trust you. Besides, hopefully my lack of fighting you over that will make my next statement go smoother."

"And what would that be? It wouldn't happen to have to do with the double date you agreed to without consulting me?" He raised a mocking eyebrow.

"Triple date, actually," I corrected, not bothering to ask how he heard my conversation with Selena from a mile away. "And it'll be fun."

"That's debatable," he muttered dryly, scratching the stubble on his chin thoughtfully.

"Oh, come on. It will be. If you don't go, I'll have to be the fifth wheel. And you never know who might come talk to me if they think I'm single?" I inquired innocently, trying to push down the smirk that threatened to spread across my lips.

He scowled, and his chest vibrated deeply with a snarl as his wolf pushed forward.

This time I couldn't push the smirk down. "I guess you better come then."

He realized what I had been doing when he saw my smirk and relaxed, his possessive growls quieting. "You make a good point. Although, I don't appreciate you conning me into agreeing."

"I wouldn't call it conning," I rebutted.

"And what would you call it?"

"Just giving you a little incentive."

"We'll agree to disagree about what to call it, but I'll go anyways. Why don't you go take a shower while I finish up in here?"

I smiled and nodded. When I stood up, I hesitated briefly before finally leaning over his desk and kissing his cheek softly.

"Thank you," I told him when I pulled away.

His face softened and he gazed at me tenderly. "Anything for you."

I gave him one last lingering look before I left his office.

I took my time getting ready since we still had two hours before we leave. After taking a shower, I slipped on a long sleeved tight black shirt, a red and black plaid skirt with black tights underneath, along with a pair of black ankle boots.

I added a bit more makeup than usual—going for a thick winged liner and ruby red matte lipstick. I left my hair in wild ringlets, allowing them to fall down my back, the front braided away from my face.

Finnian had come in just as I was finishing my makeup. He stripped off his suit, which I deemed unnecessary since he just put on another one in its place. The only difference was the color of the shirt underneath. I didn't complain though; I was just happy he was coming.

"You look beautiful," he told me once he walked out of the bathroom.

"Thanks. You look nice too."

"You ready?" He held his hand out for me to take. I grabbed my small black purse and intertwined my fingers with his.

We walked together out of the room and down towards the garage where we were meeting the others. They were already waiting once we arrived. We decided to take one of Finnian's limos so that we could all fit inside.

We had two SUVs accompanying us. One was in the front and the other trailed behind us. I complained about bringing guards on our date but Finnian said it was happening. Tyler and Matt both backed him up, so I didn't have much ground to stand on in an argument. Although he assured me that I wouldn't even realize they were around.

I chatted with Selena and Kat on the drive there. Finnian sat right next to me, his hand resting above my knee, heating my skin considerably. I twined my fingers through his, leaving them on my thigh.

It didn't take long to arrive at the restaurant. We went in through the back and were led to a private room, away from anyone else. It was a far nicer place than the bar and grill Tyler brought us to a while back. The lights were dimmed, and instead of drunken laughter and terrible karaoke, they had someone strumming a harp softly. It was definitely a high-class establishment.

We had a nervous waiter serving us. It was obvious they weren't used to serving many Royals here. He was practically shaking in his black leather shoes. I acted as friendly as I could, trying to ease his anxiety. It seemed to work after a while.

"So, I'm surprised you actually came tonight," Selena commented after the waiter took our orders.

"And why is that, Selena?" Finnian asked dryly, not looking impressed that he had to converse with my sister.

"You're not exactly a social butterfly. I figured you'd make my sister come alone."

"I'd do anything for your sister—including being around you."

Selena didn't look insulted; she actually looked rather amused.

"Anything?" Selena pressed.

He gave her a hard look, but nodded nonetheless.

"Good, because my birthday is next weekend and I'm stealing her for a girl's night," she informed him.

I looked between the two nervously, wondering how this would go down. Selena always made a big deal out of her birthday, so we had our own little tradition. Every year, Selena, Kat, a few other girls from the pack, and I would go to our parent's lakehouse.

We'd basically just get super drunk, play a bunch of drinking games, and go swimming in the middle of the night, even though her birthday was in winter and the water was freezing.

The reason for my nervousness this year was because I doubted Finnian would let me go. Not that I needed his permission, but I'd go along with what he wanted when it came to my safety. Selena was going to push this until she got her way. I was mentally preparing myself for a battle of wills between the two most stubborn people I knew.

"And what exactly does this 'girl's night' entail?" His face remained blank.

"We go to our family's lake house and spend the weekend together."

"Where?" he continued to question her.

"A couple of hours south of here; in a small lake town called Coledo Springs."

"When exactly?"

"We'd leave next Friday then come back Sunday morning."

Finnian looked like he was thinking it over, which surprised me. I wasn't expecting him to consider this. He glanced over at me, giving me a serious look.

"You want to go?" he asked me softly.

Words escaped me, so I just nodded. He held my gaze for a few more seconds, then turned back to my sister.

"If she goes, I go," he finally stated.

"You know what, I'm nothing if not flexible. We can make it a couple's trip. Babe, you can come after all," she said, turning to Tyler at the end.

My jaw dropped at that turn of events just as the waiter walked in with our food.

* * *

"Us sisters against you three bozos," Selena announced after she stripped off her shoes.

The rest of dinner had gone well, and we were now at a bowling alley getting ready for a game. The place was empty except for the employees working here. Since this place didn't have a private room like the restaurant, they had shut it down to the public.

It was actually kind of nice having the place to ourselves. We got to control the music, and we didn't have to wait in any lines or listen to other people's noise. We didn't have to wear the disgusting bowling shoes either. Instead, they let us bowl in our socks. And, to top it all off, they were supplying us with endless food and drinks.

Despite the fact that we had just eaten, I still attacked the cheese fries they placed on our table and guzzled down the cold, foamy beer.

Selena did the same.

"You sure you want to do that?" Tyler asked, stealing one of her fries.

"Absolutely. You three are going down so hard, you'll be glad that no one else is here to see the embarrassment."

"Care to put your money where your mouth is, little sister?" Matt spoke up.

"Hell yes," she agreed just as she swallowed the last of her beer and stood up to pick a bowling ball. "How much?"

"No, money is too easy. Let's make this a little more interesting."

"What did you have in mind?" she questioned after she picked a magenta colored ball. I grabbed a swirly violet one.

"Hmm." Matt pondered it over, then turned to Tyler. "You have any suggestions?"

Tyler thought it over as well. Once his eyes lit up, I knew he had thought of something interesting. "You have to tell me how you three got caught doing the silencing spell," he told her, bringing up the story that we had both denied telling him.

"No!" Kat, Selena, and I all snapped at the same time.

Matt chuckled. "I can tell you that one, man."

"I'll murder you in this very building, Matthew," Selena threatened.

"Do you think that scares me? You don't scare me."

"If you tell, you can forget about what we have planned when we get back to the castle. Does that scare you?" Kat jumped in before he could talk.

He paled slightly because he knew she was serious. The story was that humiliating for all of us. "Think of something else," he finally mumbled to Tyler.

While they were deciding that, Finnian snaked his arms around me from behind, startling me. He lowered his head and rested his chin on my shoulder. His warm breath tickled my ear as he whispered lowly, "Care to make a wager of our own?"

I turned in his arms and wrapped mine around his neck.

"What did you have in mind, King Finnian?"

"I have a lot in mind, but I don't think you're ready for any of that yet," he whispered in my ear, causing me to shudder slightly. I gulped nervously. "So instead, I'll keep it simple for you. If I win, you have to kiss me. A real kiss."

I stared into his cerulean eyes, thinking it over briefly. "Fine. But if I win, you have to take the spell off the sixth floor. At least for a few people. I want to be able to bring Kat and Selena upstairs sometimes."

He exhaled heavily. "You drive a hard bargain, but okay. Only for those two though."

"And Matt," I added.

He gave me a dry, unimpressed look. "Fine."

"Fine." I grinned as I held my hand out to his, to shake on it. He did, but not before kissing my knuckles first.

We turned our attention back to the group, who had finally worked out their deal. Kat was sitting on Matt's lap, entering our names and groups into the computer.

Selena started us off, bowling a strike to begin. She jumped up and down in celebration, and Kat and I both high fived her.

Tyler went next, bowling a strike as well. He didn't freak out and screech like his mate had, he simply smirked at her and slipped his arm around her back, which she shrugged off with a glare.

Kat and Matt went after that, both bowling a spare, keeping us tied up. Kat didn't have our natural werewolf coordination but she did have the practice. We used to go bowling every weekend when we were kids and she got to be just as good as us.

I took my time after them, taking in a deep breath before releasing the ball. I felt Finnian's eyes burning into me but I didn't let it deter me. As I exhaled, I released the ball and watched it roll down the lane, knocking over every pin.

My reaction was similar to Selena's. I jumped and squealed.

Finnian was up next, and I brushed against him sensually on my way back to the table, feigning ignorance over my actions. Hopefully that would throw off his game.

Of course, it didn't. He had to be great at everything. He knocked over every pin as well, keeping both teams tied.

This went on for a while. It started out clean, but eventually trash talking and dirty moves were added. The trash talking was first, then Selena kicked it up a notch by rubbing her ass against the front of Tyler's slacks just before his turn, way more aggressively than I had been with Finnian. He groaned and then shot her a glare, knowing what she was doing immediately.

This continued back and forth, until it came down to one player; me.

If I bowled a strike, it didn't matter what Finnian bowled after me; we would win by at least one point.

The heckling started as soon I stepped forward with my ball. Finnian was silent, but Tyler and Matt were trying to distract me. Selena and Kat were trying to shut them up, which wasn't working; so they settled for cheering me on, yelling out encouragements.

I blocked them out as best as I could and focused on the pins. I tried my best not to psych myself out.

Finally, after a few moments, I rolled the ball. It seemed to take forever to reach the end, and I held my breath as I watched.

It hit and knocked all but one over. The last pin wobbled back and forth; almost but not quite falling. I bit my lip and grabbed my hair, waiting to see what it would do.

It fell over.

I screamed and turned to my sisters. They screamed with me, and we jumped up and down together for a few seconds, then started dancing and taunting our mates. They didn't look at all pleased with the results.

I turned my attention to Finnian after our celebration. I walked over to him, leaving the girls behind. His face was blank unlike Tyler and Matt's, who both looked upset.

"Too bad you didn't bet against yourself." I snickered softly.

"At least I get to make you happy, so I win either way."

A soft blush crept up my cheeks. He had to stop dropping lines like that on me. The more he talked like that, the more he softened me up, wore me down.

"Do you want to finish?" I gestured to the lane.

"No," he muttered as he pulled me closer. I gave in and leaned into his warm body.

"Do you guys want to play again or are you ready to go?" Matt asked after a few minutes.

"Doesn't matter to me. Whatever you guys want to do," Tyler answered.

"Let's go home," Selena said since we all just shrugged in response.

We made our way to the limo, where the driver was already waiting with the door opened. As we walked into the chilly air, I shivered. Finnian pulled me closer to his body, rubbing my arm up and down.

I almost cried. It finally hit me that we could openly be together now. That he was mine now.

I remembered the time we all went to Mountain Side Bar and Grill a few weeks ago. We all walked through the cold air that night, and I had been jealous of what Matt and Kat had, how they could so openly be affectionate with each other. I had no reason to be jealous now. Not with Finnian next to me, holding me close and keeping me warm. That thought alone warmed me more than his arm ever could.

I snuggled closer to him, feeling nothing but a contented happiness wash over me.

The ride back to the castle felt longer than normal, but that was probably because I was ready to be alone with Finnian. We made idle chitchat, but I didn't participate much. I just laid my head against Finnian's shoulder, which made my eyes feel heavy.

Once we made it back, we all said goodnight and went our separate ways. When we made it to our room, Finnian started a fire immediately. That warmed my heart more, knowing that he only did that for me because I was cold.

I left him to it and walked into the bathroom to get ready for bed. I slipped out of my clothes and threw one of his t-shirts over my body. I washed my face, tied up my hair, and brushed my teeth.

I walked back out a few minutes later. He had stripped off his tie and jacket and had started undoing his buttons.

Before I could stop myself, I walked up to him, not stopping until my chest was pressed against his. I grabbed his cheeks, his stubble scratching my palms, and pulled his face down to mine. I slammed my lips over his and kissed him deeply, putting all of the warmth he had filled me with since the ball into it.

I felt like a part of my soul had finally snapped into place as soon as his lips met mine. We hadn't been affectionate in so long; I had almost forgot how it felt.

It made me feel whole. He consumed me; my senses filled with nothing but him. I loved the way he tasted when I dipped my tongue into his mouth. I loved the way he grunted against my lips and squeezed my hips gently, pulling me impossibly closer. I loved the way his scent made me feel safe and content.

After a while, I finally pulled away. His hands were wrapped around my waist and his forehead rested against mine. He looked just as affected by our kiss as I was.

"You do realize that I lost the bet, right?" he asked after a few minutes.

I giggled. "Yes, I do."

"Then what was that for?"

"I had to thank you for tonight somehow."

"I don't know what I did so right tonight, but I'll be sure to do it again if that's how you'll reward me."

I rolled my eyes playfully and smiled. "I'll have to let you figure it out by yourself then."

"If you're my prize, I'll always figure it out." He kissed my forehead before we pulled away. "Do you want to watch a movie before bed?" I nodded. "Find one while I'm changing."

I nodded again and walked over to the bed, slipping under the covers on my side. I grabbed the remote off my bedside table and searched for a movie, which I found pretty quick. I wanted to say he would like it too but he didn't seem to like movies at all. He always slept, watched me, or worked while we watched one.

I started the movie and snuggled into the bed. Finnian came out a few minutes later in nothing but boxers. I gulped when I saw him and felt my eyes change and my canines extend. I pushed down my desire, and he ignored it. Once he was under the blanket, it was easier to ignore.

He pulled me into him, intertwining my body with his. His arms wrapped around me tightly, and I rested my head on his chest. I slipped my leg between his and touched my feet to his calf, which he allowed despite how cold they were.

I watched the movie for a while but, eventually, my exhaustion won over, which was made worse by Finnian running his hand through my hair and down my arm repeatedly, which lulled me closer to sleep.

"Goodnight Finnian," I mumbled sleepily.

His hand paused its descent briefly, then started again.

"Goodnight Kendall." Was the last thing I heard before I slipped into darkness.

CHAPTER TWENTY-FOUR

Selena's birthday had expanded even further than Finnian, Matt, and Tyler. Instead of just the six of us, it was now nine of us. In addition to the guys, she also asked Dalton, Lili, and Nathan to join us.

I was only mildly surprised when Dalton decided to go. He was avoiding me, yes, but he was still Selena's best friend. He was the only guy she ever allowed to go with us, and I knew no matter what his feelings for me were, he would come through for Selena and be there when she wanted him to be. I had to give him credit, he was a good friend to her.

To avoid any awkwardness though, Dalton and I were in separate cars. He's riding in a separate SUV with Matt, Kat, and Lili. That left Tyler, Selena, Nathan, Finnian, and me in a car together.

Our vehicles were in the middle of the line of cars. Two black SUV's were in front of us and two behind, all four filled with Royal Guards. I didn't think we needed so many, but Finnian wasn't taking any chances after what happened when we went dress shopping. And he made a good point that I was more of a target now that I had been announced as queen.

Tyler was in the driver's seat, one hand on the wheel, the other on Selena's thigh, who was sitting next to him. That left me in the back seat, crushed in the middle of two of the biggest werewolves I knew. Finnian draped his arm around me before we left and never moved it, instead playing with my hair and rubbing the back of my neck tenderly.

The past week with him had been great. We had made so much progress. He may still get on my nerves at times, and we may still bicker, but he was trying. I could see that, and I appreciated it more than he knew. He wasn't pushing me, but he still let me know how much he wanted me.

On Monday, he had finally gone back to work completely. He stayed busier than I thought but always made time for me. We would have breakfast together every morning, just the two of us, which made me realize he could actually cook really well, then he would go to his office while I would go to training.

He would work through lunch, and I would spend that time with Selena and Kat. Matt and Dalton were still busy with Tyler and Kieran during the day. After that, Kat would return to training with Niki while Selena and I had settled into some of our Royal duties. We were learning and navigating our roles together, which made things much easier.

I still didn't know exactly what my job was as queen, but I was slowly figuring it out. I would spend the afternoons with members of the Royal Pack, helping the people who needed it. I was even able to visit the orphanage on the other side of the Royal Territory. That was humbling, to say the least.

All the kids there were so happy and full of light despite the fact that their families had died and their packs couldn't or wouldn't take them in. They had been so excited to see us, which warmed my heart. I'd already decided to start making weekly visits there.

After that, Finnian and I would meet back up and have dinner with everyone. That seemed to go well for the past week. Emiliya had finally started warming up to me, it seemed. I wouldn't go as far to say that we were friends, but we were friendly.

After dinner, Finnian and I would go for a run, just the two of us. His wolf was magnificent. He was so sleek and strong, deadly even, but he was nothing but a giant cuddly teddy bear around me.

It wasn't until someone else was around that he showed how intimidating his wolf really was, which was a lot.

Then we would end the night cuddling while watching TV. He usually worked until late in the night, skipping a real dinner, but he tried to cut back a bit for me. That's just one of the ways he makes me happy.

"We need to stop at a grocery store on the way," I told Tyler once we made it past the Royal boundary line.

"And a liquor store," Selena added.

"Sure," He mumbled.

The next two hours were spent with Selena and me singing and dancing. Nathan and Tyler both made fun of us, not that we cared, and Finnian just continued to hold me, only looking mildly amused. He never seemed to talk a lot when other people were around.

Once we got close to the lake house, Tyler stopped at the store. We stocked up on junk food, pizzas, beer, and whiskey. We got juice and Cokes too, for anyone who didn't drink, which was basically just Kat, Lili, and Finnian.

Finnian didn't drink. Ever. His father had been drinking while his mother was being killed. Maybe that played a part in him not being able to save her or maybe it didn't, but to Finn, he wasn't risking it. He saw drinking as a weakness, and he never wanted me or anyone to be hurt because he wasn't ready and able to fight. I respected his decision not to drink with us.

After we finished at the store, we continued on to the cabin. It was just as we left it the last time we had been here, which was after I had graduated college. We'd taken a weekend trip to celebrate.

The place was clean, as always. Dad hired someone to come clean the place every once in a while, especially before we came.

The cabin itself was beautiful and rustic. It was a six bedroom, five bathroom log cabin. It was tucked deep in the woods, surrounded by tall pine trees and nothing else. It was completely isolated from others. Even our edge of the lake was hidden in a private cove. No one ever found it and came this way.

We parked the cars in the front and exited the vehicle. Half of the guards started securing the perimeter, while the other half carried our things inside. Once inside, I could see that it was just as I remembered.

The living room had a tall stone fireplace and the back wall was made completely of windows, overlooking the lake. The back deck had a big stone fire pit and a built-in grill with a sink and mini fridge nearby. A hot tub was off to the side, away from the grill and fire pit.

Kat and Matt took thc bcdroom downstairs while the rest of us went upstairs to the remaining bedrooms. We gave Selena and Tyler the master since it was her birthday weekend, and Finnian and I took the second biggest bedroom which had its own private bathroom.

It was my favorite room in the house. It had a small balcony that the master bedroom didn't have. It overlooked the lake and, since it was taller than the trees in between the two, you could see for miles past the water. It had the most gorgeous view of the sunset.

"What do you think?" I asked after we set our bags down.

"It's nice out here," he answered.

"Yeah, I love it. I loved coming here as a kid."

"You know, I have a cabin too."

"Really?" I raised an eyebrow as I plopped down on the bed.

"Yeah. It's not near a lake, but it does have a small pond in the backyard that you can swim in."

"How long have you had it?"

"I built it about ten years ago. It took me about a year to finish, since I could only get away for a weekend every now and then."

"You built it yourself?" I questioned, feeling impressed.

"Yeah. It's a lot smaller than this place, but that's just because it's only been me who's gone there."

I stood up and walked over to him, wrapping my arms around his neck and leaning into him. "Will you take me sometime?"

"Of course. I'd love to take you," he replied to me as he pulled me closer.

"Where is it?"

"About two hours west of the castle. It's on the way to Rylan's territory. We could go a few days early, spend a couple of nights there first?"

"Really? Yeah, that sounds great." I beamed up at him.

I leaned forward to kiss his cheek but he surprised me by gripping my chin softly and pulling my lips to meet his. It was the first time since we became official that he kissed me first, and I was enjoying him taking the reins. He kissed me deeply, passionately, licking and nipping at my bottom lip before slipping his tongue between my lips, massaging mine with his.

I gripped his hair, tugging on it gently and mussing it up, making it unusually messy. His hand released my chin and moved down my body, gripping my hips tightly, locking me in place against his hard torso.

Finally, he pulled away so I could take in a breath of much needed oxygen. My lips felt swollen and heat was pooling in my lower belly. I wanted to lean forward again, take things further, but he pulled away from me completely.

"Let's go downstairs." He threaded his fingers through mine.

We walked together back to the living room. Kat and Lili were in the kitchen, putting up the food and drinks. Selena turned on the speakers around the house and was getting her party playlist ready. Tyler, Nathan, Dalton, and Matt were all sitting on the sectional couch, all four with a beer in hand already. Matt passed me one and I took it gratefully. I twisted the lid off and took a long gulp.

Selena finally settled on a song and she, along with Kat and Lili, joined us on the couches. Finnian and I were cuddled together on a fluffy oversized chair, our feet propped up together on the long rectangular ottoman.

"Let's play a game," Selena suggested as she filled her cup back up with vodka and orange juice; mostly vodka.

"What game?" Kat asked first.

"You can't go wrong with a classic. Truth or dare," she answered.

We all shrugged and agreed to play despite the childish nature of the game. I didn't really want to but did anyways since it was her birthday. The only one who didn't agree was Finnian, who just wanted to sit with me but not actually participate.

I wasn't surprised, considering he didn't want to come in the first place. And aside from that, no one ever said he was the life of the party to begin with. No one else seemed to be surprised either.

"Fine. I'll start. Kenny, truth or dare?"

"Call me Kenny again and I'll dare myself to rip out your vocal cords."

"Don't be so sensitive. Truth or dare?"

"Fine. Truth," I reluctantly answered back.

"Out of all the guys you've seen naked, who has the biggest dick?" She smirked at me.

I glared back at her. Finn growled, enraged at the thought of me seeing any male anatomy other than his . . . which I hadn't actually seen yet.

"I don't know who *has* the biggest dick, but the honor of who *is* the biggest dick is all yours."

"Funny," she drawled dryly.

"Okay . . ." I paused, looking over my options. "Katerina. Your turn. Truth or dare."

"Dare," she replied.

"Hmm . . . I dare you to jump in the lake."

"By myself?" She groaned.

"Scared?" Selena teased.

"Nope."

With that, she stood up and walked out the back door. We all followed her, with Matt flipping on the outdoor lights on the way. The back porch lit up along with the walkway down to the pier.

The pier was attached to a boat dock and had a narrow walkway, which opened up to a big deck over the water. There was plenty of room at the end for all of us, along with the two tables and swing that was already there.

Kat paused briefly at the end. She started chanting while holding her hands over the water. After a few minutes, we could see steam rising from the water in front of the ladder.

"Couldn't jump in as it was?" I asked her.

"Hell no. Not all of us have an internal heater like werewolves do. I only heated about ten feet out, though."

We nodded, and she started stripping off her clothes. We all came prepared, wearing our bathing suits under our clothes. She was wearing a cute olive-green bikini which complimented her creamy cocoa skin tone and matched her dark-green cat-like eyes.

She took a breath and jumped in, holding her nose on the way. She resurfaced a few seconds later and wiped the water off her face.

"Anyone else coming in?" she questioned us.

Selena was the first to answer; not with words, but by stripping her clothes off as well. We all followed . . . except for Finnian.

"Are you coming in?" I asked him after everyone else was in the water.

"No."

"Why?"

"I'm just here to watch over you," he grunted.

I rolled my eyes. "I don't need a babysitter. What I do need is my mate to come swim with me, though." I gave him the puppy dog face as I wrapped my arms around his waist, trying to pull him to the water, but failing. He just stared at me, not budging on his decision. I released him.

"Fine. I guess I'll have to swim by myself." I pouted then pulled my shirt over my head. His attention left my face, like I wanted.

I ran my hands down my body, making my way to my jeans slowly. I teasingly unbuttoned them and pulled down the zipper before sliding them down my legs leisurely. I grinned when I heard his deep growl. I stepped out of my jeans and flats at the same time.

"Have fun up here by yourself, Your Highness." I kissed his cheek and rubbed against him briefly before pulling away.

My new tactic worked, because he was already undressed by the time I jumped in.

The water was warm but not too hot. It felt like a hot tub but with more room to actually stretch out. My toes could barely reach the bottom, so when Finnian swam up beside me, I held on to him to stay above the surface. His feet reached the bottom with no trouble.

He held me close to him, pressing me against his hard, naked torso. In the background, I could vaguely hear the others talking and laughing but all my focus was on the man in front of me. He was so handsome that it hurt. I leaned in closer and kissed him tenderly.

Before I could deepen the kiss, a splash of water sprayed across our faces. We pulled apart; me in surprise and Finnian in anger. We looked over at Selena, who had a smug look on her face.

"Save that for the bedroom so we can finish our game."

I rolled my eyes but still listened to her. I stayed close to Finn, since he was holding me up, but I gave them my attention.

The game continued for a while. We laughed and continued to drink, since Matt had brought out a cooler at some point. After a few hours, the heat in the water wore off, which made it too cold, even for werewolves.

We were all pretty buzzed except for Kat, Lili, and Finnian. The latter of which seemed highly annoyed with drunk me.p

My mouth tended to lose all filters when alcohol entered my system.

"Why *haven't* I seen you naked yet?" I slurred out as I stumbled inside.

He shot me a glare.

"All I can do is imagine what you have in your pants. I need to see if my image is bigger or smaller than reality. I really don't think you could get bigger than I picture." I grabbed the waistband of his pants, which he'd slipped back on over his wet boxers.

He growled and pushed my hands away.

"Don't be such a grouch. Let her see," Selena yelled over to us from her spot on the couch, which was darker than normal since she sat down without drying off.

"Yeah, let me see," I complained, trying for his pants again.

Suddenly, before I could comprehend what was happening, I was upside down. Finnian had tossed me over his shoulder, which was digging painfully into my stomach. I groaned as my cheek knocked against his muscular back.

"It's time for you to go to bed," he grumbled.

I whined as he started walking, "I don't want to."

"When you start trying to take off my pants in front of people, then you're done for the night."

I pouted even though he couldn't see me. I yelled goodnight to everyone as we left the living room and made our way upstairs.

Once we arrived and the door was shut and locked behind us, he threw me down on the bed, none too gently.

I glared at him but he didn't even see since he turned away to dig out pajamas from my bag. He handed me a t-shirt and a pair of panties.

"Go take a shower," he growled out.

"Only if you take one with me." I pushed his extended hand of clothes away from me and clung on to him, pressing my body against his.

"No. Now get in the shower."

Before he could blink, I pulled my bathing suit top over my head, leaving me in nothing but bottoms in front of him. His eyes immediately lowered.

"Shower with me," I said again.

His eyes snapped back to mine. They were glowing gold. He clenched and unclenched his jaw, and I knew that his canines were extended even though I couldn't see them.

"Shower with me," I repeated for a third time, right before I slipped off my bottoms, leaving me completely bare.

"You're drunk," he stated, still holding himself back.

"I'm not that drunk. And I'm not asking you to fuck me. I just want us to shower together. We never do couple-y things like that."

He exhaled heavily. "Fine. But I'm warning you, don't touch me unless you want me to mate with you." He snarled, although there was no anger behind it, just sexual frustration.

"Of course, Your Highness," I answered and smiled cheekily.

"Get in the shower." He shook his head and didn't say anything else.

I nodded and walked into the bathroom with him on my heels. He undressed while I got the water hot. I stepped in the walk-in shower with him right behind me. Once I finally turned around, I was able to see him in all his naked glory for the first time.

I was wrong. He *was* bigger than I imagined.

"Good God, you would split me in half with that thing."

He ignored my comment. I clenched my hands at my sides, trying to keep them to myself like he had requested. It was hard though, considering he was hard as well. I gulped and tried to pry my eyes from his thick, erect length.

"Are you gonna jack yourself off since I can't touch it?" I teased once I was able to look at his eyes again. They had darkened to a sensual amber color.

"No. Now turn around." I did as he asked and was surprised when he started washing my hair. He ran shampoo through my tangled locks. He was far gentler than I ever thought he could be as he carefully unknotted every tangle. He even massaged my scalp. My head fell back, and my eyes closed in relaxation.

He continued this until I was completely clean from head to toe. He washed my body but didn't linger anywhere he shouldn't. I finally realized the amazing self-control he had; despite how turned on he was, he still didn't try anything even though he could have, since I absolutely would have let him.

"Go get dressed. I'll be out in a minute," he told me once he was finished.

"Don't you want me to return the favor?" I asked in confusion.

"No. I need you to get out so I can turn the hot water off."

"Are you sure you're not just going to masturbate once I'm out?"

"I'm sure." He grunted in annoyance. "Now go."

I pouted but finally stepped out. I wrapped a fluffy white towel around my body and went in search of my discarded pajamas, which Finnian had left on the end of the bed. I dried off quickly and got dressed.

By the time I was ready for bed, I heard a crash from the bathroom. Before I could investigate, Finnian came rushing out with nothing but a towel around his waist. His eyes were gold, but not in desire this time. No, he was enraged now. Growls slipped from his mouth before he could stop them. He looked ready to shift.

"What's wrong?" I asked cautiously as he pulled on a pair of boxers.

"We're under attack," he answered in a clipped tone. "I need to go."

"Wait." I grabbed his arm, stopping him. "I'll help."

He growled again. "No. Absolutely not. You've been drinking. You're in no condition to fight."

"But—"

"No buts. Please, Kendall, I'm begging you right now. Stay here. I know that's not your nature and I know you have authority issues, but I need you here, safe. If I go down there worried about you, I'm not going to be able to focus. Please, baby, stay in here."

I wanted to argue but something in his tone stopped me. So, against my instincts to protect my family, pack, and mate, I nodded.

"Thank you." He pulled me closer by the back of my neck and pressed his lips to my forehead.

"Stay safe. Come back to me," I whispered.

"I'll kill every wolf that stands between us. I'll always come back to you."

With that, he turned to leave the room, leaving me by myself as the fighting raged on outside the cabin.

CHAPTER TWENTY-FIVE

I wasn't alone long. Seconds after Finnian rushed out, Selena, Kat, Lili, and Nathan rushed in.

"Do you guys know what's going on?" I questioned.

"Hell if I know. Tyler told me to come up here and then took off," Selena answered before anyone else could.

"Don't look at me. I'm in the same boat as you two." Kat shrugged once our eyes landed on her.

"A small group of rebels attacked the guards," Nathan explained when we all came up empty.

"How many exactly are in a 'small group'?"

He shrugged. "Fifty or so."

"Come again, Red?" My eyebrows rose in disbelief. "It sounded like you described a group of fifty werewolves as a 'small group.' Which is ludicrous, considering we have twenty guards, which is under half, in case you forgot basic math."

"Don't be so dramatic, Kendall. With Dalton, Matt, Tyler, and Finnian out there, they only have about twenty-five more men," Nathan said.

"Are you serious? What the hell are we doing in here then? We should be helping them," I shouted, taking a step forward.

Nathan stopped me by moving in front of the door and holding his hand up. "We're not going anywhere. King Finnian gave me strict orders to keep you in this room, safe. He said to use force if necessary to keep you here. They'll be fine, I promise."

"How can you promise that?" I spat out in annoyance, at him and my mate.

"The King is stronger than any other wolf. He could take on ten normal wolves by himself. Tyler is a Royal as well, so he'll be okay. Plus, Matt and Dalton are of Alpha and Beta blood. Their strength makes up for the lack of numbers."

I shook my head, mostly out of worry for my loved ones whose lives were in danger. "How did they even find us?"

"They must have been hanging around the roads that lead to the castle and followed us here. We're lucky it's only a small group that found us. We'll know more after the fighting is over."

I nodded and walked away from the group and over to the window, pushing the curtain aside. I pulled my wolf forward, enhancing my senses. They were dulled a bit from the alcohol, which I could barely even feel the effects of anymore, but it was still enough to see into the darkness of the forest surrounding the cabin.

They weren't fighting too close to us; probably half a mile away. I couldn't make it out clearly with my vision, but I could hear it. I could hear the howls, the growls and snarls of wolves fighting, and the whimpers from those who were injured.

I continued listening but my attention was pulled away after a few seconds, drawn instead to the sound of glass being smashed. It came from downstairs. My wolf surged forward, as did my body, to find the source of danger, but Nathan stopped me again.

"Stay here," he snapped as I snarled at him.

He left the room, leaving us behind. As I looked at the people around me, I noticed how sexist all the men were being. Every girl was here, safe in this room, while they were out fighting. It pissed me off because I knew I was capable of protecting myself.

When I heard another window shatter, I decided to do just that. I could hear two of them downstairs now, and my instincts were telling me to help Nathan. I pulled my wolf forward, not even bothering to get undressed.

My bones popped and cracked, my skin stretched, and my hair, nails, and canines extended. I could vaguely hear someone talking to me, but I couldn't focus on them. My primal instincts were driving me to protect not only my mate but my pack. I was the queen now, and my protective instincts were at an all-time high.

Once shifted, I didn't waste any time. The door was closed, so I lowered my head and rammed into it. It gave in on the first try, the splintered wood allowing me enough room to squeeze through.

I rushed forward, towards the fighting wolves. Nathan had shifted. I recognized that red fur anywhere, even if I couldn't catch his scent. He was fighting off two average-sized wolves. Neither were particularly strong, but they were fast. They were using that against Nathan. He was holding his own, but I jumped in anyways.

I jumped on the back of the one closest to me. My jaws locked around his throat, my canines digging in. The bitter, metallic taste of blood filled my mouth. I ripped out his throat before he knew what was happening.

He fell to the ground in a lifeless heap, his blood spilling out and staining Mom's living room rug.

Nathan finished off the wolf he was fighting, then turned to growl at me. I growled back but it didn't seem to faze him. He started butting me with his head, trying to push me back upstairs. I wanted to listen to him. I really did; I promised Finnian I would stay in our room. But my wolf instincts had taken over completely. I couldn't stop myself.

So, I knocked him out of the way, which was easy since he didn't see it coming, and jumped through the smashed window, careful to miss any glass still remaining.

The window was located on the side of the house, between the lake and the road back to town. I darted in the direction of the fighting, ready to find my mate. Since I wasn't going to listen to him, Nathan decided to follow me, right on my heels.

I didn't have to look back to know that Selena had joined us as well. I didn't smell Kat and Lili, which was good. They needed to conserve their energy in case anyone needed healing.

Selena made her way to my side, while Nathan stayed behind us to guard our flanks. It didn't take long for us to reach the fray. Everywhere I looked was covered in blood. Dead wolves were scattered across the ground to our left. We wove our way through to reach the wolves still alive.

It was a brutal sight. I knew Harrison trained his army well, but this was a bloodbath. The rebel wolves didn't stand a chance. They were tearing into them, ripping them apart limb from limb. If I were still a human, I would have thrown up.

My eyes were immediately drawn to my mate . . . my lethal, dangerous mate. He tore out two throats at the same time, one with his canines and one with his claws. His eyes found mine while he was doing that.

He growled menacingly and as soon as their bodies hit the ground, he sprinted over to me. Before I could comprehend what he was doing, he had my smaller frame under his, growling at anyone who got too close.

I tried bucking him off, but he didn't move an inch. He was unwaveringly insistent on protecting me, not that I needed it. There were only a handful of rebels left alive, and the Royal Guards were more than capable of fending them off.

And they did just that. They continued to destroy them until the very last one. For some reason, they didn't kill him. He kept fighting, far more skilled than the others, but he wouldn't go down. They wouldn't let him run either. They had him surrounded.

After a few minutes of defending themselves, but not delivering the final blow, I noticed Lili coming out. She walked over to the edge of their circle and raised her hands. She chanted a few words and, before I knew it, the wolf fell to the ground, unconscious but alive.

And with that, the battle was over.

Finnian finally moved away from me, allowing me to stand up from my position on the ground. He snarled at me for a second but it didn't last long. Then he started licking my face.

I noticed from the corner of my eye Tyler standing up from Selena as well. She snapped at him with her teeth for holding her down, but Tyler ignored it and starting licking her as well. She eventually relented and let him do it.

Kat ran out after a couple of minutes, not far behind Lili. She ran over to Matt, who shifted back just in time to catch her in his arms. It was a sweet moment, but I couldn't look considering my brother was butt ass naked.

Finnian pulled away from me and shifted back. I didn't get to check him out for long because one of the guards handed him a t-shirt and a pair of jeans, which he swiftly put on.

"Go back to the house, Kendall. Now," he growled out at me, which I returned with one of my own.

I shifted back as well, not caring about my nudity. He did though, considering he snarled again, ripped off his own shirt, and threw it over my head, all in the space of two seconds. The shirt was too big for me, which allowed it to cover the majority of my thighs.

"Don't talk to me that way." I crossed my arms over my chest angrily.

He clenched his jaw and sighed furiously through his nose. "I am trying very hard to not lose my temper right now, Miss Keating, but I am so fucking angry at you. I can't even look at you right now; so go back, before I say something I regret."

I suddenly realized how he felt when I kept calling him King Finnian. I felt like a five-year-old being scolded by a disappointed parent. And we all knew disappointment hurt a hell of a lot more than anger.

"Fine," I snapped, half in anger because of him and half in shame for myself. I turned on my heel to walk away, but his hand grasped my elbow, stopping me. He spun me around to face him.

Before I could question him, he pulled me into his hard body, one hand tangling in my still damp hair, cradling my head, the other resting on the small of my back. I wrapped my arms around him as well, my anger melting away. I rested my head on his bare chest. He rested his chin on my head, occasionally pressing kisses to my forehead.

He moved his hand from my head to my chin, lifting my head up from his chest. He leaned down and kissed me deeply, before pulling away completely.

"I'll be up in a minute," he added.

I nodded and continued my trek back to the cabin. Selena followed me. Tyler was nowhere to be found, leading me to believe that he stayed behind with Finnian. Kat and Lili also stayed behind, already focusing on healing the severely injured guys . . . not that there were many. Most would heal completely on their own within the next few hours.

Once we made it back, we went past the living room, still filled with dead wolves, and made our way upstairs. We separated to go to our own rooms.

I had expected to be wracked with guilt about killing that wolf, like I had the first time I had taken a life, but I didn't feel anything. Maybe it was the shock that caused the guilt the first time or maybe I was just becoming desensitized, but I was damn tired of people trying to kill me and the people I loved. I refused to feel guilty about killing someone who would have killed me.

I paced around the room, waiting for Finnian to return. It didn't take him long. He strode in and pulled me into him again, breathing in my scent.

"What happened?" I breathed out, not able to expand what I meant by that.

"I'm not sure how they found us. They must have spotted us leaving the castle. I should've had Nikolina spell our vehicles to be hidden."

"You know that would have been almost impossible with so many cars. Don't blame yourself," I tried to soothe him when I heard the self-directed resentment in his voice.

"You could have been hurt. I should have done everything in my power to prevent that."

"Stop that. I wasn't hurt because you kept me safe," I countered.

His anger turned on me now. "I tried to, but it's hard to do when you don't listen to me." He glared down at me and put a couple feet between us.

"You're right; I'm sorry. I made a promise and I should have kept it. In my defense though, they got into the house. I had to go help Nathan. He was down there alone."

"Nathan can handle himself," he interrupted.

"Well, still, he was alone and I wanted to help. And I never planned on going outside, but by that point, my wolf was in control. She wanted to protect you and everyone else."

His eyes softened when he heard that. "You wanted to protect me?"

"My wolf did," I denied weakly, causing his smug grin to grow.

"Come on. We need another shower. You're covered in blood now."

"Yeah? Whose fault is that?" I glared at him.

"If you hadn't been out there, I wouldn't have been able to jump on top of you." He shrugged carelessly before walking to the bathroom.

I joined him once I heard the shower running. We bathed in silence for a few minutes before he spoke again, "We're leaving in just a few minutes."

"What? Why?"

"Because we don't know who they alerted before they attacked. For all we know, there could be more on the way. I need to get you back to safety."

"What about that guy Lili knocked out?"

"He was their leader. I made sure to keep him alive for questioning. We got lucky; usually the leaders die along with the rest. With him and the wolf Rylan captured, we just might figure out something useful about who their alpha is," he explained.

"That's a long drive back," I complained weakly. I understood why we needed to leave, but all I wanted to do was curl up in bed with him and sleep.

"You can sleep on the way back." He kissed me softly then stepped out of the shower.

I turned off the water and did the same. Once I was dried off, he handed me underwear, a pair of black leggings, and one of his t-shirts. I thanked him and slipped them on. I was grateful that I could at least dress comfortably on the way back.

The next thirty minutes passed quickly. Lili and Kat finished healing the last of the seriously injured. Thankfully, Finnian was completely unharmed.

The bodies stayed as they were for now, but Finnian had already made a call about someone coming to clear them away and clean up the cabin. The leader, who was still unconscious, was being carried in the back of another car. Lili had set up an invisible barrier to keep him in so he couldn't attack the guards in the car or try to escape should he wake up.

By the time we left, both Kat and Lili were exhausted, so we had to unfortunately make the drive back while we were exposed. The seating arrangements were the same as they were on the way. Selena and Tyler were in the front while Nathan, Finnian, and I were in the back.

Unlike the last time though, I wasn't in the middle. Instead, I was sprawled out on Finnian's lap, only my feet resting in the middle.

He was holding me close to his body, not letting me move an inch. He was taking being protective to the extremes, considering he growled at Selena for reaching back to slap me. He never let her hand make contact. I knew his protectiveness would pass.

He usually never interfered with mine and Selena's spats. Neither did Tyler. Both of them knew that our sisterly quarrels didn't concern them. But when Finnian's wolf was in control, it was another story. I didn't comment on it, and Selena let it go knowing that it was a normal reaction. Tyler was acting the same way for her.

Eventually, I dozed off to sleep, my head leaning on his shoulder. It wasn't hard to do, especially since it started raining. The smooth ride of the car, the sound of pattering rain hitting the metal roof, and the soothing feel of Finnian running his hand up and down my arm; all of it lulled me into sleep.

When I woke up, we were back at the castle. We had just pulled into the garage, and Finnian exited the car with me in his arms.

"I can walk," I mumbled, swatting his chest gently to put me down.

"And I can carry you," he countered, not budging.

I didn't argue. I was too tired to argue. I just let him continue carrying me as I relaxed in his arms.

"Is everyone safe?" Niki asked once we made it inside. She looked worried for once.

"Everyone is fine, Nikolina. I told you that earlier," Finn answered her.

All she did was nod. Once Lili walked inside, she rushed over and pulled her into a hug. I smiled at the sight. Niki was always so motherly towards Lili, especially since their own mother abandoned them to return to Bulgaria. As far as I knew, they hadn't spoken to her in years.

"I'm glad you're okay, brother," Kieran said, drawing my attention away from the two witch sisters. "You too, Kendall."

"Thanks Kieran." I smiled at him. Finnian just nodded.

"I've moved the wolf to the cells. We'll question him in the morning."

With that, Finnian left the room, halting any further conversation. He walked up every flight of stairs until we reached our floor. Once we made it to our room, he gently placed me down on the bed. I shivered and immediately burrowed under the covers. Finnian walked across the room, starting a blazing fire.

I pulled off my leggings, and Finnian stripped down to his boxers. He curled up in bed with me, pulling me close to him.

With the warmth from the fire and the pattering of rain against the window, I fell back asleep quickly.

* * *

I didn't wake up until noon the next day. Finnian was gone, and his side of the bed was cold. His scent was stale, telling me he had been gone for at least a few hours.

I sat up and stretched my arms over my head. I yawned and got out of bed. I went into the bathroom to get ready for the day. I dressed casually in an oversized sweater and a pair of fleece leggings. I pulled a beanie over my messy curls.

I was just leaving the bathroom when I heard a knock on our bedroom door. I frowned since no one but Finn and I came up here, and he wouldn't knock first. I inhaled deeply and relaxed once I smelled Kat.

"Come in," I called as I plopped down on the bed again.

She came in, carrying a tray of food. "I thought you might be hungry."

"Yes! I'm starving. You're seriously my hero." I took the tray from her hands and eagerly dug in. It was a bowl of homemade chicken soup and a couple of grilled cheese sandwiches. It was comfort food, which I needed. "Thanks."

"No problem. Finnian asked me to come check on you."

"Where is he anyways?" I asked as I bit into my sandwich.

"He's . . . questioning the leader of the rebels."

"Why'd you say it like that?" I asked when I noticed the way she hesitated saying the word.

"I wouldn't exactly call it questioning."

"What would you call it?"

"Honestly?" I nodded. "I would call it torture."

"How do you know what they're doing? Were you down there?"

"Yeah. It was for training. It isn't often that you have someone available to practice your torturing skills on. Finnian had Niki come down to get information from him. She delegated the task to me and Lili. We were down there for like three hours, and he still didn't talk."

"So, what did Finnian do? Just keep torturing him?"

"Pretty much. I'm pretty sure he would have left him alone for a while, let him stew in his cell. But then he started saying all kind of horrible things about you. Finnian went crazy after that. I'm surprised he didn't kill him, to be honest. But then again, I think that's what the guy wanted. He can't talk if he's not breathing. Whoever he works for, he's loyal 'til the end."

"Hmm . . ." I bit the inside of my cheek and pondered her words. "I may be completely off, but do you think whoever is leading the rebels might be related in some way to the guy who killed me in Niki's vision?"

She looked intrigued for a split second, before her face went blank and her eyes turned a cloudy off white. It filled her entire eye, covering the green of her irises. I wasn't confused about what was happening, though. She was having a vision. She had been sitting on the edge of the bed. When she started falling towards the floor, I grabbed her and laid her down. After that, all I could do was wait.

It took about five minutes for her to come to. I finished eating in that time and turned to face her. She blinked hard a few times as her eyes cleared and went back to normal. She groaned as she sat up. She held her head in her hands for a few seconds, waiting for the aftereffects to clear.

"It's the same person, Kendall," she said after a few minutes.

"What?"

"I don't know who it is, but I do know that the Alpha of the rebellion is the same guy who killed you in Niki's vision."

"Did you see anything?"

"No. It was just a feeling. I wish an image came with it, but we'll have to work with what we have."

I nodded. "I need to tell Finnian this. Is Matt still with him?"

"Yeah."

I closed my eyes and concentrated on pushing on the connection with my brother. Finnian could mindlink me, because royals could mindlink with anyone. Finnian and I either had to mate and mark each other or complete the coronation ceremony before I had the same abilities as him. He could mindlink me, but I couldn't do the same yet.

"Yeah?" Matt asked through mindlink after he dropped his shield.

"Can you tell Finnian I need to see him? Like, right now?"

I didn't hear anything back for a few seconds, so I waited. *"He's on his way."*

"Thanks, bro."

"No problem."

After that, we closed our link.

"How do you think he'll react?" I turned my attention back to Kat.

"Oh, he'll be pissed for sure. I actually feel a little sorry for the prisoner. If he was harsh before, he'll be a nightmare now. If he sees an opportunity to stop the vision from coming true, he's going to take it."

"You're probably right. I hope he realizes I'm going back down there with him."

She laughed, loudly. "Yeah, good luck with that."

I frowned at her. "You were down there," I stated.

"Yeah, and Matt freaked out. He tried to send me away, but Niki said I needed to be there. He didn't really have a say since she outranks him. Finnian has a say for you, though."

"We'll see about that," I commented.

Before either of us could say anything else, the door opened and my mate strolled in, frowning at me.

"You summoned?"

I cracked a grin at that. "It's important."

"Do tell."

"Kat had a vision. It related to Niki's." At my words, he looked ten times more alert and interested. He turned his attention to Kat.

"It wasn't a visual vision. It was just a feeling. Whoever is the leader of the rebels is the same guy from Niki's vision. I don't know who it is, but if we can find the Alpha of the rebels, we can stop the vision from happening."

"You didn't get any other clues to who it could be?"

"Sorry, no. I might get more later. I'll meditate longer tonight, to try and get something. But I might not, so I wouldn't depend on that if I were you."

"Alright. Thank you, Katerina." He nodded once to her.

"I'll leave you two alone to talk," Kat said as she stood up and walked out the door.

"Are you okay?" I asked him when I noticed how tense he was.

He pulled me into his embrace, breathing in my scent. "I swear to you, I'm going to find this guy. I'll never let anyone hurt you."

"I know you won't. We'll find him together. Which is why I'm going back to the prison with you."

"No. That is no place for the Queen."

"Get over yourself. This is the twenty-first century. I'm not your submissive little housewife. We're a team. I'm going."

He narrowed his eyes at me, sizing me up. Finally, he exhaled heavily. "Fine. It can get intense though. Don't say I didn't warn you."

"I won't."

* * *

Turns out, I didn't actually get to see how intense it was. I did get to see Finnian throw a fit though.

It happened just before we reached the prison. The guy killed himself.

Apparently, when I called Finnian away, they left him in the interrogation room alone to grab some coffee. Finnian was pissed at them for leaving him alone.In their defense, the guy was handcuffed to the table.

I guess they were only tight when his thumb wasn't broken. He broke it and slipped the damn things right off. Then, he ripped his own throat out.

It was a horrible way to die for a werewolf. We were predators. Our claws and canines were supposed to be used to defend ourselves, not harm ourselves. Ending our own lives by our own claws was a disgraceful way to go.

Which led me to believe that fear was driving his actions. Whoever he worked for must have scared the shit out of him. I didn't know how he could possibly be more scared of someone who isn't King Finnian Cahill, the man who spent the better part of eight hours torturing him. Whoever we were up against was surely a force to be reckoned with.

I sighed as Finnian slammed his fist into the wall yet again, creating another long crack in the stone.

After he destroyed half of the prison and nearly killed Matt, Dalton, Kieran, and Tyler, I dragged him back up to our room. From there, he just continued his temper tantrum. He shifted—twice. The chairs in front of the fireplace were destroyed, and there were multiple cracks in the walls. His hands were bloody and raw, his bones probably demolished as well, but he just kept going. The pain didn't even faze him.

"Please, calm down. You're overreacting." I tried once again to get him to relax.

"Overreacting?" He turned and snarled at me. "That was our best chance at finding the motherfucker who wants to kill you. I think my reaction is just fine."

"Finnian, you need to stop," I finally commanded. "We'll find him. Our best chance to do that, though, is to stay calm and stick together."

"I won't let him hurt you," he repeated for the second time today.

"I know. I trust you. Trust yourself, okay? This won't be our only opportunity. We still have that guy Rylan captured."

He nodded. "You're right. I already mindlinked him and told him to watch the guy closely. He's going to have three guys with him at all times."

I nodded slowly. "Okay, come on. Let's get Kat or Niki to heal your hand." I grabbed his good hand and dragged him out of the room in search of a witch.

All I could think as we walked was that I hoped I wasn't just spewing bullshit. I hoped we could find the guy in time.

CHAPTER TWENTY-SIX

"What are your plans for the day?" I asked when Finn walked out of the bathroom. His eyes found mine as he tied his tie.

"I'll be in my public office all day."

I nodded in understanding. I had come to discover that he did different things in different offices. If he needed to work on something for his work in the human world, he used his private office down the hall. If he had work to do as the King of werewolves, he typically worked in his public office or, if he needed more privacy, his meeting room.

"You need any help later?"

"You're not going to training this afternoon?"

I walked past him, into the bathroom, leaving the door open so we could talk.

"No. Harrison and I decided we'd do training on Monday, Wednesday, and Fridays. I'm surprised you didn't know that already," I answered as I slipped on a pair of dark-olive leggings and a cream sweater.

"I had a conference meeting yesterday," he explained how he didn't know as he leaned against the door frame. He crossed his arms over his chest and watched me get ready.

"Oh. Well, we decided just three times a week is enough for now. He's impressed with my improvement. And besides, I've been so busy, it's hard training six hours every day."

"What are your plans for today then?"

"Um, let's see . . . I'm going to meet with Niki now. She wants me to pick out a dress for my coronation. I think she wants me to pick flowers and a menu today too. It's really starting to feel like a human wedding."

"Do you want a human wedding?" he asked, raising an eyebrow.

I snorted as I slipped on a pair of combat boots. "Hell no. A coronation is hard enough already; I don't need a wedding to plan too."

"Just checking. I want to give you everything you want."

"That's sweet." I kissed his cheek on the way out of the bathroom. "After that, Selena and I are going to the orphanage, then I figured I'd come help out in the office until dinner."

"Speaking of dinner, I want to take you out tonight."

I froze in shock, then turned to raise an eyebrow at him. "Like a date?"

"Yes."

"You want to take me on a date tonight?"

"Yes," he repeated.

"Like, just the two of us, out in public?"

"What part of this aren't you understanding?" His lips tilted up in amusement.

"All of it, I guess. I had to practically blackmail you into the group date last time."

"I don't want to go out with them; I want to go out with you. A group date didn't appeal to me, but a night alone with you does."

After a few seconds, I beamed up at him. "In that case, I'd love to go out with you tonight."

His smile grew just a bit as he walked up to me. He grabbed my hands and kissed me gently. "Good."

"I have to go meet Niki now," I told him, yet I didn't make a move to pull away from him.

He kissed me for a few more minutes. His lips moved from mine, down my jaw and neck, then back up. He ended with a soft kiss to my forehead. "Come on, I'll walk you." He laced our fingers together as we left the room.

Niki was having me meet her in some room I had never been in before. It was on the first floor, near the gym. Once we reached it, I noticed it was basically just a room that seemed to be for planning events. One area was like a little dressing room with mirrors covering the walls. The other half of the room was filled with tables.

Niki was already in the room with some other woman I didn't know. They were in front of the dressing room area, already riffling through the half-dozen racks or so of dresses that had been brought in.

I sighed inwardly, not ready to look through them, especially without Kat or Selena there to help. Kat was practicing with Lili on Niki's orders. Selena said she would come but I had yet to see her this morning.

"Perfect timing, my queen. The dresses arrived no more than five minutes ago," Niki said once she noticed me.

We walked over. The second woman bowed her head in greeting, not lifting it until I spoke.

"I'm Kendall. It's nice to meet you."

"It is such an honor to meet you as well, Queen Kendall."

"Kendall, this is Cynthia, the Royal Stylist. She oversees getting the Royals ready for big events," Niki explained.

"Oh, okay. I didn't know you had a stylist."

"Yes, Cynthia wasn't around for the ball, but she usually is around before events. That didn't stop her from helping us then, though. All of the dresses we tried on that day were dresses she chose for us."

"I have a conference call in five minutes," Finnian butted in before we could dive into the gowns. "I'll see you at lunch."

I nodded and returned his kiss before he turned to leave. Then I turned my attention back to Niki and Cynthia.

"Why is there so much red?" I questioned when I finally looked at the dresses.

"It is tradition for the new queen to wear red for her coronation," Niki explained.

"Why? What's the symbolism behind that?"

"It was said that Finnian's great-great-great-grandmother wore red for her coronation. She chose it because of what the color red represents: passion, strength, power, love,and determination. She explained in her coronation speech that she would embody those traits in her leadership. And she did just that. She is said to be one of the greatest queens to have ever ruled the werewolves. That she started a revolution where the queen was more than just a submissive figurehead. She was a real leader, and she influenced the shift in women's role in the werewolf world."

"Wow, that's awesome. She sounds like a badass."

"Indeed, dear girl, she was. The color red is still worn to show that that future queens will honor those leadership traits."

"Then, I'll wear it with pride," I replied.

"I have a feeling you will make your mark in the history books as well."

"I hope it's not for being the worst queen ever," I joked weakly, trying to hide how choked up I was feeling.

"Never, my queen. You'll make your mark in the best way possible. I have a feeling."

"Thank you, Niki," I told her honestly.

"No need to thank me. I speak nothing but the truth."

I nodded. "Alright, let's find a dress then."

We turned to the racks and started looking through them.

"Okay, we can narrow it down a little. I don't want long sleeves or anything off the shoulder. I don't really like one sleeved dresses either. I just want something simple but classy."

They nodded to me and continued to look through the racks, searching for a dress that meets my criteria. Every once and a while, one of them would hold up a dress for me to see but none of them jumped out to me.

Finally, I found the one. I pulled it off the rack and walked over to the mirror, holding it in front of my body.

"That one is beautiful, Kendall," Niki told me when she saw it. "Try it on."

I nodded and walked behind the curtain into a separate changing room. I stripped off my clothes and replaced it with the dress.

It didn't fit quite right, but it was pretty close for an unaltered dress. It was a deep ruby red. It had thin straps with a sweetheart neckline. The top of the dress was tight, and it had silver jewels that looked like real diamonds. Knowing Niki, they probably were. About halfway down my stomach, it loosened, the soft tulle flowing down to the floor, pooling by my feet and behind me slightly.

It was perfect.

I pulled the curtain back and showed them.

"That is gorgeous," Niki commented.

"I agree. I don't think we're going to find one better than that," Cynthia added.

"What are you thinking for hair, makeup, and accessories?"

They both looked over to examine me again.

"You have beautiful hair, but I think an up do would look best. A crown braid, maybe?"

"Absolutely. With a few curls left out to frame her face."

"Just what I was thinking. For makeup, I'm thinking a bold brow, cat eye liner, and a matching red lipstick," Cynthia suggested.

"Yes, yes. Perfect. And we should keep the accessories to a minimum, since the dress is covered in diamonds," Niki chimed excitedly.

I knew it.

"I agree. Maybe a silver hair accessory and a simple bracelet or ring."

"And what about shoes?"

My head was swimming. They were talking so fast about things I couldn't care less about.

"Strappy silver platform heels, perhaps."

"Umm, I don't think I'm really needed anymore, so I'm just gonna g—" I interrupted and, in turn, was interrupted.

"Nonsense, Kendall. We're just getting started," Niki informed me, turning her attention back.

"I mean, I don't really care about hair and—"

"We'll figure that out later. For now, we need to take your measurements, then we'll discuss the menu."

I turned as Cynthia came up to me with pins and a tape measure. "I don't really care what we eat, so I'll leave you to deci—"

"The chef is bringing cake samples for you to try," Niki stated knowingly.

I paused and looked back at her.

"Did you say cake?"

* * *

"Where were you this morning?" I asked Selena on our walk back from the orphanage.

I had been debating if she was even going to show up for the visit, but she finally did about thirty minutes after I had arrived. I hadn't had a chance to ask her why she hadn't shown up this morning with all the kids around.

"I was busy," she stated simply. She had a little smirk on her face, which clued me in that she was hiding something. She was a terrible liar.

"With what? It must have been pretty important for you to miss the cake samples. There was this one white chocolate raspberry cake . . . when people describe food being better than sex, that cake was what they had in mind."

"Oh, that sounds good. Think they have any left?"

"You didn't show up, so you don't get any," I said as I stepped over a wayward log that had fallen onto the trail in the forest.

"You'd give me some if you knew what I know," she said in a singsong voice.

I glanced at her in scrutiny. "Well, tell me."

"Sorry, baby sis, no can do." She smirked again. "It's a secret for now."

I huffed in annoyance. "Then why even—"

"I'm pregnant!" she cut me off with a squeal of joy.

I looked at her in shock, not comprehending her words. She had a giant grin on her face as she was jumping up and down and clapping stupidly.

"You're going to be a mom?" I asked. She just nodded excitedly. "Damn, I feel bad for your kid."

Her joy turned to shock, then fury. "Why the hell would you—"

My laughter cut her off. "I'm kidding, relax. I'm happy for you, but I am a little curious."

"About?"

"You and Tyler have known each other for four weeks. It usually takes at least a month before someone knows they're pregnant. How soon were you two screwing?"

"Well, he wouldn't do it back home. But the night we got back to the castle, I had my way with him."

"Were you trying to get pregnant?"

"Not really, but we also didn't use protection, so it's not surprising. We're excited though. I took the test this morning and it was positive."

"Well I'm excited too," I told her as I pulled her into a tight hug. "I can't wait to spoil the little pup once she's born. You know you're going to have to name her after me if she's a girl, right?"

She scoffed and pulled away from me. "In your dreams."

* * *

"Are you almost ready?" Finnian rapped his knuckles against the bathroom door.

"Almost," I answered as I glanced at my appearance one last time in the mirror.

He had told me that our date wasn't going to be super fancy, so I kept my outfit cute and simple. I was wearing a black turtleneck and a plaid skirt. The bottom of the turtleneck was tucked into the skirt. I pulled on a pair of black tights under the skirt and a pair of black ankle boots over my feet. I had my hair fixed in a messy side braid, and my makeup was soft and natural.

After I deemed myself ready, I walked to the door, the heels from my boots clicking lightly against the dark concrete floor. Finnian was sitting in his chair in front of the fireplace, which had been replaced since he destroyed the previous chairs, watching a nonexistent fire. He stood up when he heard me walk out and turned to face me.

"You look beautiful, Kendall."

"Thanks." I kissed his cheek. "You look nice too."

I grabbed my purse and linked my arm through his. He guided me out of our room and down the hall.

"So, where are we going?"

"It's a surprise."

"You hate surprises," I argued.

"It's your surprise; not mine," he countered.

"*I* hate surprises."

"You'll like this one."

He helped me into a black Range Rover and walked around to the driver's side. I was a little shocked to see him driving since he usually had someone else chauffeuring him around.

"Oh, I forgot to tell you before we left." I suddenly remembered and bounced in my seat in excitement.

"Tell me what?"

"You have to keep it between us. I'm not even supposed to know this yet," I warned.

"I don't willingly converse with anyone other than you," he muttered dryly.

"You have a point. Anyways, Selena is pregnant."

His eyebrows raised a fraction of an inch but other than that, he had no reaction. "Already? Tyler works fast."

"Right? That's what I was saying. It's only been a little over four weeks."

"What about you?" he asked cautiously.

"What about me?"

"Do you want kids?"

My look of confusion faded and my eyes softened as I gazed at his worried expression. "I do. Not yet, but eventually. Do you?" I didn't really need to ask to know his answer, but I wanted to see what he would say.

"I want a pack of kids."

"Woah, slow down buddy. My vagina, my rules. Three at most."

He surprised me by chuckling loudly. His laugh was so rare, it caught me off guard whenever I heard it.

"It's a good thing we have forever to decide."

I smiled softly at him and grabbed his hand. I brought it to my lips, kissing his knuckles gently before resting it against my thigh. "Forever," I agreed.

He gave me a loving look and squeezed my hand lightly.

The rest of the drive was made in silence, just enjoying each other's presence. After about twenty minutes, we finally seemed to reach our destination. He had driven up the mountain and down an unfamiliar road, one I wouldn't want to take with anyone but him. It hugged the edge hazardously, the turns sharp and dangerous. Luckily, we didn't go far up the mountain since the road ended less than half a mile up.

We stopped at a small clearing. Finn parked the car in front of the dense row of trees. The opposite side of the clearing ended with an abrupt drop. The view was gorgeous. Below us was nothing but green from the forest in view.

Across from us was another, bigger, mountain, the top of which was snow covered. Behind the mountain, the sky was an inky swirl of cobalt and magenta, with a soft lilac afterglow. It took my breath away.

Once I was able to tear my eyes away from the view, I looked at the rest of the clearing. Soft twinkling lights were strung up from the trees behind us and candles dotted the ground, along with rose petals. In the center, there was a plush red blanket spread across the ground, a picnic basket on top of it, along with a few pillows and another blanket.

"Do you like it?" I heard Finnian ask from behind me.

I turned around and threw my arms around his neck, pulling him to me tightly.

"I love it. This is perfect. Thank you."

"Anything for you."

I smiled as I kissed him, and he returned it fervently. After a few seconds, he pulled away.

"Let's eat."

I nodded and let him lead me to the blanket. I tucked my legs to the side. Finnian plopped down next to me and opened the picnic basket. He then proceeded to pull out all of my favorite things. We had beer to drink. Or rather, I had beer to drink; he had water. There were a variety of foods, everything from Oreo cheesecake to spicy chicken pasta.

I obviously started with dessert.

Finnian grabbed a fork and scooped some onto it, then lifted it to my lips. I opened eagerly and accepted the delicious swirl of chocolate and cream cheese.

"That's so good," I moaned out as I swallowed and licked my lips afterwards.

I glanced up at him when he didn't reply. His eyes were a deep gold, and his canines extended.

"Sorry," I mumbled as I lowered my head, hiding a blush.

"Don't apologize. You didn't do anything. I just don't think you realize how alluring you are."

I looked up at him when he said that, taking in his features. He was beyond handsome. His strong jaw was covered in dark stubble, adding to his dark sex appeal. His lips were full and luscious, just waiting to be kissed. His nose was long and straight, his cheek bones high and sharp. His almond shaped eyes were a swirling mixture of cerulean and gold, sitting under thick, dark arched eyebrows. His hair was falling messily in front of his eyes, as it did at the end of every day, after he would spend the last few hours of the day running his fingers through it.

I swallowed harshly and ran my tongue over my own extended canines. Before he could do anything, I launched myself at him.

He caught me easily and held me against him, our bodies flush together as we laid horizontally. My lips found his and I kissed him frantically, everything I felt for him behind it.

He returned it just as passionately.

We kissed for a while, when I decided to go further. I raked my nails lightly down his chest, which was still covered in a dark blue button up. My hand worked its way down to the waistband of his pants. Before I could find his zipper, he flipped us so that he was covering me. He pinned my arms over my head and held himself up with his elbows.

"Not here. I want you so damn much. No, I need you, but not here. Our first time will be special for you."

"This is special," I argued.

"We're out in the open, where anyone can wander up, and it's going to get cold soon. Not here," he repeated.

I huffed an annoyed breath. "Fine."

He kissed me softly one last time, which eased my attitude a bit.

"Soon. I promise. Now, let's finish dinner."

I nodded and we sat up. As I continued eating the cake, I knew I'd be holding him to his promise.

CHAPTER TWENTY-SEVEN

"How long are you gonna be gone?" Selena asked.

"Three days," I informed her as I folded another shirt into a small suitcase.

"I just don't understand why I can't come," she whined for the hundredth time this morning.

"Because we're spending the night in his cabin first. And I don't want you there."

"That's so rude. You can't be rude to a pregnant woman."

I rolled my eyes. "No, I can't *hit* a pregnant woman. I can be rude all I want."

"You shouldn't even be going. Last time we went somewhere, we were attacked. His dumbass should leave you here."

"First of all, he can't leave me here alone. The person trying to kill me might be here. And second, he has more guards going this time. He has like thirty already at the cabin, making sure no rebel is within at least sixty miles. And we have another thirty going with us. He's taking extra precautions this time; we'll be safe."

"Why couldn't Alpha Rylan bring the rebel here?"

"Why can't you stop whining? Why do you want me here so bad anyways? We don't even like each other."

"I may not like you, but you entertain me. Kat and Lili are always busy with Niki, and Tyler will be extra busy since your precious mate isn't here. And Dalton and Matt are always off doing

God knows what with Kieran. Who am I supposed to hang out with?"

"How about you work on building a bridge and getting over it?"

"Okay, the 1990s called. They want their joke back," she drawled dryly.

"They called again and want their eyebrows back."

"Aren't you a comedian. That was over a year ago. They've grown back." She covered her eyebrows defensively, pouting as she did.

I grinned at her as she complained. I shook my head at her hateful glare and walked back into my bathroom to finish packing. I always tended to over pack, so my suitcase looked like I was leaving for a week and not just two nights. But I couldn't help it; I never knew what kind of clothes I would feel like wearing until it was time to get ready.

After a few minutes, I zipped up my suitcase and left the bathroom just as Finnian entered.

"Please, Selena, why don't you make yourself at home on my bed," he said, deadpan, once he saw her.

She was sprawled out, pigging out on a pack of Oreos, which were leaving little chocolate crumbs on our sheets.

"It's my sister's bed too, and she doesn't mind. She is actually considerate and hospitable."

"Actually, I'm not. I told your fat ass to stop eating on my bed like thirty minutes ago."

"You can't call a pregnant woman fat," she snapped.

"You can't keep pulling the pregnant card. As long as you tell me I look like a ten-year-old boy, I'm going to keep calling you fat."

"It's not my fault you didn't get any curves. Maybe you'd be pregnant by now if you had."

I didn't dignify her with a response; instead, I simply flipped her the bird and went about my business.

"Are we gonna leave soon?" I asked Finnian.

"I just need to pack."

"Okay, I need to go see Kat first, then I'll meet you in the garage?"

"Sure. I'll bring your bag down."

"Thanks," I replied with a smile when he grabbed my suitcase handle from my hand.

I turned to leave the room, and Selena scrambled out of the bed. She followed behind me, leaving a trail of Oreo dust in her wake. I figured she'd veer off at some point, but she stayed close behind me.

"Why are you following me?"

"I'm nosy and I want to see what you need to talk to Kat about."

I sighed. "Well, at least you're aware of your awful personality traits."

"I'm aware of all of yours too."

I rolled my eyes but didn't respond. After a few minutes of walking in silence, we made it to Niki's work room. I knocked twice and smiled as Kat pulled it open.

The room looked exactly the same is it did the last time I came here. The walls were still lined with bookshelves, which were filled with spell books, relics, and ingredients for potions. The furnishing remained the same; tables in the corner and a large round dark oak table in the center, which had an ancient basin in the middle and spell books lying open. Once I got closer, I realized the basin was filled with a murky tawny liquid.

"Is that it?" I asked Kat, who was the only one in the room.

"Yeah, but there are a few things you need to know first."

"What is that?" Selena asked.

"It's for the wolf that Kendall and Finnian are going to interrogate. It's a truth potion. But like I said, there are some things that you need to be aware of."

"Okay, shoot," I told her. We all took a seat around the table.

"Okay, so first, it should be a last resort. You two need to try everything possible to get him to talk before you use it."

I nodded in understanding.

"There are drawbacks to using it. The biggest one is that it causes death. All of the information Niki has about it says that you have about sixty seconds maximum before he dies. He'll talk during that time but he'll be in immense pain, so it will take him a few seconds to answer, especially if he is fighting it."

"So, what do we do to make sure we get what we need before he dies?"

"You need to have a specific question. And it needs to be something that has a short answer. Time is limited, and so is the information you'll be able to get. You'll do better trying to get him to talk without a time limit."

"Okay, I understand. Thanks for doing this for me."

"Yeah, no problem. Anytime."

"Alright, well, I'm sure Finnian is already waiting for me, so I better go."

"Okay, be safe," she replied to me as she pulled me into a hug. After we pulled apart, she handed me the potion. I tightened my fingers around the cool glass vial.

"Always. I'll see you in a few days."

Kat stayed behind to clean up, and Selena walked out with me, continuing to follow me down to the garage.

Once we arrived, I noticed everyone seemed to be gathered there. Finn had loaded our bags and was standing around the Range Rover, chatting with Niki, Kieran, and Tyler.

"Queen Kendall," Niki greeted, her head bowed.

"Hi, Niki."

"I trust Katerina gave you the truth potion?"

"She did. She explained how it works too."

"Excellent. I wish nothing but good outcomes with it."

"Me too." I smiled weakly at her.

"Are you sure you don't want me to come, brother?" Kieran asked once Niki and I finished talking.

"I'm sure. I need you and Tyler taking care of things here."

"With all due respect, I think I could be of more use to you at the interrogation."

"Maybe so, but it's not happening. I'm taking my mate to my private cabin, and I won't have anyone else bothering us. I can handle the interrogation on my own. You'll stay here."

"Yes, my King." Kieran bowed his head in submission.

"I'll see you in a few days, brother."

"Stay safe, Finn."

Finnian nodded to his brother, then turned to Tyler. "Take care of your witch while we're gone."

Tyler cracked a grin, not at all offended by the insult towards his mate. I giggled a little too once I saw Selena's face.

"I'm not a witch, you fucker." She seethed.

"My mistake." His lips tugged up ever so slightly, hinting at his amusement.

"That's a little insulting to witches, Finn," I whispered, knowing Selena could hear me.

"I suppose you're right. I know I'd hate to be compared to her."

She didn't respond verbally; she just held up both hands, flipping us her middle fingers instead, much like I had earlier. I grinned and wiggled my fingers in goodbye.

I said goodbye to everyone else, then we got in the car. I buckled up and waved again as Finn reversed out of the garage.

Immediately, six cars surrounded us; three in the front and three in the back. We settled into the drive after a few minutes, the radio playing softly in the background as we made our way through the winding roads of the Royal Territory.

The evergreen trees, covered in a thin layer of frost, canopied over the road. There was a biting chill in the air, and the dark-grey storm clouds threatened the fall of snow at any second. I cranked up the heater and got comfortable for the long drive.

* * *

After a few hours of driving, we finally pulled up to the cabin. There was no distinguishable road, but the trees had been cleared enough for a vehicle to fit through. Finnian parked right beside the house.

The guards stopped a couple miles back. Instead of following us in their cars, they followed in their wolf form. I could see a few of them, but once Finn opened my door and helped me out, they scattered to give us some privacy. I didn't think for a second that they weren't close by, guarding us.

Once I was out of the car, I finally observed the cabin closely. It was small, but cozy and cute. It was nestled deep in the forest, nothing around for miles. The metal roof was covered in a thin layer of snow, which started falling not long before we got here.

Finnian grabbed our bags with one hand and rested the other on the small of my back, guiding me towards the porch and unlocking the door, letting us inside and freeing us from the falling snowflakes.

The small stone fireplace was the first thing I saw. Finnian walked over to start a fire as I looked around. The living room and kitchen were combined into one big room. There was no technology of any kind, and the only furniture in the living room was a couch and a couple of wooden tables.

Inside the kitchen was an outdated refrigerator and oven. The sink was small, but it still took up almost half of the counter space. There was just enough room for one person to cook supper. The table to the side was made with glossy dark oak. It looked strong and sturdy, the way that only a true craftsman could make it. I made a mental note to ask Finn later if he made the furniture too.

I walked further inside and took a left, through the only door in the room besides the two exits. It led to the bedroom. The king-sized bed was placed directly in front of the sliding wooden double doors and was covered in burgundy bedding. I noticed that there was a skylight above it, with rays of orange from the sunset seeping through the parts of the glass not yet obscured by snow.

To the left of the bedroom was a small bathroom, with nothing but a small sink and countertop, a toilet, and a shower-tub combo. It was smaller than what I was used to, but I adored it, especially since he built it all.

"It's beautiful, Finn. I love it."

He walked over and lifted his hand, stroking my cheek gently. "Good, I'm glad you like it."

I kissed his palm and smiled at him softly.

"Come on; I'm going to cook dinner for my mate."

I nodded and followed him back to the kitchen. He pulled out my chair at the table and I took a seat. He moved over to the kitchen, pulling out various seasonings, a pack of meat, and other ingredients. He cut up some veggies, then grabbed a mixing bowl from one of the cabinets and started mixing the ingredients together.

"What was it like for you as a kid?" I asked after a few minutes of silence, just watching him work.

"It was okay. My father was harsh at times. He taught Kieran and I how to be leaders from a young age. We didn't have much of a childhood when it came to him."

"And your mom?"

A small smile tugged on his lips. "My mother was amazing. She was warm, and tender, and loving. She gave the best hugs, and always told us that it's okay to be vulnerable, to be human sometimes. Especially with your mate." He paused and swallowed audibly, not meeting my gaze as he continued mixing ingredients studiously. "She would be so disappointed in me for how I treated you."

"Finn . . . Your mom would be proud of you. You had the courage to fight for me even when you were terrified. The woman you just described would have been so proud of that."

I stood up and moved behind him, barely having enough room for both of us in the small kitchen, but that just made it easier to be close to him. I slid my arms around his waist and laid my cheek against his back, squeezing him softly.

He paused and turned around, wrapping me in his strong, warm arms. "I hope you know how sorry I am about everything I did and said to you, Kendall."

I pulled back just enough to look up at him. "I forgive you."

His eyes squeezed shut, and he pulled me in again, resting his cheek on the top of my head.

I pulled away after a few moments. "Now, get back to work. I'm starving." He grinned down at me and turned back to the food. I slapped his ass and walked back to my chair.

"Tell me about you guys as kids. You, Niki, Tyler, and Kieran. You all grew up together right?"

"Right. We were all very close growing up. There was a game we all used to play together. Niki was still learning magic from her mother at the time, so she would practice on us. She would cast a spell on an item and then hide it in the forest. You couldn't see or smell it unless you were within three feet of it. Whoever found the item first, Niki would deem the winner and allow them to pick one spell for her to perform."

"It sounds like she was really good, even as a child. Who usually won?"

"She was. She's always been extremely powerful. And it was a mixed bag. We all won at times. Although, I wish I could claim that I was the sole winner."

He grinned over at me, more at ease than I'd ever seen him. "What about Emiliya and Lili?"

"Emiliya is about ten years younger than us. She left when she was thirteen to attend a boarding school and didn't return until a few years ago, which is when Kieran discovered she was his mate."

It was subtle, but he grimaced just slightly. "You don't like her, do you?"

"She is . . . prickly. She has abandonment issues, I guess you could say. Her mother left after I became king and appointed Niki as my royal witch. Emiliya was still a child then, and Lili was merely a toddler. Niki raised Lili, and Emiliya decided to go away for school. I would like to say that Kieran is the same brother I grew up with now that he is happily mated, but I'm afraid he hasn't been the same since our parents died."

"You two went through something super traumatic and then had to be leaders for an entire species. I think that would change anyone."

"I suppose you're right. Kieran and I were close as children . . . that seems like another lifetime now."

"You may not be able to have that same relationship with him, but that doesn't mean you can't be close again."

He nodded absentmindedly and continued telling me stories as he cooked. After a while, he dished up the piping hot stew into two bowls and placed a plate of buttermilk biscuits in the middle of the table. He grabbed a couple of spoons and fixed us both a glass of iced tea.

"Thanks," I told him as I started eating. The stew was chock full of beef, potatoes, carrots, and onions, all mixed together in a thick dark gravy. I grabbed a biscuit and dipped it in, letting it soak up the liquid.

"You're welcome."

"This is delicious," I said through a mouthful of food.

His lips tugged up in delight. "Glad you like it. It was my mother's recipe."

I smiled affectionately at him. We continued to talk as we ate. We discussed our niece or nephew that would be making an appearance in about eight months. He seemed excited, but that could have been because he could tell I was. He told me more about his childhood, and I told him about mine.

After about an hour and a second round of dinner, we finally decided to get some rest.

. . . Only I didn't intend on getting any rest.

I had been planning this since we decided to take this trip. I was beyond ready, and this was the perfect romantic getaway.

There were no rebels nearby, so I knew it wasn't likely that we would be disturbed. This was the perfect opportunity, and I was taking it.

Once we made it to the bedroom, I shut myself in the bathroom to get ready. I brushed my teeth and took off my makeup. I usually felt prettier with it, but I wanted to be completely bare for him. We were linking our souls together, and I didn't want anything between us.

I stripped off my clothes, took a quick shower, and stepped into my lacy white lingerie, which I didn't intend to wear for long. I ran my fingers through my hair a couple of times. My curls were wild and messy, but I knew he loved my natural tresses.

I took one last deep breath and exited the bathroom. Finnian was dressed in nothing but his boxers, and my mouth watered at the sight. He didn't notice me at first but when he did, his eyes darkened to a deep amber and his canines extended.

"What are you wearing?" he growled out.

"Maybe you'll be able to figure it out if it's on the floor."

"Don't test me, Kendall. I only have so much self-restraint."

"Well, stop. I don't want you to restrain yourself; I want you to ravish me."

Faster than I could comprehend, he was standing in front of me. He wrapped his arms around my waist and pulled me towards him. His lips descended to mine, his kiss needy and desperate; different from our usual affectionate kisses. All our need and want for each other was in this kiss. He nipped at my bottom lip. I opened for him, and he slid his tongue in, battling for dominance with mine.

He moved us backwards, and I felt the back of my legs hit the bed before I fell towards it. He fell with me and landed on top of me. He supported himself with one hand and tangled the other in my hair. His lips left mine and began trailing down my jaw, then my neck. He sucked and nipped the skin gently. His canines scraped against the spot where his mark would be in a matter of minutes.

His hand left my hair and began descending down my body, leaving a trail of fire in the wake of his palm. His hand went all the way down to my thigh; he gripped it roughly, lifting it and wrapping it around his hip. His excitement pressed against me through his boxers and my panties. A low moan tore from my throat at the feeling.

His lips went lower, and he peppered kisses along my collar bone. As his lips went further down, his hand made its way to my back in a tortuously slow pace. He grasped the back of my bra but didn't unhook it.

"Are you sure?" He pulled away to look at me.

"I wouldn't have said it if I wasn't," I drawled. He gave me an unimpressed look, so I dropped the sarcasm. "I'm positive. I love you, Finnian."

"I love you too, baby," he said, gazing lovingly into my eyes.

That was all he needed; his fingers unclasped my bra. I lifted my arms from around his neck and he pulled it off of me. He growled as he looked down at me, but I didn't feel self-conscious.

"You're perfect," he murmured. He pressed a kiss to the top of my breast and looked at me through sooty eyelashes. He smiled wickedly at me and lowered his lips again.

He sucked the top of my breast and slowly made his way down. He took my puckered nipple into his mouth and kneaded my other breast with his hand. I gasped at the sensations that ran through me. He pulled away and blew on the sensitive bud. His warm breath hitting it made it even tighter than before, almost painfully so. He switched to the other breast and gave it the same attention. My breath came out in short pants.

I pulled him away from my chest and pulled his lips back to mine, kissing him passionately. I put all the love I felt for him into the kiss. His bare chest pressed against mine, my skin burning pleasurably from the touch of his, nothing separating our upper bodies.

As he continued to kiss me, his hand slipped down. His fingers skimmed the top of my panties teasingly before he slipped his hand inside and started stroking me softly. I moaned into his lips at the new sensation that hit me. Pleasure filled my whole body, and an ache started between my thighs, only alleviating at the brush of his fingers.

I lowered my hands and tried to push his pants down, but couldn't get them very far from our position. I whimpered in frustration as he pulled away.

"Someone's eager," he teased. His hand left my panties, causing another whimper to slip through my closed lips as the ache increased, begging for his touch. "Don't worry. I'm not anywhere close to done."

My heart sped up even more at his words. He lifted himself off of me and slid his boxers off. He stood in front of me, and my eyes took him completely. He was glorious. His manhood stood erect, and a bit of nervousness filled me. He would definitely be painful at first.

He slowly pulled down my panties, his fingers trailing down my legs with them until he pulled them completely off. He took one ankle in his hand and lifted it, kissing slowly, teasingly up my leg. Once he reached my inner thigh above my knee, I couldn't take it anymore.

"Finnian, please," I begged breathlessly. He knew exactly what I needed.

He moved up my body, planting another kiss against my lips. He reached for his wallet on the bedside table and pulled out a condom. He rolled it on and positioned himself at my slick entrance.

"Tell me if you want me to stop," he whispered, pressing a sweet kiss to my forehead. I nodded.

He slowly entered me, and I gasped at the foreign feeling of him filling me, stretching me. My eyes watered, but I blinked the tears away, not wanting to worry him or cause him to stop.

"You okay, Kendall?" he asked once he filled me completely. I nodded, and he started moving inside of me slowly. After a few minutes, the pain subsided, and I got used to his length.

"Faster," I moaned out demandingly.

He complied and started moving into me faster, harder. I gripped on to his back, digging my short fingernails in. I moaned lowly, which caused a groan to leave his lips. He kissed me again hungrily, then moved his lips down my jaw and neck, kissing, sucking, nibbling on the tender flesh.

He continued thrusting in and out of me at a fast pace. I arched my back, meeting him thrust for thrust. My lower belly started to tighten, and I felt pressure building inside of me. My breathing was coming out in short pants, and a sheen of sweat coated my body and his, despite how cold it was outside. I felt his muscles tense and bunch under my hands, and I gripped him harder.

The feeling continued to build. When he reached his hand between our bodies to stroke my clit, I finally exploded. A guttural moan left my lips as I came undone. I was so caught up in the feeling that I didn't notice his canines extend, until they cut through my flesh like hot butter. The feeling wasn't painful; in fact, it just made my pleasure increase. When he pulled back, I sunk my teeth into his neck in the same spot.

As I rode out my pleasure, he seemed to do the same. A low groan left his lips as I pulled my teeth out of his neck, and he thrust into me wildly a couple more times before finding his own release.

Once he was done, he rested his forehead against mine, our harsh breaths mixing together. Eventually, he pulled away from me, bringing my exhausted and spent body into his. I curled into him, my breathing still heavy.

My heart was beating erratically, and I could feel his heartbeat match mine as I laid my head on his chest. He tightened his arm around my waist and pulled me as close as I could get. My neck throbbed but it wasn't painful. A could feel a trickle of blood, which he wiped away with his finger, but the wound had already healed.

As our breathing evened out, he finally spoke.

"That was amazing," he murmured, his thumb stroking my waist gently.

"Yeah, it was. It was perfect," I mumbled in agreement. I pressed a couple of kisses to his chest and intertwined his other hand with mine.

We laid in silence for a few minutes, just enjoying each other's presence. After a while, he pulled away and was suddenly on top of me.

"Time for round two." He grinned mischievously at me.

Before I could think, his lips were covering mine again. Our lips moved in sync, and my body reacted to his once again. Any tiredness I was feeling left me, and eagerness took its place. It would definitely be a long, pleasurable night.

CHAPTER TWENTY-EIGHT

I woke up the next morning to sunny rays warming my face and Finnian kissing my shoulder. The small cabin was nice and toasty, thanks to the fire he lit in the early hours of the morning. It had stopped snowing at some point during the night, leaving the sun shining over a couple of inches of snow.

I was still naked from the night before. The sheets were bunched up around my navel, and my upper body was exposed to him.

Finnian was lying on his side, propping his head up so he could look at me. He was slowly trailing his fingers from under my breasts, down my stomach, and back up again.

I squealed in delight when his fingers made contact with my ribs—my ticklish area.

He grinned down at me, a rare sight to see.

"You're ticklish?" he asked devilishly.

"Nope," I quickly replied, biting my lip to conceal my grin. He smirked mischievously and ran his hand back up before I could stop him.

I squealed again. "Not ticklish, huh?" he teased.

"You caught me. I guess you know my deepest secret now."

"I know all your secrets now." He tapped the side of his head.

"You know all of my emotions and feelings, not my thoughts. There's a difference," I confessed as I scooted closer to him, wrapping my arms around his neck. His hand found my hip and his other moved under my head.

"I suppose you're right. I'm glad to know that you feel so happy right now."

"How could I not? You make me happy."

"You make me happy too, Kendall. More than you know."

"Oh, I know. The bond works both ways, remember?"

"I remember." He leaned forward and kissed me gently before he pulled away completely. "We need to get up. We still have a few hours left to drive. Let's take a shower. One of the guards will bring breakfast here by the time you're ready."

I nodded and tossed the covers off of my legs. I followed him into the bathroom. He started the hot water, waiting for it to heat up before he turned on the shower head.

It was a tight fit, considering the shower was far smaller than the one back home, but we made do. It took longer than usual for us to finish, since neither of us could keep our hands off of each other. After over an hour, we finally finished.

Finn got dressed quickly and left me alone in the bathroom to get ready.

Once my hair was braided back, my body covered by a sweater dress with thick leggings, and my makeup applied, I went in search of Finn. He was in the kitchen, drinking a cup of coffee and waiting for me.

"You look beautiful, Kendall."

"Thanks. Are those doughnuts?" I gestured to the box in the center of the table.

"Chocolate," he added.

"Yum, my favorite." I took a seat at the table and opened the box, surprised to see that it was still full. "You didn't eat yet?"

"No, I was waiting for you." My heart swelled at that.

"I love you, you know that? You're so sweet sometimes."

"Only for you. I love you too." He reached out and cupped my cheek from across the table. After stroking my cheekbone with his thumb a few times, he pulled back.

I distributed the doughnuts and made small talk while we ate.

After we finished eating, we finished packing. A couple of the guards came and loaded our bags up. Once we were packed, we hit the road.

If I only I had known that this trip had been the beginning of the end.

* * *

By the time we arrived in Alpha Rylan's territory, it was well past noon. We had been greeted by the warriors of his pack.

His territory was by far one of the most beautiful lands I had ever seen. I grew up surrounded by vibrant oak trees and warm, humid air. On some days, it got so thick that it was difficult to breathe.

Finnian's territory was surrounded by mountains with a combination of spruce and pine trees. The air was frigidly cold, and the humidity made it seem twenty degrees colder at all times.

Rylan's territory was different though. He had set up a cute little town, like something out of a Hallmark movie. The shops around the town square were styled after old Victorian architecture. The air was cool and crisp, and the trees were a vivacious blend of red, orange, and yellow. I wanted to take a picture of the the town and hang it in my living room.

I wasn't sure what I had been expecting, but the welcome we got felt a little exaggerated. His warriors followed us to the town square, where Rylan's office and prison were, howling as they ran alongside our cars. Once we made it to town, every member of his pack was waiting for us.

"Are you ready?" Finnian asked, drawing my attention away from the 2000 or so wolves in front of us and back to him.

"Why are they all here?"

"Respect. It's tradition for every wolf in a pack to gather together when a member of the Royal Family visits. They'll submit to us as soon as we get out."

"I'm a little nervous. This is a lot of people. I still don't feel much like a queen."

"That's one of the things I love about you. You're not a traditional queen, and I wouldn't want you to be. It makes you more relatable that you're so down to earth."

"Are you sure?" I bit my lip as I asked worriedly.

"Positive." He brushed his thumb against my lip, pulling it from my clenched teeth. He kissed me one last time. "Let's go."

He got out of the car and before I could blink, he was in front of my door. He pulled it open and helped me down, lacing our fingers as we started moving towards the town hall.

Before we could make it three feet away from the car, every wolf kneeled down on one knee and exposed their necks. They held one hand over their heart, indicating that their loyalty was to Finnian, their king.

I felt overwhelmed by the support we were receiving. I could feel pride swelling in Finn as well, although his face remained stoic. After a few seconds, Finnian raised his hand, signaling them to stand.

Collectively, they all stood. Once every wolf was up, Rylan, who I recognized from the mating ball, walked towards us.

"Your Highnesses, it is such an honor to have you here."

"Thank you for having us, Alpha," Finnian stated.

"It's a pleasure to see you again, Alpha Rylan."

"You as well, Queen Kendall."

"Where is the prisoner?" Finnian asked, immediately getting down to business.

"He is in the prison, waiting for you. Perhaps, Queen Kendall, you would like to explore the town while we attend to the prisoner?"

"Take Nathan with you. I don't want you around when I question the rebel," Finn answered.

I raised an eyebrow. *"What do you mean you don't want me around?"* I asked through my newly established mindlink.

"You don't need to see what I'm going to do to him."

"We're partners, King Finnian. We do this together or not at all. Besides, I have the potion from Kat."

He glared at me when I called him King, but he seemed to be considering my words.

"Fine," he spoke aloud. "Rylan and I need to discuss a few things first."

I nodded. We followed behind Rylan past his pack members and up the cobblestone stairs into the town hall. He closed the door behind us as we walked in his office. Finnian and I sat together on a small love seat.

"So, you've finally found your mate." Rylan smiled, looking between the two of us. His demeanor became much more relaxed and familiar once his door was closed.

Finnian surprised me when he returned the easy smile. "I did. I see you still haven't."

"Not yet, but thanks for the reminder, you lucky bastard."

My eyes widened at his words, but Finnian just chuckled in response. "I would fight you for that comment, but I still owe you for saving Kendall from that heinous Alpha at the mating ball."

"Hey, I wouldn't say I needed saving. I am perfectly capable of saving myself," I commented.

"She's right, Finn. She didn't need me to save her. She has a warrior spirit, I can tell."

I nodded gratefully to Rylan. Finnian beamed down at me, pride in his eyes that made my heart swell.

Finnian turned away after a few seconds, clearing his throat. "Tell me about the rebels you found."

"There isn't much to tell that I haven't already told you. It was a small unit of rebels, less than two hundred. We captured their leader, but he has yet to talk."

"Well, I suppose we should change that."

*   *   *

"Stay close by, Kendall," Finnian instructed as Rylan led us down into the basement, where the prisoners were kept.

As we walked through, I noticed most of the cells were empty. They were high-tech, like something I would picture in a maximum security prison. The walls were made of thick fiber glass with clear liquid wolfsbane. The only way to enter the cells was to punch in a ten-digit access code. Every cell had a different code, making it nearly impossible to break out.

We walked down a row of cells, then turned down the next row and walked through a dimly lit narrow hallway. There was a door every ten feet or so, but we stopped at none of them. Instead, we walked to the very end, going in the very last door after Rylan entered the code.

Once it was open, Rylan went in first, then Finnian. He looked around the room for a moment, then ushered me in once he saw it was safe. There was a chair, one that I would picture in a dentist office, and the rebel wolf was tied down to it.

He looked furiously at each of the men in the room, which consisted of Finn, Rylan, Nathan, and two of Rylan's guards, but I could smell fear seeping out of his pores. He was yelling around the tape covering his mouth, his words indecipherable, sweat beading on his forehead and upper lip.

Finnian stripped off his suit jacket and tie, undoing the first few buttons of his crisp navy blue shirt. He rolled up his sleeves, showing off his muscular forearms.

"Are you sure you want to be here?" Finn's voice entered my mind.

"I'm sure. We're a team."

He nodded subtly, then turned his attention back to the prisoner. Nathan grabbed me gently by the elbow and guided me over to the corner.

One of the guards ripped the tape from the guy's mouth. He turned his hateful glare to Finnian.

"So, you're that king everyone always raves about. You look like a pussy to me. Your queen over there though . . . damn. Just wait until the rebellion attacks. They'll kill you quick, which you'll be happy about considering the things they'll do to that fine piece of ass before they kill her too."

I had to give Finnian credit. For as enraged as I could feel that he was, he stayed composed on the outside. Instead of showing his anger, he calmly turned to the table to his right. A sick feeling coiled in my stomach at what I saw. There were an assortment of tools, including pliers and a drill.

Finnian chose the pliers.

"Who do you work for?" he questioned evenly.

"Do your worst, your royal highness," he spat out.

I could feel his annoyance spike through our bond before he grabbed his hand. Before anyone could comprehend what he was doing, he ripped off the guy's thumb nail.

To give the guy credit, he stayed relatively composed, only letting out a short groan.

"Who do you answer to?" he questioned again.

He looked up at Finnian and spat right in his face. Finn still stayed calm and collected outside. He simply wiped the saliva from his cheek and pulled off three more fingernails in rapid succession.

"Do you want to try that again?"

"Fuck you!"

Finn upped the number even more, by ripping off the remaining pinky nail on his right hand, then doing the next five on the left hand as well.

"Ahh, mother . . . fucker . . ." the wolf grunted, spit flying from his lips as he breathed heavily through the pain.

I clenched my fists and bit the insides of my cheek, trying to keep the contents of my stomach where they were.

"You okay, Kendall?" he asked through mindlink. *"You can leave anytime you want."*

"I'm good. Keep going," I lied, not wanting him to have to do this alone.

I knew that as pissed as he was, he didn't enjoy this. He actually despised doing it. But he also didn't want to have another wolf do it. He didn't want it on anyone else's conscience. As his mate, it was my job to help him get through it.

"You ready to change your answer yet?"

He just received a scowl.

He put down the pliers and picked up a drill.

"You're going to wish you had just answered me."

*   *   *

"Please . . . please. No more . . ." the rebel slurred, barely conscious. Blood coated every inch of his body, except for his face. Finn avoided going above the neck.

I kept the bile in my stomach for the first hour, but once Finn started cutting off toes, I started retching violently. That was the one time he stopped. He cleaned the blood off his hands and came over to me. He held my hair back until I was finished, then held me gently until I calmed down. He tried to get me to leave again then, but I convinced him to keep going with me still here.

"Give me a name and it stops."

He exhaled harshly a few times, struggling to bring in a breath.

"I took an oath. I'll take it to my grave."

Finnian sighed heavily. "Enough of this. Kendall, do you have the potion?"

I nodded and pulled it out of my cardigan pocket. I handed it over to him. He didn't hesitate to unscrew the cap.

"Wait, no. What is that? No, I—" He didn't let him finish his protests. He gripped his chin harshly, pulled it down, then pushed his head back to pour the thick murky liquid into his mouth. Finnian held his jaw firmly shut. The rebel tried to resist, but it was no use; he eventually swallowed the contents of the potion.

Almost immediately, the screams started. The cries were different from before; more guttural.

He sounded like he was being burned alive from the inside. His harsh cries continued and blood vessels started to pop in his eyes, turning the whites red.

"Who is the leader of the rebellion?" Finnian repeated the same question he had been asking the last four hours.

"Ah!" He continued screaming, the noise getting louder and harsher. Blood started gushing out of his eyes first, red tears pooling in his mouth. The ears and nose were next. Blood streamed down from both, eventually mingling in with the blood covering his torso.

"It's . . . Ugh!"

"Tell me who it is!" Finnian yelled, finally losing his temper.

"I don't know him! I only know his name!"

"What is it?" Finnian questioned again, calmer this time.

"Ivaylo," he answered, moments before his harsh breathing and spasming body both stopped, blood flying from his lips at his last exhale.

CHAPTER TWENTY-NINE

"I appreciate you all coming three days earlier than you originally planned. I would not have convened this Council meeting had it not been an urgent matter that we need to attend to," Finnian stated from the front of the room, right next to me.

The room was filled with Alphas that Finn trusted enough to put on his Council. We had gotten back three days ago, and he called for a meeting as soon as every Alpha could make arrangements to get here.

The Council room was one I hadn't seen before. It was actually underground, which was news to me. I never even considered that the castle had a basement.

There was a long table at the front of the room. Finnian sat in the center, the chairs along the table were for his royal advisors. I sat on his immediate right, while Kieran took his left. Niki was next to me while Harrison sat next to her. Emiliya was beside her mate, and Tyler was next to her. A couple other people that I wasn't familiar with were at the ends of the table.

On the other side of our table were five rows of tables, each holding ten people. As his Council was still growing, only the first two and a half rows were filled. They were facing us, watching Finnian closely but not making direct eye contact.

"As you all know, the rebellion has gotten significantly bigger in recent months. We have discussed at length what to do about them in recent meetings. There was not a lot we could do about it at the time, however, as we lacked the knowledge of their leadership." He paused.

My eyes drifted across the room, taking in every familiar face. The first one I saw was Rylan, who came back with us from his territory. He'd been helping Finnian search records for the name Ivaylo. They hadn't found much.

My eyes also landed on my father and brother. Technically, the screening process for dad to join the Council wouldn't be over for another week, but Finnian made an exception. He trusted my family, since he knew they would never hurt me. Since the people he could really trust these days were in short supply, he needed everyone he could get.

Dad arrived here with mom yesterday. Brody was back at home, running the pack until after my Coronation in three days. All of the alphas would be staying for that, as it was mandatory for all alphas to attend.

"The dynamic has changed as new information has been obtained. We now know the name of the leader. His first name is Ivaylo. His surname has yet to be uncovered. The issue we are currently facing is figuring out who this Ivaylo is. We have searched every record we have, and we have yet to find anyone with that name.

That leads us to believe that this is his alias and not his birth name. That, or he was born into the rebellion and his birth isn't on record. It is likely, though, that Ivaylo is an alias since we have never heard a murmur of that name before, and we have a record of many wolves in the rebellion. I'll open the floor to thoughts or information on the subject."

Finnian sat down once he finished.

"King Finnian, did you get any other identifying information besides the name?" an older alpha that I wasn't familiar with asked.

"We didn't. We only know that members of the rebellion are extremely loyal to him. We only got the name because of a truth potion," he answered.

"That sounds foreign. Perhaps he's originally from another continent and came to America recently," my father suggested. "Do you know the origin of the name?"

"It's Bulgarian," another alpha answered, likely the oldest one in the room.

At that, all eyes turned to either Niki or Emiliya. Mine turned to Niki, since Emiliya wasn't fond of me and Niki was right next to me.

"I cannot help you on that front. I do not even speak my native tongue. My mother never educated me in my Bulgarian heritage," Emiliya informed everyone looking in her direction.

All eyes turned to Niki.

"Ah, I have looked into that actually. I looked through a few of my mother's books that she didn't take with her to Bulgaria. I wasn't able to translate much because the dialect was centuries old, but I was able to find out a little about the name."

"What is that Nikolina? And why wasn't I informed sooner?" Finnian raised an irritated eyebrow at her.

"I apologize, King Finnian. I have been searching for days. I only discovered this information in the early hours of the morning."

"Very well. Proceed."

"Ivaylo loosely translates to wolf. The story is that Ivaylo was the original werewolf. His betrothed was from the original witch family, Tatiana, the eldest of ten children. She was distraught when his wolf didn't have a connection to her like his human half did. She had cast a spell on herself to be bonded to him on a primal level. This was the first mating. She meant it for just herself and her beloved, but she underestimated her power. She accidentally created the mate bond. It has since grown so powerful that no magic can diminish it."

"What was their demise?" Finnian inquired, a thoughtful expression on his face.

"There was no great demise, my king. They procreated rapidly. Their offspring were all werewolves, except for their first born—he was a wizard. Every wolf can trace their lineage to Ivaylo and Tatiana. They both died peacefully in their sleep, together, at eight hundred years old."

"Do you have any idea why someone would assume his name?"

"I have nothing concrete, Your Highness, but I do have a theory."

"Which is?"

"The night before their passing, Tatiana had a vision. She saw a future wolf rising above all else. He had the spirit of Ivaylo within him. He defeated a great enemy and laid ground for a new werewolf frontier. My theory is that the current Ivaylo knows his Bulgarian witch history. He believes himself to be the wolf from Tatiana's vision. Her vision was documented in a series of journals written by Tatiana's youngest sister, Nadejda. Witches are the only people who have access to Nadejda's journals. Therefore, I believe the leader of the rebellion is either the mate of a witch or has a witch working for him."

"Do you have any idea who it could be?" I asked her.

"I have no idea. Record keeping is something werewolves do. Witches don't do it. The only records kept of witches are done by werewolves, but so many witches these days are living away from packs. There is no way to find out who the witch is by records alone."

"There are no records of who has Nadejda's journals?"

"I can guarantee that almost every witch family has a copy. They are one of the most common documents for witches. There are millions of them. Many have been translated. I have a copy in old Bulgarian, so I had to translate it myself."

"Is there anything else we should know?" Finn spoke up again when he saw I didn't have any more questions.

"I don't believe so. I am certain about none of this, but I believe that if you find the witch, you find Ivaylo."

* * *

"Are you going to come have lunch with us?" I asked Finn once we left the Council meeting.

"I can't; I'm sorry. I have a conference call in twenty minutes. Nathan will be going with you though."

"Why?"

"I've assigned him as your new guard. I had Niki read his aura and she cleared him."

"She can read auras? Why doesn't she just do that to everyone until she finds the guy we're looking for?"

"That would take too long. And even if they do have a dark aura, that doesn't mean that they are involved in the rebellion. Something as little as being jealous can taint someone's aura."

"Does that mean yours is tainted since you get jealous all the time?" I smiled cheekily up at him.

He playfully narrowed his eyes and pulled me closer into his side as we walked. "I already told you this before. I'm not jealous, I'm territorial. Jealousy is wanting something you don't have. Being territorial is protecting something that's already yours. You're already mine."

I grinned up at him, remembering his words to me before I went to the bar and grill with Kat, Tyler, Dalton, Matt, and Lili. We had come so far since then.

"I guess you have a valid point."

We stopped outside of the sunroom where my family would be having lunch. He turned me to face him and pulled me into his chest.

"I'll see you this evening for dinner. Stay with Nathan. I'll be in my office if you need me for anything."

He paused to press his lips to mine, kissing me gently.

"I love you, Kendall."

"I love you too."

He kissed my forehead quickly before pulling away and walking in the opposite direction.

Once he rounded the end of the hall, I entered the sunroom. There was no sun to be seen; instead, a soft patter of freezing rain rapped softly against the glass. The sky was a gloomy dark grey, and there was a layer of slush on the ground.

The round table in the center of the room was already full. Mom and Dad sat next to each other, and Selena sat across from them. Nathan was one seat down from her. I sat in between them, right across from my father. Kat and Matt were on the other side of Selena. Dalton was, unsurprisingly, absent. He had been avoiding me.

"Hey, sweetheart."

"Hey, Dad. What are you guys talking about?"

"I was just telling them about the meeting."

After Niki's story, the meeting had lasted for another forty-five minutes. Not much else was discovered; they mainly discussed safety measures to be taken.

"You did great, Dad. I never would have guessed that you were a new member if I didn't know already. I know you impressed Finnian, which is hard to do," I told him as I dished out lasagna onto my plate. I had requested that they just bring something in and leave it, so we had more privacy than we would have had if they served us.

"I appreciate that, Kenny. That means a lot."

I just smiled at him before I shoveled a bite of lasagna into my mouth.

"Kat, were you familiar with that story?" Mom turned her attention to the only witch in the room.

"I vaguely remember it. Nadejda's journals are basically the equivalent to human bedtime stories. My mom gave them to me to read before bed when I was a kid, but there were so many, it's hard to remember them all. She practically documented her whole life."

"Do you have any copies of them?"

"I do, back at home. My family actually has two copies; one for my mom and one for me. One is translated to English and the other is translated to Hausa, which is my mom's native language."

"So, they really are as common as Niki made them out to be?" I asked once I swallowed my food.

" 'Fraid so." Kat shrugged.

"That's too bad. You could have done a locator spell if it was rarer."

"I know. We'll figure something else out."

I nodded and continued eating.

"So, Kendall, do you need any help getting ready for your coronation?" Mom turned her attention to me.

"Not really. We finally finished planning everything yesterday morning before you guys got here. Niki basically took care of everything; she just made me make the final decisions."

"What does your dress look like?" she asked, excitement in her eyes.

I pulled out my phone and opened the picture of the final result. It had been altered and fitted to my liking, so I had to try it on yesterday. It fit like a glove.

"Kendall, that is gorgeous. You will truly look like a queen." She looked up from my phone with tears in her eyes.

I smiled softly at her. "Thanks, Mom. I'm glad you'll be there. I just wish Brody could be there too."

"I know, sweetheart. But you'll see him soon. I'm sure of it."

"Well, in other news, I'm pregnant," Selena randomly announced, drawing the attention to herself.

Immediately, everyone started yelling at her at once. Some in joy, others in outrage. My attention remained on her as I laughed about Dad and Matt's reaction. I didn't pay much attention to Mom's last words to me.

I'd see them soon.

It seemed so normal, such a casual thing to say. Something I'd never think twice about hearing.

I suppose I should have, though.

If I had only known that her words would be incorrect.

I wouldn't be seeing them again.

Soon enough, I wouldn't be seeing anyone again.

CHAPTER THIRTY

I woke up to screaming, followed by growling.

I pried my sleep ridden eyes open and groaned in annoyance. Finnian's arms were impossibly tight around my body. They loosened, and his growling stopped once we saw the source of the screaming.

"Wake up, Kenny Kens. It's coronation day," Selena announced, mere moments before she dove onto our bed, crushing both Finn and me.

We moved in synchronization and pushed her off of us and towards the foot of the bed.

"You make me regret allowing you up here every time I see you, Selena," he muttered dryly.

He threw the covers off of his body and moved gracefully from the bed into the bathroom, where he proceeded to slam the door as he mumbled bitterly about in-laws.

"I'll never know how he moves around so easily with that stick shoved up his ass."

I smirked lazily at her and leaned against the headboard. "What are you doing here so early? The ceremony isn't until five o'clock."

"We have lots to do."

"Like?"

"Like, breakfast for one. We're having a big family breakfast."

"Since when?" My brows furrowed in confusion.

"Since I planned it. I thought it would be a nice surprise. It's not just family. Lili, Niki, Harrison, and Nathan will be there too."

"If it's a surprise, then why did you tell me, you idiot?"

She shrugged carelessly. "What can I say, my secret keeping skills are subpar at best."

"Okay, let me get ready and I'll meet you down there."

"Okay. It's in the Northern sunroom."

I nodded and walked into the bathroom when she left the room. Finnian was already in the shower, so I slipped out of my clothes and joined him. He immediately wrapped me in his arms, pulling me close to him.

"I'm glad you decided to join me, my queen." He smiled lazily against my neck before he sucked on the skin where his mark was.

I inhaled sharply, barely withholding a moan of desire. His lips left my neck and found mine. His hands snaked around to the backs of my thighs, then lifted me gently as he deepened the kiss. My legs wrapped around his hips tightly, our bodies grinding together at the movement.

My back touched the cold stone wall of the shower. One of Finnian's hands left my thigh and tangled itself into my hair, pulling my head back gently. He playfully nipped and sucked on my neck and collarbone.

I ground into him harder, his hardness pressing against my clit. He continued to tease me; kissing, licking, and biting my skin. It wasn't until I started teasing back that he gave me what I wanted.

I slipped my hand between our bodies and down to his manhood. I stroked it gently, softly; he wanted more.

He growled and pushed my hand away. In one quick thrust, he was inside of me. I gripped his shoulders, my nails digging in as he moved.

I met him thrust for thrust, the friction building and building as we moved in sync.

"Finnian," I whimpered as he increased his pace.

"What, baby? What do you need?" He nipped at my jaw teasingly.

"Faster, please," I panted.

He kissed me deeply, halting my pleas. He gave me what I wanted. His pace increased, driving me to the edge.

I cried out, reaching my climax as he continued to plunge into me. He pushed into me one last time and grunted deeply. We rode out of climax's together, our bodies one as we embraced each other.

"I love you, Kendall Keating." he whispered once his breathing slowed.

"Kendall Cahill," I corrected, looking into his dark pools of blue.

"You want to take my name?" he asked, his face unreadable as he clenched his jaw.

"Of course." I kissed him one last time before sliding down his body. "I love you too, by the way."

We didn't speak much after that. He washed every inch of my body, and I returned the favor. He would occasionally pepper kisses along my shoulders and back; I smiled softly every time. I would never get used to that. I would never get used to him. No matter how long we were together, I knew it would always feel like it was new. I would never grow tired of this—of him.

Once we finished showering, we dried ourselves off and got dressed. He dressed himself in a charcoal colored suit, my favorite of his excessive amount of suits, and I dressed myself in a pair of skinny jeans, a red plaid flannel over a black tank top, and finished it off with combat boots. I braided my hair over to the side and left my face bare, since I would get my makeup done later anyways.

Once we were both ready, we walked out of our room and down to the first floor, his fingers laced through mine.

The room was already pretty full when we got there. Everyone was standing around and listening to a story Dad was telling. Everybody, minus the witches, had a mimosa in their hand. A familiar looking waiter handed me one. Finnian got coffee.

"Easy on the mimosas this time, killer." Finnian smirked down at me, reminding me that I drank a little too much at the last brunch.

"I have nothing to be angry about this time. I don't need to drink when I have you," I whispered in his ear and kissed his cheek.

"Kenny! If it isn't the girl of the hour. Get over here," Dad bellowed.

I smiled and walked over. He pulled me into a tight bear hug, which I returned just as tightly.

"I'm so proud of you, sweetheart. You're going to be an amazing queen." He gripped my shoulders tightly as he pulled away from our hug and looked me square in the eyes.

"Thanks, Daddy."

Brunch went by pretty quickly after that. It was nice to have a couple of hours just spending time with my family before the big ceremony. The food wasn't bad either. Finnian stayed the whole time. I discovered that once my family got past how he treated me in the beginning, he fit in perfectly.

After we finished eating and were just sitting around talking, I noticed Dalton ducking out early. I hadn't had the chance to talk to him lately, so I quietly slipped out as well after letting Finnian know where I was going.

"Dalton!" I yelled, running to catch up with his fast steps.

He slowed, hesitation in his steps, then he stopped completely, turning to face me, his eyes remaining downcast.

"How's it going?" I asked once I was standing in front of him.

"Fine."

I exhaled heavily. "Okay, enough small talk. We need to work this out."

He mimicked my sigh. "I figured this was coming. You're annoyingly persistent."

"Walk with me," I told him, rolling my eyes at his insult.

We took a detour, leaving the castle and walking into the crisp and nippy air, strolling slowly towards the forest.

"So, tell me where you're at. You know, with the whole crush on me thing," I instructed after we made it a ways away from the castle.

He let out a breathy chuckle and shook his head, looking at the ground. "You know, one of the reasons I fell for you in the first place was because you had no filter. There was never any fakeness with you. You've always been so brutally honest and genuine. That's a quality I'm starting to hate in this moment, though."

I grabbed his arm, stopping him just as we entered the line of trees. "Dalton, come on. I know we've never been best buds, but I do consider you a friend. I don't want to lose you just because I don't feel the same way about you. You annoy the shit out of me, but I want you in my life."

He finally met my eyes. "I'll always be in your life, as long as you'll have me."

He stopped talking, but I didn't reply. My gut was telling me that he wasn't finished, that he just needed a minute to continue speaking.

"I . . . I should probably tell you the truth."

"Okay." I lowered myself on a tree stump, and he did the same.

"There is a reason I was able to fall in love with you. Most wolves find it impossible to fall in love with someone other than their mate."

My eyebrows furrowed together. "Yeah, it's rare. Unless a werewolf loses their mate . . ." My eyes widened as I looked back up at him.

His face confirmed my thoughts.

"I felt her die when I was ten. I wasn't sure what was happening at first. I just felt this ache in my chest. I asked Kat's mom about it and she told me that I had lost her."

His eyes glazed over and I remained silent. I grabbed his hand, squeezing it tightly in mine.

"I asked her to show me how she died. She was able to do a spell and find out about her. Her name was Jules. She was two years younger than me; only eight when she died. Her pack was attacked by the rebellion. She was caught in the crossfire."

"I don't know what to say, Dalton. I'm so sorry that you had to go through that."

"Don't be sorry. I'm a firm believer that things happen the way they are supposed to happen. I had to believe that, or the grief would have overwhelmed me. I think part of the reason I was so drawn to you was that you, unknowingly, helped me wade through that. You helped me forget, and all you had to do was be yourself."

"I'm sorry I couldn't be more for you."

"I'm not. You would've never been happy with me. Not like you are with him. It hurts, but I really am glad that you're happy."

"Thank you. That means a lot to me."

We sat in silence for a while, lost in our own thoughts. His hand was still held on tightly to mine, and his eyes were glazed over.

"Why didn't you ever tell anyone?"

"I guess I liked pretending that it never happened. It's easier to deal with loss if no one around you reminds you about it."

I thought back to all the times he had talked about his mate. My eyes widened when I recalled all the times I had talked about his mate. I had constantly said that I felt sorry for her for getting stuck with him.

I was a horrible person.

"I know what you're thinking. Don't. You didn't know. We gave each other crap. It was our dynamic. Don't feel guilty for talking about something that I never told you about," he said sternly before I could apologize.

"I'm still sorry though. I never would have . . ."

"I know, Kendall. We're good."

Finally, I nodded. "So, what's next for you?"

"What's next? I think it's time for me to go home. Work on putting my attention on something besides you and Jules. Get more involved in the pack and training to become Beta. I just have to believe that someday, I'll meet someone who is capable of loving me back."

"You will. I know you will."

He slowly bobbed his head up and down before smirking and looking up at me. "You know, I didn't think you were capable of a heart to heart," he teased, lightening the heavy mood.

I pushed his shoulder softly and rolled my eyes.

Things may never go back to normal with us, but maybe they could be better.

* * *

"Kendall, my dear, we need to go over your part one last time," Niki stated as she walked into the room I was getting ready in.

I was currently in the middle of having my hair braided into a crown braid. The woman doing it, Mikayla, was far more skilled than I could ever hope to be. She twisted my curly mane into an intricate braid that far exceeded my average at best French braiding skills.

"Niki, please tell me why? We've discussed it so many times already. A monkey could do it at this point. Or a better analogy; Selena could do it."

That earned me a glare from Selena, who was sitting right next to me, reading a magazine. She wanted Mikayla to do her hair and makeup as well. Something about wanting to be the prettiest Keating sister there.

I didn't bother to correct her delusions.

"Just humor me," Niki practically begged.

"Fine. One more time."

"Okay, so you have seen the arena that it is taking place."

"Correct." I rolled my eyes. I had only seen it every day for the last two weeks.

"Excellent, you already know the set up."

I nodded again, just slightly so I didn't disturb Mikayla.

"You will be entering through the south tunnel. You will walk towards the center of the arena. But you must walk slowly, to give everyone a chance to recite their Loyalty Pledge. The Loyalty Pledge, as you may already know, is the pledge to honor, protect, respect, and be obedient of the Queen's command; your command. It should take about sixty to ninety seconds for every alpha in attendance to recite it."

"Again, Niki, I am aware. In fact, I've already heard the Loyalty Pledge three times."

"Brilliant! I'm delighted that you are already familiar with it. As I was saying, you will walk to the center then stop in front of King Finnian. He will ask you a series of questions. You must answer with 'I swear.' After that, you will recite your personal vows. You have written them, correct?"

"I have. I even have them memorized."

"Outstanding! After your vows, King Finnian will cut his hand. He will then proceed to cut yours as well. You will hold your hands together over the Royal Chalice. I will come and say a spell to bind your blood to his. Your blood will officially become Royal Blood after that. Once that is complete, you two will leave together through the same tunnel that you entered from."

"Okay, got it." I shot her a thumbs up just as my hair was done.

"You look absolutely marvelous, my queen," Niki told me once I turned to face her.

"Thanks, Niki." I grinned at her.

"I have to admit; you do look pretty good," Selena added, speaking while her mouth is full with a burrito.

"Thanks. You look like E.T.'s long-lost brother."

She shot me the finger and ignored me; instead, she turned around to face Mikayla, who was starting her makeup.

I snickered and turned back to Niki. Just as she was about to speak, a knock sounded from the door.

"Come in." I announced after I put on a robe, since my torso was bare except for a strapless bra.

Kieran entered, smiling at me as he shut the door behind himself.

"You look gorgeous, like the queen you are. My mother would have loved to see this day. She'd be immensely proud."

"Thanks, Kieran. I wish I could have met her."

"I wish that as well. Do you have a few minutes to talk?" He gestured to the door.

"Sure. I just have to put my dress on. I have plenty of time."

He nodded and I walked out, following behind him. Nathan was sitting outside the door, sticking to me like glue all day. He stood up when I closed the door behind me, ready to follow.

"Don't worry, Red. We'll be right back. Besides, Kieran is practically my brother now; he's not a threat."

Nathan reluctantly nodded and sat back down while Kieran and I walked in the opposite direction.

"So, what did you want to talk about?" I asked as we rounded the corner.

"I wanted to give you a gift for today. From Emiliya and me."

He pulled out a small red velvet box from the pocket inside his jacket. He flipped it open with his thumb and handed it to me. It was the most beautiful—and expensive—ring I'd ever seen. It was a blood-red ruby ring with a solid white gold band. The jewel was shaped like a teardrop and was bigger than my thumb nail.

"It's beautiful, Kieran. I love it. Thank you so much."

"It's my pleasure, Kendall. We're family now, after all. I am beyond happy that my brother found you."

"I appreciate that more than you know." I slipped it out of the box and on my right ring finger.

"Good luck today. And welcome to the family."

"Thanks. I'll see you at the ceremony."

Kieran continued walking and I turned and walked the other way. Once I made it back to the room, Niki was gone and Mom had joined us. She helped me finish getting ready. It wouldn't take long now.

* * *

I let out a deep exhale and shook my hands, trying to rid myself of my nerves. I was standing at the edge of the southern tunnel, waiting for my signal.

I glanced down at my dress again, making sure it was perfect. It was even prettier than the first time I saw it. The deep ruby color looked amazing against my tanned complexion. My makeup and hair were both done flawlessly. My eyes were framed in dark false lashes with sharp black winged eyeliner. My lips were covered with a ruby matte lipstick. A few curls had been left out of my braid, resting against my cheeks and neck, and diamond encrusted pins were weaved throughout the braid.

My jewelry was kept simple. Just the ring Kieran had given me, a pair of ruby studs in my ears, and a white gold ruby bracelet. My feet were encased in a simple pair of silver open-toed stilettos.

I felt beautiful.

I breathed out deeply again, just as I heard Uilleann pipes begin to play. The Uilleann pipes were a Royal tradition, since the Cahill family originated from Ireland. The Royal Ballad drifted throughout the arena, and I slowly started walking forward.

The arena was decorated wonderfully. It was sort of set up like a football field but much classier. The seating area was raised away from the middle and formed a circle around it. The entire place was a mixture of dark marble and stone, with silk ribbons draped around the walls, and white and red roses covering the center of the arena. The seats were filled, thousands of Alphas and Royal Pack members here to see me officially become Queen.

Slowly, but surely, I became visible to those people and the Loyalty Pledge started. Throughout the arena, everyone chanted in unison.

"I pledge my loyalty to Queen Kendall. I pledge my support to Queen Kendall. I pledge that my pack will remain loyal to Queen Kendall, or they will face the full repercussions of committing treason. I pledge to always respect and admire Queen Kendall. I pledge to always faithfully trust in Queen Kendall. I pledge to always honor and protect Queen Kendall. I pledge these things until the end of her reign. May it be long and peaceful."

I was feeling choked up as I walked. I felt my eyes mist over at the show of support I was receiving. I blinked the tears away and kept walking. Just as the pledge was over, I made it to Finnian.

He looked beyond handsome in a black tuxedo with a red tie that matched my dress. He had a ghost of a smile on his lips, one that no one but me would be able to detect.

"I can't wait to take that dress off you later. You look stunning, Kendall." he told me through mindlink.

"You can undress me as long as I get to undress you, King Finnian." I smirked slightly, and he growled in my head.

"Deal."

"I would like to take a moment to officially introduce my mate, and your queen, Kendall Taylor Keating Cahill, formerly of the Keating Pack," Finnian spoke to the crowd.

Cheers and applause erupted around us. Finnian waited until they died down before we continued.

"Kendall, do you swear to lead the Werewolf Kingdom with honor and dignity?"

"I swear."

"Do you swear to uphold the laws of the land?"

"I swear."

"Do you swear to put the needs of the Kingdom above your own needs?"

"I swear."

"Do you swear to go above and beyond for any and every wolf in need?"

"I swear."

"Do you swear to be fair and kind in your ruling?"

"I swear."

"Do you swear to be the best queen that you are capable of being?"

"I swear."

"Then, as King Finnian Cahill, I accept you as my queen. You may now give your vows."

I smiled at him and turned to face the crowd, or at least one side of it.

"I've always been a firm believer that actions speak louder than words. I've witnessed the power of action while I was growing up and watching my father run his pack. As an adult, I've watched my mate and king do the same. Both of those two particularly important men in my life always made sure to follow through on their promises. It is easy to say you're going to do something and never do it, but following through on those promises is the sign of a great leader."

I paused, my eyes finding my dad's. His eyes were shiny with tears and crinkled in the corners because of the huge smile on his face. He gave me a subtle thumbs up to keep going.

"I know I have some big shoes to fill, but I will spend my life trying to fill them. I will do everything in my power to make not only every single werewolf proud, but also try to make those who came before me proud as well. I never had the honor of meeting my late mother-in-law, and that saddens me more than words can express, but I have heard stories about her leadership. She was graceful, kind, and fair. That is all I can hope to be and everything I will strive to be.

"I will spend every day of my life trying to be a better queen than I was the day before. I know these are all just words, and I look forward to proving that my actions will always match these words. Thank you so much for honoring me by being here today. I love all of you, and I hope to personally meet the leaders of every pack."

As soon as I stepped back to Finnian, the cheering and applause started again. Finnian had a soft look in his eyes, one that is filled with pride. He pulled me closer and kissed me softly until the cheering died down.

Once it did, we continued with the ceremony.

"I will now bind our blood together," Finnian announced.

He grabbed my hand and walked us over to the table where the golden Royal Chalice was placed. Niki was already standing on the other side of it, smiling encouragingly at me.

Finnian grabbed the knife with the Cahill insignia on the blade. He held his hand over the chalice and dragged the blade along his palm, causing beads of blood to well up immediately. It healed quickly, but plenty dripped inside before that.

Next, he grabbed my hand. He hesitated dragging the blade down, not wanting to hurt me.

"It's okay. Do it," I reassured him through our mindlink.

He looked up at me for a few seconds, then nodded and did the same to me. Mine wasn't as deep, since I didn't heal as fast as he did yet. My body couldn't do that until our blood was bound.

As my blood was in the process of filling the chalice, a shift in the air occurred. A series of events happened, all within a span of a few seconds; although it felt like everything was going in slow motion.

A series of howls sounded first. They were coming from everywhere. Close to us, far from us. From the east, the west. Everywhere. They were howls of battle.

The next thing that happened was that the arena was immediately filled with members of the Royal Army, Harrison among them. Some were shifted, some were in human form.

The arena became chaos after that. Alphas attacking other alphas, blood being shed, and snarls filling the air.

"King Finnian, we're under attack. It's the rebellion. We underestimated them. They're attacking us on every border except the north," Harrison informed Finnian once he reached us.

He looked panicked, which was a bad sign. Harrison was always the picture of calm, cool, and collected. It had to be bad for him to be freaked out. I grabbed Finnian's arm, fearing for him, my family, and friends. All but one of my family members were here.

"Which side was hit the worst?" Finnian asked.

His emotions were moving so fast that it was hard for me to detect one. I could vaguely sense anger, worry, fear. Fear for me . . .

"The southern border is probably the worst. The eastern side is pretty bad too."

"Okay, you take the eastern border. I'll take the south. I'll send Kieran to the west border. Where's Nathan?"

"He's out there fighting. What are you going to do with the Queen, Your Highness?"

"She'll go to the safe room with Niki. Nathan will meet them there when he is able."

"What? No, you have to stay with me. We need to find my family. They're here somewhere." My hands, one still bloody, gripped his jacket. My voice was shaky, the words barely squeezing past the lump in my throat.

A cold sweat broke out across my skin; fear coiled through my body like a venomous snake, wrapping itself around my heart and throat, squeezing like a vice.

I glanced around, trying to locate my loved ones. All I could see was blood. It surrounded me, it paralyzed me. I knew if I lived through this, it would haunt me.

My breathing increased, to the point that that was all I could hear. Everything around me disappeared, only the sound of my ragged and desperate attempts to take in oxygen remained in my head.

They were all here, in this arena.

Mom and Dad. The people who shaped the person I am. The people who always loved me unconditionally. The people who taught me what true love and respect looked like. The people who I tried to be like.

Matt and Selena. My siblings. My older siblings. Two of the three people who I shared such a unique bond with. The people who I grew up with, who I learned with. The people who became my best friends the day I was born.

Kat. My chosen sister. The girl who I admired and respected. The girl who always had my back. The girl who my brother fell in love with. The girl who had been the voice of reason for me since I was five.

Tyler. The father of my unborn niece or nephew. The guy who had quickly became one of my best friends. The guy who adored my sister. The guy who my sister adored right back. My mate's best friend.

Finnian. My mate. The only man I'd ever loved. The only man I'd ever wanted to be with. The man who made me feel things I didn't ever think were possible. The man who snuck past every defense I had. The man who wormed his way into my heart and wove himself around it. The man who I would die without.

I wasn't worried about myself. I was worried about them. The people who I couldn't live without.

"—dall! Kendall, listen to me!" Finnian yelled, his panicky voice breaking through the fog in my head.

He grabbed my face in his hands, my wide, misty eyes taking in every movement of his. I could feel hot tears rolling down my face, in rapid succession.

"Kendall, listen to me. I need you to go with Niki. Can you do that for me, baby?" he asked desperately.

"Finnian, no. Please, don't leave me."

He pulled me closer and kissed my forehead. "I have to. Niki will keep you safe. I have to stop them before they reach the castle."

"I have to find my family."

"Tyler has them. He'll keep them safe."

"Finnian, please," I begged.

I squeezed my eyes shut, causing more tears to cascade down my cheeks. A sob wrenched from my throat.

"Hey, hey. Look at me. This is what needs to happen, baby. I can kill ten for every three that my best warrior kills. Niki can protect you. She's the only one I trust. Trust my judgement on this, okay? You'll be fine. I'll be fine. Please, go with her."

Reluctantly, I nodded.

"Thank you." He kissed me again. "I love you more than anything in this world, Kendall. I'll be back soon."

"I love you too, Finn. Please be safe."

He nodded once, then he was gone.

Niki took his place not a second later. She grabbed my elbow and started pulling me towards the north tunnel. I lifted my dress and pumped my legs faster to keep up with her.

"Where are we going?" I asked once we were out of the arena and in the tunnel.

"There is a safe room at the base of Mt. Cahill. It is the only border that's not being attacked. We'll be safe there. It's half a mile from the end of the tunnel."

"Is my family there?"

Niki gave me a saddened look. "I'm afraid not, Kendall. The room is only for members of the Royal Family and their mates. There is a spell that doesn't allow anyone without Royal Blood to enter. I cannot undo it for so many people in such a short time. Only for myself and Nathan to keep you safe."

"I need to find my family, Niki!" I screamed and stopped running, jerking her back because of her grip on my arm.

"Kendall, I understand your worries. I have the same worry about my sisters. But now isn't the time. We have a job to do just like everyone else. We need to keep you safe. God forbid, if anything happens to Finnian, you will become the ruler. You have to be protected. Now, let's get to the safe room and I'll do a protection spell for them."

My chin wobbled as my bottom lip shook, but I still nodded.

We continued on, until we finally made it to the mountain safe room. It didn't look like anything was there, but we were able to walk through the stone. It just looked like the base of the mountain, but that was the point. It was hidden.

"Okay, now do the spell," I instructed.

She nodded and found a source of water at the back of the room. She poured the bottle of water on the stone ground.

Before she could do anything, someone else joined us. I was momentarily excited, thinking it was Finnian, but that vanished the moment I saw it was just Nathan.

"How did you get here so fast?" Niki questioned, hesitation in her tone that I didn't understand.

"Where's Finnian?" I added before he could answer.

"He's a bit tied up at the moment," Nathan answered.

I looked at him in confusion. He was my friend, my trainer. Why did he sound so . . . cold all of a sudden? Niki moved to stand in front of me, adding to the confusion.

"It's you," she mumbled.

"What's me?" he asked, sounding amused now.

"The one who wants to kill the Queen. It's you," Niki accused.

"I didn't realize anyone knew, but yeah; it's me." He chuckled.

My eyes widened, betrayal running hot through my veins.

This was Nathan. He had become one of my best friends since I started training with him. What could possibly possess him to do this? To betray my trust, Finnian's trust? To want me *dead*. How did Niki not realize if she read his aura?

"Why?" I whispered.

"Why? Maybe because Finnian isn't fit to rule. He's a joke. He's soft, just like his father. It got his father killed, and now it will get him killed. The kingdom needs a real leader."

"You bastard . . ." I trailed off, anger seizing my throat.

"Don't take it so personally. You're a great friend and I love our banter, but this had to happen. The only way to get to him is through you."

My hands started to shake, a mixture of fear and fury.

"You forgot one little thing, Nathan. You have to get past me to get to her. I won't be so easily defeated." Niki sneered at him.

He smirked back. "It'll be easier than you think."

Niki didn't let him affect her. She raised her hands to him and started chanting.

Nothing happened. She stopped and looked down at her hands in shock.

Nathan snickered and gestured down to my waist. No, not my waist. My hand. My ring, to be specific.

"Kendall . . . I'm so sorry," Niki spoke after she saw my hand. Realization dawned on her face as she saw the ring, and horror and guilt followed.

Before I could question anyone, Nathan made his move.

In the blink of an eye, he grabbed Niki's head and twisted it. A sickening snap resounded around the small room.

My eyes widened in horror as she fell to the ground, her lifeless brown eyes staring back at me.

CHAPTER THIRTY-ONE

Chaos.

That was the only way to describe it.

Pure chaos.

Blood covered the streets, buildings and homes burned, and billowing smoke polluted the air. Bodies littered the ground of the small town just south of the castle, the town that housed the majority of the Royal Pack. The town was filled with women and children, which was why the rebellion chose to attack it; it was a weak point.

A child, no older than three, let loose a blood curdling scream, tears streaming down his ruddy cheeks. He screamed for his mother who would never answer him again. He was alone.

Howls of sorrow filled the air, their grief palpable. Some howls were angry as well, promising vengeance.

They wanted justice. They wanted revenge.

It was answered when the King arrived.

He tore through like a tornado, ripping out jugulars and decapitating wolves who would dare turn on the Royal family.

The rebel wolves continued to pour in heavily. But for every wolf that stepped foot on the Royal Territory, King Finnian killed three. He was unstoppable. He was a killing machine.

He was pissed.

His mate was in danger, and he couldn't be there with her. The nightmare that was Niki's vision continued to haunt him. It was what was driving him. Driving him to finish this and find her.

The rebellion underestimated his desire to protect her. They underestimated his strength and his courage. He wasn't like the kings of the past. He didn't sit in the castle during a battle, letting his solders fight for him.

No, Finnian was a real leader. He led his men to battle, fighting right alongside them. Watching their backs, saving them from sure death.

But who had his?

He got his answer when three wolves flocked around him.

One he had grown up with. He'd never admit it, but Tyler helped mold him into the king he was today. He admired Tyler's calm demeanor. And, if he was honest, he often looked to Tyler for advice with Kendall. He claimed to only trust Kendall and Niki but deep down, he knew Tyler was good.

The other two wolves he didn't have such a lengthy background with, but he did have a connection to them. Jefferson and Matt Keating. His father-in-law and brother-in-law. He was unsure if he would fit in with his mate's family, but he had proven that he could.

They had his back.

And that meant more to him than anything.

The fighting continued. Once they cleared the southern border, they made their way to the eastern border, where fighting was still raging on.

Once they made it to the eastern border, they jumped right back in. Finnian fought ferociously, bravely.

But then it stopped.

His world stopped turning. His universe darkened.

He couldn't feel her.

She was gone, and he wasn't there.

Jefferson, Matt, and Tyler protected the broken King, keeping him safe as he whimpered in the center of the circle. He wished they would move. He had nothing to live for now.

He released a sorrowful howl. The kind only a king who had just lost his queen could make.

*   *   *

Life is made up of choices.

It could be a simple choice; like did I want pizza or tacos for dinner? I usually picked both.

Or the choice could be more complex. It could be a choice that could drastically alter your life or the life of someone close to you.

We make choices every day. Sometimes we don't even think about it. We don't think of the consequences of those choices. Sometimes we may even believe that there are no consequences. There are always consequences.

A few weeks ago, I made a choice. I saw Niki's vision and I chose to stay with Finnian anyways. I chose to fight.

I was an idiot.

I thought I had a choice. I thought our destiny was shaped by choices.

I thought wrong.

At the end of the day, fate determined everything. Fate controlled our lives. Fate had every single one of us by the balls, and we didn't even realize it. We stupidly thought we would change the outcome of things.

It was naïve thinking, really.

I never had a choice. I never had a chance in hell at changing things. Whether I had accepted Finnian or not, this was always my fate. Did I regret accepting him though?

Hell no. If I had to die, then at least I had a few amazing weeks with him.

I just hoped that fate had other, better plans for him. Because it sure had a shitstorm in store for me.

I was fate's bitch, and it was ready to screw me.

But it wasn't in my nature to go down that easily.

No, if fate were to take me down, then I would go down fighting.

Even if it killed me.

* * *

My glassy eyes stayed locked on Niki's. She was my friend. She was there for me and protected me. From the beginning, she had been my number-one confidant at the castle.

She deserved better than this.

"You're a monster," I whispered as my eyes moved back to the traitor in front of me.

He shrugged. "I'm not a monster. Just a man fighting for what is right."

"What did you do to the ring?" I demanded, my skin burning from the inside out as fire ignited in my blood.

"Emiliya cast a spell on it so that Niki couldn't use magic when she was near it. Personally, I didn't think it would work. I figured Niki would sense the magic when you got near her. But she didn't. The timing of the attack was perfect as well. It was actually supposed to happen as soon as you entered the arena, but they were a little late. Lucky for me, they arrived before Niki did the blood-binding spell. That would have ruined everything if she realized she couldn't use magic around you."

I forced down the tears, not wanting him to see me cry. I ripped the ring off my finger and threw it against the wall so hard, the ruby shattered.

"You and Emiliya . . . who else is involved?"

He smirked again. I wanted to slap the smug look off his face. "All will be explained, Kendall. For now, it's time to go."

He was right in front of me in the blink of an eye, gripping my bicep and pulling me. I fought back. I extended my claws and took a swipe at his face, leaving three long claw marks down his freckled cheek. When he looked back at me, his eyes were golden; even as the wounds healed.

He grabbed me by the throat and squeezed. My feet left the ground, and I scratched his hand, to no avail.

Black spots started to dance across my vision. I was about to pass out but a voice stopped him.

"Nathan, I told you, you can't kill her!" a bitter voice snapped from behind him, but I barely heard her over the whooshing sound in my ears.

He dropped me to the ground. I gasped for breath, taking in large gulps of air as I held my throat gingerly in my hand.

I looked up and saw the owner of the annoyed voice. Emiliya.

"At least, not yet," she added.

"Fine. Keep her contained then," he growled at her and wiped the blood with the back of his hand.

I didn't even recognize the man standing before me. I didn't see the sarcastic, loyal ginger that I'd known him to be. Instead, he was cold, calculating, and easily angered. He trained me; he knew every move I would make before I could do it.

"Did she suffer?" Emiliya asked as she glanced down at Niki, a snarl distorting her elegant features.

"It was quick."

"That's a shame. I hoped she would suffer first."

A felt a similar snarl on my face. "I'll make sure you pay for that, you evil bitch."

I shouldn't be surprised that Emiliya was involved. She had been awful from the very beginning, but I couldn't believe she could possibly hate her sister so much that she would want her to die a painful death.

I lowered my barrier, trying to reach out to Finnian or my family. I pulled back from my link when I realized I couldn't connect to anyone.

"You really are an idiot. Do you really think we would leave your mindlink intact? You deserve to die for your own stupidity." She sneered at me.

"I'm going to kill you," I promised, even though it was one I wasn't sure I could fulfill.

"I can assure you; you will die long before you have the opportunity."

"Let's go." Nathan gripped my arm again, even tighter than before if that's possible.

I moved to attack again until a wave of searing heat crawled over my skin. It was eerily similar to the time in the limo when Emiliya attacked me. It lasted a few seconds, then let up.

"Try it again, you arrogant imbecile," she told me.

I clenched my teeth and glared at her. I had to bide my time and come up with a plan. I let him drag me from the safe room, which ironically was the least safe place I could be in, and out into the cold. We continued around the mountain. I wasn't sure why, since there wasn't anything that way for sixty miles.

I stumbled behind Nathan constantly. He was basically dragging me. With the heels and his fast pace, I couldn't keep up. After a while, he threw me down, my shoulder adsorbing the impact.

"Take off the shoes. They're slowing us down."

I glared and refused to move. Heat exploded across my skin once again, burning me from the inside.

I whimpered softly then did as ordered once it died down.

I kicked off the shoes and continued walking barefoot. There was a light layer of snow dusting the ground. I guess fate did me one solid by giving me werewolf heat.

I glanced down at myself. Not that it mattered, but I was a mess. My dress was ripped and tattered, blood and dirt covering it. A spattering of bruises covered my throat and my arms.

"Are you going to explain anything, you piece of shit?" I growled out to Nathan, trying to distract myself from the situation I was in.

"Enough of your insolent chatter." Emiliya lifted her hand, like she was about to use magic on me.

"Emiliya, enough. She'll be dead soon anyways," he told her before she could do anything. "As for you, I suppose I could ease your confusion before you die."

"How considerate," I drawled sarcastically, a look of repulsion on my face.

"I am the leader of the rebellion, although very few are aware of it, even in the rebellion."

"Are you Ivaylo?" I questioned.

"No. Ivaylo is my second in command. Most wolves believe he is the leader. He answers to me though."

"Who is Ivaylo?"

"I'll let him reveal himself, if he so chooses."

"What about Kieran? Where does he fit into this?"

Emiliya turned back and scoffed. "That idiot knows nothing."

"You're betraying your own mate?"

Nathan chuckled softly. "Kieran isn't her mate. He was so desperate to find love, he didn't see through the magic used to fake the bond. I almost pity him."

Gears turned in my brain, trying to piece together the story. Trying to figure out how a royal werewolf would have fallen for their mind games. I wanted to kick myself for never getting to know him better, but he was always stuck up Emiliya's ass. Maybe that was the point. Maybe she isolated him from everyone, including his brother, so no one would notice what she was doing. It didn't help that Finnian isolated himself too.

"What about the ring?" I questioned, trying to figure out where that puzzle piece fit.

Emiliya scoffed again, but it was Nathan who answered, "Emiliya worked Kieran like a puppet. All she had to do was mention getting you a gift and he went along with it. Once he discovers the truth about Emiliya, death will be a mercy for him."

"What about the two attacks that you two were present for?"

"Well, the first time, they were idiots and got too close. They were supposed to be watching out for Emiliya, *from a distance*. And at the lake, I was testing Finnian to see how he would react. I knew I had his trust when he left me behind to guard you. Exactly what I wanted."

"So, what's your plan now?"

"Well, your little witch friend Kat ruined our original plans."

"Which were?"

"We were going to kill you close to the castle, let Finnian find you, then kill him in his moment of grief. Emiliya would have killed Kieran, and the entire Cahill line would have been dead."

That was the original vision. "What changed?"

"Niki and Kat cast a spell on you. It is a spell where whoever kills you will die in return. Since I don't want that, nor do I want my witch to perish, we must come up with an alternative. Had it just been Niki who cast the spell, it would have broken upon her death, but like I said, your friend was involved. We tried to kill her too, but your brother had her very well guarded."

I felt a weight lift off my shoulders, just the tiniest bit. At least I knew one person I loved was safe.

"What's your alternative?"

Before he could answer, we stopped. Nathan's head snapped around, searching the trees behind us. I didn't see or hear anything but obviously he was able to. Before I could ask more questions, he shifted into his giant red wolf.

A few moments later, I saw what had his attention. A large grey wolf emerged from the trees—a wolf I was very familiar with.

Dalton.

My eyes widened in horror as Nathan advanced on him, growling deeply.

"Dalton, leave, now! He'll kill you!" I yelled.

He ignored me and instead growled at Nathan right before they leaped at each other.

"Your friend isn't very smart, is he? He never should have come looking for you." Emiliya cackled from behind me.

I ignored her and watched the fight. I took a step forward and pain started again. It stopped and I glared back at her. I tried to shift but nothing happened.

I hated it, but he was alone in this.

I had to give it to Dalton, he was holding his own. He was just a beta-in-training fighting against an alpha. That wasn't an easy feat, but he was managing.

He lunged at Nathan, aiming for his throat. He missed but he did get a hold of his ear and ripped the tip off with his teeth. Nathan growled in return. It oddly felt like Dalton had just poked the bear.

Nathan jumped at him. Dalton dodged and rolled to the side. He didn't get up fast enough, though. Nathan took advantage of that. He jumped on him while he was on his back. He swiped his paws down his underbelly, causing Dalton to whimper.

Nathan responded with a bite to his front paw.

Dalton swiped his other paw down Nathan's face. It didn't hurt him, but he was able to push him off and stand back up. He limped around, obviously hurt. Blood dripped from his belly, turning the stark white snow red, melting it with the heat of the fresh blood.

Nathan jumped again and somehow, with pure luck, Dalton evaded it. He answered with a pounce of his own. He landed on Nathan's back and clawed down his rib cage. Nathan howled in pain.

Dalton didn't stand a chance after that.

Emiliya started chanting, causing Dalton to whimper.

"No!" I yelled, running at her to stop her.

It caught Nathan's attention. As Emiliya kept Dalton down with magic, Nathan knocked into me from behind. I fell face first into the ground, my head bouncing up, then hitting against the hard ground again. Black spots danced in my vision. I tried to blink them away but to no avail.

I felt teeth puncture my upper arm, hitting bone. I tried to pull away, but I was too weak from the hit on the head.

From the corner of my eye, I saw Dalton stand through the pain and try to make his way over to us. That pulled Nathan's attention away from me. He walked back over to Dalton, who collapsed in my line of vision.

Nathan stopped in front of him, but Dalton didn't look at him, his eyes meeting mine instead. We couldn't mindlink, but we were communicating in our own way.

His eyes said it all. Love shown deep in his brown eyes, as did regret. He regretted not being able to save me. He loved me, and he couldn't stop Nathan from killing me.

"I'm sorry," I mouthed.

He nodded his head, forgiveness in his eyes. He didn't blame me.

Right before I blacked out, I saw Nathan rip his throat out. I saw the life leave his eyes.

* * *

When I came to, my head felt like a thousand pounds. I groaned at the pressure built up, causing it to pound viciously.

Before I knew it, I was on the ground.

I looked up as I rubbed my throbbing tailbone.

"About time you woke up," Nathan barked. I was disappointed to see he was completely healed.

The same treatment wasn't extended to me, though. I gingerly touched my forehead and felt a bump the size of Russia under my fingers. I hissed and pulled away. Nathan had apparently been carrying me over his shoulder for quite a ways. I wasn't sure exactly where we were, but I knew we were close to the border of Finnian's territory. I couldn't get any hints that anyone was nearby for at least a few miles.

As I gathered my wits, my mind went back to what happened before I passed out.

Dalton.

He was dead.

Tears welled up in my eyes, grief weighing down on my chest. A sob bubbled up from my throat before I was able to stop it.

I closed my eyes to stop the tears and bit my lower lip to stop it from quivering.

I wouldn't give Nathan the satisfaction of seeing me break.

But I was breaking. I was losing hope. I couldn't win. I was alone. He'd beaten us. Nathan was smarter than us.

I just wish I didn't have to bring people down with me.

Niki and Dalton were good people. They were my friends, and I loved them both. Yet, they both died trying to protect me. And in the end, they failed anyways. I wish they would have stayed out of it. They didn't need to die with me.

I thought of everyone they left behind.

Niki had Lili. She was basically her mother. Emiliya may be a horrendous sister, but Lili wasn't. Lili would be devastated.

Finnian would be too. Other than Tyler, Niki was his best friend. He trusted her more than anyone. He would need her to get over the loss of his mate. She was probably the only person who could wade into the grief of that and pull him out.

But now he'd just be grieving her too.

And then there was Dalton.

He had so many people that loved him. I couldn't even imagine how distraught Selena would be when she found out. She didn't need that stress while she was pregnant.

Matt, Brody, Dad . . . they all worked closely with Dalton over the years. They would have trouble hearing the news.

I didn't even want to think about how his family would react. His mom . . .

I blinked away the remaining tears. As much as I loved those two, I needed to stay focused on the present. My attention had to stay on this if I wanted to avenge them.

"Get up, we need to keep moving."

I gritted my teeth and did as he said. I brushed off the snow stuck to my dress and continued to follow him.

"Where are we going?"

I was ignored.

"You're kidnapping me, with the intentions of killing me. The least you could do is answer my questions."

He sighed heavily, like he was annoyed. "We're going to a cabin that Emiliya uses. Once she finds a loophole to your friend's spell, then we'll kill you."

"Mm, fun," I grunted.

We continued on for a few more miles. My feet were freezing and close to being frostbitten. My head still pounded, and black spots continued to dance in my vision no matter how many times I blinked them away.

I was running on pure adrenaline at that point. I had to stay conscious. No telling what they would do if I were asleep.

I just bided my time and kept following them.

Finally, we made it to a cabin. It wasn't like Finnian's cute little cottage in the woods. No, instead, it was just creepy. It was covered in vines, and the wood was rotting off in some places. The windows were boarded up, like it hadn't been used in years.

I could picture it as the basecamp for a serial killer in some slasher movie. My guess wasn't far off.

Emiliya said a spell, which unlocked the door. We entered, and I glanced around. There were spell books spread around the room. There was a table in the middle that had potion ingredients surrounding it.

It looked like Niki's workroom but much creepier.

"Do you have her?" Nathan asked Emiliya. "I'm going to go do some scouting. Find Ivaylo."

"Of course, I have her. The pathetic bitch is no match for me." She scoffed, as though he offended her.

"Just checking. No need to get snippy." He held his hands up in surrender and she rolled her eyes. It didn't seem like they were particularly fond of one another.

I plopped down on the musty old couch in the corner when Nathan left. She sorted through spell books, flipping through them in concentration.

"You know you're not going to win, right?" I added after a few beats of silence.

She didn't answer, just continued her search.

"How could you do that to your own sister? My sister may get on my nerves, but I would die before I ever hurt her."

That got her attention.

"My sister was a pathetic excuse for a witch. I was stronger than her. I was always stronger than her, even without mother's help. I should have been made the Royal Witch. If Finnian were even half the king you claim him to be, he would have made me his Royal Witch."

"You're delusional, bitch," I snapped.

"Coming from the girl whose witch was so easily killed." She sneered. "Now stop talking or I'll put you to sleep."

She started flipping through her books again, and I started forming a plan. Now was my time to strike. I couldn't take out Nathan; he was of Alpha blood. I was hurt and couldn't shift because of Emiliya. I needed to take her out so I could stand a chance against him. I just needed to wait until she was distracted. If I could move fast enough, she wouldn't have time to use magic on me.

I needed to do it perfectly though. So, I waited.

She flipped through book after book and I remained patient.

"Hm, here's something. I could change her spell to kill her instead of whoever killed you. That would work out perfectly."

At that, I couldn't contain my rage. Before she could even start the spell, I was on my feet and running towards her. I fell to ground halfway, holding my head in pain.

"You'll never beat me, you ignorant buffoon. I will always be more powerful. I will always be stronger," she spat out.

I screamed, trying to push the pain aside.

I thought of Kat. I had already lost two friends; I couldn't lose my best friend.

I thought of my family. I needed to protect them. I needed to fight like I had never fought before. They didn't raise a quitter.

They raised me to overcome every challenge laid out in front of me. They raised a warrior.

I thought of Finnian. He needed me now. If I died, if I let them win, he would be in danger. It happened to his dad, but I wouldn't let it happen to him. He was always so protective of me, but now I needed to be protective of him. I needed to fight for him.

Thinking of them was all the motivation I needed.

I took a deep breath. My head snapped up to look at her, my rage overwhelming the pain I was feeling.

I stood up, although I was a bit wobbly. The pain increased slightly, but I stayed standing. I winced and pushed it to the back of my mind, ignoring the feeling of my organs melting inside my body.

Instead, I let my claws elongate and lunged at her.

Her heart dropped to the floor at the same time her body did.

The pain stopped. I let out a breath of relief. This was my chance.

As I ran out of the cabin, I heard a howl of fury in the distance.

Nathan.

He would be coming for me now.

I tried to shift but, for whatever reason, I couldn't. Emiliya's magic should have worn off when she died. I didn't know the mechanics behind witchery, but maybe she was able to find a loophole for that.

Either that, or she had someone helping her like Kat had helped Niki.

But now wasn't the time to dwell on that. I pumped my legs as fast as I could, running in the direction opposite of Nathan.

The sun had long since gone down, nothing but the light of the moon guiding my way. The temperature had dropped considerably, and the ground remained covered in snow. The wind bit my cheeks as I ran, whipping my hair that had fallen from the braid behind me.

I was clumsier than usual. I kept tripping over tree roots. Branches kept lashing at my arms, feeling like whips at the speed I was moving. Blood started dripping down my arms and face from the impact.

I didn't know how long I ran. It could have been minutes, could have been hours. All I knew was that I couldn't stop. Not until I reached safety. I had to find Finnian before Nathan found me.

That was easier said than done though.

Not only was I clumsy, but my sense of direction was way off. I couldn't tell which direction I was heading, only that it had been opposite of the way Nathan was heading. I could have been going towards the castle or the small mountain road.

I found the answer to my question as I saw the road up ahead. It was a small backroad, barely big enough to fit one vehicle. There were no streetlights or cars to be seen. If I stayed on the road, I would eventually end up at the castle.

Before I could make it to the road, I was flung down to the ground, claws raking down my back, ripping through the delicate material of my dress. I withheld a scream of pain and somehow managed to flip over, my blood soaking into the snowy ground, melting it and creating a thick sludge under my body.

Nathan was in his wolf form on top of me, growling menacingly, his eyes filled with fire. He wanted to make me suffer.

He shifted back, his naked form on top of me.

"I was going to kill you quickly. It would have been a painless death. But now, I'm going to make sure it's agonizing. You'll be begging me for death."

Before I could respond, his fist slammed against my cheekbone, tearing through the tender flesh. I could feel blood rolling down the side of my face, pooling in my ear.

"I'll make you beg for mercy, but you won't receive it. I'll torture you until you don't even remember who you are anymore, then I'll end you. I'll put you down like the bitch you are."

He punched me again, this time in the nose. I heard the sick crunch of the bone snapping.

He drew his fist back to hit me again but before he could follow through, the sneer on his face turned blank. For the fourth time that day, I saw life leave someone's eyes.

Nathan fell off of me, into a heap on the ground. I pushed his legs off of me and backed up into a tree, fear consuming me.

It took me a minute before I realized it was Rylan standing in front of me. I wasn't sure whether to be relieved or terrified.

"Good to see you again, Kendall." He smirked down at me, then dropped Nathan's heart, leaving his hand covered in blood.

"Rylan . . ." I trailed off, not sure what else to say.

"You don't have to be scared. I'm not a barbarian like my partner here." He glanced at Nathan. "Always so easily angered, this one." He tsked down at Nathan's body.

"You won't hurt me?" I asked hesitantly, although I probably wouldn't believe him either way.

"Only when I have too. I don't enjoy hurting pretty girls, so you're safe until it is necessary for me to harm you."

"You're Ivaylo," I stated, the puzzle pieces fitting together.

"I'm impressed that you figured it out."

"Why?"

"It is much more fun to let you discover things on your own, so I'll let you figure that out yourself. In the meantime, I sincerely hope you don't fight me on this."

He pulled a clear vial out of his pocket, a thick green liquid inside.

"No—" Before I could protest, he grabbed my head, not letting me move at all.

He was a lot stronger than I would have thought. I was of Alpha blood too, therefore I should have been able to put up a decent fight. But I was no match for him. I scratched at his hands, but it was useless. He poured the disgusting, vile liquid into my mouth and then held it shut, forcing me to swallow.

Once I did, he released me.

"What did you give me?" I screamed, my voice shaky and high-pitched. I was scared.

"I suppose I can tell you. You'll forget momentarily anyways."

"What is that supposed to mean?"

"Since Emiliya is—I'm sorry, was—incompetent, we had to improvise since we couldn't kill you. This potion will mimic your death. All your links will be cut off. Your mate bond to Finnian, your familial link to your family, your pack link, your Royal link, etcetera. They won't be able to feel you any longer. They will think you're dead.

"It will also erase your memories. When you wake up, you will have no idea who you are. You won't even remember your name. In human terms, amnesia. And speaking of humans, you will also be one. The potion won't kill your wolf, but it will put her in a deep sleep. You'll think yourself to be just another average human."

"Why would you do that to me?" I whispered in horror.

"Hey, don't sound so upset! That's better than death, don't you think? Anyways, the only way any of this can be undone is by drinking the same potion. Which is unfortunate for you, considering only two witches in the world know the spell, and one of them is dead. But don't fret. I'll make sure you're taken care of."

As he spoke, I could feel the effects of the potion. I could feel my connection to Finnian and my family shrinking. My wolf was receding further and further into my unconscious. My brain became fuzzy as I tried desperately to remember who I was. I was losing myself. I only caught one last thing before my mind turned into a black hole, sucking out everything that made me, me.

"Don't feel bad that you couldn't beat me. I'm a Royal wolf, after all. Hopefully, my brother won't be too upset that I stole his mate."

I gasped right before I lost consciousness.

Right before I lost myself.

I think I'd have preferred death to this.
But then again, I guess fate doesn't really give you a choice.

ACKNOWLEDGEMENTS

I want to start with thanking my family and friends for always supporting my dreams and reading the words I poured my heart into.

I also want to thank all of the people who read Changing Fate on Wattpad. I felt so supported sharing my work for the very first time.

AUTHOR'S NOTE

Thank you so much for reading *Changing Fate*! I can't express how grateful I am for reading something that was once just a thought inside my head.

I'd love to hear your thoughts on the book. Please leave a review on Amazon or Goodreads because I just love reading your comments and getting to know you!

Can't wait to hear from you!

C.J. Alexis

Do you like werewolf stories?
Here are samples of other stories
you might enjoy!

ASHLEY MICHELLE

His to Claim

CHAPTER 1

SCARLETT

"—Shift."

I was jolted out of my daydreaming by the sound of a loud voice ringing in my ear. I turned around with raised brows to find Darlene, the shift manager of the small family-owned diner, staring at me expectantly with a tray of dirty dishes in one hand. I had clearly missed the important parts of whatever she had been saying to me.

A sheepish grin worked its way up my face. "What was that?"

She rolled her eyes and blew a stray hair out of her face. "I *said*, do you mind covering the end of my shift for me? My babysitter called. Apparently, Graham is running a pretty high fever."

I nodded my head. "Sure, no problem." It wasn't like I had any plans for the evening anyway, other than obsessively checking the mail. There were only two weeks left before graduation, and I was yet to hear from any of the colleges I had applied to.

Darlene let out a small sigh. "Thanks, Scarlett. I owe you."

I waved my hand. "Don't worry about it. I know how hard it is on you being left to take care of Graham while Troy is away. I'm happy to help lighten the load." Her husband had to travel a lot for his job, and that left Darlene with extra parenting duties.

She gave me a grateful smile as she turned away with the tray of dishes. "You're truly an angel, Scarlett."

I snorted at her comment. "I already agreed to cover you. You don't need to kiss my butt anymore, Darlene."

She gave me a playful wink before turning away, disappearing through the kitchen door. I slowly turned back around with a sigh. This was going to be a long night of nothing but the virtual emptiness of the diner.

I was happy when a familiar face shuffled through the front door of the diner, setting off the little bell that hung above the door. He lifted his hand to his head, ruffling his dark hair which was starting to look shaggy around the edges. This boy would look like a mountain man if it weren't for my constant influence in his life. He met my gaze briefly as he reached out and grabbed one of the cheaply made menus from an empty table. He flipped through the pages quickly before setting it back down.

I pulled the pen and pad from the front pocket of my stained apron. "What can I get you, Wyatt?"

He shrugged as he moved closer toward me. "I think a cup of coffee will be fine. It's been a long day."

"It's going to be a bit longer. Darlene asked me to cover the end of her shift," I commented with an apologetic smile. Wyatt had promised to pick me up after my shift ended while I was running out the door this morning.

He let out a sigh, running his hand through his hair. "Of course, she did. Well, there *is* a meeting tonight. Guess it's going to be extra long for both of us, sweetheart," he replied with a sarcastic grin as I poured him a cup of coffee and placed it on the counter in front of me.

Darlene approached us carrying her purse, her jacket slung over her arm. "You know the coffee here is shit, Wyatt. I don't know why you keep ordering it when you only ever have a sip and leave the rest."

Wyatt ignored her comment. The two of them were always at each other's throats for reasons unknown to me. He pressed his hands to the counter, breathing in deeply. His nose scrunched up a bit, and he looked over at me. "You smell." I frowned at my cousins greeting as he sat himself down on a stool at the breakfast counter, grabbing the coffee.

"Gee, you really know how to compliment a girl," I grumbled, my voice dripping with sarcasm. My cousin and I had a very close relationship, considering that my parents had taken him in after his father ran off and his mother got sick. He returned the favor when my parents died, taking me into his home and raising me like I was his kid sister.

"God, Wyatt…" Darlene remarked as she threw her arms into the sleeves of her jacket, pulling up the collar. "Even if a woman does stink, you shouldn't comment on it. And you wonder why you're still single."

Her words brought a smile to my face, and I gave him a sharp look. I snickered as I turned away from my cousin who was pouting at the blunt reprimand he had received. I could see Winston, our cook, slaving away over the grill through the small hole, singing along to some garbage being gurgled out of the old boom box he kept in the kitchen. The diner was my home away from home, and its motley crew was my self-created wolf pack even if they were only humans.

"Wyatt," she said his name in a flat tone. Darlene had never cared much for my cousin. Maybe it's because he had a knack for putting his foot in his mouth… or maybe because they had gone "grown-up" together and he'd been quite the fool back in his younger years.

"See you tomorrow, Scarlett. Thanks again," she called.

I turned around to give her a quick wave. "See ya, Darlene. Tell Graham I said hello and hope he feels better," I called back as she exited the front door, the bell ringing again.

Wyatt lifted his gaze to mine, staring at me expectantly with wide eyes as if he was waiting for something. I stared back at him, shifting my hands to my hips. "Why are you looking at me like that? Do I have something on my face?" I reached up with a hand and wiped it across my cheek, checking to see if there was any food splatter. It was a hazard of the job.

"Can't you feel it, Scarlett?" he asked me in a soft voice so that no one else could hear. Hell, if it weren't for my extra-sensitive senses I probably wouldn't have heard him either.

I narrowed my eyes in confusion at his question. "What are talking about? Are you feeling okay, Wyatt?" I reached out and placed my hand on his forehead. He pulled back with a furrowed brow and looked at me as if I had two heads.

"After all the complaining and whining I had to listen to from you… are you seriously telling me that you don't feel even the slightest bit different?" he asked a little louder in an exasperated tone, waving his hand in the air dramatically. I had no idea what he was going on about or why he seemed so upset.

I looked around the small room at the other patrons who seemed content to ignore his outburst. I leaned forward, stuffing my notepad back into the pocket of my apron. "I don't know why you think I should feel different, but I feel the same as I always do. Unless you want to count the fact that my feet feel like I've been walking barefoot on hot coals. These ten-hour shifts have been killing me," I whined at him.

He gave me a slow blink, shaking his head. "Seriously, Scarlett?"

"What?" I questioned with a tired tone.

"Your scent—"

I held up a hand, cutting off his thought mid-sentence.

"I know. I know. I smell, but in my defense, you would smell too if you worked with greasy food all day," I snapped at him, growing tired of the conversation he was having with me. If I wanted to be insulted, I'm sure I could easily find one of my peers to satisfy that need without a problem. Human or shifter, they were all eager to tear someone else down to elevate themselves.

He shook his head at me. "No, your scent has changed, Scarlett. Your wolf has matured. I can smell her on you now."

I stared at him blankly as I digested his words. Had my wolf finally reached maturity without me noticing? I searched my mind for a sign of my wolf's presence. I had been waiting for this moment since I hit puberty. Most of my peers had already matured, leaving me like an outsider when it came to the pack.

All shifters had to go through two stages of puberty: the natural human one and the beast underneath. It could happen at any time, but basically, it meant that the connection between human and wolf was fully formed. It wasn't until this happens that we were allowed to attend actual pack events. Most of my friends had already matured. I had been left in the group of late bloomers. Sometimes, it happened that a wolf never matured. These people were seen as Omegas. They were still a part of the pack, but they would never be considered true wolves.

I shifted back and forth on my feet, concentrating hard. "I don't feel any different."

Wyatt took a sip of his coffee. "You will trust me." He pulled the mug away from himself, peering down into the cup with a small look of disgust before setting it down. "But you know what this means?"

"What?" I questioned with a raised brow.

He met my gaze with a knowing look. "You don't have to wait in the car like the other pups during the meeting tonight. You're a true wolf now," he teased as he gave me a wolfish grin. I rolled my eyes at his comment, but on the inside, I felt a bubble of excitement.

* * *

I had only ever seen the pack house from the outside, having never been allowed to enter it before. I found myself getting anxious as I followed Wyatt down the dirt driveway and around the side of the house. In the back, there was another building, about the size of a guest house.

I could hear the sound of happy voices carried on the gentle evening breeze. My palms felt sweaty in the pockets of my sweatshirt as my nerves got the better of me. Wyatt gave me a grin as he opened the door. "So it begins."

I rolled my eyes at him as I walked past him into the large open room. The smells of other pack members overwhelmed me for a moment. My eyes scanned the crowd warily, looking for familiar faces. I found my gaze gravitating towards the front of the room where the stream of bodies seemed to be moving.

That was the first time I saw *him.*

He stood near the front, greeting people with a friendly smile. My heart hammered in my chest as I watched him from where I stood at the back of the room. I had no idea who he was, but I knew he was perfect. His dark hair was shaved close to his head as if it had been shaved bare at some point and was finally being allowed to grow out. My eyes followed the length of his body, taking in every part of him. He had a lean body that spoke of endurance-honed muscles.

Wyatt elbowed my side. "Don't just stand there, Scarlett. People are starting to look at us." He urged me to move forward. I had to force my feet to move from where I had been anchored. My whole world seemed to be shifting on its axis, and I couldn't be sure I was standing on solid ground anymore.

My heart was in my throat as I approached my mate—at least that was what my wolf was telling me. This perfect male specimen was our mate, the one that the Goddess had ordained for us at birth. But what if he hated me? What if I wasn't what he was expecting? Insecurities that I had never felt before began to flood my brain.

I dug my heels into the floor. "I can't do this. Let's go home."

Wyatt grabbed onto my elbow and led me on. "You're being ridiculous. We all had to go through this, Scarlett. Consider it your official initiation into the pack." I gritted my teeth as every step brought me closer to the finality of my situation.

The Alpha and his mate were standing together, greeting the other pack members as they filed into the room, grabbing seats for the meeting. I remembered them from the times they had visited my home when I was much younger, way back when my mother was still alive, and my father held a prominent position in the pack. They looked older and a little more worn down, but that had to be expected of people in their positions.

"Alpha Aaron," Wyatt spoke formally as he reached out a hand, a standard human greeting. I danced on the balls of my feet, wishing that I hadn't accepted Wyatt's offer to join him. I was still in my work uniform, smelling like grease and probably looking unkempt from the busy workday… not the way I wanted to make my first impression on the pack.

"Wyatt," he replied, shaking the hand that had been offered to him with a firm grip, "it is good to see you again."

Wyatt beamed at the acknowledgment, turning his eyes toward the female beside the Alpha, bowing his head. "Luna Victoria."

She gave him a kind smile. "Wyatt."

Alpha Aaron's dark gaze shifted in my direction, a smile still on his lips. "And who is this beauty?" he questioned, lifting a brow as he examined me further. My cheeks rushed with heat, and I felt the sudden urge to hide behind my cousin like I did back in my younger years where I would cling to my mother's leg.

Wyatt wrapped his arm around my shoulder, pulling me in protectively to his side, and that only made me feel more embarrassed. "This is my cousin, Scarlett."

Luna Victoria gave me a knowing glance as she leaned into her mate's side. "Sweetheart, it's Conrad and Elizabeth's daughter."

"Of course, she is," he replied as if he had already known. My lips twitched with the urge to smile when she looked at me with a playful eye roll at his expense. Alpha Aaron crossed his arms over his wide chest, leaning forward toward me. "I can see it now that I've gotten a closer look. You've got Conrad's eyes."

"And Elizabeth's beautiful face," Luna Victoria remarked. "If I recall correctly, your mother was a late bloomer as well." I felt my head sink a little lower at her comment.

"David..." Luna Victoria called, turning toward my mate with a smile, "come over here real fast."

She glanced back at me. "Conrad helped train David when he was a young boy. I'm sure he will be very interested in meeting you." I felt my nerves spike as he turned in our direction, and I realized that he wasn't an average member of the pack. This was *their* son, the next heir: an Alpha born male.

I wanted to run, but my feet kept me firmly rooted in place. I was afraid to look up from the ground. What would I see staring back at me? I swallowed hard, trying to prepare myself for what was about to happen.

His shoes came into view, and I felt my wolf stirring under my skin. Wyatt elbowed me in the side. "Scarlett…" he hissed under his breath in a warning tone. I lifted my face to meet his gaze with bated breath.

His dark eyes widened in surprise as we drank each other in. Something in my mind snapped. I could feel it all, everything everyone had tried to explain to me about having a wolf. Her emotions and thoughts surged through me as I watched the corners of his mouth lift upwards into a smile.. a heart-stopping smile that was meant for only me.

I felt my own lips begin to mimic his. There were nothing and no one else in the room for us at that moment. This is what it felt like to have a mate, and I knew he was feeling the same sensations by the look in his eyes.

The moment was broken when a tall dark-haired female placed a kiss on his cheek. "I'm sorry I'm late, David. My shift went into overtime. I had to help Doctor McCarthy deliver the Johnsons' twins. Those pups are going to be a handful. I can tell you that now." She finished with a soft chuckle of amusement.

I hadn't even seen her approach us I had been so lost in a different world. My smile faded quickly as my brows furrowed in confusion as I glanced between the two of them. He looked rather stiff as she grabbed hold of his hand with hers, turning her face in my direction.

"Hello. I don't think I've seen you before." She tilted her head to the side.

"That's because she's only just matured, Eva," Luna Victoria commented toward her, both of them sharing a look of understanding like two people who've already been through it.

"This must be very exciting for you then," she remarked with a bright smile, completely unaware of what had happened between me and the male she was holding onto as if he were hers. My wolf was growling possessively in my mind, struggling to free herself so that she could eliminate the competition.

"David, this is Scarlett," Luna Victoria introduced me. "Conrad's daughter," she supplied as if it were my own special title.

I felt like the rug had been pulled out from under my feet and I was falling without anyone to catch me. My stomach was in my throat, but I forced myself to speak. "Hi…" I replied in a tense voice, finding it hard to hold his gaze.

David pulled his hand free from Eva's grasp and took a step towards me. He lifted his hand slightly like he wanted to reach out to me, but he thought better of it, deciding to stuff it into the pocket of his slacks instead.

"It's nice to meet you, Scarlett." Goosebumps rose on my flesh, and I watched his pupils dilate a bit as he took in more of me. "Your father was a great man. The pack lost a great warrior when he passed away. I lost a dear friend," he added, trying to keep things from getting strange in front of all the onlookers. None of them seemed to know what had transpired between the two of us.

I gave him a small smile that didn't reach my eyes. "Thank you." He looked like he wanted to say something more to me, his lips parted slightly. Alpha Aaron stepped forward, his dark eyes calculating as he glanced between myself and his son. I lowered my gaze to the ground, clenching my jaw tightly.

"Well, we should get this meeting going." He wrapped his arm around his mate and pulled her into his side. "It's wonderful to have another true wolf added to the pack."

Wyatt grabbed my elbow, and I tensed slightly at the touch. Now that I could connect to my wolf, the world seemed too overwhelming. Every sensation moved through me like an exploding bomb. I let him lead me away to some empty seats, but my mind was adrift as I looked around the room. I had matured and met my mate, only to find out that he already had someone at his side. How could I compete with her?

My gaze focused on the female in question, Eva. She was a fully matured female compared to myself, who was still growing into my body, which was mostly knees and elbows. She seemed kind, and she didn't waver under the gaze of all the people in the room. She looked like a queen. I certainly wasn't much compared to her. That was why she was the one standing on the stage, holding his hand.

I sunk down lower in my seat. I could hear Alpha Aaron's voice as he spoke to the group, but none of the words were able to pierce through my racing thoughts.

"We are happy to announce that the mating ceremony of Eva and David will be held at the end of next month," Alpha Aaron said with pride in his voice, clapping David on the back as he stood next to a smiling Eva, hand in hand. My heart dropped, and I sucked in a painful breath. This wasn't how things were supposed to go. I was his mate, not her.

I couldn't sit in that room for another moment and listen to any more words. I leaned over to Wyatt. "I need to go," I whispered. He looked over at me in confusion as I rose up out of my chair and hurried toward the exit. I didn't look back, but I felt David's eyes on me, my body heating up everywhere his gaze drifted to. It was getting hard to breathe as I pushed open the door and flung myself out into the night, letting the cool air wash over me.

I sucked in ragged breaths as I tried to overcome the ache in my chest. No one had warned me maturing would be so painful.

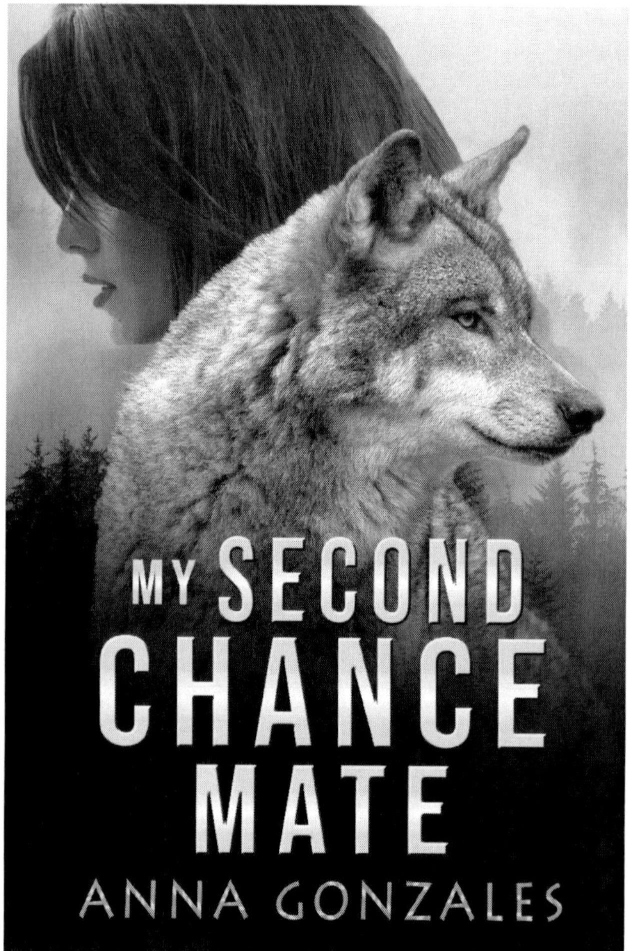
MY SECOND
CHANCE
MATE
ANNA GONZALES

CHAPTER ONE
Rejected but Moving On

HARMONY

Waking up in the morning has never been easy for me and now it feels as if there's no point in doing it at all. I didn't always feel this way. I used to love life. I enjoyed hanging out with friends and even going to school. That changed the day I met my mate. What is a mate? It's supposed to be the best part of being a werewolf, which is what I am. We are born in human form and can transform into a wolf at the age of twelve. From that point on, it's a waiting game until we find our mate. A mate is a special someone who completes you; the one you was made for and vice versa. I should be happy to have found mine. Unfortunately, my story is unique and I don't mean that in a good way.

*   *   *

One Year Ago . . .

I met him at the age of sixteen. He was everything I could've hoped for. Seventeen years old, 6"1', gorgeous gray eyes, dark black hair, nicely tanned skin, washboard abs, and strong long legs. Perfect, right? I thought so too. We found each other outside the airport baggage claim area. Our eyes met and it was electrifying. We moved towards one another as if pulled by some force until we were only a foot away.

"Mate," we both whispered. He reached out to touch my cheek and I leant into his palm. It felt right; like home. I was so happy that I closed my eyes to savor the moment when he suddenly tensed and dropped his hand. I opened my eyes to ask what was wrong just as he took a big step back. I stared at him in confusion and was about to ask what made him move away when the sound of a familiar voice made the words freeze on my lips.

"Babe, I see you've met my sister. Isn't she adorable?" My older sister, Megan, gushed as she gave me her usual too-tight, can't breathe type of hug.

"Did you say babe?" I asked.

"Yes, silly! Aiden, you didn't introduce yourself?" She laughed while playfully swatting his chest. "Harmony, meet the best thing to come out of this whole mandatory wolf camp that mom and dad sent me to. My boyfriend, Aiden James," she announced happily while grabbing his arm.

My wolf growled at the sight of her touching my mate, but I couldn't say anything right now. I love my sister. She's my best friend and she looked so happy. I couldn't do anything to ruin that. Don't get me wrong;I had some serious questions to ask but I would get my answers when the time was right. Even if I had to tie Aiden to a chair to do it. There was a satisfactory rumble from my wolf just by picturing it. I couldn't believe that, out of all people my sister could have met at this camp, she had to meet and fall in love with the one wolf meant for me.

The camp they attended was a first of it's kind. It was created for two types of wolves. The first was for someone like Aiden, a future alpha. These types of wolves would one day be the leaders of their pack and had to be taught to control their added power and authority so that it wouldn't be misused. The second was for wolves born from two werewolf parents who both carry the recessive gene. It causes their child to be born completely human, and my sister was one of those children. The whole thing was complicated enough as it is, and finding out I was the mate of a future alpha my sister was currently dating only added to the complication.

Aiden and I quickly exchanged hellos as if the spine tingling encounter between us never happened. We grabbed their bags and headed to the car. The ride was uncomfortable mainly because the love birds decided to share the back seat and cuddle. I exchanged looks with Aiden a couple times in the mirror, and though he would smile at my sister, the looks he gave me seemed sad and resigned. His mood confused me but I expected to get an explanation soon.

We made it to our pack house where they were having a big barbeque to welcome my sister and Aiden back. Aiden is the only nephew of our alpha, and because our alpha's mate is human, she could not conceive a child. Our law states that the next male in line would be the alpha's younger brother, Aiden's dad. However, he was killed by rogues when Aiden was thirteen so by law, Aiden is the next heir. It is strange that we never had the opportunity to meet before but that's due to the fact that Aiden's mother took him back to her pack shortly after his father's death. She was unable to deal with the memories of her lost mate that surrounded her wherever she went. Her story was sad and was still used today to teach young pups the ups and downs of mating.

After about an hour into the barbeque, my sister made a run to the store with our mom, and it finally gave me a chance to get Aiden alone. I dragged him to a clearing, a little far down from our pack house, and laid above him.

"So, what are we going to do? I love my sister to death but we're mates. We can't deny that. I don't want to hurt her but the pull I feel for you is so strong I can't ignore it," I started rambling.

"I can," he said.

I continued, not quite hearing him. "I mean, I know this is going to be difficult and create a lot of drama but I'm so happy I've found you a—"

He cut me off and repeated those two words, loud enough so I could hear them. "I can."

"You can? Can what?" I asked, confused.

"I can ignore it. This pull between us," he stated. He proceeded to rip my heart out of my chest with the rest of his words. "I never had a choice in many things in my life. I didn't choose to lose my dad, or have to leave my pack, or be put into the role of alpha but I chose your sister. I fell in love with her all on my own with no influence from anyone. I refuse to change how I feel just because my wolf wants me to. I want to be with the one I love because I say so and not because a bond is forcing me to."

I stared at him. I was shocked and hurt. "Are you saying what I'm thinking? Are you rejecting our bond?"

He sighed. "Look, I don't want to hurt you, Harmony. I spent time with your sister, and I got to know her and fell in love all on my own. If I'm with you, it's not by choice anymore but by fate. I refuse to let fate control anything else in my life. I'm sorry but that's just how it has to be."

To say I was hurt was an understatement. What came next was just anger. "You refuse? What about me? Do you know how long I've dreamed of meeting my mate and finally feeling the love only he can give me? Only you can give me? And now you tell me I can never feel that because fate has dealt you a cruel hand and you're rebelling? And so I'm the one who has to pay for your misfortune? I have never done anything in my sixteen years of life to deserve that, but does it matter to you? Obviously not!" I cried out.

"Look, Harmony. I—"

"No, you look. I'm sorry you had to go through all that but that's what I can be here for. I can help heal the pain you've been through and support you through the role that was forced onto you. No one will be able to understand you like I, your mate, can. Let me do this for you. For us," I pleaded.

"I just can't, Harmony. I've already chosen the future I want, and that future is with your sister," he replied firmly.

"What about our bond? It's going to be hard to fight it. My wolf is trying to get through, and I'm sure so is yours. How are you going to deny him?" I questioned.

Nothing. And I meant nothing could have saved me from the pain his answer caused. "Well, I'll fight him off until I completely mate with Megan. Once I mark her, he will be easier to control, and as more time passes, our bond will eventually weaken."

"True, but you forgot one important detail. Or maybe it's not so important to you since you won't be affected but what happens to the rejected mate, Aiden? What will happen to me? Let me remind you, being that I don't have a choice in the rejection," I lashed out in anger, "my wolf will weaken. When you mark Megan, I will feel as if my chest has been ripped open. You will have your love for Megan to help get you through the weakened bond, but I won't be able to find another wolf mate since we are only given one in our lifetime. Even though the bond will deteriorate, I will still hurt every day. I will have to see you together and be reminded of my rejection time and time again. Is that really what you want

for me? I know you feel something for me. I saw it at the airport. Are you absolutely sure this is what you want to do?"

"It's what I want," he whispered. "I've thought about this my whole life."

I tried one last plea."What about kids, Aiden? Megan is human. You won't be able to have a pup with her. How will you carry on your alpha line?"

"I'll deal with that when the problem arises."

"So you'll give up your mate and any future blood children just to spite fate?" I asked, hurt and shocked.

He nodded. "Yes. I'm really sorry. I just can't be with you." There was a hint of sadness in his voice.

"It's not that you can't. You just chose not to," I whispered in defeat. "So you're finally getting to choose for yourself, and that choice forces me into a life of pain and misery," I said as I looked him in the eyes. I thought I saw some indecision and pain, but it was quickly replaced by resignation and determination. I looked away as the tears started to fall. "Fine." I turned back to face him. "I will accept your rejection of the bond but only because like a mate should; I only want your happiness. You see, that's what mates are supposed to do: Protect each other, care for one another, and put each other first. I will endure the pain of the future for you, and I hope that it haunts you every night while you live your happily ever after with my sister." And with that said, I shifted into my light brown wolf and ran further into the darkness of the woods.

* * *

Shaking my head of the unwanted memories, I think about my life since then. I haven't done anything drastic to my appearance. I still wear my brown hair long and straight, no contacts cover my light green eyes, my full lips are still only covered in clear lip gloss, and I haven't changed from skinnys and tanks to ripped jeans and grungy t-shirts. No, the only change is my attitude. The sweet carefree nature is gone. I now know how real life can be and it isn't a fairytale. My enthusiasm for life is gone. When you look into my eyes, you'll see emptiness that hides the constant pain.

I no longer live with my pack. Six months after my rejection, Aiden marked my sister and the pain was unbearable. I couldn't be around him and see him happy anymore. Yes, there were times when I was near him and could feel his wolf fighting for control but Aiden always pushed him back. I begged my parents to let me leave the pack and join my maternal aunt's pack— Her mate's pack in Hawaii, to be specific. My parents didn't understand why at first because I never told anyone about my rejection. I made up the excuse of it being hard to be around Aiden and Megan knowing I haven't found my mate yet. At least it was half true.

That's where I am now. A new pack, a new school, and hopefully, a new life. I should have an optimistic attitude, but I no longer have the illusion of happily ever after. Hope is something I seriously lack in the present. There is one good thing to come from all this.

"Harmony, get your lazy ass up so we can get to school. I don't want to miss all the fresh meat awaiting me. My game is on fire today. Just don't stare too hard at me 'cause you might be blinded by all this hotness."

There it is. My cousin Jared. He's the only one who knows about my rejection because, unlike my aunt and uncle, I can't hide the pain from him. He knows me too well, and it took all of my wolf strength to stop him from jumping on a plane to beat the crap out of Aiden. It's good though because he constantly takes my mind off of things with his crazy man whorish ways and wise remarks. His friends are awesome too. And are total eye candies. A few tried hitting on me when I was first introduced to the pack, but Jared gave all them death glares. He warned his player friends that I was completely hands off unless any of them were planning on putting a ring on my finger. I laughed at all the deathly ill expressions in the room after that announcement. Commitment is equal to a bad case of crabs in their minds. I can't wait 'til they meet their mates. It'll be fun watching them get tamed.

I get dressed in some black skinnys and an off-shoulder white top with a black tank underneath. I put my hair in a loose bun, gloss my lips, and slip into a pair of black gladiator sandals. As I'm tucking a fly away hair behind my ear, the opening of the front door announces Jace, Nate, and Brad's arrival. I make my way to their voices and find them in the kitchen as usual.

"Bro, I'm telling you. This year we're gonna score so much pu—"

"Lady in the room!" I shout, interrupting what I'm sure was gonna be one of Nate's more colorful terms for *vajayjay.*

"Right. Sorry, Harm. As I was saying, we're gonna score so much chicks because we're now seniors," Nate corrects himself excitedly.

"Well, I know I will, but I'm not too sure about you ugly mutts. Just don't stand too close to me and you'll have a chance since my sex appeal is just too massive," Jared boasts, a l in his usual arrogant self.

"Really, Jared? I know what's massive about you, and it's not your sex appeal or your weiner. Don't try to deny it. Our moms showered us together when we were little, and if I remember correctly, which I do, it was very, very, very tiny," I say, making sure I emphasized the size with my thumb and pointer fingers.

"Hey, that's because I haven't changed yet. Trust me. Massive isn't even a big enough word to describe it now," he argues, a tiny bit offended.

I cringe. "First of all, gross. And second, your ego is the only thing that's massive. I'm worried if you don't bring it down you might not be able to fit your fat head out the door."

"She's right. Besides, we all know my sexiness outshines all of you," Brad informs them.

"No way. I score the most ass . . . I mean chicks every year," Jace argues.

"That's only cause you don't have standards and will screw anything with two sets of lips," says Nate with a raised brow.

This sets off a whole new conversation about what's doable and what's not, followed by pushing and headlocks. These boys are too much and, even though I'm not excited about the day ahead, it promises to be entertaining.

ABOUT THE AUTHOR

My name is C.J. and I was born and raised in Texas. I'm a proud cat mom who loves to write. I've been a chronic daydreamer since I was a young child, but I didn't start writing until I was eighteen. I started Changing Fate almost a decade ago when I was twenty years old, and I never planned for it to turn into what it is now. I'm passionate about self-care, and spending time with family and friends, traveling, watching movies, writing, and reading are all important for my self-care routine. I'm a classic Enneagram type 4, and it shows in my writing consistently.

Made in United States
North Haven, CT
02 January 2025